Head to Heart Talks

Walking a Sacred Path

VICKY KELM WILLIAMS

PUBLISHED BY FIDELI PUBLISHING, INC.

ISBN: 978-1-955622-58-5

Published by

Fideli Publishing, Inc.
119 W. Morgan St.
Martinsville, IN 46151
www.FideliPublishing.com

Dedication

This book is dedicated with a grateful heart to the "Seekers of Truth" who believe in the power of possibilities; and the dreamers, visionaries and artists that bring it into Reality. To the Magic and Mysteries of Life, and to those who are willing to "never give up" until the call of their *Heart* is answered and the questions of their *Head* are satisfied.

To my beautiful family, who has taught me what unconditional love looks and feels like. As diverse as we are, it is *Love* that keeps us together, and *Respect* that helps us accept our differences. They are my greatest teachers and supporters of my *Heart*.

With abundant Love and Respect I wish to acknowledge the following gifted editors and artists who took the words of my *Heart* and put them into form:

- Barbara Dulmage, editing genius: songispirit@aol.com,

- Jill Freeman, artist, creator of all artwork: whisperedartdesigns@gmail.com,

- Victoria Williams Steen, artist, "prettied up" the Mandalas: www.artthouinspired.com,

- Robin Surface, artist and Mastermind, Fideli Publishing, www.FideliPublishing.com,

- And, the many beautiful souls that courageously shared their heart's stories and made this book possible.

Table of Contents

Introduction

To experience living on Earth takes courage. While it is an absolutely magnificent place full of beauty, diversity, and opportunity, it also opens the door to the human experience, and one is never quite certain what will unfold! For just as no two humans are alike, no two humans will view life in the same manner.

Book two of the *Head to Heart Talks* series explores some simple, yet profound Truths that will offer the readers some "food for thought." The complex world of human civilization offers a plethora of views from which to choose how to live life on Earth, which can often be a daunting task. Our practical *Head* digests, regurgitates, and attempts to decipher these views in order to make sense of life, which raises questions. Where do I fit in? How can I get the most of life?

Our curious *Head* mind and our creative, loving *Heart* collectively help us to truly create a way to embrace the human experience. That path can be a slippery slope to maneuver; however, if we bravely follow our inner guidance we will gather the "tools" needed to enjoy an exciting, adventurous journey through life, and to find our way to that peaceful place of balance.

Book one consists of individual, stand-alone stories from which to randomly choose. In this second book you will note various words in italics with an asterisk in front of them. These are references to stories from the first book, *Head to Heart Talks: Rediscovering Your Authentic Self.*

Book two follows the journey of two characters from the first book, Jim and Ruth, for whom the old woman becomes a Teacher of the ways necessary for *Walking a Sacred Path.* Stories within the chapters support her teachings, and you will no doubt find yourself rereading some chapters in order to fully comprehend and embody the teachings. These tools she offers, if used, will enrich *your* Sacred Walk.

This book demonstrates how the Sacred Web of Life connects all of us when we pay attention, trusting and allowing our hearts to guide our path. Remember that whatever you do for yourself, you also do for others!

We invite you to discover that everything you need is already within you! Equipped with the tools offered in this book, you will discover that *Walking a Sacred Path* is forever an adventure! And, that the value of community is immeasurable!

Reflection Pages

His Holiness, the 14th Dalai Lama ended a public talk suggesting that perhaps he may have said something they might like to "think some more about," but if not, that was okay, too." That seemed an excellent idea, so here is an option for you!

"Hitting the pause button" serves as a powerful way to quiet a thinking, practical mind while offering our emotional, creative heart the opportunity to really *feel.* A few "reflection pages" are included here to offer you, the reader, the opportunity to consider what you might want to "think some more about." These pages will open the door to a deeper relationship between the "what if's" and "yeah, buts" of your ever-chattering mind, and the "voice" of your beautiful heart. That is important, because the relationship between your *Head* and your *Heart* is the most important relationship you will ever have!

As you continue on this journey with the old woman in the woods, remember this suggestion from Book One, *Head to Heart Talk: Rediscovering your Authentic Self*:

> "Put your mind in your pocket, place your hands on your heart, and take a few deep breaths. Tell your mind that its job is to simply remember what it hears and your heart 'listens' to the teachings in each (chapter)."

A journal is an invaluable tool to help you connect your thoughts with your feelings. Do not "think" about what you want to write, or worry that is grammatically correct or makes sense. Whether you choose a Super Hero spiral notebook, or something else that catches your eye, let your writing be free and uncensored, and see what unfolds!

Here we go! Time for some *"Head to Heart Talks!"*

Old Friends

Many moons had passed since the old woman had received any visitors to her cabin. Seven winters, seven planting seasons, and seven growing seasons, before the old woman realized the seventh harvesting season was about to begin. She knew it was time to once again open her heart and her home to those who sought her stories.

The much-needed rains forced the leaves from their homes on the Standing Ones before the change of color was even in full swing. The old woman stood and observed the colorful display that covered her front yard, and admitted to herself that she had probably kept herself too busy to have time for visitors. It was as though the universe knew she had some personal work to delve into within her own heart before she would be a clean vessel through which the stories others needed to hear could be told.

I wonder, thought the old woman as she looked beyond her front porch, *how the rest of the world is doing?*

She had, of course, made her way to town for necessities; however, the trips generally consisted of shopping from a specific list to pick up what was needed, and then she promptly returned to her cabin. Rarely was there a time during those trips when the old woman engaged in what she referred to as idle conversation. Once in a while she made her way to a favorite park bench that overlooked the small community in which she lived, and she occasionally sat in her favorite pew at the church she had attended while she was raising her family. Both of those choices occurred randomly, whenever the old woman felt a pull in her heart to do so. They were certainly not preplanned occurrences.

The morning clouds that had filled the sky during an ever-so-gentle rain began to part, giving way to the afternoon's blue skies. She pulled the tie of her sweater snuggly around her waist.

It's nearly time to bring some firewood into the house so the cabin is nice and cozy for our first visitor.

As if on cue, a young man appeared through the clearing to her yard, and a smile quickly spread across his face. The old woman returned his smile with an enthusiastic wave.

Jim picked up his stride, and within a few steps was close enough to extend his arms and receive a big hug from the old woman of which he had become quite fond. She received his open arms with affection for this man who had become a most trusted and helpful friend. Jim was eager not only to assist with routine chores, but to also make certain the old woman had plenty of wood for the winter season. His impromptu visits seemed to come at precisely the time she most needed them, for both the chores and for her heart.

"How have you been, my friend?" asked Jim. "Are you ready for me to bring some wood into your cabin, and stack some on the porch for you?" He scanned the yard, checking out the branches and twigs that had fallen from the strong winds of the late summer storms.

"Why, it appears the storms have gifted you with enough wood so that I won't even need to split much of the bigger pieces for kindling."

He stretched his body. "Hey, my body likes that!" He flexed the muscles of his right arm. "These muscles are in shape and ready to be used!"

"You're looking fit to me; I'd say Sarah's taking pretty good care of you," responded the old woman with a smile.

Jim laughed and patted his belly.

"That she is; however, I've also become quite the chef at home these days. You should see how well Sarah and the kids look! I reckon you could say I have developed some cookin' skills."

Enough idle talk.

The words echoed in both the old woman's and Jim's heads. Jim knew he was lucky to have more than a few sentences from his elder friend; he wasn't going to push her past her comfort zone, and it was obvious she had nothing more to say at the moment.

The clouds began to part as Jim busied himself with the task of cleaning up the yard and stacking wood, while the old woman busied herself in the kitchen. She knew Jim loved her biscuits and was most partial to her strawberry preserves. She liked to help Jim remember his affection for his grandmother since he had mentioned it the very first time he came to meet her.

It's always good to remember one's grandparents; it helps to understand one's family history in order to better understand one's own self. It helps to gain clarity around the "thinking" patterns of past generations that perhaps need to change, in order for future generations to grow and flourish. Fact is, it's part of the evolution of life.

Her thoughts brought a tiny smile to her face. Her smile wrinkles deepened, revealing the rich love and enjoyment for life she had experienced throughout her life, and the tremendous gratitude she felt to have been privileged to share in both the joyous and sorrowful moments of life with so many in her community.

She kneaded the biscuit dough and reflected on how life is much like making good biscuits: gently moving things about with tenderness and strength while allowing the ingredients to work their magic. Indeed, life needs to be handled with balance, doing things that serve the family with gentleness and love, and on occasion "kneading" to stretch beyond one's comfort zone in order to rise to a new level of knowing and being.

Perhaps it is similar to using an old family biscuit recipe that is tried and true, creatively integrating some new ingredients, such as cheese with a bit of garlic, or adding some raisins, cinnamon and pecans, then drizzling a thin white icing over them, all for warming the hearts and bodies of our families. To make biscuits like Jim enjoys them, and to have ample strawberry preserves and butter available for him to smear on as he wishes, she does especially for him. Then he is nourished in Body, Mind, and Spirit.

The old woman knew that every human being wants to really be seen; not just recognized by appearance, but rather, really noticed, so that they are remembered by their likes and dislikes, what warms their hearts, and what pushes them away. They want someone to see their strengths, in addition to the areas that are ready to be refined and developed. And, they want that honest Truth so they can become successful human beings within their families as well as within their communities.

People need to pay more attention to each other; to notice facial expressions, and how they react to certain topics, foods, and situations in general, in order to really get to know a person at the deepest level.

The old woman pulled an old jelly glass from her cupboard. She then dipped it in a small amount of flour beside the rolled-out dough and began to cut the biscuits and place them on a baking sheet.

I have faith in the human heart; I just know we're going to start really "seeing" each other very soon, before the world turns even more cold and removed from human actions and reactions.

She slipped the baking sheet into a 450-degree oven and set the timer for twelve minutes. She peered out her kitchen window to see how Jim was doing when she heard the door to her cabin open.

"I do believe you are ready for the colder temps," said Jim as he entered with a large armful of wood. "If you'll get the door I'll bring in enough to fill your wood holder and kindling basket."

The old woman nodded, wiped off her hands and moved toward the front door where she held it open for Jim. After about three loads of split wood had been brought in, the timer on the oven buzzed.

"You can take care of those biscuits," said Jim. "I could smell them from outside!"

His belly began to growl. "Goodness, seems my belly is letting me know it's time to be fed! That's my last big load, and I'll bring the kindling in and put it into your big bucket."

When Jim had finished his task, he placed a couple of handfuls of dry leaves underneath the iron fire base, added several good handfuls of the kindling from the bucket and placed several small twigs on the top of the base. He reached into his pocket for some matches and carefully lit the leaves, lightly blowing on them to encourage the fire to ignite the twigs that had been placed on top. It was a sight to see this man work with the fire as he softly spoke words of encouragement and gratitude for the warmth it was about to bring.

The old woman watched Jim, impressed with his relationship with the fire. *There's an art to bringing forth the best in all things, and a fire is no exception.*

This said much about Jim. She knew he was a man of solid personal ethics; it was evident in everything he said and did, and she knew that was a result of how he thought about life.

As Jim continued, the old woman noticed the way in which he seemed to dance with the fire. There seemed to be a rhythm of movement between Jim and the fire.

Jim is obviously very in tune with his heart's rhythm.

She noted every detail of his face. His lips formed a circle as he gently blew on the embers, to bring forth the flame needed to create a bond between the three elements he had placed at the base of the fireplace. His bodily position was strategically in alignment with the leaves, kindling and small twigs, and he was bent on one knee in an almost prayer-like position.

He seemed to coax the flames ever so gently to embrace the small kindling, so the larger twigs on top could ignite.

The old woman observed the energy that ran between Jim and the fire.

It takes patience, gentleness, and knowledge of one's heart to bring life into balance, and Jim knows this. Why, you can almost hear his heart speaking to that fire, and the fire seems to be observing him as well.

She shook her head ever so slightly as her heart felt great joy to observe such a precious and sweet relationship.

His actions indicated he and Sarah have moved through their differences and learned what love is all about.

The old woman felt tears burn her eyes. She quickly blinked them away, took a small breath, let out a quiet sigh, and brought herself back to the fire. It was time to step away from such an intimate moment.

As the fire began to burn an orange and yellow, a purple edge appeared that seemed to frame the entire flame. Jim knew it was ready for some larger pieces, so he placed a couple of medium sized logs on top, then stood up and dusted off his hands.

"That oughta take the chill off for this evening. This will probably be all you need for tonight, and it's supposed to be warm tomorrow."

He turned to sit in his usual designated chair, and as the two friends sat in front of the roaring fire, nothing much was spoken. Jim busily fed his face with hot biscuits and strawberry preserves while the old woman sipped a second cup of coffee. Warmth filled the room almost as much as the biscuits and coffee filled their bellies, and only the crackling fire broke the silence.

The old woman suddenly realized in a single beautiful moment, that she had been in great need of company. While she loved the serenity of the woods and the peacefulness that comes with being at home, she was beginning to realize she'd spent more years alone than she had living with a family. That felt a bit sad to her; she hadn't considered that it would one day bring a feeling of loneliness.

She then did what she did best, and got busy. She pulled out the black velvet bag that held her tatting. Regardless of any situation, the old woman knew that staying busy always cured whatever ailed her. As she tatted away, Jim began to speak.

"You know, I've been thinking about when I first met you. My life was pretty stirred up, and I wasn't certain how I would maneuver my way through it. Heck, now that feels like a lifetime ago and what's it been … seven years or so?"

He glanced over at the old woman, who was lost in her handiwork. He didn't want to interrupt her thoughts, so he simply poured himself another cup of coffee and sat in silence with her. He had been around her enough that he knew whatever she was thinking about would best be moved through the silence of her heart.

Within a few moments the old woman began her story.

"Once upon a time, not so long ago, there lived a couple that had a deep love for one another, for their community, and for the three children they were privileged to raise. They lived in an urban city filled with cars, shopping centers, tall buildings that housed many businesses, and what seemed like a church on every major street corner. While it was not a major big city, it seemed to never sleep. That is to say, it was constantly abuzz with traffic and sirens. People came and went at all times of the day and night, kept busy with places to go, things to do, people to see, and always some event that would enrich one's life; that is, according to whomever needed the various sorts of activities.

"While the time was filled with busyness, it seemed there was rarely time to just spend time with the family together. And when the family was together, it seemed all they did was talk about other members of the family, or about their friends and their family businesses.

"One day the Mother and Father decided to try an experiment. They wanted to see how the family would react if the car was not accessible for 24-hours, so they parked the car at a safe location, locked it up, and took a taxi home. They both had to chuckle at how they felt their kids would react when they found out there was no way to go anywhere for 24-hours.

They were prepared for the fussing and fuming they were sure would ensue once they told their children, and the utter despair that would fill the next 24-hours.

"Well, would you believe it, when they got home and told their kids they would all be homebound for the next 24-hours, much to their surprise the kids seemed almost relieved that they had nowhere to go. Practically in unison the three kids exclaimed, 'That's okay!' The three of them looked at each other and started to laugh.

"'How about getting out the board games?' the oldest finally suggested. 'I know it's no fun to play when you know you'll get your socks knocked off, but maybe I'm rusty and one of you will win,' he smirked.

"The second oldest headed toward the hallway closet with the third child close behind. 'Oh, you wish,' he said. 'We'll see about that!'

"The parents looked at each other in amazement, shrugged their shoulders, and then commenced cleaning off the kitchen table to make room for the games to begin!

"What those parents learned that day was that sometimes our children cherish being at home together, playing games, eating meals, watching a movie, and just enjoy being with each other.

"While our friends are indeed important to us when we are young, there really is nothing like being with one's family. Truth be told, friends come and go; it is the family unit we will forever be connected with, and age has nothing to do with it. Parents need to remember this even when the older kid is moaning about being too old to hang out with his or her parents or younger siblings. Inside each of us is a smaller version of ourselves, yearning to reconnect to simpler times, when all that mattered was knowing that we are of value and importance to our family."

The old woman bit the thread from the shuttle, knotted the end, and handed the chain to Jim.

"Thank you for your help today, and for showing up to let me know you had been thinking of me."

She picked up the tray with the cups, the remains of biscuits and strawberry preserves, and headed to the kitchen. Just before entering the kitchen she turned to Jim.

"These are my words."

Jim savored the sweet moment that was filled with memories of his visits to the old woman's cabin. He was grateful for her presence, and for her willingness to share her insights with anyone who took the time to find his or her way to her cabin.

He glanced around the room that looked precisely like it did the first time he had made his trek there. Two chairs sat in front of the fireplace with a beautiful, small walnut table between them. The fireplace mantle had the same items in the precise order they had always been. Starting from the far left, there was an unusually large piece of clear quartz crystal that supported one side of a few small books. An antique black iron secured the other end. About four inches further down the mantel was a pair of jeweled picture frames that held the pictures of people the old woman no doubt held dear. A feather with tan leather securely wrapped around the stem, a colorful rattle, and a most unusual piece of wood were next. At the very end of the mantel was a green glass kerosene lamp.

The clamoring of dishes brought Jim back to the moment.

Guess I'd better get moving or she'll be wondering why I'm still sitting here, although I'd like to know the answer to that myself.

With that thought, Jim inhaled and exhaled a deep breath, moved in his chair, and stretched his legs to prepare to stand up.

Why am *I still here?*

As he stood, he cleared his throat loudly enough that he thought the old woman would hear him, and almost immediately she walked through the doorway wiping her hands with a kitchen towel.

She looked up at Jim. "You must be very comfortable since you're still here."

He looked down at her beautiful face, wrinkled with lines that indicated the wisdom she had gained over the years.

"I have a question I'd like to ask you if you have time." He patted her shoulder ever so gently. "If another time would be best for us to continue this conversation, just let me know and I'll come back later."

He removed his hand from her shoulder and stood squarely in front of her.

The old woman finished drying her hands and placed the dishtowel on a dining chair.

"Now is always a good time."

Jim felt a sense of awkwardness as he glanced toward the fire.

Why do I feel awkward? I've known this woman for some time now, and she's as close to my heart as my grandmother. And, what do *I want to ask her?*

The old woman sensed his hesitation; she felt for her friend, who didn't quite seem comfortable with what he wanted to say.

"You seem uneasy."

Jim cleared his throat. "Well, I know you are a woman of few words and seem to be a very private person, so I do not want to cause you any discomfort."

"If there's something you want to tell me, just spit it out. It's the idle chatter that's a waste of time. I'm listening."

Jim felt a small smile cross his lips at his friend's words. In all the time he'd known her she had just said more words than she'd probably said altogether over the years.

"Okay, I gotcha. Well, you have so much wisdom, I was wondering if you would be willing to tell *your* story."

There it was. Jim had just opened his mouth, and out came the words. He felt a sigh of relief as he closely watched for his friend's reaction to his question.

The air in the cabin was filled with a silence that seemed to fill the room with a cozy feeling. It was like being bear-hugged by someone who really loved you.

Strange, Jim thought, as he visualized a bear coming close enough to him to give him a big embrace.

He brought himself back to the moment and glanced down at her. She was smoothing out the apron she still wore. The small blue print appeared very old, like it had been made from the old flour sacks from years ago. It was stained from all the cooking and canning she had done over the years, and the white lace trim around the front pocket had begun to unravel. No doubt this apron had witnessed many a meal preparation for people the old woman loved.

She breathed deeply.

"Reckon I knew this time would come." She fidgeted with the bow in front that wrapped the apron tightly around her petite body, and silence once again ensued.

Jim knew to just wait for her response. She was not one to be pushed or hurried into anything. While it was obvious she had been a very spirited young woman, the years had mellowed her into the quiet, contemplative place maturity often brings.

After what felt like ten minutes, the old woman inhaled deeply and nodded.

"Reckon I could do that."

Jim was shocked. He just stared at her as she smoothed her hair and stared directly into his eyes.

She said she would do it! Oh, my gosh, I can't believe she agreed to do that!

Something very magical happened in that moment; it was as though time stood still and a door had just opened. Both Jim and the old woman knew. They stood at the threshold of something that was ready to be birthed, and they were brought together for this very moment.

The air moved with a gentle flow of warmth that was also a mystery. Jim stared at the fire, which was now only a few burning embers. He knew the windows and doors were closed; yet, something stirred the air. The hair on the back of Jim's neck felt the flow and the old woman merely nodded ever so slightly. A smile began to deepen the creases in her face, and became wider as she nodded more vigorously.

"Okay," Jim said. "So when would you like to do this?"

"How about I get some guidance from my heart," she responded. "These sorts of things just unfold, so there is no sense in rushing things with planning."

Jim nodded in agreement.

She picked up the dishtowel and turned toward Jim.

"Reckon we've said all we need to say for now."

Jim smiled. "Reckon you got that right."

He was still shocked that this woman of few words had agreed to tell her story. Like a child with a secret, he moved toward the door. The moment felt surreal.

I knew she liked me but I had no idea she would share her life with me.

They walked to the door together in silence. Jim reached for his hat that hung on the deer antler nailed to the wall, and pulled it snuggly onto his head. He reached for the doorknob as he turned to the old woman.

"Thank you so much; I hardly have words. Just send me a note when you are ready for me to come back. It's all up to you. I'm just grateful you're willing to do this. We'll see what happens."

He opened the door and turned to the old woman one more time. She stood directly behind him, which was another first. Generally, the old woman was already in her kitchen when he left. Now, here she was, standing right behind him.

He couldn't help himself. "Is there anything you want to say, or anything you need?"

She simply responded with an affectionate smile and shook her head.

As Jim closed the door behind him, he gazed across the orange sky in the West where the sun had begun to descend. It was a brilliant hue of orange and purple, as though the sky were on fire.

This has been an unbelievable afternoon; the sky must be on fire. Maybe like the sky, the fire is burning to herald in the newness that change brings forth.

As these thoughts rambled through his head, he quickly headed back to his truck in order to get there before the sun completely set and the path disappeared into darkness.

Jim got into his truck and started the engine. He could feel the numbness from the shock of the entire evening begin to subside as he relaxed his body in the comfort of his old truck.

"Once again, her story hit home. We've been wondering how to keep our family close."

And, she's going to tell her story.

Then he glanced in his rearview mirror at the woods from which he had just emerged.

"Good grief. I didn't see this coming at all." His focus turned from the woods. He looked directly into his own eyes and took a couple of deep breaths.

"Where did that idea come from? Who in the world asked her that question? Hmmm … maybe it wasn't someone of this world!"

Meanwhile, the old woman tidied up her kitchen, and put away the silver tray, coffee cups and dishes from the evening treat with Jim.

Much like the rest of the cabin, the kitchen was small and compact. The cabinets looked white-washed, when in reality they were probably worn from years of use. There was a small turquoise refrigerator that looked like it was from the 1950s, with only two magnets on the door. One had a picture of a little boy that stared out toward the horizon, a white scarf flowing around his neck. Beneath him was written "The Little Prince." The second magnet had a mirrored front that said, "You are loved."

On the side of the refrigerator was a picture of two people holding hands. One cannot tell who they are because only their backs are visible. A man stands facing them, and one might assume the couple is getting married. The picture was yellowed on the edges, which seemed to indicate that it was a very old picture.

The old woman finished up her tasks at the sink, hung the dishtowel over the handle of the oven, and turned off the light. The only visible light now emanated from a small, stained-glass turtle lamp. It was a cozy kitchen that held the warmth of love and tenderness with which the old woman fed those who found their way to her home.

She exited the kitchen and moved into a very large, open area, past an oak dining room table and chairs, and paused in front of the fireplace where she and Jim had been sitting. She stood for a few minutes and observed the slowly burning embers, then sat down to watch them for a bit.

Life is so very interesting. I've done my best to keep my life to myself, and then tonight happens.

She shook her head and stared at the brilliant orange, sparkling embers.

Why have I kept to myself? Reckon it doesn't matter. If it's time to reengage in life, things will simply fall into place.

She began to look at each item on her mantel as though reflecting on her life. The old woman felt a tear trickle down her cheek, and the silence of the moment was broken only by the sound of her heartbeat.

She was nervous, though she had no idea why. Yet, she was clear that these feelings were real, intense, and beckoned her to cross the threshold before her. She looked at the glowing embers more intensely, as if to ask for guidance.

Just then, a small flame danced from amidst the center of the embers, as if on cue.

I'm listening, she offered in response. *What is it you wish to say?*

Without a moment's hesitation she knew.

"I know, it's time for me to re-emerge and give back to the world what it has so sweetly given to me."

While her heart knew, her head began to consider.

You know what will happen if you engage in the world. Those who knew you when you were young will think you have lost your mind. You will only confirm what they told you would happen if you continued along the path you were taking.

Are you ready to embarrass your family and be completely honest about what you know to be true? Think about that: are you really willing to return to that world of reality that clings to fear, self-doubt, and an endless stream of questions for which you are expected to provide explanation?

Her stare was broken when the flame disappeared. She glanced up at the mantle once again, took a deep breath, and then released it with a heavy sigh.

"Yes, I am!"

She stood up, and with both feet firmly planted on the braided rug beneath her, she spoke.

"With both of these feet and the help from all that have supported and sustained me throughout my life, I am ready."

A sense of joy moved through her heart as she felt herself stand taller than her 5'1" height. From the bottoms of her feet she could feel energy moving upward through her calves, thighs and buttocks, straight up her spine and all the way up her neck to the base of her head. When it reached the top of her head she felt a crown appear. The band tightened around her forehead, and the Sacred One with whom she had been connected since she was a small child appeared directly in front of her, and placed a mark on her forehead. It was the opening of her third eye, and she knew precisely what that indicated. Her heart was activated, and a surge of warmth moved through her veins, permeating every cell of her body.

She continued to stand very straight. She seemed to stand outside her body, and watched as an observer. It was as though she witnessed a momentous initiation that would prepare her to cross the waiting threshold.

Soft colors began to swirl about her as billows of white begin to gently spiral in a cylindrical shape in front of her eyes, and she knew.

It is time to do the work in front of me and, with your support, let us enter into that magical energy of love that always brings more love, peace, and joy into the world.

She had no idea what was going to come of all of it. It wasn't hers to know. All that was required of her was to show up and pay attention. She closed her eyes, took three deep breaths, and relaxed into the moment. Her lips parted as a sigh released, and her lips became a small circle through which the breath exited her mouth with direction and purpose. Another breath was taken in through her nose, pulled up from her belly and into her diaphragm, and once again, released through her parted lips. She stood relaxed and receptive to a third breath, and when it was released she knew yet again.

It is done!

She had crossed the threshold, and now stood firmly in a place she knew very well. The landscape was familiar; the scent of the air filled her lungs with loving memories of her true home. Cedar and sage scented the air that surrounded her like a lover's embrace. She was being cleansed and purified of any fears, apprehensions, or self-doubt.

This was something greater than her human understanding could explain or comprehend. Her heart knew, though, and she was joyful to once again be home with her *Old Friends.*

Stand in the Gap

The roar of the giant silver grain bins filled the air with the reverberating sound of drying grain. The deep hum blanketed the empty fields for miles.

The old woman watched the long line of semis that pulled the grain trailers that awaited the fresh dried bounty of corn and soybeans.

This year's harvest has been very successful, she observed.

From early dawn until long after dusk the tractor-trailers were filled, as farmers scurried about to get their goods to market before the predicted rain and snow mix moved in. Grandfather Sun had heralded in the day with brilliant, orange-red skies. Now, at mid-afternoon, steel gray clouds filled the sky with ample warning of the ensuing rainy weather.

As smoke billowed from the exhaust pipes of the diesel trucks, green John Deere tractors held the grain shoots that waited to fill the next trailer with the rich gifts from Earth Mother. The old woman observed the fast pace of the farmers as she gazed at the work in progress behind her cabin.

They look like they are in a hurry, and maybe a bit worried.

She paused her thoughts and honed in on the men that checked tires on the semis and chatted amongst themselves.

Or, maybe they are excited about this annual event for which they have waited all year.

One of the farmers noticed her, and with a wide smile, waved at her. She raised her hand and waved back at him.

It's sorta like a man in competition with the elements of nature.

She loved the richness of the Midwest and the genuine, down-to-earth nature of the farmers. She had much respect for the ancient, life-giving gifts provided by the rich Midwest soil, and for the generations upon generations of farmers that had devoted their lives to the tending and care of Earth Mother.

She turned and looked at her empty garden space. Everything had been pruned back, raked, and the trimmings placed in a large pile to be burned. The ashes would then be recycled back into the garden to enrich the soil for the next year's planting season.

She continued around the cabin to the front porch and made her way to the front door. As she reached for the handle on the screen door she reminded herself to cover the door with the plastic used to keep out the cold.

Once inside, she made a fresh pot of coffee, and took a loaf of banana bread out of the refrigerator. She retrieved a saucer out of the cabinet and placed a generous slice of the bread on it.

Thoughts of her conversation with Jim entered her mind as the coffee pot alerted her that the coffee was ready to warm her belly. With that, she quickly dismissed the thoughts and focused on spreading a dab of butter across the banana bread.

How I remember helping Mother churn butter. While it was not one of my favorite things to do back then, at this moment I would enjoy such a task, simply because of the time I would get to spend with her.

With a tender smile, she put the knife in the sink.

Such time-consuming tasks are no longer shared. Interesting how experiences are viewed differently, given time for the memory to ferment and grow into wisdom.

She poured a cup of coffee, placed it on the tray next to the buttered banana bread, and headed back to the porch.

The old woman could hear the farmers in the fields behind her cabin as she sat on her porch swing with the tray in her lap. She noticed the various hues of red, orange and brown leaves that blanketed her front yard. It was a reminder that the Standing Ones utilized the natural process of autumn in order to prepare for winter.

The Harvest has been gathered, and the busyness of life is about to become very still. Another cycle is concluding along the spectrum of life many refer to as the Sacred Walk.

She then proceeded to enjoy the slice of buttered banana bread and sipped her hot coffee.

Ahhh, banana bread; yet another treat offered by my mother and grandmother. Wonder how many grandmothers in my ancestral line made this?

Her thoughts moved to the stories her mother had told her about her great-grandmother. She and her family had made the pilgrimage to this "land of plenty" during the great immigration from Ireland, and had made their way halfway across America where they had set up a new home in Illinois.

I cannot imagine giving up your country and trekking across the oceans to find a better life. It must have been a traumatic experience for the entire family. It had to have been both terrifying and exciting for them.

Her great-grandmother had died before the old woman was blessed to meet her; however, her mother had told her several stories about this unique little Irish lady. As the stories go about the Irish culture, one story about Great-Grandmother was that she apparently practiced indulging in the brew on a daily basis. She would spend a great deal of time in the basement acting as an entrepreneur in order to make certain she and her family had an ample supply of ale.

She was a petite woman who barely weighed ninety-five pounds. She loved the homemade ale nearly as much as she loved her coffee. Each morning Great-Grandmother brewed a pot of coffee that sat on the stove all day until she finished the last drop, despite the fact that by that time it looked like motor oil. The thought brought a smile to the old woman's face.

Guess that's where I get my love for coffee. And, of course, my small frame, auburn hair, freckles and feisty personality could also be attributed to Great-Grandmother.

She felt the cold air coming in on the North winds as she finished her morning treat, and her thoughts once again returned to the season of winter. She stared at the Standing Ones that still held leaves, and those that had already dropped theirs in preparation for winter. She watched the squirrels scurry about at lightning speed, flitting their bushy copper-colored tails about like whips. Their cheeks bulged with the nuts they had gathered as they scampered up the trees to their special hiding places.

A smile widened on her face as she watched the squirrels fuss over fallen nuts, then generously share their finds with those most insistent.

Silly little fellas, they know they're going to share what they have. I think it's a part of the sport of the season they enjoy, rather than hoarding away to keep the food from others.

She then considered other critters of the Forest, and all that they were busy doing in preparation for winter. She remembered that, just as the bear prepares to go within the cave to hibernate for the season, humans must also gather what they need in order to stay warm and cozy for this final season of the year.

Autumn offers us the opportunity to contemplate the events of the past year, and, like the trees, shed the things that no longer serve us. It is a time to courageously allow ourselves to be vulnerable to the releasing of old habits, beliefs, and ideas, in order to spend the stillness of winter to dream.

She glanced straight ahead at **The Magnificent Oak* that had to be over one hundred years old, and fixed her eyes on the Ancient One.

I can only imagine how many dreams you have held in the roots of your being. Reckon we all can dream visions for the next round we will walk as we move around the Sacred Wheel of Life, and seed them in our hearts to bring forth in the spring.

The old woman pondered her thoughts of winter and wondered what new dreams she would like to consider.

"Maybe it's time to repaint the garden shed in the back," she softly whispered. "That old thing looks as old as the trees that stand around it. Guess if I want it to shelter my garden supplies for another year I'd better let it know I appreciate it by giving it a fresh coat of paint."

Only a few crumbs of her bread remained, and she sipped the last of her coffee, while her feet continued in the steady rhythm that synchronized with the porch swing.

It's a dance, you know. Deciding when to take action, and when to let each moment move you along the path. Sorta like this old porch swing and me.

Her pink colored lips parted in a smile that added definition to the wrinkles on her face. White hair now framed her face, while hints of auburn still streaked the gray braid that hung halfway down her back.

She was beautiful. It had taken her many years to finally realize that. She always knew she had a beautiful heart; she just never saw her physical beauty. Her parents used to watch her like a hawk when she ate, and would remind her that if she got fat no one would want her. She had carried those words for most of her life, and to her they had meant that no one would choose her unless she was absolutely perfect, which she further interpreted to mean that she would be unloved.

Such things parents tell their children. Of course, they are meant to help their child find someone to love, to get married, and to have a family. Most parents want their children to know love, but those words can often be interpreted in drastically different ways.

The old woman of course now understood that her physical beauty was a direct reflection of her heart, which was what she held most important.

A glow of peace and calm now replaced the often-furrowed brow that appeared when such memories emerged, or when she was concerned about a situation someone she loved and cared about was confronting. Oh, yes, she knew the person would be just fine; however, being human often hinders one's sense of well-being. That is, until one can surrender the events of life to something greater than human understanding. At least that's how the old woman viewed life.

"Feels like that cold front is here," she told her cat, Gracie as she shivered. "Reckon we'd better get the winter clothes and blankets out of the cedar chest."

"And you, missy," she said to Gracie, "had better get that coat of yours thickened up!"

She rose from the swing and took time to let her old bones feel the wooden floor beneath her as she steadied herself. She glanced down again at Gracie.

"I'll grab that old wool blanket of yours for you to use until that coat gets thicker."

As she turned and moved toward the front door, something caught her eye. She stopped and squinted her eyes until her furry canine friend, Tom, came into focus.

Tom approached the cabin with the same lumbering pace and hungry look he'd had when he had first appeared many years ago at the edge of the wooded land that surrounded her property. She remembered when she had first set eyes on him. He had been covered with briars from head to toe, a scrawny little puppy so skinny that his ribs protruded. How could she have ignored this pitiful little fella that seemed so lost and alone?

Since that time, he had randomly come and gone, checking in to see what treats the old woman might have for him. She had grown quite fond of him over the years, always welcoming him with a bowl heaped with leftovers from her refrigerator.

"Well, for goodness sakes, Tom, you're a sight for sore eyes! Reckon you've been gone most of the summer playing around with your other buddies. Now that the cold weather's coming in, you're finding your way to a steady source of food and shelter."

Tom backed up a bit as she walked to the edge of the porch.

"Oh, no need to get jumpy; I know to only get so close to you. Gracious, you're like a lot of men can be, scared to be too close to a loving person."

She smiled and silently sent her love to him to assure him that he was safe.

"I have your old dish in the kitchen, so I'll see what sorts of leftovers I have in the refrigerator for you. You know," she teased, "it's nice to have my 'garbage disposal' back! I can only put so much in my yard or I'll have an abundance of skunks and raccoons pilfering around the yard!"

With that, she did a balancing act with the tray as she gingerly opened the front door.

Jim's question resurfaced in her mind as she entered the cabin. She carefully closed the door behind her, and on the question. However, as she washed up the cup and saucer the question persisted, and seemed to intensify.

"Would you be willing to tell your story?"

Let me take care of Tom first, she silently replied. *He's outside waiting for some leftovers, and I certainly want him to know he's loved.*

She opened the refrigerator door and scanned the available options. There was a small portion of meatloaf, some green beans and a bit of mashed potatoes.

Not certain Tom will care about the green beans. But, if he doesn't eat them another critter will.

With that, she scraped the leftovers into his usual bowl, placed the storage container in the sink and headed to the front door.

Sure enough, Tom sat erect while he waited for what in his mind was no doubt a gourmet meal. With a wide smile, the old woman opened the door and greeted her furry friend with a delectable dish of goodies. He did not move until she had placed the bowl in front of him and backed away.

"Why, you are most respectful, Tom; it is good to see that you have not lost your manners. It sure is good to have you back home," she said with much affection for her loyal friend. "I'll just leave you to your meal, and there will be something for you tomorrow when you return."

She turned and walked back into the cabin, and went to the kitchen to wash the leftovers container.

"I've missed ol' Tom; he certainly is a welcome sight. Better check and see how he's doing with his meal."

She turned and walked to the front door. Sure enough, he had scarfed up the food and was long gone. She went out to pick up his dish, then returned it back to the kitchen and washed it as well.

Reckon he liked those green beans … they're gone!

"Okay, Tom's taken care of. Now let's take care of that question."

She moved to her chair in front of the fireplace, and took a deep breath from low in her belly. Her lips parted as she released a sigh.

"Okay, I hear you," she whispered.

She inhaled another deep breath and slowly released it.

"I know now is the time."

She sat as still as she could while her thoughts began to go into action. She was not one to share her most intimate feelings with just anyone in the physical realm.

What are you doing? You're opening yourself up to be completely exposed. People will know everything about you, and you know what happens as a result of that.

She felt a knot in her stomach as her pulse raced and her heart seemed to pound out of her chest. Her practical mind was taking her into fight-or-flight mode.

Without a moment's hesitation her heart began to speak.

"Don't listen to that fearful head; you know it's afraid of everything."

The old woman turned her eyes to the picture on her right and stared at the colorful painting on the wall. She blinked and allowed her eyes to come into focus on the sailboat in the painting, in which two people sat next to each other. The water was calm, and beautiful blue skies were dotted with billowy white clouds. The picture was framed in dark oak, and a small metal piece was attached to the center of the bottom of the frame, on which the words *The Trout* were embossed in Old English style cursive.

"*Life can be as simple and serene as that painting,*" she heard from her heart, and she felt peace.

She rose from her chair and moved directly in front of the painting. She stood very still with her feet firmly planted on the wood floor beneath her, and took in every detail.

"*Are you really sure you want to do this?*" her head asked again.

The old woman nodded.

"Everything that has brought joy to those around us has come from our heart, she whispered. "While I appreciate your ever cautious words, I request that you do what you do so well; that is, simply listen, and remember what my heart has to say. It will always guide us to the peaceful balance we've achieved throughout our journey."

At that very moment, her heartbeat returned to its regular pace, her breathing became fluid and easy, and she felt calm.

The old woman glanced at the fireplace.

Now might be the time to have the assistance of a small fire.

She slipped on her leather gloves, picked up the fireplace shovel, and gathered the small black pieces into a pile. She then placed some bark, leaves, and very small kindling onto the pile, and topped it off with a couple of pinecones.

The old woman retrieved a very old, small wooden box that sat beside the firewood. It had been left in her twig gifting basket on the porch by one of her guests, and she smiled as she picked it up and tenderly traced her fingers across the word 'Always' on top of *The Wooden Box*. She remembered the young man that had left it, and that he had said his grandfather had carved the word into the top with a screwdriver.

"It was his way of telling my grandmother that he loved her," he had told her.

She lifted the lid and retrieved a match, lit it, and placed it at the base of the items gathered for the fire. Then she carefully bent over and blew ever-so-gently on the flame.

I ask your assistance with igniting the creation of this fire, and with whatever is to be brought forth by what lies before me.

After a few moments the fire began to grow, and the old woman gingerly added a couple of handfuls of the medium-sized tree branches that had been cut for starting a fire.

"*Remember,*" whispered her heart, "*through the wisdom of uncertainty you will find your security. This is the only inevitable moment and this is where Joy resides: in this inevitable moment.*"

Of course, the old woman knew this Truth. Her head wanted to be of assistance in order for her to have the peace she already had within. It's just that the human mind is conditioned to what society deems important to keep a sense of order and balance; and yet, it is the culprit from which doubt enters. She knew this all too well.

"Be still, my beautiful head. Our heart has this under control. Let us surrender to the wisdom of our heart; you know it always guides us to our highest good."

She placed a couple of rolled up newspaper logs on top of the slowly burning flames, then turned and sat down in her chair in front of the fire.

She adjusted the pillow in her chair to support her back and wiggled a few times in order to sit fully erect, and settled in for whatever was to appear. With her feet flat on the floor, she took a few deep breaths and focused her eyes on the flames in front of her. They seemed to dance in colors of yellow, orange, and dark grays, outlined in a purple hue. She focused on each inhale and exhale as she watched the dance of the fire coordinate with the rhythm of her breathing.

With only the sound of her breath and the crackling of the fire, the old woman felt her body become light. After all these years her head knew to simply be the observer rather than to offer a dialogue of continual questions, answers and assumptions. Her head knew by now that its only task was to remember what she would witness.

The relationship between her head and her heart supported the Truth, and this meant to simply be present in the moment. It had taken many years to weed out the beliefs she had learned as Truth, and to realize they were merely *illusions* of Truth.

Her teacher had helped her develop her gift of discernment by suggesting that, when she asked her heart a question, if the answer she received prompted more questions, they most certainly came from the head. And, that the questions were likely based on certain beliefs she had been taught. That is, if she called up a belief she had learned while growing up, her thoughts or words generally included the word "should." She "should" do this or that. Or, *someone else* "should" do this or that. In an attempt to solve the "should" situation, more questions generally needed to be asked in order to be certain she was doing the *right* thing. Heaven knows, she must do things perfectly or there would be severe, often irrevocable consequences.

Moreover, during such head ranting, if doubt or fear reared its head as an uneasy feeling in her belly, she knew it wasn't the Truth. For when Truth is spoken, there are no further questions and the gut feels calm.

The old woman closed her eyes as the flames continued to dance, and white billowy clouds began to spiral before her. She felt at home, for she knew the destination well. Her body became of less importance as she felt her soul move upward among the white spirals that continued to roll, becoming brilliant reds and purples. She knew the journey well; it was the portal to the Divine and to those waiting to assist her.

As a child she had stared with excitement and curiosity when those white puffy cloud-like shapes moved about her room. She would look over at her dresser to make certain she was awake, and her dresser would appear so tiny that it could have fit inside her dollhouse. At other times she would quickly close her eyes out of fear and confusion. When that happened, she would open them again to find the dresser back to its regular size. She did as she had been taught and simply prayed for Jesus and her angels to protect her.

The old woman's body sat in the chair in front of the fire; however, her Spirit was now in the sacred place she goes to when she needs guidance from a higher realm. She sat in a circle with those from that dimension that had agreed to help her maneuver her way through her incarnation on Earth. It was an agreement she and her Allies had made before she made her transition to this planet.

The place always looked precisely the same, with each person in the exact same position. This was further assurance that she had not been tricked; rather, she was mindful of every detail. And, she always concluded her prayer, "As Above, so Below." This was how she learned to be impeccable in both worlds.

Once in the light energy of the Spirit realm, she took her seat in the circle with her Allies around a fire, the Ally directly in front of her initiated the usual acknowledgement, which also served as a greeting.

After a few quiet moments the old woman asked for guidance pertaining to Jim's question. No words were spoken, as everything was communicated through thought. After about five minutes the Ally beside the old woman nodded, and she knew this meant, *"It is as it needs to be."*

To those who come from their head this is a confusing answer. However, those who, like her, are comfortable working from their heart, understand very clearly what this statement means.

During the next fifteen minutes or so the old woman and her Allies shared insights into the request, and possible outcomes of her choices. She was given all the information needed to move in the direction she chooses with Jim's request.

Armed with the wisdom of Spiritual Truths, her time with the Allies was complete. She would take the dialogue with her Allies into her heart as she reentered the Earth plane, for her Allies are not attached to what she chooses to do. They respect and trust her to make the choice that best fits the circumstances once she is back in the dense energy of Earth.

The old woman felt a tremendous sense of gratitude for her Allies, and for their continual guidance and support. Most importantly, she was grateful for their unconditional love and patience throughout her Earth walk.

She often reminded her Allies that being in the physical realm had many limitations, one of which was the lack of acceptance by many, of things that cannot be seen. That is, unless it is supported by organized religion, where it is often taught in a very structured, controlled manner. People are strongly urged to read the sacred scriptures, the *Holy Bible* in the case of Christianity, for example, and are taught that only those appointed by God can accurately interpret its meaning. This is supported by the anointing of such gifts to a select few who are appointed to be the leaders of the church. They alone have access to communication with the unseen world. Anyone not anointed who claims to hear from that world is cautioned that demons may be attempting to trick him or her into following false doctrines. Those who claim to have the gift to speak to, see into, or hear from the unseen world are considered blasphemous, and are labeled as disrespectful and dishonoring of those chosen by God.

Many mental health professionals declare that, if a person claims to have encountered a deceased loved one, remembered a former lifetime, and/or to have had a dialogue with a nonvisible source of any kind, he or she most certainly has a mental disorder, and is hastily medicated.

Residence on Earth can be a very peculiar experience, and is certainly not for the faint-hearted. The old woman had tremendous gratitude for her ability to "Stand in the Gap" between the worlds, or, as it is often referenced, "Walk between the Worlds." In addition to offering an open heart to others, she considered this to be one of the most precious gifts she had to offer this world.

She realized that Christianity taught about the Holy Trinity: Father, Son and Holy Spirit. Perhaps what she was introduced to so early in her life was the Holy Spirit, and as she matured she understood more deeply that part of the Trinity. Whatever the case, she felt at home with that essence, and it was there that she found her gift to bring to the world.

The old woman began to feel and hear her breath as she became aware of her body. She felt the floor beneath her feet as she returned from the Spirit world.

The return to the physical world gave her a feeling of richness on many levels. While there was sweetness in that dimension that demonstrated purity and Truth in their most natural states, she also felt recharged, renewed, and eager to return to her physical body in order to complete the work she had agreed to do while on Earth.

Her hands felt the armrests of her chair as her fingers traced the curved edges. She ever so gently allowed her senses to return to her physical body, as her heart sent a loving "thank you" to the world from which she had returned. She moistened her lips with her tongue and smelled the wood scent in the air from the logs that burned in the fireplace, as she allowed her entire body to be filled with the love she had received from her Allies.

She straightened her spine, and her neck regained an upright position as she moved her head a bit and allowed her eyes to slowly open. She was in her second home, and it felt as warm and loving as the one from which she had just returned.

She rolled her shoulders, bent her arms at the elbows, and brought her hands to her heart. In the tenderness of the moment, she looked directly into the slowly burning fire and noticed the logs were now half burned.

What an amazing life.

She moved her head from side to side, blinked her eyes several times, and inhaled deeply, then slowly exhaled through parted lips.

I'm such a blessed woman! So much love, so very much love.

In the stillness of the moment with only the sound of the crackling fire, her eyes burned with tears.

It has been a very long time since I felt such deep gratitude for life. I guess the busyness of life has kept my feelings at bay. I knew I had put the wants and needs of others before my own for most of my life. It was, of course, because I saw what I needed as a young person through the eyes of the Allies from the Spirit world that came to speak to me. Like myself, those others needed someone to listen, someone to care, someone to really "see" them.

With her feet firmly on the floor and with the support of the arms of the chair, she stood up.

What I have done has only been possible with my Allies as my constant companions.

She glanced at the items on the fireplace mantle from left to right and remembered the importance each item held in her heart. When her eyes reached the end of the mantle her gaze focused on *The Trout painting.

Everything in my life that I have surrendered to Creator has brought me to where I am. For this I am most grateful!

She touched the painting for a moment, then placed her hand on her heart.

"Thank you," she whispered. "It is my honor and privilege to *Stand in the Gap* between the worlds."

Fire Starter / Fire Keeper

S ilence hung in the air as the clock on the nightstand flashed 3:45 a.m. The old woman moved from a fetal position and stretched her legs. She didn't need to look at the clock; she awoke nearly every morning around the same time.

The air in her bedroom was cold.

That cold wave must have come in last night, and I didn't turn on the furnace. She snuggled the down comforter close around her. *Maybe I can go back to sleep.*

"*That's not going to happen, but enjoy the comforts of your bed for a bit,*" responded her heart.

"Oh, I will!" the old woman softly whispered.

Early mornings had always been her favorite time of the day. The stillness of life adds a peacefulness that, according to the old woman, can only be experienced in the wee hours of the morning. It has been called the "bewitching hour," probably because the veil between the worlds at that time is so thin. Except for the nocturnal animals, even the critters still rest.

She loved her old cast iron bed; it was the bed that her grandmother had used as long as she could remember. The foot and head of the bed were adorned with ornate curves, pineapple-shaped points topped each of the four posts and each leg was supported by sturdy, looped cast iron.

The old woman had spray-painted the bed gold many years ago, to remind herself that she was a Queen. It was now a brushed gold from years of use. Somehow, she simply could not imagine her home without its presence. It was a constant reminder of her strong and wise grandmother, who had also taught her many old and beautiful crafts.

Her grandmother had been a rather stern woman who said precisely what was on her mind, and exactly as she perceived things. She also remembered her grandmother's insistence on perfection. Numerous times after her grandmother had taught her a new knitting pattern, the old woman had returned to show her how she was doing, only to have her grandmother begin to unravel the stitches.

"You call that knitting?" she would ask, as she rewound the whole piece into a ball for her to take home and start over. Yes, whether it was quilting, crocheting, sewing, or any other handiwork, her grandmother expected perfection.

However, despite her grandmother's gruff tone and critical words, she knew her grandmother had loved her. In fact, even as a young girl she knew her grandmother adored her. She had always felt "seen" by her grandmother; that is, she saw who the young girl was well before she actually became that person. Truth be told, that was why the young girl became the person her grandmother knew her to be. She was that loved, that her grandmother could be so honest with her. There was a bond between them, and an unconditional love that fed them both.

When someone sees the best in us, that person can be completely honest even when we mess up, and we will receive their words as helpful, rather than with fear that we have been a disappointment. This allows for an ebb and flow in the relationship that creates a mutual love and respect for each other, and, over the years, will help us also learn to love ourselves. This happens when each person in the relationship knows that whatever is said is intended only for the betterment of the other person. Such words are not meant as criticism; rather, they are spoken because the person can see our true potential, and their words are meant to help us to be the best we can be.

Such honest interactions can actually deepen trust in the person with whom we are speaking and, ultimately, in the relationship. When honesty can be heard from the place of love that it was offered, that helps a person learn to not take things personally, and instead to simply be grateful for the Truth. This is how a person develops the ability to look in the mirror and be honest with him- or herself, which in turn builds strong confidence in both oneself and in other relationships. It was the old woman's grandmother that had first taught her these important Truths.

Time to get up. As cozy as this is, the house needs to be warmed up. She noted that it was now 5:30 in the morning.

Goodness, where has the time gone? Ready or not, here we go.

She threw off the comforter and sat up, then reached for her robe at the foot of the bed and put it on. She tied the belt securely as her feet found the slippers on the floor. She stood up and steadied herself before moving to the living area to check the thermostat, which read fifty-five degrees.

Oh, my goodness, it must be freezing outside! She clicked on the furnace and tightened the belt of her robe.

How grateful I am for the promptness and ease with which heat is present! Thank you, my faithful furnace.

She glanced over toward the fireplace.

Guess I'll get a small fire going. Sure can't sit on the porch this morning.

She swept the coals from the night before into a pile, then covered the pile with small kindling, and topped it with several twigs. She brushed off her hands and picked up a large abalone shell that lay beside the fireplace opening and filled it with white sage. She held the shell in her left hand and placed her right hand above it, then bowed her head and whispered a few words.

She pulled a match from the old wooden box in front of the fireplace and struck it on the side of the matchbox. She lit the sage in the shell, and white smoke rose from the shell as the scent of sage filled the air.

She retrieved the feather wrapped with leather from the mantle and waved the smoke over her head. Once she felt enveloped in the sacred smoke she moved about her house, gently infusing every room in the cabin with the smoke.

After she had thoroughly smudged the cabin, she stood in front of the fireplace and once again examined the small pile of fire starter in the center of the opening. She mumbled a few words as she returned the feather back to its place on the mantle, and placed the shell in its usual location between the fireplace opening and the old wooden box.

"Reckon we're ready," she whispered. "I'll be right back."

She went into the kitchen and, using only the light from a small stained-glass lamp, she moved about with ease.

There was a gentle rhythm to each movement she made. As simple as her morning routine was, every step she took seemed to have intention and purpose. It was as though her physical body moved about in a routine manner while her soul flew among the stars. With only the hum of the furnace, the silence of the moment provided an avenue by which she could travel between the worlds.

She stared out the kitchen window at the skies, dark but for the stars that sparkled like diamonds. They seemed to remind her that her ancestors watched from afar, and that her presence on Earth was merely a temporary visit. When the time was at hand, she, too, would return to her rightful place among her ancestors.

As she continued to gaze at the night sky, her eyes were drawn downward.

"Oh, my goodness, it snowed last night!" It was a magical moment for her to see the ground blanketed by the first real snow of the season.

Oh, the gifts from heaven look like diamonds in the light of Grandmother Moon. As long as I live, the first snow will always bring a sense of wonder and amazement to my youthful heart!

"I guess it *is* nearly Christmas, and time for the kids to wake up to such a beautiful sight. Of course, they'll be more interested in missing school and having the day off to play in this white, fluffy snow."

The old woman once again scanned the darkened sky. Her eyes then moved back to the sparking snow.

"It looks like millions of the sparkling fireflies of summer are lying on the ground. Yes, sir, a million fireflies; yet another amazing reminder that we're watched over and blessed from Above."

The rumble of the furnace sent forth warmth of heat that brought her attention back to what she had come into the kitchen to do.

Better get busy making my coffee. She turned from the window and began to gather what she needed to make her morning brew.

She placed a coffee mug and a napkin on a wooden tray, and once the beep of the coffeemaker sounded, she placed the coffee pot on the tray next to the mug. She moved gingerly from the kitchen to her chair in front of the fireplace, and carefully placed the tray onto the small walnut table beside her chair. She turned to the fireplace, then removed a match from the wooden box.

"With gratitude I invite the strength of this fire to ignite warmth, and to fill my heart and this room with love," she whispered as she lit the kindling.

As the fire from the ignited match broke through the kindling, the small twigs received the fire and became a series of dancing flames. She stood for a few moments with her hands in front of the fire and slowly brought the warmth to her heart. All was at peace in her home.

She sat down in her chair and filled her mug with coffee. The morning was set, and she savored her first sip of coffee as it warmed her belly. Now to focus on the fire in front of her, and to receive information for the day.

Reckon that fire is like the warmth in my tummy; it's beginning to warm my entire being.

She took a couple more sips of her coffee and set the mug on the tray, then stood up and retrieved a couple of small pieces of the split wood. Reverently, she placed the first piece on top of the flames, and the second one at an angle over the first one.

She stood back a bit, brushed off her hands, and once again extended her hands in front of the fire. It was obvious this old woman had a tremendous amount of respect for the partnership she enjoyed with the fire that brought warmth to her home.

She poured a bit more coffee into her mug to warm it, and carefully took a sip.

"Mmm, that's some mighty tasty coffee this morning," she whispered. "I'd say all is well this cold morning."

She glanced at the large iron wood holder that was filled to the brim and smiled.

"That Jim has made certain we will stay warm this winter."

And so the day had begun, very much like every morning when the weather was cold. Her drapes were still closed to keep out the cold air, which helped the fire to warm the cabin more quickly. She would open them when Grandfather Sun officially began to ascend.

She loved watching Grandfather show his face to the inhabitants of Earth; it was such a reminder that all of nature has a very predictable pattern that also offers certainty to human life.

It was now close to 8:30 in the morning, and the old woman sensed that Grandfather was about to begin his ascent. Her hunch was confirmed by the red-orange glow coming in the East window next to the fireplace.

She picked up the tray with her mug and coffee pot and hurried into the kitchen. As she placed the tray on the counter in front of the window above the sink, she noticed the sky beginning to lighten in the West. She quickly moved back to the window beside the fireplace and flung open the curtains, allowing the warmth of Grandfather to come through.

"It takes my breath away," she whispered. "No matter how often I witness Grandfather's ascent, it amazes me!" Her heart felt rejuvenated by the warmth of such beauty, as Grandfather's golden reflection streamed across the ground's brilliant white glow.

"Yet another day to experience joy, peace, and the simple gifts of beauty that surrounds my heart and home." She felt tremendous gratitude for the abundance of critters, Standing Ones, creepy crawlies, winged ones, and the many different sizes and shapes of foliage that framed the pathway to her home.

"Let the warmth of Grandfather fill my home with the beauty of his Light," she said softly, as she moved throughout her cabin and carefully opened the rest of the curtains.

As the old woman glanced out the window, her eye caught a movement in the distance. She squinted her eyes to focus, and a smile appeared on her face.

"Well, I'll be darned, it's Jim! Wonder what brings him here so early?"

She quickly cleaned out the coffee pot and prepared a fresh brew. She pilfered through the breadbox, took out some homemade raisin bread, and placed it beside the toaster just in case Jim was hungry.

She then noticed someone was with Jim. It was a woman.

Hmmm, wonder who that is with him? Well, it doesn't matter who she is; they'll be here in a few minutes, so I'd better get some mugs and dishes ready.

She glanced down at the bedclothes and robe she still wore and quickly wrapped her apron snuggly around her waist.

Just as the old woman's coffee pot beeped to let her know the fresh brew was ready, there was a knock at the front door. She carefully placed the mugs, saucers, cream pitcher, and a beautiful glass dish filled with sugar cubes onto a wooden tray.

After a light tap on the door, the door opened ever so slightly.

"I know you're awake; you're the early bird." A wide smile crossed Jim's face. "Not to mention, I noticed smoke rolling out of your chimney. It appears those broken branches have come in handy."

Jim and his guest quickly entered the cabin and secured the door tightly to keep the cold air outside where it belonged.

The old woman walked in from the kitchen, carefully balancing the tray. She nodded toward a chair at the dining room table, then motioned her head toward the fireplace. Jim knew his friend well enough to know she wanted him to bring an extra chair to the fire for his guest.

Jim and his guest hung their coats and hats on the deer antlers beside the door, and they slipped off their boots. The old woman glanced at the rather round lady with streaks of gray in her hair, smiled, and carefully carried the wooden tray toward the walnut table between the regular comfy chairs.

Jim noticed that she was still in her bedclothes, but certainly did not want to risk embarrassing his friend by drawing attention to it.

"Do you need help with anything else?" he offered. He sniffed the air like a hungry dog.

His guest quickly nudged Jim and whispered, "Be polite; we didn't come here to eat."

"Oh, I am being polite! This lovely lady loves to feed people. Even if you aren't hungry, one sniff and your tummy will let you know that something good is waiting to be devoured."

He leaned toward the old woman and whispered, "Are you ready for a few questions about your life, or do you want to wait?"

She simply replied, "There's a platter of cinnamon toast with lots of butter on the counter in the kitchen."

"Gotcha," responded Jim with a smile.

"Wait until you put these delicious morsels into your mouth," he said to his guest, with a quick wink and a playful pat to her knee.

He turned and headed toward the kitchen. "I got this!"

Now, keep in mind the old woman had never made cinnamon toast for Jim; however, he knew from his good sniffer that whatever she had made would be outstanding.

He brought in the platter of goodies with great pride as the two women sat in silence and stared at the fire. Both looked up as Jim approached.

"Hope you're ready for a treat, Sarah," he said.

The old woman blushed a bit when she realized it was Jim's wife, Sarah, who was his guest. She recalled the very first picture Jim had shown her of Sarah. How she had changed over the years.

There's something about wisdom that brings out the rich fullness in a person as they mature. She appears very relaxed and happy. That warms my heart. Her eyes twinkled at the thought.

Silence followed, interrupted only by delightful groans and moans as they enjoyed their delicious treat. Jim patted his tummy and looked over at the old woman.

"Sarah's a great cook and, like I told you the last time I saw you, she's taught me to be handy in the kitchen as well."

"We have all benefitted from your culinary skills!" chuckled Sarah. She looked over at the old woman, "Our children are as round as we are!" Jim and Sarah simultaneously let out a laugh.

The old woman's heart was about to burst from her chest.

Jim has finally opened his heart!

She remembered all too well the first time he had come to sit with her. He had admitted to having a great deal of *Fire Within* that his family had evidenced in his quick temper. Her eyes closed in a prayerful moment of gratitude.

Relationships were designed for such moments of playful banter, laughter, and sharing joyful memories. My heart is happy for Jim and Sarah. Sarah certainly was patient while Jim allowed a new story about Love to enter his heart.

The old woman retrieved her tatting as the laughter began to settle. Jim reached for Sarah's hand, and they looked at each other with deep respect and fondness. The sounds of the crackling fire were all that could be heard, and the air was filled with the peacefulness that comes from truly being connected to another soul. The three of them brought a calm abiding that seemed to connect with the fire as the flames became smaller, and a gentle rhythm that seemed to sway with the logs that were embraced by the fire.

"Jim tells me you are going to tell your story," Sarah finally said to the old woman.

Jim quickly straightened up and looked at Sarah as if to say, "Shhh." She promptly leaned back in her chair.

After a few very awkward moments, Jim cleared his throat.

"I hope it's all right that I told Sarah what we spoke of the last time we were together."

The old woman continued tatting away at the long chain that had begun to extend beyond her hands.

Jim rose from his chair, picked up the fireplace poker, and stirred the burning logs until they were brilliant amber. He then strategically placed a couple of the split wood pieces carefully on the slowly burning logs. When he was certain the fire was precisely as it needed to be in order to burn well for another couple of hours, he returned to his chair.

The old woman began her story.

"Many years ago, a very spunky baby girl was born into a strict Christian family. They were thrilled that this second baby was a girl, although they really had no idea just how lively this little princess would be. Her mama made most of her clothes and dressed her in everything pink. She carefully embroidered tiny flowers on the fronts of her dresses. And, crochet, goodness, how her mama could crochet! That baby girl had all sorts of pretty, prissy clothes, sweaters and booties; whatever she wore easily identified her as a girl.

"It was a good thing her mama did that, because the next three babies that came were boys. So, here she was, the only girl in the family, with four brothers. Needless to say, that little girl was not very prissy once she could stand on her own two feet. And stubborn? Lordy, that girl was strong-willed! Her daddy was in quite a quandary about the fact that he couldn't control his precious princess.

"That's how this little girl came into the world, and that is how she has lived her life as a grown woman: by her own grit, determination, and patience. Gracious, that girl had patience. She never knew the meaning of the word 'can't,' even though it was a word she heard a lot. Instead, the word served as fuel for her fiery nature."

The old woman stopped and looked at the fire. The flames seemed to dance with delight in the presence of the three people that sat in the audience enjoying their performance. They began to stand taller, and then appeared to wave back and forth.

"Glad you are enjoying the show!" they seemed to say.

The old woman once again returned to her tatting, and continued her story.

"'Spare the rod, spoil the child' was practiced in her home; however, her strong will served as a motivator for whatever she decided to do. Yes sir, 'no' became the 'yes' she needed to make something of herself. Her only hindrance was her youth. Once she became a grown woman, the sky was the limit."

She paused. Jim and Sarah sat very still, mesmerized by the old woman's fingers that moved at warp speed, as a very long chain of delicate, looped thread piled up.

"Reckon that little lady lived her life precisely as she desired," she continued. "It was many years before she truly stepped into her fullness, but that can be said of all of us. She had always been kind and compassionate, sometimes actually to a fault until she matured. While her heart was broken a few times, she lived from it as fully as she could.

"Yep, even with a broken heart, she'd dry up those tears and get on with helping someone else who was a lot worse off than she was. She learned very early that to be of service is to be about God's work, and that is where she found her solace until her heart mended.

"She also had a fierce love for, and devotion to, all sorts of critters. She had a special place in her heart for dogs in particular. Didn't matter the size, color, or age; she simply loved dogs. She saw them as loyal, faithful, and always willing to love you despite your actions. There wasn't a stray that didn't find a home if they happened upon where she lived. Fact is, when she began to date, one of her first requirements of a young man was that he love dogs if he wanted to even be considered for a second date."

The old woman bit the end of the thread and tied a knot on the end of the very long chain. She returned her tatting items to the black velvet bag and stood up.

"Reckon life has been a very sweet one for that precocious little girl," she continued. "True, a bitter taste has been thrown in from time to time, but it has been during those times that she has learned to walk by faith rather than to lean on her own understanding."

The old woman placed the long chain in Sarah's left hand, closing her fingers tightly around it.

"It has been my privilege and honor to have witnessed yours and Jim's lives. You have a steadfast and patient heart. Treasure it, keep it open, and always appreciate the love you receive." She held Sarah's hand tightly and smiled at Jim.

"You have done great work, my friend. It is good to see that you have turned the *Fire Within* into something very beautiful. It has touched my heart to witness how you have transformed that inner fire into such an amazing gift. You have learned how to tend the fire in Sarah's heart, while your own continues to burn. Being a Fire Keeper takes a great deal of persistence, determination, and selfless giving. Above all, you must develop the ability to pay attention. You have learned how and when to feed the fire, and when to stand back and allow it to burn to a simmer, and you do it extremely well."

Sarah and Jim sat very still. The flames in the fireplace burned brightly, though they paled in comparison to the fire present between the two of them. The old woman placed the platter onto the wooden tray and carefully balanced the items.

"I'll be glad to carry that for you, my friend," Jim offered.

"Thank you, I got this," she smiled. Then she bent over and whispered to him, "And, I have started on our project."

She turned and moved toward the kitchen.

"These are my words," she said, and disappeared into the kitchen.

Jim knew this scene very well. He simply sat very still and observed the fire. He gave Sarah's hand a firm squeeze and leaned over to kiss her forehead.

Tears rolled down her cheeks. She had never experienced such amazing gentleness and strength from a total stranger. She had known the old woman was an important person in her husband's life. Now she knew why.

As she sat quietly and allowed her tears to flow, she felt a release from deep within her soul. The old woman seemed to know her better than she knew herself; yet, all the old woman did was tell a story about a young girl growing up. It was hard to wrap her mind around the emotions she felt. Nothing was said about the story being about Sarah, so why would her heart feel such a sense of being seen?

Perhaps Jim told the old woman about my life growing up.

She turned to her husband and whispered, "Did you tell the old woman about my life growing up? Did you tell her about Max?"

"We didn't have Max then," he responded. "I did tell her about my Shiloh, though. But, Honey, I would never speak of your life. You know I feel that it's your choice to tell her or anyone else about any aspect of your life. I respect your right to tell people what you want them to know. That is, unless it pertains to our life together, and then I'm very clear that what I say is my own perception. If someone wants to know your take on a situation, they need to ask you. I will not speak for you, Sweetheart; I have too much respect for you." He placed his hand on hers.

"Besides, I believe she was talking about her life. Remember," he whispered, "she's going to tell her story. She told me she has started our project. Maybe this is the first installment?"

He kissed her hand and glanced toward the fire.

"It's all such a mystery, and it makes my heart happy. Almost as much as you do!"

"You say the sweetest things," smiled Sarah. "And, you are correct; I certainly know I wasn't the only precocious little girl." She sat back in her chair, glanced at the fire, and took a deep breath.

Besides, there's no explanation for her knowing those things about me. Still, it's very strange.

And then she remembered her husband telling her that most of what happened at the cabin rarely made logical sense. He used to say that it was just something one needed to experience.

Jim stoked the fire and put on a couple of logs to keep it burning for awhile. Then he and Sarah moved toward the front door and put on their coats, hats and boots.

Sarah knew the teaching about giving back energy after receiving a gift. She dug into her pocket and pulled out a beautifully wrapped, shiny foil box with a red bow. She gently placed the gift in the twig gifting basket. Then Jim pulled some money out of his pants pocket and carefully placed it underneath Sarah's gift.

With that, they slowly sauntered down the path that led to their truck.

"Slow down, Honey," said Sarah. "I need to take in this place." She closed her eyes and took a deep breath.

She felt the air around her and smelled the smoke from the chimney. As she released her breath, she slowly opened her eyes and scanned the

Forest around her. Winter was upon them, and most of the ground was covered with newly fallen snow. The only remaining green was on the cedar trees that seemed to reach toward the heavens. She took one more deep breath and closed her eyes again.

"I smell the pines! Oh, Jim, what a magical place!" She opened her eyes and reached up to hug his neck.

"'Love' is not a big enough word for how I feel about you, my sweetheart, my anchor, my ... Fire Keeper."

She gave him a passionate kiss. "Let's go home. You have a fire to tend! Get my drift?" she teased mischievously.

Jim grabbed his wife and pulled her close as he moved her hair to one side.

"You bet I do, you ornery vixen!"

After a few affectionate and playful hugs they turned and, with their arms around each other's waists, walked to their truck in peaceful harmony.

Their journey was like most couples' stories that have endured the ups and downs of a relationship. Sometimes one person's heart is more invested than the other's, and it flip-flops a few times until both realize that it is safe to trust their hearts with each other. Fortunately for Jim and Sarah, they had confidence that they would be able to maneuver their way around and through whatever they might face.

Jim opened the door for Sarah and she hopped into the seat like a sixteen-year-old. She grinned broadly at Jim.

"Come on, you Fire Keeper!"

Jim smiled from ear to ear and carefully closed the door. He got into the other side of the truck and leaned over to Sarah with puckered lips. She promptly accommodated his request before he started the engine, backed up the truck, and paused before putting it into forward.

"You know, Sarah, I may be the *Fire Keeper*; however, you have your role as well." He placed the gearshift into drive, put his foot on the brake, and turned to her.

"You, my dear, are the *Fire Starter!*"

Let's Do This!

It was mid-afternoon in late February. The old woman had just finished cleaning the cabin when she heard the howling, blistery winds of winter. She put away her broom and dustpan, quickly washed her hands, and hurried to the front window of the cabin.

The strong North winds had blanketed the old woman's front yard with snowdrifts. As she scanned the yard and observed the many drifts, her eyes were drawn downward to the porch in front of her.

"That wind must be very fierce," she observed. "Why, just look at those small drifts on the porch. That has not happened in all the years I've lived here. Never! Looks like an ocean of snowcaps!" she said excitedly. Her eyes widened as she observed the beauty of the *Unblemished Snow* that fell.

"What a wintry wonderland!" she whispered with childlike playfulness. "From the looks of this we'll have a foot of snow by morning." She paused briefly. "Sure wish my grandchildren were here to enjoy this."

She sighed deeply and smiled. "When this snow storm has released all it's going to gift the Earth, I'll be out there! The little girl in me still loves to play in these gifts provided from Above. Truth is, she's the one that keeps me feeling young and free!"

A red cardinal streaked past her and landed on the edge of the porch rails.

"Hello, Granny!" she whispered, as the bird stared directly into her eyes.

"I know you are loving this weather as much as I am."

She remembered in a flash the year she had painted a red cardinal on a frosted glass Christmas tree ornament for her grandmother.

Oh, how thrilled Granny was when she opened that gift!

Each year Granny had expected a handmade gift for Christmas; it didn't matter what it was, she loved it. But, then there was the year she had given her granny a gift that had been purchased from a store.

The look on Granny's face told me to never repeat that choice.

From that point on, a handmade gift was presented every year to her beloved granny.

As if in response to the old woman's thoughts of her granny, the brilliant red cardinal flew off toward the North.

"Goodbye, my sweet granny," she whispered. "Take your place with the other Elders and *Wisdom Keepers."

Don't forget to give Mom and Dad my love.

She sighed deeply, and warmth filled her heart as she considered the beauty of the distant memories.

What a gift those memories offer me when I am confronted with a similar situation in the here and now.

She paused her thoughts and scanned the view in front of her.

I am grateful to have learned to "look over my shoulder," rather than to stare at my past from a place of fear that I will offend someone or mess up something. It is much more peaceful for me to bring what I have learned into the present moment, and use it to make a conscious choice rather than a reactive one.

"The Spirit within me grows in wisdom when I use my past as a resource, rather than as a whipping stick. I am most grateful for that awareness!"

Her eyes once again surveyed the freshly fallen snowflakes that made up the beautiful blanket of innocence and purity that fell from the heavens. She recalled the teaching that snowflakes carried the dreams and hopes sent through human prayer. The winter snows returned those prayers back to them, to be birthed in the spring.

"Again, something from the past comes to the present moment, to be used by those who pay attention." She took in a deep breath to bring herself from her head to her heart.

"I suppose it's the gift of remembering that helps all of us appreciate what we have, to feel confident about ourselves, and to be more willing to live in the present moment," she said softly. "For when we are grateful, we free our hearts to create new dreams and visions for our lives, and for the world."

The old woman's heart embraced the gift the wintry snow had put before her, and she suddenly remembered Tom and Gracie.

"Oh my, I wonder where those critters are stowed away?" she whispered.

She moved closer to the window to scan the yard for signs of her furry friends.

"Nope, don't see any paw prints."

She moved from the front window that faced South, to the window in the kitchen that faced West and looked out, but no paw prints were visible there, either.

"Hopefully, they are together in the back shed. Each winter they somehow manage to squeeze themselves through the small crack in the back. Of course, I'm certain Tom has dug a bit of a hole to help with access; he does that every winter."

She grabbed the ends of the thickly woven shawl that draped over her shoulders and tightened it snuggly around her.

Ahhh, that feels better.

She filled the tea kettle with water, placed it on the stove, and turned on the burner.

The old woman moved into the living room, slipped on her leather gloves, and grabbed a couple of pieces of split wood. She placed them on the edge of the fireplace, then stirred the simmering chunks of wood with the poker. She pushed the coals close together into a pile and strategically placed the two pieces of wood over the burning coals.

She then retrieved a pinch of tobacco from its tin and sprinkled it over the wood and coals.

Thank you for your warmth, she silently prayed, with gratitude for what she knew was about to appear.

The tea kettle signaled that the water was ready, so she placed the poker back in its holder, removed her gloves, and moved toward the kitchen. After she made a cup of hot tea, she headed to her chair in front of the fireplace.

She sipped a bit of tea while the fired burned gently, then looked at the mantel, where sweetly decorated Valentine's Day cards made over the years by her grandchildren were displayed. The homemade cards were mingled among the purchased cards they now sent as adults.

It is nice to know that my grandchildren have grown into thoughtful human beings. My children have taught them well how to love, and to be considerate of others. Reckon I have loved them well, too! She smiled.

"*Such sweetness,*" whispered her heart, "*to see homemade cards made with crayons and colored pencils.*"

Memories filled her head and her heart as she recalled the number of cards she had received over the years, from her children, and from the many students she had encountered.

I have received thousands of cards from thousands of different faces, each as unique and special as the next one. I have, indeed, been a very blessed woman.

She reflected on the numerous other people she had met across the span of her life. Some were there for a moment, some for several months, others for years. And, then there were those that would forever be embedded in her heart.

She thought of Jim. For some reason, he was one of those people who held a special place in her heart. She had watched him grow from a man with rage in his heart, to a man who had become a source of tremendous support. Whether six months or a year passed between his visits, he always showed up precisely when tasks around the house needed attention, or when her heart simply needed company.

As the old woman sat in front of the now flaming fire, she considered the matters of her heart.

How quickly life has flown by.

She glanced at the mantel above the fire and felt warmth within her entire being. It was interesting to recall the memory attached to each individual piece that now sat on display.

Each one is a reminder of a special moment, event or person in my life, and the richness of each experience taught me to trust. Mainly, to trust myself. Of course, ultimately, I learned to trust others, as well. It helped to give me hope for the next generation, and to live with the faith of a mustard seed.

She thought back to when she was a young girl in grade school, and recalled a small necklace her father had given her. It was a clear, square piece of plastic about an eighth of an inch thick, and held a tiny mustard seed in the center.

I don't know why that piece impressed me, except I remember that Dad said it was to remind me "to have the faith of a mustard seed."

She could almost feel the weight of the tiny necklace around her neck as she touched her neck where it had hung for so many years. She remembered it as clearly as if it were still in her jewelry box.

A black edge framed that small square piece of plastic. Goodness, I kept that necklace most of my life. I don't know where it could have gone; I treasured it as though it were a diamond necklace.

She continued her journey down memory lane.

Money did not really seem to matter to our family back then; I suppose it was because everyone lived on limited funds. Mamas stayed home and Dads went to work as the breadwinners.

Of course, my mama kept busy with sewing our clothes, tending the needs of a garden, canning and freezing food for the winter, keeping the house spic and span, and forever doing whatever was needed to make her family run smoothly. Her list of duties was endless. Why, I can remember that Mama didn't get her driver's license until the year I got mine. Until then, Dad was the resident chauffeur."

A picture of their home in Oakley, Illinois came into her mind. The small, two-bedroom, one bath home sat on a knoll that seemed like a "giant" hill when she was young.

She and her three brothers had always eagerly awaited the arrival of snow. They would get their heavy winter clothes ready in anticipation, and she remembered her older brother carefully and gracefully gliding an old rag across the blades of the sled in preparation for the next morning's magical trip down the slope.

As she now sat in front of the fire in her cabin, she could still feel the flutter of excitement in her belly as she recalled those memorable annual winter events. She felt as though she again stood on that knoll, looking down at the adjacent farmhouse that sat at the foot of their hill. It seemed to be miles away, far enough that it appeared as small as one of the metal houses used in a Monopoly game.

"Lightning speed," she whispered. "That's how fast that old sled used to fly down the slopes of that old knoll." She took a deep breath.

Of course, the trip back up the hill was never as much fun; however, it was worth every achy muscle the next morning. Whatever price we paid paled in comparison to the thrill of the lightning speed ride down that magnificent hill.

She blinked a few times to bring the fire in front of her back into focus.

"Such a daydreamer! I suppose a daydreamer never really gives up that gift." She smiled. "And, it is a gift, despite what others may think."

The flames had become few and far between, so the old woman got up and restocked the fire with small pieces of wood to bring it back to a steady burn. Then her mind returned to Jim's request.

Okay, step one is complete; we've made contact with the Allies. We'd better get to it and see what shows up with this endeavor.

She returned to her chair and retrieved a good sized, tightly woven basket from a shelf just below the top of the small walnut table. She placed the basket in her lap.

I guess this is the most likely place to start. Everything of any importance to me is in Mother's old basket. Truth is, it held all of her treasures as well.

She took a few deep breaths as memories flooded her heart. Both the lid and the basket looked like they had seen more years on Earth than the old woman had.

She carefully lifted the lid, uncovering a bright, shiny red fabric. She gently parted the fabric, revealing a plethora of items. There was an old, well-worn thimble that had probably belonged to her grandmother, and a set of jacks with a small red ball, that appeared as old as the thimble. Also among the treasures, were miscellaneous buttons, ribbons, old coins, a beautiful brooch with green stones, a couple of yellowed envelopes stamped from 1971, a small black bag tied at the top, and several wallet-sized pictures.

She dug a bit deeper and found an interesting large ring that she had not thought about in many years. Her Uncle Mike had given her the ring when she was about eleven. She couldn't recall the reason for the gift; it was just something he said he had made for her.

He was a sweet, loving man, who had carried many troubles in his heart. From time to time he had believed he was another person, generally someone famous, and then he would get into trouble. While he had never harmed anyone, his personality disorder had caused a great deal of grief for him and for his family. When he was simply Uncle Mike, he was kind and generous.

He had presented his niece on one occasion with this prized ring he had carved from a small chunk of wood. He had carefully notched a rather large indentation on the top, and glued a bright red plastic "stone" neatly in place. Small indentations had been carved along the sides and across the bottom of the ring, and assorted colored stones had been glued into each notch.

It was a sight to behold; yet, the young girl had felt the love her mother's brother had had for her, to have made her such a unique ring.

It was a beautiful gift from his tender, yet troubled heart. It is sad to see what happens to some people's hearts from their life's experience. He died at the age of 56. I guess he was done living with life's uncertainties.

For that reason, the old woman had kept the ring in her basket of treasures.

"I think I've seen enough. I'll leave the other assortment of odds and ends for my next treasure hunt. It'll be my next mystery to uncover." She smiled tenderly.

Her heart whispered, *"How I love exploring the mysteries of life in search of hidden treasures."*

As she sifted through the items on top of the basket, and it was the small black bag and the green brooch that she kept out. She held the brooch up to the light and stared into the green stones. The stones looked like emeralds. Of course, they were just semi-precious stones; nonetheless, the brooch obviously meant a great deal to the old woman.

She carefully placed the wooden ring back in her basket and neatly returned the other items. She covered them with the shiny red fabric, put the lid snuggly back on top, and returned the basket to its shelf.

She held the brooch in front of her and examined the beauty of the antique pin that looked like a sparkling green leaf. Marquise cut green stones created the body of the brooch. Round green stones were strategically spaced between nine large pearls in two places within the brooch, which gave the appearance of two stems. It was an amazingly beautiful pin.

She held the brooch up to the light of a lamp to her left, which enabled her to see the clarity of the green stones.

"What do I tell them, Granny?" she whispered. "What will be of significance to whomever reads the stories?" She felt a tug at her heart. "My life has been an interesting one, with many ups and downs; however, that's what most people experience here on Earth. My life is certainly no exception."

She turned to her left and saw that the snow had begun to subside. She looked through the dining room window that faced South, and a beam of sunlight caught her attention. She noticed that the light streamed downward from the sky onto the glistening snow, and seemed to spotlight the sparkling beauty.

Intrigued by the picturesque sight, she got up from her chair and moved it to face the dining room window so she could absorb the beauty of winter. She sat down and held the brooch toward the golden light and stared at the brilliance within the stones. She felt a pull at her heart as a gentle nudge seemed to move her through the green glass stones, and she felt her body encased in the emerald green color that moved her toward the heavens.

Within a few moments, she stood in front of a doorway, her eyes fixed on the deep, translucent green. She stepped over the threshold, and the green hue became the grass that blanketed the land around her granny's old farmhouse.

The brick house rested on a grassy hill that overlooked two small ponds just down the slope of the land. There were many very large, sturdy trees that surrounded the entire area, so that the house had been visible from the road only during the winter after the trees had shed their leaves.

It was an old farmhouse that had been built sometime around the late 1800s. She remembered it well from the numerous visits she had made with her children, mostly on Sunday afternoons and for occasional summer vacations.

This farmhouse is where she had learned the gifts of her grandmother's busy hands, everything from gardening, canning, and sewing, to various handicrafts. This is also where the old woman's children had explored the landscape and made new discoveries, from the surrounding coalmine pits to the various types of birds and animals that had made their homes on the farm. Many memories were made on this land for all of the children, grandchildren and great-grandchildren of her grandmother's family.

As she moved around the land, she noticed that her feet did not touch the Earth. That was when she knew she now "Walked between the Worlds," and that her task was to pay attention to any messages she received, or emotions she felt during her time on this land. Her eyes filled with tears as she focused on her heart.

She inhaled deeply and her chest moved upward, allowing her heart to reach for the heavens. She did this in order to keep herself composed. She knew if she started thinking about her experience she would return to the physical realm, and she was not yet ready for that. She knew there was a message to be communicated to her on this visit.

She placed her left hand on her heart and called to the Spirits of the land.

"What is it you wish to share with me?"

As if on cue, a brilliant red cardinal landed on the tree branch to the left of her, just south of where she stood.

"*Where is your faith?*" the old woman heard. "*Have you forgotten how to trust yourself? Why do you minimize the wisdom you have gained over the years? It is time to remember what you came here to learn, and what you are to do with those teachings.*"

Within seconds, two hummingbirds landed on a tiny twig that reached upward from the branch on which the cardinal was perched. Their tiny bodies were now perched beside each other. They were almost an iridescent green, and one had a red ring that adorned its neck.

The old woman considered how the iridescent green of the birds resembled the brooch, and she quickly dismissed the thought in order to stay present in this dimension. Once again, she remembered that if her mind went into action, she would be back in the physical realm. She quickly focused her eyes on the tiny beaks of the hummingbirds.

"What is it?" she whispered. "What do you wish to tell me?"

With their tiny toes hanging onto the twig, they stared at the old woman.

"*Why do you ask that question?*" they asked. "*Do you not remember the importance of not asking questions to which you already know the answer?*"

"Thank you, wise ones," she said softly. "I remember that teaching. I suppose I ask questions when I am afraid of the answers."

She blinked her eyes to clear the tears that blurred the tiny creatures, and inhaled deeply.

"I also know that when I ask questions to which I know the answer, it is because my human self does not want to take the action. I've made some silly choices in my life for which I have not yet forgiven myself, and it is time to forgive both myself and those involved in those situations, so that I can set all of us free."

A cool breeze swept the old woman's hair in front of her eyes. She quickly moved her hair behind her ear in order to have a clear view of the tiny creatures. Almost immediately, the hummingbirds began to flap their wings at warp speed, and with an ever so gentle hum of their wings, they flew away.

I guess they agree with my words, so that's settled!

She looked again at the red cardinal that seemed to simply observe the scene before him. A gray female cardinal flew in from the West and perched close to the red one. The old woman smiled.

I do believe this is a tag team event.

"*You have grown into a very wise woman,*" whispered the gray cardinal. "*We remember the young woman who constantly questioned herself and her worth. Your love for your children warmed all of our hearts on this land. We knew it would be through those relationships that you would find your gifts, and the unconditional love you needed in order to claim and embody your personal strengths.*"

The old woman felt a lump in her throat and she allowed her tears to flow.

"I certainly did doubt my self-worth most of my life. I was so very disappointed with the conditional love I had experienced, until my children arrived. When my children left home, my heart felt empty. It was then that I sought to find and reclaim my personal Truth. Meeting my Teacher helped me to realize that what I had heard when I was a child from all the critters, the Standing Ones, and the Spirit within my heart, was what was true and real. When I reached school age, I was taught to grow up and to not use the world of make-believe."

Her eyes moved toward the first pond on the land. The water was clear, with only a few ripples from the bullfrogs that leaped from the water lilies to the edge of the pond. She felt tenderness within her heart for the young girl who did not understand why adults would tell her that what she had experienced was make-believe, and she remembered the sadness and the loneliness that had ensued.

She recounted the many stories she had heard over the years of young adults who, like her, had been stripped in their early years of such inner Truths and knowing by well-intended parents, caregivers, teachers, and religious leaders.

Her eyes moved back to the pair of cardinals in front of her.

"The faith I was taught gave me a sense of security, in that I knew I was never alone; however, the rigid, demanding teachings also kept me from seeing my worth. It is a sad state of affairs that has to be dealt with as children grow up and become adults."

She took a deep breath and felt Earth Mother beneath her feet.

"Thank you all so very much for 'seeing' me when no one else, including myself, truly saw my worth at such a tender age," she said softly. "Their teachings did not support the gift of seeing that I had experienced so early in life." She felt a brief moment of sadness from the memory.

"If I had continued to access the assistance that stood directly in front of me, I would have avoided many painful teachings that I walked into. And, yet, I know it is what we choose to experience before we agree to make this visit to Earth."

The cardinals sat steadfastly and stared directly into the old woman's eyes.

She continued, "I am grateful for the patience and guidance that all of you have provided, and for the continued support that has allowed me to open my heart and my eyes." She took a deep breath and wiped her tears.

"It has also helped me to know and trust that the young people I worked with all those years would eventually find their way back to their own gifts and personal Truths, as I did."

The cardinals, like the pair of hummingbirds, simply stared at the old woman as they communicated.

"Now you know why you were brought here. It is time for you to share what you have learned. Always remember how very loved and supported you are!"

And, with that, they flew off into the North.

The old woman watched the pair of cardinals soar toward the heavens. From her vantage point, the white billowy clouds seemed to pull the pair from the blue skies into the softness of their loving care.

As she scanned the skies above her and the vastness of the universe they occupy, her eyes were distracted by a very large, red-tailed hawk. She immediately knew this would be the next winged one to bring a message to her.

Within a few seconds, the giant cedar trees swayed in the wind, and the old woman was drawn into the vibrant green color of these tall Standing Ones. She remembered the teaching by the Native Americans.

"The Cedar trees were among the Evergreens that were allowed to keep their green foliage because they had shown themselves to be faithful to the teachings of the Creator."

At that moment she felt her feet touch the Earth, and her eyes began to blink. She took a deep breath as the scent of cedar and sassafras filled the air, and the fire that burned to her right welcomed her back into the physical dimension. She took several additional deep breaths, and as she opened her eyes she felt the brooch in her right hand.

She stared straight ahead at the snow that continued to blanket the Earth, and was once again reminded of the teaching that snowflakes are the prayers and dreams of Earth's inhabitants. They return to Earth Mother to feed and nourish her with the richness of their dreams.

It is good that I remember this important teaching; someone may visit that needs to hear these rich Truths offered by those that walked before us.

The old woman looked down at the brooch she held in her hand.

"Well, thank you," she said to the beautiful brooch. "That was a very special journey. I wonder if anyone knew you could time travel with an old brooch?" She laughed heartily as she brought the brooch to her lips and kissed it.

Her eyes turned to the old hands that held this delicate pin.

My hands look as weathered and deep-veined as my grandmother's did; guess it's only appropriate that they do, since I'm the age my grandmother was when I noticed her wrinkled hands.

She then remembered her mother's hands.

"They, too, had deep veins in them as she aged, only her hands were still soft and smooth." She stared at her own aged hands.

My hands worked the land and garden as my granny's did, while Mama's stayed softer from all the inside work for which she used them.

She attached the brooch to her teal-colored sweater, smoothed her white blouse beneath it, and picked up the small black bag that sat in her lap.

"I reckon you're next."

She inhaled deeply and slowly exhaled.

"I do believe I need to move these old bones; perhaps we'll save you for later today or tomorrow. I need to get my hands in the snow and my feet on the ground in order to be fully back in this physical world."

She stood up, walked to the fireplace mantel, and placed the small black bag beside the old black iron that secured a few special books on one end. She then stirred the coals a bit and placed three split logs on the slowly burning fire, to ensure that she would return to a warm home.

The old woman headed to the utility room, where she found her snow pants and boots. After she slipped on her snow pants and heavy coat, she pulled a pair of heavy wool socks from the boots and put them on. She felt like a kid stuck in clothes that were two sizes too small as she attempted to put on her hat and gloves. She completed the ensemble with a knitted scarf wrapped snuggly around her neck. Donned in all of her winter regalia, she was ready to bring herself solidly back to this beautiful white wonderland on Earth.

She retrieved a walking stick next to the back door to keep herself steady and exclaimed, "Think I'm ready to play!"

She exited through the back door of the utility room, tightly gripped the walking stick, and placed it in the snow. She carefully took one step, and then another, and her boots disappeared into eight inches of snow.

Well, so much for making snow angels! I'd be buried alive in this white wonder, ahhh, what a way to leave Earth! She giggled.

"Nope, not ready for that, there's too much snow left to explore!" And, she took the next step with a big grin on her face.

After a nice hot bath that warmed her old body from the wintry exploration of the land around her cabin, she slipped into her favorite pair of flannel pajamas and furry slippers. She wiped the steam from the hot tub water off the bathroom mirror and noticed the rosy color on her cheeks.

How about that? That wintry wind left a youthful pink blush on my face!

She retrieved cold cream from the medicine cabinet and wiped a thick layer all over her face and neck.

"Oh, that feels better!" She reflected on the image in the mirror, and then noticed how red her hands were.

Oh my, looks like you could use some heavy moisturizer as well!

With that, she slathered her hands with an abundant amount of the cold cream.

"Good ol' Pond's cold cream. I sure remember that Mother applied it every night before she went to bed. Maybe that's why her skin stayed youthful looking well into her eighties."

After completing her nightly routine, her belly reminded her that it needed to be fed.

"Okay, okay, let's warm up a mug of that chicken and rice soup from yesterday."

She grabbed her robe and tied it firmly around her waist.

"I'm cozied up and ready to tend to my belly's request!"

Once in the kitchen, she retrieved the soup from the refrigerator and ladled a couple of scoops into a small saucepan.

"That ought to do it."

Her belly rumbled loudly as if to say, "Thank you, it will indeed."

When the soup came to a soft boil, she turned off the stove burner, grabbed a rather large mug from the cabinet and ladled the soup into it. Steam rolled above the mug, filling the air with the scent of homemade chicken and rice soup. As if on cue, her belly rumbled again as the old woman gathered a spoon, a few saltine crackers and a glass of water, and placed them on the tray that held her mug of soup.

She moved to her chair in front of a low burning fire. She settled into the chair, placed both her hands over the tray, bowed her head and mumbled a few words. She placed both hands on her heart as she finished, then commenced enjoying the warmth of her meal.

After about thirty minutes, the old woman noticed that the fire beckoned for attention. She drank the last of her soup, placed everything on the tray, and rose from her chair as she spoke to the fire.

"I'll be back to attend to you in just a few minutes."

She disappeared into the kitchen, and returned within ten minutes. She stirred the embers and completed the necessary steps to bring the fire back to a medium burn.

"That'll take care of you for as long as you're needed for the work we have to do. Then I'll let the furnace give you a rest for the night."

She stood up and retrieved the small black bag she had placed by the antique iron bookend and went back to her chair. The fire began to crackle and pop, shooting up small flames from the bottom of the gathered wood.

"My, my, you all certainly are cooperating with each other," she said to the fire. "I must say, I am grateful for your beauty, and for your example of what collaboration looks like."

She went back to her chair and sat down carefully, wiggled a bit to get comfortable, and again addressed the fire.

"I am requesting that you all assist me with this work."

The flames began to slowly emerge as the old woman felt the object in her right hand. She raised her arm, opened her hand, and spoke to the small black bag.

"Let's see what you have to share with me." She took a few very deep breaths and closed her eyes. She continued to breathe steadily as she felt the floor beneath her feet.

The fire blazed as the wood crackled and popped. Warmth from the fire now moved toward the old woman, and she ever so slowly opened her hands. She untied the small black bag with steady hands, and paused for a few moments.

Settle in, she told herself, *and breathe.*

Her hands were now a bit shaky as she carefully opened the top of the bag. Again, she glanced at the fire and asked for assistance. Her head attempted to analyze the situation and make up a story about what was going to happen, but her heart was peaceful and even a little excited about the possibilities.

She gazed steadily at the fire that now burned gently, and she began to breathe with the fire's rhythm. Within a few moments her eyes moved from the fire to the opened black bag that revealed the top of a gold object.

I know what this is. Be silent, my head, your only task is to remember what we witness, and any words that are spoken to us.

She removed the gold object from the bag and held it up to the fire. After a moment or so, she pushed the stem at the top of the object. The face of the piece opened and a Compass was revealed. The double pointed arrow shook and moved as she held the piece in front of her heart. She glanced down at the quivering arrow that rotated clockwise and counterclockwise until the perfect North direction was located.

The intricacies of the face of the Compass were engraved in black on the gold. Beginning at the far edge of the circumference of the Compass were numerous tiny straight lines and numbers. An arrow was affixed in the center with a tiny gold piece that had an even tinier green stone on top. Eight lines radiated evenly from that center, and each line narrowed to a point. Black letters were engraved into the gold face around the center, respectively: N, NE, E, SE, S, SW, W, NW. One tip of the arrow was black; the opposite tip was red. It was a reminder of the ancient ways in which humans navigated their way through the landscape of Earth, as they hunted, gathered, and moved about to find a place they could call home.

As the old woman held the Compass she recalled how primitive civilizations were guided by the sky scape; that is, the location of the sun, moon and stars. Nature was the guide that led early civilizations as they moved about on Earth, and to wander the various terrains in search of a place to settle down and build a community.

If nature brought torrential rains and floods that made their land unable to grow the food needed to feed the community, or if they lost a particular species of animals to be used for food or other resources to support the community, they would pack up and move. The relocation was often a significant distance from their current homes, which required that they use the stars to guide their travels.

She felt the smooth surface of the Compass. *Imagine what courage it took to live during those times.*

She stared at the small round object that was like those used to guide early humans on their journeys.

"What courage it took to use this little piece of metal; and, yet, it certainly made life easier than relying only on the sky scape for direction."

The old woman felt her heart quicken and her stomach flutter. She felt surrounded by a very familiar warmth that was not from the fire. It was the movement of her Allies, giving her a nudge. It was how they guided her.

"Okay, I'm listening," she softly whispered. "Is this Compass to be a part of the story I'm to share?"

The words were barely out of her mouth when the wind howled outside. She leaned forward toward the fire, and the room was filled with the scent of sassafras as the fire began to dance.

"I'm listening," the old woman repeated.

After what felt like five minutes, she rose from her chair and went to the front window. The snowfall had suddenly ceased as quickly as though someone had just pulled the plug on it. She smiled as she gazed at the dark sky that sparkled with the full array of stars. Grandmother Moon was full, and her beautiful rays of light on the freshly fallen snow looked like thousands of sparkling diamonds.

Her eyes glanced down at the gold Compass, and she stared at the beautiful instrument in her hand. Her eyes filled with tears and tenderness enveloped her heart as she began to recall how the Compass had come to her.

Many years ago, the old woman had had a very dear gentleman friend who had touched her heart deeply. It was a very significant relationship to her, especially since she had lived alone for over thirty years. They had shared many things in common, in particular, the desire for a simple life that held a deep love and affection for the ancient ways that valued and appreciated the *Wisdom of nature.

On one of her gentleman friend's visit to another part of the country for which he had a deep affinity, he had purchased the Compass. She remembered the day he had returned from his trip and handed her the small black bag. He had explained that when he saw what was inside he immediately thought of her. It had moved her heart deeply to know that he had thought of her on his travels, which made her eager to discover what was inside. When she opened the bag and discovered the gold Compass, her heart had nearly jumped from her chest.

"Oh, my gosh," she said as her eyes filled with tears. "You have no idea what this means to me. Thank you so very much!" And, she hugged him.

While he knew her well, there was much more he did not know, or, maybe did not want to know about her. The significance and importance of the sacred directions was one of those unexplored areas. To her, this could only mean that a Divine Source had guided him to the treasured antique Compass that was to find its way to her.

That had been many years ago, and to the old woman this Compass was not only a part of a deep love she and her gentleman friend had shared; it was also an indicator from the Divine that when the time was at hand, this gift would be used for something very important.

Well, I'll be darned!

She let out a small giggle, shook her head, and kissed the Compass.

"Okay, I'm ready and willing! Let's see where this takes us."

The Divine Magic of Life; how it continues to use the wisdom of nature to keep me doing my work.

Her eyes glanced back at the glistening beauty outside the window and her heart filled with gratitude.

Just look at that gift from Creator!

"Your guidance has been made clear, thank you!" she softly whispered as her eyes moved toward the heavens. "I trust your wisdom to begin this journey."

After a moment of silence, she inhaled a deep breath and held it, then slowly exhaled.

If there is one thing I have depended on my whole life, it is our relationship. Let's do this!

I wonder, the old woman thought as she pulled the down comforter over herself and settled in for a good night's sleep, *how my friend in Oregon is doing?*

She curled into a snug fetal position to allow her body temperature to warm the cold sheets.

Heaven knows, I hope his heart has finally found a home.

The wind had subsided and she once again thought of her critters.

Hopefully Gracie and Tom are keeping each other warm on this frigidly cold night.

She turned over to the opposite side and once again curled up into a tight ball.

"Ahhh, this is nice! Let's hope my critters are as snug and warm as I am, wherever they are."

She thought of her friend again.

Maybe he has found someone to really open his heart to.

A momentary lump in her throat caused her to swallow the sorrow that still lingered from the loss of his presence in her life.

"Everything works for the good," she reminded herself, "and this is no exception."

Okay, enough of those thoughts. Time to shut down and allow our body to rest. We have work to do in the morning.

"I know!" her heart exclaimed to her head. "Since you love to be of assistance, how about you work at remembering our dreams tonight? I've called in some guidance for where and how to begin the work with our Compass. If you could witness those dreams and hold them until morning, we can get busy on this assignment first thing tomorrow."

A deep yawn ended the conversation between her head and her heart. She readjusted her pillow and pulled the comforter still closer around her body. A last yawn expelled everything from her mind and body as she drifted off to journey among the stars.

A distant rumble woke the old woman from her sleep. She quickly opened her eyes.

What in the world is that? She sat straight up in her bed and glanced at the clock.

Oh, my goodness, it's nearly 7 o'clock! That must have been some journey last night!

Not one for jumping out of bed first thing in the morning, she grabbed the pillow beside her to prop herself up. After a few yawns, she focused her eyes back on the clock.

"That surely could not have been thunder after that snow storm last night," she mumbled. "Perhaps Tom and Gracie have emerged from their shelter with a bang!"

Still, it didn't make sense, so the old woman grabbed her robe from the foot of the bed, put it on, and tied it snuggly around her waist. She slid out of bed, slipped on her house slippers, and steadied herself as she stood up.

She exited her bedroom and moved toward the front window to check things out. Sure enough, there were Tom and Gracie, who looked at her as if to say, "We made it. Could you spare a bit to eat?"

"Oh, you pitiful looking little critters," she said with a wide smile. "You are a sight for sore eyes!"

Her eyes drifted toward the front yard, only to find it obscured from her sight by a very dense fog.

"Well, my lands, I didn't know such fog could be present after a heavy snow storm." She squinted to focus through the fog.

"What is that?" She strained in an attempt to have a clearer vision of an appearing dark object. She felt a flutter in her belly as a warm breeze swept across her.

I know that feeling, she mused. *Yes, indeed, I know.*

Just then the fog began to move as the dark object took another shape. Was the object actually taking another form, or was the fog lifting to unveil what was present?

"Let's not try to figure this out," she said to her head. "My heart knows what is present. Besides, you certainly know by now there are no words to describe matters from the Spirit world. We just have to wait, and it will be revealed."

She blinked and glanced down at her critters.

"Okay, I will be back directly; then we'll take care of what beckons for attention." She looked back up at the large object that was still very muted from her vision. However, she knew it carried some information for her.

"I see you," she whispered to the object, "I'll be right back."

She returned with a tray that held two small bowls; one bowl held cat food for Gracie, and the other was heaped with leftovers for Tom. The old woman carefully opened the front door, stepped out, and placed the bowls in front of her beloved critters.

She stood up and glanced again toward the area where the dark object had been. As the fog continued to lift she noticed that the "unknown" dark object was the Magnificent Old Oak in her front yard. Beside it was a large branch that had fallen during the snowstorm.

"Hmmm, now isn't that interesting," she said, as she scanned the yard. To her surprise, the snow had leveled out.

"What a beautiful sight," she whispered, as she noticed Grandfather Sun began to peek through the fog that was now moving West. She shivered and quickly moved back into the cabin.

"Brrr, it's cold out there! It's good to know that Gracie and Tom are keeping warm." She shivered again and closed the door tightly behind her.

She carried the tray into the kitchen, then moved to the fireplace and got a fire started. Then she went into her bedroom to change from her bedclothes into something warm for the day.

"We've got some instructions waiting for us," her heart told her head. *"Are you ready to tackle this one?"*

"I'm ready for anything!" replied her head.

She chuckled as she slipped into a pair of khaki colored corduroy pants, tucked in a black camisole, and layered over it a black turtleneck and a variegated turquoise and black sweater. She went into the bathroom and "painted the barn" with a bit of blush, and finished with a pink shade of lipstick.

She pulled on a pair of Smart Wool socks, slipped her feet into fleece-lined slippers, and moved back into the kitchen.

"I can't believe it's nearly 8 o'clock and I am just now preparing my morning coffee!"

She prepared the coffee pot and put a slice of cinnamon bread into the toaster. While the coffee brewed and the bread toasted, she covered the tray on her counter with a towel. Once everything was ready, she reached into the cabinet and pulled out one of her favorite delicate cups that she had brought back from England many years ago.

It feels like a special day, and one that will add even more richness to the beginning of the next chapter to be told.

She carefully moved toward her "contemplation" chair and placed the tray on the walnut table. Warmth filled the air as the fire burned brightly.

"Oh, how grateful I am for all the blessings and protection this home and hearth provide."

Steam rose from the hot coffee as she recalled the dark object that had been hidden by the dense fog. She remembered the wave of warmth that had moved through her body, and the flutter she had felt in her belly when she had acknowledged the object's presence. Her head began to let her know that it was simply the Old Oak and nothing more, when her heart intervened.

"You know by now that we are not going to try and figure out what it means. All we need to do is be still, and we will be shown."

After a second cup of coffee, the old woman dusted the toast crumbs from her hands and took a deep breath.

"You know," she said, "it's a full-time job for me to keep you from incessantly speculating about everything. I love how brilliantly we work together, now!"

Her mind thought back to the many solutions it had offered that had made her life what it was today; and, from the mind's vantage point, they felt unappreciated. The old woman used the "ears" of her heart to listen, rather than to rely only on what she felt, in order to truly understand what her head had just communicated.

"The thing is, my beautiful and supportive practical head, if you continue to speculate, dissect, and analyze everything, it exhausts me, your loving and sensitive heart. And, that has only caused experiences to be delayed!"

With lightness in her heart, she continued, "We have spent our life coordinating this relationship in order to support our visions and our dreams. Let's not go into reverse now. We stand in the North direction, the final phase of life on Earth. Now is the time to accept that we *are* elders and, more importantly, to act like it!"

The old woman suddenly knew precisely what the dark object was that had been muted by the fog. It was her shadow side, the side that feared being incorrect or misunderstood. It was the practical side that was concerned about how others would perceive what she had to say, and that somehow, she would be judged as a crazy old woman who used the Spirit world as a place to hide when life made no sense.

Well, nonsense!

"Let's get about doing what we know it is time to do. Let's take the wisdom we have learned from first-hand experience, and the faith in our heart, to present what we have learned during this time on Earth. Nothing is coincidental; everything offers an opportunity to share, to grow, and to develop and enjoy every beautiful experience we witness and participate in while on Earth."

She placed her items on the tray and set the tray on the walnut table. She then looked directly into the fire and picked up the black bag that held the gold Compass.

Her heart called to Jim.

"Okay, it's time for us to get about this work!"

She held the black bag to her heart and repeated what she had said the night before.

Let's do this!

The Giveaway

With a partially filled brown bag in hand, the old woman exited her cabin through the back utility room and headed toward the shed. She wore a pair of baggy bell-bottom jeans that looked like something from the seventies, and a very worn flannel shirt with a quilted red and black checkered vest layered on top. A purple bag hung from a belt loop on her jeans, and on the opposite side a knife sheath was strapped through her belt. Her hair was pulled back into a tight braid, and a very faded Atlanta Braves ball cap was placed snuggly on her head. Her hands were clad with a pair of leather gloves, and an old pair of hiking boots protected her feet. She was ready to tackle the task in front of her.

The air was cool and calm on this early April day. Clouds dotted the blue skies, while warm sunbeams from Grandfather Sun streamed through the broken clouds, awakening the slumbering plants within the Earth.

The grass that surrounded the cabin began to reveal signs of green among the winter brown, and tiny blades of plants emerged from within the Earth. The bare branches of the Standing Ones were now dotted with buds, as were the bushes that surrounded the perimeter of the old woman's cabin. Earth Below was nourished through a beautiful collaboration between Grandfather's warmth and moisture from the Cloud Beings from the Sky Nation Above.

Father Sky, Above, impregnated Earth Mother, and her willingness to receive these gifts brought forth an abundance of beauty Below for all to receive and be nourished. This Divine union offered the inhabitants of Earth a promise that warmth and beauty would soon blanket their lives with a rainbow of color brought forth by the awakening of spring.

The season of spring heralds in a time of new growth, and the opportunity to realize the dreams that were created during the stillness of winter. Bulbs lie dormant within Earth Mother during the winter months, as tiny seeds of future leaves lie within the branches of the Standing Ones until warmth returns. At that time, all of nature experiences a grand reawakening, and the inhabitants of Earth Mother yawn and stretch with the instinctive awareness that it is time to begin another walk along the Sacred Path of the Medicine Wheel that we call Life.

This beautiful April day had summoned the old woman to complete her portion of the collaboration. Her task was to release the remnants of autumn and winter that no longer served Earth, and to state her intentions for this year's garden.

She loaded a four-wheeled cart in the shed with the items needed to complete her task, picked up a metal rake with her free hand, and brought everything to the edge of the garden. Her eyes sparkled like a child's on the first day of school as she approached a large pile of broken branches, twigs, and leaves with a look of determination. This was clearly a task she had routinely executed dozens of times with the onset of spring, and from the look on her face she would enjoy every minute of it.

Her garden area beckoned her presence as she pulled the cart to the awakened land that waited to be of service. Once in place, she untied the string that held the purple bag on her belt loop and pulled out a pinch of tobacco. She carefully lowered herself to her knees, placed the tobacco on the edge of the garden, and softly prayed.

"Thank you for the abundance of gifts provided by you that nourish the souls of those who come to visit, and that also keep my own body strong and healthy. May my thoughts, words and actions be of service to those who inhabit you, sweet Mother."

She then kissed the Earth and whispered, "*Aho, Mitakuye oyasin*, I love you!"

Warmth filled the air as Grandfather parted the clouds to witness this annual event. The old woman looked up.

"As Above, so Below," she said softly. "Thank you for the warmth; it's a good day to witness the remains from the Standing Ones to be offered up with my prayers of thanksgiving for the abundance we are given."

Her eyes now focused on the large mound of winter's fallen debris.

"These twigs, branches and leaves represent the things that have served those who reside on this sacred Earth, and they are now ready to return to heaven." She glanced upward. "With deep respect, I offer up these gifts through the smoke, and ask that they be carried to Creator with gratitude. May the remaining ashes feed and enrich Mother's soil."

"As Above," she said, lifting her hands toward the sky, "so Below." She bent down and touched the Earth.

As she completed the words, a red-tailed hawk flew across the point of focus for which the prayers had been sent. The old woman felt a flutter in her belly and a quickening in her heart. She knew this messenger from Creator was present to let her know that her prayers and gifts had been accepted and gratefully received.

She further knew the teaching that the presence of the red-tailed hawk acknowledged the role of the one it flew over to be a Guardian of the Earth, and one who was respected for his or her awareness of the interconnectedness of all things. This red-tailed hawk was, in essence, recognizing the old woman's inner reverence for all of life, and her gift for knowing that everything that happened in life had a purpose.

Again, she lifted her hands to the sky.

"I also offer up some old beliefs that had greatly impacted my life, and that were made clear to me during winter's hibernation. It is with a grateful heart that I offer them to you, Creator God. While these teachings were given to me when I was young as a means to help me maneuver my way through the human experience, they no longer serve me.

"The gift brought through my tears during these winter months cleared the way for me to become aware of yet another layer of old habits, and old ways of thinking. Released with those tears, the light of awareness revealed the *Shadows* that had been hidden within my heart. It is with abundant love for what those old beliefs and ways offered, that I ask you now, Creator God, to take the remnants of my old life and receive them with the Light of your Love."

She moved her hands from the Sky Above and placed them on her heart Below, as she stood in silence with Grandfather on her face and a cool breeze at her back. This moment of stillness received her emotions of Joy that what was now behind her had brought her to where she was at that very moment.

From that place of peace her future stood directly before her. Whatever she chose to do with the next moment was where she would *be* in the very next moment. Life was always about what she chose in every thought she had, every word she spoke, and in every deed she performed.

Once again, she retrieved tobacco from the purple bag, held it first to her lips and then to her heart, and scattered it over the pile in front of her.

"Thank you for your willingness to carry those Giveaways with love to the heavens within the smoke. May they return to Earth Mother illuminated by the Divine Light of Love from which it was sent, to enrich the lives of all the inhabitants on Earth."

The air was crisp as a breeze moved in from the North. She inhaled deeply as she pulled up from her heart the intentions she had for this year's garden, and held them for a few moments. She exhaled slowly and blessed the garden space and the fire she would soon ignite, for their generosity and willingness to work with her very able hands and heart.

She then requested Earth Mother to work in collaboration with her, to create an abundance of nourishment for her Body, Mind and Spirit. She made a commitment to continue to be a good steward of the land.

Stillness hung over the land until the silence was broken by the whisper of a strong warm breeze from the South. It surrounded the old woman's body and sent a surge of warmth to her heart. She closed her eyes and remembered one of her favorite phrases from "The Little Prince."

"For it is only with the heart one can see clearly, what is essential is invisible to the eye."

Warmth from Earth Mother moved upward from the bottoms of her feet, all the way to her heart. She closed her eyes and allowed the flow of energy to continue to move upward from the top of her head, all the way to the heavens. A gentle shudder moved through her entire being, which she received as confirmation that the bond was secured. She opened her eyes, glanced toward the heavens, then touched the Earth and took three deep, cleansing breaths.

The agreement sealed, she began to prepare the annual Giveaway that offered up her portion of the collaboration. She lifted the paper bag from the cart, and retrieved from it wadded up pieces of recycled paper, a dozen or so fallen pine cones from the richly scented pine tree in her side yard, and a half dozen treated fire sticks to help ignite a fire.

The old woman was busy very carefully and strategically placing the items within and around various cubbyholes in the debris pile, when she sensed a presence. She looked toward the movement, and two turkeys stopped in their tracks. Her thoughts immediately went to the "medicine" of the turkey.

"The turkey is the Giveaway bird," she whispered.

She acknowledged their presence with a smile, and they stared back at her as if to say, "We see you!"

The old woman immediately turned her eyes to the woodpile, lit a match, and placed it on a rolled-up piece of paper. As the paper began to burn, she carefully placed it in the cubbyhole located in the East direction and began to hum a tune.

She repeated this three more times as she acknowledged the four sacred directions. Then she stood and lit another rolled up piece of paper, raised it to the Sky, and carefully placed it in the center of the woodpile.

She stood back respectfully, pulled off her leather gloves, and began to sing, touching her heart and her head to reflect the words as she sang:

> *These hands are strong, this heart is wide,*
> *this mind, this mind is wise.*
> *These hands are strong, this heart is wide,*
> *I am on, on your side.*
> *There is work to be done; there is word to be done,*
> *With these hands, this heart, this mind.*
> *There is work to be done, there is work to be done,*
> *I am on, on your side.*

The old woman continued singing as she slowly moved around the newly lit fire three times.

As she began her fourth round, her eyes again caught sight of movement. She kept her stride and focused on the song, but allowed a quick glance toward the distraction, and saw a dark shadow enter the path West of the cabin. It was too far away for her to recognize anything more than that it was human. As she completed the fifth round, the image became clear.

It's Jim!

She smiled, and felt a sense of elation. The sight of Jim was confirmation that he had heard her call. The sixth round was completed, as was the old woman's singing, when Jim emerged from the East side of the cabin.

He slowed to a standstill out of respect for the work with which the old woman busied herself, and simply looked down at the ground and stepped back. Jim knew when something sacred was in progress, and that to stare or stand too close would infringe on that person's personal work.

The fire now burned with a fury as she completed the seventh round. The old woman put on her gloves again, grabbed her rake, and began to clean the debris from the edges of the fire. She pushed the loose pieces toward the fire around the perimeter of the burning brush pile with the back of the rake. Then she used the teeth of the rake to pull any debris of leaves and small twigs from the edge of the ring outward about two feet all the way around, so that a clearing was formed away from the burning fire.

The fire now burned evenly, and the old woman glanced in Jim's direction and smiled. She set the rake aside, removed another pinch of tobacco from the purple bag, and gently tossed it into the fire. She then touched the Earth, stood up, and removed her gloves as she walked toward Jim.

"Looks like you are busy as a beaver this lovely spring day," Jim said with a grin.

The old woman returned his smile and pointed to the shed. "There are two lawn chairs on the right side as you enter; if you'd fetch them we could rest a bit."

"You mean you can rest. You're the one that's been busy," he said as he turned and entered the shed.

He glanced to his right and, sure enough, there sat the two lawn chairs. He noticed a small basket that had some rags, so he pulled one out and stuck it in his pocket, then returned with the chairs to where the old woman stood.

"If you'd watch the fire a bit, I'll get us something to drink," she suggested. "Would you want coffee or tea?"

He opened one chair and set it by the cart.

"Coffee, please."

The old woman stopped at the back door and watched as Jim moved to the fire, leaned over, and mumbled a few words. It warmed her heart to observe him.

Yep, that man will understand what I have to share with him.

Once inside the cabin, she pulled off her work boots, washed her hands, and set the coffee pot to brew. While she waited for the coffee, she pulled out the wooden tray and placed on it a couple of coffee mugs and a few napkins.

No need for sugar or creamer; Jim likes his coffee black.

She went to the cookie jar and grabbed a few chocolate chip cookies.

He'll definitely like these, bless his heart!

Meanwhile, Jim had unfolded and dusted off both chairs and placed them on each side of the cart. He moved the few remaining items in the cart off to one side and dusted off a section of the cart for the tray.

If I know that lady, she'll bring out that wooden tray and some sort of goodies, and she'll need to set them down somewhere.

He then stepped toward the fire and noticed a container of yellow cornmeal.

"Hmmm, she must use that to bless the fire or something. I do know that everything she does has a purpose."

He saw the door open and quickly moved to hold the door open for her.

"Can I help you with something?"

She handed him the tray. "You can take this for me so I can slip on my boots, and I'll be out directly."

With a grateful smile, he took the tray to the cart he had prepared for it.

The old woman closed the door behind him and headed into her bedroom. She went into her closet, and emerged with something she placed in her vest pocket. Then she returned to the utility room and slipped on her boots.

As she exited the back door, her eyes immediately went to the fire.

It looks good; no doubt Jim's been talking to it.

Jim had neatly set the wooden tray onto the cart. He held the back of a chair as she approached, and motioned with his hand for her to sit down. The old woman had to smile; it was evidence that chivalry was still very much alive.

After both were seated, the old woman poured each of them a mug of coffee.

Jim smiled. "It is good to be here, and especially to be sitting outside by this fire with you."

She removed the orange napkin from the top of the basket and revealed the chocolate chip cookies.

"Oh, hush, my beating heart!" he exclaimed. "You certainly know how to add sweetness to a visit. Please, help yourself first. It appears you've been quite busy today."

The old woman placed a cookie on a napkin and took a big bite. She had clearly worked up an appetite!

Jim placed a couple of cookies on a napkin, sipped a bit of his coffee, and almost devoured a cookie in one bite.

"How in the heck do you make everything so delicious? Mmm!"

While the fire gently burned, Jim and the old woman sipped their coffee and enjoyed their cookies, comfortable in the stillness of the moment. She smiled.

There's something about sharing food with others that fills our hearts as well as our bellies.

The fire crackled and popped as the remnants of winter filled the air with a symphony of sound that seemed to harmonize with the dance between these two special friends.

Within a few moments, the old woman set her mug on the tray and moved to the fire. She picked up the rake and repeated her routine of pulling the fire together and cleaning the space around it. When the task was completed, she pulled a small handful of the yellow cornmeal from its container.

She faced the fire from the East and offered a sprinkling of the cornmeal, then moved clockwise around the fire, pausing to offer a sprinkling of cornmeal at each of the directions. When the ceremony was complete, she placed the rake behind the cart and sat down in the lawn chair.

The breeze had turned brisk, so the old woman offered Jim a bit more coffee. He gratefully accepted, and she filled both mugs.

Jim watched the fire as it gently moved through and around the broken pieces of tree branches.

"Here it is, spring, and those remnants are still of service."

All was in harmony on this special, sacred land, and a sense of peace filled the air. The old woman finally broke the silence.

"I guess you heard me call to you awhile back."

"I believe I did," said Jim. "I wasn't certain until I got here today, but from the looks of the work you're doing with the fire, I'd say you're ready to 'spring forth' into something. No pun intended," he chuckled.

She couldn't help but smile; Jim just had a way of being a happy soul. He had developed an attitude of lightness over the years that warmed the old woman's heart.

There are times when life offers the opportunity to refuel one's faith. To witness a person transform their life and become the person they were meant to be ... it gives me great hope for the next generation.

"How's the story of your life coming along?" Jim finally asked.

Silence hung suspended in air for a few moments. The old woman ignored his question, sipped her coffee, and observed the fire, which now needed constant attention to make certain all the pieces would be completely burned.

She placed her mug on the tray, and once again picked up the rake and began to pull the pieces close together. Tiny flames revived the now small fire as smoke rose and beckoned attention.

She moved around the fire for another twenty minutes or so until it became very small. She retrieved some tobacco from the purple bag and kneeled down in the East.

"Thank you for your patience and love," she whispered. "I now ask for assistance with the task in front of me." She bowed her head and silently completed her prayer.

Guide me through this next phase of our journey together. Use me as the physical vessel to share your Truths to the inhabitants on Earth, so that they understand what it means to see the good in others, and so they may restore balance on Mother and be in right relationship with All their Relations.

She spread the remaining coals into an extended circle with the rake, then motioned for Jim to join her. He promptly rose from his chair and stood beside where she knelt.

"Like thousands of bright, shiny stars, millions of diamonds that sparkle in the darkness," she whispered.

The old woman reached up for Jim's hand and pulled him down beside her.

"These coals are like everyone on Mother," she said. "They each have various shapes and sizes. They each burn in ways that are uniquely theirs. No two are alike; yet, they all come from the same source, from the Eternal Flame of Love. Even when darkness comes, the pieces of Love, regardless of their size, bring light to the darkness and allow beauty to sparkle."

Jim hardly knew what to do. His heart pounded as tears dampened his eyes. He inhaled a few deep breaths as softly as he could, and yet, what his heart wanted most was for him to burst into tears.

"It's okay, Jim; the Truth brings tears because it comes from the heart."

A tear slid down Jim's cheek and he simply bowed his head.

There are no words. How can one describe such a moment?

There was something about that precise moment that felt familiar. It felt like something he had witnessed before, and yet, he knew he had not. He told himself this was not the time to figure things out; he needed to stay present and witness whatever unfolded. Something at his very core told him to pay attention and simply observe, rather than to waste time to trying to understand.

The old woman was obviously with Jim, and yet he felt her somehow distant. *It's like her body is here, but she's not.*

After about ten minutes, he felt her move, and she exhaled a very deep breath. He stayed as still as he could, keeping his breathing easy and light so as not to distract her.

She'll come around when she's ready. Be patient, and be still!

She raised her head within a few moments and looked directly into the space where the fire had been. The coals were now mostly black and gray as the cool air helped to extinguish the fire.

She glanced over toward Jim and patted his knee. "Thank you."

The old woman lifted both of her hands and held them just above the coals, and felt just a bit of warmth. She sprinkled one last pinch of tobacco over the coals, then opened her hands and lowered them onto the coals. They were lukewarm to the touch, so she slipped on her gloves and stirred them with both hands until there was no warmth left.

Once the coals were completely cool, she glanced over at Jim. "Since you are here, will you help me stand up?"

Jim immediately stood up, leaned over and held her arm at the elbow. "Are you ready?"

She nodded and leaned on Jim's arm to help pull herself up. When both feet were firmly on the ground, she looked at Jim.

"I think we're done here."

The tray was removed from the cart so that the items used for her task could be loaded onto it. Jim folded the lawn chairs and offered to pull the cart. The old woman accepted his offer and extended the handle to him. Then she picked up the rake and began to spread the black and gray ashes into the garden.

"That ought to help enrich the soil for this season," she remarked as she turned and walked behind Jim.

After everything was neatly placed back in the shed, she picked up the container of cornmeal, exited the shed and secured the door. Jim stood at the back of the cabin with the tray and scanned the garden area to double check for any items that might have been overlooked.

"It looks like everything has been picked up. Is there anything else that needs tending?"

The old woman shook her head and opened the back door as Jim handed her the tray. She took the tray and motioned for him to come in. He felt a bit awkward, as he supposed that only family and friends generally used the back door.

Guess she considers me a friend, and after today I reckon it's official!

After they had both removed their boots and washed their hands in the dry sink in the utility room, the old woman led the way into the kitchen. She turned to Jim.

"Do you have time to chat?"

Jim nodded. "Sure do; however, I'd imagine you're pretty tuckered out after all that work."

She simply filled the tea kettle with water, and put it on the stove to heat. Jim leaned back on the counter to stay out of her way as she gathered what was needed for them to have tea.

"Can I help with anything?"

She retrieved the silver tray without a word, and placed on it two cups, two spoons, sugar and creamer dishes, and a couple of napkins.

Wonder if a snack is needed?

She quickly dismissed the thought.

"If you're cold, you might start a little fire. Nothing big, though, since I'll be in bed early tonight."

"I'll bet you will be. I'll get on that fire," he responded as he exited the kitchen.

The old woman appeared in front of the fireplace within ten minutes or so. Jim quickly jumped up.

"May I help you with that?"

The old woman merely gave a nod toward the walnut table between the chairs.

Now, Jim knew her well enough to know not to touch items that were not his, so he suggested, "May I take the tray and let you clear the space?"

She smiled as she handed him the tray. When everything was in order they both sat down, and the old woman poured each of them a cup of chamomile tea.

"I hope you like chamomile tea. There's no caffeine in it, so it won't keep you awake." She took a sip of her tea.

"By the way, thank you for showing up today."

Jim drank a bit of his tea as his eyes expressed gratitude for being there.

The Giveaway was complete, a friend sat beside her by the fire, and the tea warmed her soul, all of which topped off an absolutely rich and abundant day.

Jim poured more tea for himself and offered some to her. She nodded. "Jim, this story that's brewing in my heart may look different than you may have anticipated."

He looked at her and said nothing; he knew she had more to say.

She stared at the fire, yawned, and softly continued. "Sometimes I have no idea what I'm doing. I just know when something needs to be done and I allow it to unfold."

Jim watched her closely. He noticed the softness of her skin, the creases in her face, and the calmness that emanated from her. He also noticed something he had never seen before. She wore a white gold band with a pear shaped blue stone in the center on the ring finger of her left hand.

"I bought this ring for myself as a commitment," she told him, noting his observation. And that was all that was said about the ring.

It's probably a good thing that I'm going into this adventure knowing nothing!

The fire now burned slowly, and she yawned again.

"Jim, how about you come back in another week or two? Whatever day suits you will be perfect for me." Another sip of tea emptied her cup.

"That sounds great," he agreed. "I look forward to beginning this journey, wherever it takes us." He yawned. "I believe that yawn of yours is contagious, because I didn't do nearly as much as you did today."

He placed his cup and napkin on the tray, then stood up, picked up the tray, and held it in front of the old woman.

"May I take your cup? I think by now I know where the kitchen is," he chuckled.

When he returned from the kitchen the old woman didn't so much as flinch. He cleared his throat so as not to frighten her, slowly moved toward the fireplace, and glanced at her.

Yep, she's awake. He picked up the poker to spread out the coals a bit.

"Like thousands of bright shiny stars, millions of diamonds that sparkle in the darkness," she softly whispered.

Jim offered her a hand. "May I help you up?"

Too tired to even raise her head, she extended her hand to his. As she began to get up, he held onto her elbow for additional support.

Once steady on both feet, she reached into her vest pocket, pulled out a small round object, and reached for Jim's left hand. She placed the object into his hand and closed his fingers around it as she looked into his eyes.

"Thank you," was all she said, and without another word went into her bedroom and closed the door behind her.

Jim slowly opened his hand, and a large, round cat's eye marble was revealed. Swirls of green and blue floated inside the crystal clear glass, while a fine thread of red snaked around the colors.

I haven't seen one of these since I was a very young boy. Interesting. I wonder what this is for?

He stuck the marble in his pocket and turned toward the fireplace.

No doubt it means something, and I'll know soon enough.

Jim double-checked the fireplace to make certain the embers were cool. He stood for a moment and listened to be sure his friend was settled down for the night. He felt warmth in his chest as his heartbeat raced.

What is it about this place? In all of my life I have never experienced such a place of … what is the word?

"Hmmm …"

I believe the word is magic. Yeah, that's it, it's magic!

He heard a faint sound from the old woman's bedroom, so he quickly headed to the front door, quietly opened the doors and secured them behind him. Then he dropped a gift into the twig basket and stepped onto the Earth. When he reached the edge of the yard, and just before he stepped onto the wooded path, he turned and glanced back.

"I have a hunch my life is about to change dramatically."

His stomach flipped as if to confirm his words. He shook his head and grinned.

You know, come to think about it, I can remember having a dream about such a place when I was a young boy.

Eureka! That was it!

Good Grief! Somehow, I knew this place existed way back when I was very young. I can remember that as I got older, I became frustrated that life seemed to have become so … dull.

He felt excitement as his heart quickened. The spirit of young Jim had returned!

I did know such a place as this existed; it just took me nearly forty years to find it!

He shook his head as he turned and walked the path back to his truck.

"Can't wait to tell Sarah about today … no, I'd better just keep this to myself for now. I mean, I really don't know what I'd say, anyway."

He arrived at his truck and slipped inside.

"Magic, plain and simple! I can hardly wait to see what happens next!"

He leaned over and patted his dog. "I can tell you, Max, you're my most faithful friend."

Jim started the truck, put it in gear, and just before he pulled onto the main road he looked over at his *Best Friend.

"What do you say, buddy?" He gave Max's head another pat. "Want to hear an interesting story? First, though, let me tell you about my grand *Giveaway*. I've decided to quit being so grown up. I can live in the magic of life and still be responsible!"

As he pulled onto the main road, Jim began, "Now, about that story..."

Untold Stories

The old woman sat on her porch swing and tatted as she revisited the memories of her heart. Pictures flashed across her mind like the rewind of a movie.

I wonder what Mary did with her life … or John. What a corker he was. And, I certainly can't forget Matt and his southern accent. Such shenanigans those boys played!

"I'm certain their lives must have taken as many twists and turns as mine has," she giggled.

So many young people with so many different stories; I wonder what happened with Grace, or with Patty? Of all the thousands of students over my career, those two really kick started my own life into another Reality.

"Truly!" she exclaimed.

"I wonder how they all turned out as adults?" She stared ahead at the Magnificent Old Oak, which seemed to hear her words and to acknowledge her question as the breeze gently swayed the branches.

"It's anyone guess," she replied as she completed another inch on the tatted chain without missing a loop.

I never could have imagined this journey.

She paused her tatting once again and stared straight ahead at the Old Oak.

"Oh, yes I could!" she whispered. "I believed anything was possible and everyone around me knew that. From the time I was a young girl I knew there was so much more to life, and I wanted to learn first-hand about every bit of it.

"Thank you for your support with keeping the dreams of my youth alive," she said to the youthful spirit of the South. "It is because of your assistance that I have always had faith in what I could not see, but what I knew to be true without a shadow of doubt. From that childlike place I trusted that what was to happen *would* happen, regardless of what the big people would say. Thank you for 'seeing' me! That is why I have been able to keep my dreams alive."

She pushed forward on the porch floor with her feet and the swing began to move.

Ahhh, the porch swing; it will forever be a place of comfort to me.

Her eyes caught sight of Jim on the walking path to the West. She smiled as he approached the edge of the yard.

Right on time!

When he saw that she had noticed him, he gave her a wave and picked up his pace.

Grandfather Sun shone directly overhead as blue skies welcomed Jim onto the land. The old woman felt lightness in her heart. She knew within her core that Jim knew the ways; that was quite apparent, especially after his last visit and the support he had shown for her work with the Giveaway. He just needed a nudge to remember those ways.

He stopped just before he reached the porch steps and turned to scan the front yard.

"Why, I can't believe how full everything has become in just a week." He smiled.

"Mmm, I smell lilacs," he said as he closed his eyes and inhaled, "and there is nothing like the smell of lilacs to let you know that spring has officially arrived!"

She set her tatting aside and went into the cabin. She didn't need to say anything to Jim; he knew she was going in to get a mid-day treat for them.

He stepped up onto the porch and turned to gaze out at the multitude of plants that had popped up through the Earth. The daffodils had already dropped their flowers, as peonies took center stage and stood tall in large bunches, awaiting the warmth of mid-May to bring forth their full beauty.

Only a couple more weeks, and those colorful, puffy balls of beauty will be visible in her yard.

He glanced toward the redbud trees that were in full color.

What a sight to behold!

He lifted his eyes toward the tops of the trees.

"Would you look at those dogwoods? I know she doesn't use fertilizer; it must be her magic that creates such an abundance of richly colored blossoms."

Yep, spring's in full array!

He quickly turned as he heard her return from inside. He hurried to hold the door open for her as she gracefully carried a large tray that was covered with a brilliant orange cloth.

"That's quite a tray you have there. Need any help?"

She shook her head, so Jim hurried around her and placed a small folding table between the swing and the willow branch chair. Once they were seated and the tea had been poured, they sat in silence as they enjoyed some fudge brownies with walnuts.

"Got to tell you," he mumbled through a mouthful of brownie, "those are the best brownies I have ever eaten … like, ever! Mmm! And, do I taste black walnuts?" He smacked his lips and closed his eyes as he slowed his chewing in order to savor the last few bites.

She nodded affirmatively.

"You sure know how to spoil a person! I must make those for Sarah and the kids."

"No need to do that; I boxed some for you to take home."

Jim smiled. There really were no words to describe the deep affection he felt for this woman. He knew his mother was a wonderful woman, as was his wife; and, yet, the old woman that sat beside him offered something that was profoundly different. He couldn't understand it, let alone put it into words.

Grandfather moved ever so slowly toward the West, indicating that it was about one in the afternoon. Jim looked at the old woman.

"Is there anything you wish to speak about today?" he asked.

She sipped her tea without response. He waited a few more minutes, then pulled a notebook out of his shirt pocket and set it on his lap.

"You won't need that," she replied. "That is, unless you have questions written down for me."

"I have many questions in my head that I want to ask you about, but nothing is written down. Just thought maybe I'd take a few notes about what you share with me."

She poured another cup of tea and offered some to Jim, which he declined.

"Have you written down what we have already talked about over the last few years?"

"No."

"Then what makes you think you need to write anything down now?" she asked.

That's a very good question, he thought. *And, she's correct.*

He knew it wasn't about the details; it was about what happens when the two of them are together. To be more precise, it was about what he experienced first-hand, and how he interpreted the occurrence. It was his personal perspective that would then create a story about what he had witnessed or heard.

It's always about what I know to be true, according to how I was taught and what I experienced throughout my life. That is what has influenced my understanding, which is true for everyone.

He knew this for certain: he could recall nearly every aspect of what they had talked about, as well as what he had observed. All of it was forever buried within his heart, to call up when he needed the information.

"You're correct," he finally responded, as he slipped the notebook back into his shirt pocket. So, where would you like to start?"

"Where do *you* want to start?" she replied after a long pause.

Jim had to smile. Of course, she was going to let him lead the way; it was his idea.

Within moments, the scent of skunk moved through the air. Both Jim and the old woman sat in silence, waiting for the culprit to become visible. As the scent became stronger, they both looked to the East, where a large skunk appeared.

He was a very large, robust critter. He waddled to the edge of the yard and stopped behind a large bridal veil bush just shy of the clearing. His jet-black fur starkly contrasted with the white fur, which made him very visible.

"Does he really think we can't see him?" whispered Jim. "I mean, he stands out with that green bush in front of him." They both sat very still, waiting to see what Mr. Skunk was going to do.

Without moving a muscle, the old woman whispered, "He has a message for you, Jim. Listen."

Puzzled, Jim attempted to absorb her words, and remained very still so as not to flinch and frighten Mr. Skunk.

What does she mean?

A flutter in his belly got his attention, and he attempted to take in a deep breath through his mouth to avoid taking in the smell. He sat as still as he possibly could, so as not to frighten the animal into defense mode, which might have resulted in unpleasantness.

He released the breath through his mouth, then inhaled and exhaled again. On the second inhale he held his breath as long as he could, then slowly exhaled as he tried to calm his gut.

Stay calm, stay centered, and take this in.

He felt the floor beneath his feet as he slowly released his breath.

We're fine. Just stay in the moment.

Jim took another slow, deep inhale, paused, and held the breath for a few seconds. Then with a slow exhale, his belly relaxed.

He slowly moved his eyes away from Mr. Skunk and focused on the Old Oak directly in front of him.

Jim's breathing was now even and steady. He felt a tingling in his hands and warmth on the back of his neck. He caught a whiff of Mr. Skunk and was tempted to look in his direction.

The old woman never moved a muscle as she whispered, "Sit still, Jim, sit very still, and listen."

A gentle inhale and exhale told Jim Mr. Skunk was close. He kept his eyes focused on the Old Oak as he began to feel the presence of something else. It was not the skunk, and he wasn't certain what it was. He sat as still as he could, and tried to remain calm.

I am not afraid. I am safe. The old woman is beside me. Stay calm; you are safe.

A deep tone began to sound in Jim's left ear. His instinct was to bolt off the porch and run for his truck, but he just kept breathing.

Jim, stop this! You are safe! Where is your courage?

And then he heard a strong voice.

"It is time for you to come out from behind the bush. Not everything is black and white, Jim. We see you! We know who you are, and we need for you to reclaim your gifts. Fear not about your reputation; those that judge you have yet to wake up."

He could feel the warmth envelope his body, and he somehow knew the old woman's energy had expanded to include him. Tears filled his eyes as he relaxed into her energy, and he had an urge to bury his face in his hands and let them release. And, yet, something told him to *"Be Still and Know."*

Jim then remembered that when his grandpa and grandma had taken him to church, the preacher would speak of how the Holy Spirit would move people. That always frightened him. While he loved his grandparents, he did not agree with many of the sermons he had heard while attending their church. Nonetheless, he knew his grandparents were definitely good people who had lived in a loving manner, and for that reason he had trusted in what they believed.

He remembered the phrase, "Be Still and Know." His parents and grandparents had used those words many times, but he had never fully understood the meaning until this moment.

So, this is what they meant: to simply be still and pay attention, and I will hear what it is time for me to hear.

Peace fell over his entire being as the Old Oak in front of him came back into focus. Once again, he felt the floor beneath his feet, took a couple of breaths, and began to open his eyes.

He slowly moved his eyes toward the bush and, of course, Mr. Skunk had disappeared. He then turned his head a bit further to the left to check on the old woman and, as usual, she tatted away as a long chain formed beneath her hands.

Jim let out a big sigh, and stretched out his arms as he released a deep yawn.

"Oh my, I do believe I've been in the *Twilight Zone,*" he said with a chuckle.

The old woman paused her handiwork and looked at him. "Reckon that's a good name for it."

"What would you call it?"

She smiled. "Reality!"

"Reality; hmmm, that's an interesting word to use."

When his words were met with silence, his thoughts kicked in. *No doubt I'll learn more about that when the time's right.*

He then stood up, rotated his shoulders, and moved his head clockwise to loosen his neck. "My body is very stiff, as though I'd been in bed for a week! I suppose it's from tension."

He peeked into the teapot. "There's still some tea; would you like a cup?"

"As a matter of fact, I'd like to make a fresh pot," she said as she set aside her tatting and stood up. "Would you like to join me in the kitchen?"

He bent over and picked up the tray. "Lead the way!"

Once in the kitchen Jim placed the tray beside the sink.

"What can I do to help?" he offered.

The old woman filled her tea kettle with water, set it on the stove and turned on the burner. She pulled out a drawer that revealed a dozen or so various flavored teas.

"You can pick out a flavor; I have no preference."

"You certainly have an abundance of options," he said. He rummaged through the boxes of tea until he found one labeled "Mystical Moments."

"This one sounds interesting," he said with a smile. "Do you drink this one often?"

He removed the box from the drawer and held it up for the old woman to see. She glanced at the box and grinned.

"I'm not surprised you picked that one."

"What does that mean?" he asked with a smile. "Is that something that can help me understand what just happened on the porch?"

Just then, a sunbeam emerged through the West window. They both looked at the intensity of the light that pierced through as it landed smack dab on a quartz crystal on the window ledge. Neither said a word, but they both knew it indicated something.

"Whoa!" Jim finally said. "Your crystal just got supercharged! What does that mean?"

The tea kettle began to whistle and the old woman turned off the burner without response, leaving Jim to think about his question.

"If you want that flavor of tea, take out two bags and put them in the teapot."

He hastily pulled out two tea bags, placed them just inside the teapot, and wound the strings around the handle. She promptly filled the pot three-quarters full with the boiling water, and placed the lid on top to let it steep.

"Would you like me to keep the brownies on the tray or are you done?"

Jim chuckled. "That's like asking a bear if it poops in the woods!" They both laughed. "Of course, you can leave those brownies on the tray."

"You first," he said as he picked up the tray.

She wiped her hands, grabbed a sweater off a kitchen chair and led the way to the front porch.

The air was warm and Grandfather burned brightly as they sipped their tea and enjoyed the playfulness of the squirrels. Many birds hopped along the ground until they found a good spot to bury their beaks into the soil and pull out a nice, juicy worm, while others scavenged the ground for bits of straw, string, and various odds and ends that would fill in the spots of the perfect nest to hold their babies.

Jim finished a brownie and turned to the old woman. "You sure don't need any form of electronics to pass the time. You have all the entertainment you need right here in your front yard!"

She nodded. "People often ask me how I live out here all alone. They ask if I ever get lonely." She scanned the yard. "I suppose for those that live in the city it would seem a lonely and boring place. However," she motioned toward the yard, "this is my extended family."

Jim smiled. "It's certainly a peaceful, yet lively place to be. If you don't mind, I do have a question."

"And, what might that be?"

Jim fidgeted a bit as he set his cup on the tray and readjusted himself in the chair. A few moments passed before he turned his chair so he could look directly at her.

"Would you be willing to tell me more about what happened a while ago with that skunk? Specifically, how did you know that critter had something to tell me? And, how did I hear his message?

"I know I'm only to ask one question, but I have many. I guess since this is a different situation than normal, is it okay to ask several questions?"

A cool breeze blew in and the old woman slipped on her sweater. It felt to Jim like ten minutes or so passed before she responded.

"You may ask as many questions as you wish. Just make certain to not ask questions to which you already know the answer."

A puzzled look came over his face. "Hmmm, that's an interesting statement. I'll have to think about that one."

"And try not to think too much, Jim; it'll just get in the way."

Okay, now I'm really confused, what does she mean, "it will get in the way?"

"I'll do my best," he responded. "However, I'm not certain how I will learn if I don't ask questions."

And, at that moment, he understood.

"Never mind; I take that back. What happened earlier was a perfect example. You spoke about the skunk having a message for me, and I didn't ask you any questions. It just happened, and that was how I realized what your comment meant."

She smiled and nodded.

He paused for a moment and watched her as she stared straight ahead. She seemed to be somewhere else, so he waited in silence for her to comment.

"That's exactly correct," she finally said.

Jim smiled. "Where did you go?"

A wide smile came across the old woman's face as she glanced at him.

"To Reality."

"I have a lot to learn," said Jim as they both chuckled.

"No, you have a lot to remember," she responded. "Let me tell you a couple of stories." She paused. "But first, do you have another hour or so?"

Jim nodded. "I have all afternoon."

With that, she picked up her tatting and began her story.

"There were two significant situations that came into my life once I surrendered to and accepted the Call. These were exceptional situations that occurred when I was a guidance counselor at a junior high school, where students began their Rites of Passage from grade school into the beginnings of full-fledged adolescence. During the two years they spent in seventh and eighth grades, they grew from young children into teenagers, complete with all the physical and psychological changes that come with puberty.

"The first experience occurred with a girl named Grace. Like most students, Grace entered this new environment with mixed emotions. While she was uncertain of herself, she was eager to experience all that junior high might bring.

"Grace came into my office for the first time with a look of curiosity as to why I had called her in. She wasn't very warm, and quite frankly exuded a sense of caution. She was a bright child who had done very well scholastically in grade school; however, she lacked friends.

"I noted that Grace had a different look in her eyes than most of the other seventh grade students, and there was something intriguing about her. About two months into the school year, she began to come to my office for a random chat, though she did not stay long.

"Then one day, Grace peeked into my office with a smile and asked if she could talk to me. I indicated that was fine, so she entered my office and closed the door behind her.

"This was unusual since it was standard procedure to leave the door open; that is, unless it was a private conversation. I had not had such an experience with Grace prior to that time.

"I immediately felt my belly flip, and all my senses went on high alert. Grace eagerly sat on the edge of the chair beside my desk, and turned to face me directly as she leaned forward on the desk.

"My gut told me, 'Pay careful attention!'

"With great excitement Grace said, 'They told me I could talk to you.'

"My whole body was now on high alert. I had no idea what my uneasiness was all about; however, I knew to trust what I heard and to turn off my practical thinking head.

"I responded to Grace that it was good that her classmates trusted me, although I knew it was more than that. I remained as calm as I could while my gut cautioned me to brace myself.

"Grace had an 'I've got a secret' look on her face as she said, 'No, that's not who told me.'

"By now my heart was thumping out of my chest, my mouth was dry, and I called to the heavens to stand with me. Somehow, I managed to stammer, 'Well, it's good the teachers told you that.' Still, I knew it was someone or something else.

"Grace leaned closer and said with excitement, 'It's my friends.'

"Okay, I had no recourse but to allow my higher self to guide me through this, so I responded, 'What friends?'

"Grace smiled and said, 'My *special* friends. They told me I could trust you. They told me you would believe me.'

"She then began to describe three friends that only she could see and said they were her very *best* friends."

The old woman paused both the story and her tatting as she took several deep breaths and glanced toward the Old Oak. After several moments of silence, she put her tatting aside and stood up.

Jim wasn't certain what he needed to say or do, if anything. It was all so much, so unusual, and so *very* extraordinary. How could what she just told him be true? And yet, he knew it had to be. He glanced at the old woman and saw a tear slide down her cheek as she took deep, even breaths, and placed her hands on her heart.

She shook her head and wiped away the tear as she sat back down.

"Is there anything I can do for you?" asked Jim.

"You know," she responded, "I could use a glass of water."

Jim immediately jumped up. "I'll be right back. Is there anything else I can get you?"

"Thank you," she nodded. "If you would take the tray inside, I'd be grateful."

"You got it. I'll be back directly."

Jim returned to the porch within ten minutes, carrying the tray with two glasses, a dish with sliced lemons, and a full pitcher of water. He placed them on the portable table between them.

"Hope you don't mind that I snooped and found a few items I thought would be useful."

The old woman simply smiled.

Jim poured water in both glasses, placed a lemon in his, and offered her a slice, which she accepted.

She immediately drank nearly half the water in her glass and placed it back on the table.

"That was just what I needed, thank you."

She picked up and resumed her tatting as she cleared her throat and continued her story.

"From that day forward Grace dropped by as often as she could, and would talk in detail about her friends. This was a dilemma for me as a public school representative; such topics were, and probably still are, forbidden to discuss. And, yet, my loyalty was always to the students, to do whatever it took to help them learn to trust their instincts in order to maneuver their way through life.

"Grace frequently spoke of her deceased grandmother, who often visited her to remind her that she was loved. Grace also spoke of how her hands would get really red and feel like they were on fire from time to time, especially when her grandmother or her three friends were around. I mostly just listened to rather than encourage her stories; yet, never did I plant a seed of doubt that what she had experienced was not real. As is true with most relationships, Grace was there to teach me things as well.

"She continued to tell me everything about her life growing up with her three friends, and that until she reached third grade her parents had thought it was just her imagination. But, when she entered fourth grade her parents took her to a psychologist, who put her on medication to cease the experiences. She said it didn't work, though; she just learned to not speak to her parents or anyone about her experiences, and by the fifth grade they took her off the medication.

"She told me she felt great relief that she finally had someone to talk to about it. She was, however, certainly not going to let her parents know, or they would put her back on medication.

"And so the school year came to a conclusion, summer came and went, and the new school year began in the fall. Students usually came in to share their summer's experiences with me, but this time Grace did not. By the middle of the first grading period I called her into my office to check in with her.

"She was not the same girl. Her hair was disheveled, and her face was sad as she walked into my room with her head down. I took one look and asked her directly what had happened over the summer, and she simply replied that she had lost her three friends.

"I asked what had happened, and she proceeded to tell me that her parents had sent her to a Christian summer camp. She said she had shared her secret with a few of the kids her age. When word got around to the camp counselors, a minister was called in, who performed an exorcism on her. She could no longer access her friends after that. To make matters worse, her parents had put her back on medication.

"It was a sad year for Grace. Try as I did to encourage her, she could not muster up enough hope that life would be any different when she got older. Truth was, she didn't care about much of anything. The rest of the year she only came to my office when I called her in. Grace had a broken heart, and there was nothing I could do to help.

"About eight years later I saw Grace in the grocery store. She came over to me with a big smile, and happily reported that she had finally found a group that supported her spiritual beliefs. She thanked me for my support and said she always hoped to see me again, so she could let me know how grateful she was that I had believed her."

The old woman placed her tatting next to her on the swing. She looked up and smiled broadly.

"I would love to know what Grace did with her life, and would love to let her know how she impacted mine."

She picked up the lemon water and drank the rest of it. Jim held up the water pitcher as if to ask if she wanted more. The old woman nodded, so Jim filled both glasses again.

He didn't know what to think about her story; it was beyond anything he had ever heard and, quite frankly, it *was* beyond belief. Yet, Jim's gut told him that what she had just shared with him was, in some strange way, very much the Truth.

She then picked up the chain and tatting shuttle and began her next story.

"The second story is about a young girl of about fourteen, named Patty. I saw her around school from time to time; however, she was on the other counselor's list, so I did not know her well.

"One morning the school nurse called and asked me to speak with Patty. She said Patty had attempted suicide over the weekend and, for some reason, the nurse felt that I was the one who could best handle the situation.

"The school nurse and I were friends, and she knew my way of viewing life was quite different from the norm. Patty's counselor was a man who viewed life from a more traditional perspective. And, she also felt that Patty might feel she could speak more freely to a woman.

"She brought Patty into my office and introduced us, then pulled the door closed behind her as she left. The young girl appeared frightened and confused as she timidly sat in the chair beside my desk.

"Our communication began in an honest and forthright manner. I told her I had heard that she hadn't had such a good weekend. At first, Patty lowered her head and did not respond. Then, after a few more attempts to make her feel comfortable talking with me, I told her directly that I had heard she had attempted to kill herself over the weekend. She nodded her head and began to cry. I asked her what hurt so badly that she wanted to die.

"After shedding many tears, Patty finally said that someone had told her to kill herself. Once again, my gut let me know this was an unusual situation, and to pay attention. After a few more inquiries, Patty finally told me it was 'just a voice she heard that had spoken to her before.'

"I got up and placed an empty chair directly in front of her, and instructed her to put that voice in the chair. Almost immediately I saw an image of a man with dark hair and a beard, who sat staring directly at her. Patty would only look at the floor and cry. I asked her if this man had dark hair and a beard. She quickly lifted her head and looked me in the eyes.

"'You see him! You really see him!'

"I asked her to look at him and tell him he must leave, and that he must never come around her again. Her tears began to dry up as she just stared at me.

"'You see him, you really see him,' she repeated. It was very apparent that she knew what he looked like, and to have someone else see him validated his existence.

"I asked her directly, 'Do you want him to leave?'

"She nodded vigorously. 'Yes!'

"I then looked directly at the man sitting in the chair and told him to leave and to never bother her again. He did not look at me; he simply continued to stare at Patty. I told him again, more sternly, to honor her words and to leave her alone. He finally looked directly at me, and then disappeared.

"I told Patty he was gone, and to look at the chair for confirmation. Slowly, and *very* cautiously, she moved her eyes from me to the chair, and her huge sigh of relief was reflected in her face.

"My head immediately reminded me that I was in a public school building, and that I needed to know how I planned to handle this situation. I took a few deep breaths, felt my feet on the floor, and called for assistance from the unseen world. Almost immediately a thought entered my mind.

"I looked at Patty and asked her if their family attended a church. When she told me they were Pentecostal, I knew precisely what to do. I made a phone call to her mother and told her that I had spoken to her daughter, and that I believed someone not of this world had indeed told her to harm herself. Her mother immediately asked if I thought it was a demon. I suggested she discuss that with their minister.

"Patty's mother and father were in my office within thirty minutes. Their faces showed great relief as they thanked me and took her with them.

"A few days later, Patty came into my office and thanked me for helping her. She completed that year, moved up to high school, and to my knowledge was never plagued by that voice again.

"At that time, I had no idea where all of that came from. Somehow, forces beyond my human understanding had guided me through both of those situations. What I learned from the experiences was to trust my inner guidance. Those experiences led me back to the source I had known as child, and I asked to be guided to someone who could teach me more about such things."

A long chain was wound into several circles in the old woman's lap. She bit the end of the thread, tied a knot and held it to her heart.

"Those experiences are forever burned into my heart. They were the beginning of the end of my life as I had known it up until that point."

She looked at Jim, who could only stare at her, and offered him the chain.

"Let's see what happens to your life."

Jim sat up in his chair and stared at the beautiful chain.

"Whoa, not certain I want to accept that…"

"The choice is yours, Jim. Everyone has free will. It takes a great deal of courage to accept in faith what you cannot see. Fear often holds us back, and

Jim, fear can be a very good companion. We need a sense of healthy fear to allow us to step back, take a deep breath, and ask our heart for guidance. It is when we allow that fear to engage our minds into a continual stream of 'what ifs' and 'yeah, buts' that we step away from the Divine source that is ready to guide us toward our purpose in being here. When that happens, our earthly bodies and worldly teachings will take the helm and be our guide.

"The bottom line to true happiness and purpose requires us to go into our hearts, our true source, and bring forth the gifts of trust and faith that will support and illuminate the path to our soul's purpose, and to the very reason we came to Earth Mother at this precise moment and time. Just make certain, Jim, that you always work with the Light that brings healing Love to the planet."

With the chain still extended to Jim, she paused a moment in thought, looked him in the eyes and said, "It requires us to be willing to 'Follow the Snake.'"

After a moment of silence, she concluded, "These are my words."

Jim sat very still.

Follow the snake; whatever does that mean? As quickly as the thought appeared he dismissed it. He knew that in time he would understand.

He felt suspended in time and space, and in that moment, he knew what he needed to do. His mind immediately kicked into gear and began asking a series of questions about what he would do with these teachings. How might his parents receive them? And, while he was fairly certain Sarah would stand by him, he wasn't absolutely sure. Whatever choice he made, he still wondered, *What if?*

Jim reached out his hand and accepted the tatted chain offered by the old woman. He shook his head and smiled.

"You do know that I have never trusted anyone in my entire life like I trust you."

She nodded. "Trust the Divine Light of Love. We have enough darkness, and it is Light that will bring harmony to the Earth."

And so, the journey officially began. Neither Jim nor the old woman knew what was about to happen. They did, however, know that whatever it was, it would change not only their lives, but it would also change the lives of those around them.

The old woman had complete faith and trust in this Reality, although she had no idea what would transpire, or how. Truth was, she didn't need to know. She had complete confidence and faith in the Divine guidance that had brought her to this moment, and she knew that she only needed to show up.

Jim was quite baffled and bewildered by it all. And, yet, his trust in this beautiful old woman, coupled with what he had experienced that day, was all he needed. If he could become as wise as she had become, he, too, would simply show up!

Everything that needed to be said for the moment had been said. She set aside her tatting bag, stood up, and with the tray in hand, went into the cabin.

Jim placed a gift in the twig basket as he left the porch and, as he walked back to his truck, his thoughts moved to the mysteries and magic that were about to unfold. He recalled the *Untold Stories* that had been shared.

"Amazing … simply amazing!" he slowly whispered.

Ruth's Heart

Grandfather Sun's light filtered through the lush new growth of the bushes in front of the porch on this exceptionally cool, early May morning. The old woman watched the sifted sunlight move upward from the horizon until its brightness began to emerge just above the treetops in the East.

She sat on her porch swing, wrapped in a purple chenille robe over a pink thermal shirt and pastel checkered flannel pants. Her feet were clad in thick socks and a pair of fluffy black slippers, and a very well used quilt lay across her lap. She sipped her coffee and observed the critters as they scurried about in preparation for a new day.

"What a beautiful way to begin a new day!" she sighed. "No matter how many times I witness early mornings, I am always amazed by the vibrant colors brought forth by Grandfather's presence."

Young birds of various colors and sizes bravely perched on the edges of their nests, mustering up the courage to take flight. They chirped and looked toward nearby branches to make certain their mamas and papas were close by. They seemed to be thinking, "Dare I leave the only home I've known?" Their parents simply observed. They knew they had done their job, and had prepared their young to venture off on their own. It was time; the nest was now considerably too small for the growing birds.

She watched as baby rabbits playfully scampered and chased one another about the front yard. They looked like they were playing leapfrog as they made their way through the maze of the new growth of perennials that now began to fill in the spaces of her flower garden.

And then a thought occurred to her.

Looks like the vegetable garden needs a sturdy fence around its perimeters; we have an abundance of rabbits this year.

She steadied herself as she stood up.

"You know, it's not so much that the fence is needed to keep something out; it's more about protecting what is within."

She picked up her coffee cup and went into the cabin. She entered the kitchen and dropped a slice of raisin bread into the toaster.

Better fuel up before we get this day in motion. Let's see what today brings!

When the bread popped up from the toaster, the old woman spread a generous portion of butter across the top and poured one more cup of coffee. She glanced out the kitchen window while she ate her toast and sipped her coffee, and suddenly noticed something flitter by. She focused her eyes, and within seconds an emerald green color with a splash of red flashed passed the window.

"Oh, I believe that was a ruby throated hummingbird!" She finished her toast and took her last sip of coffee.

Time to get the feeder cleaned out and hung up ... they're back for the summer!

She filled the sink with warm, soapy water, and smiled as she washed her dishes.

"Today is a good day for a warm soup."

I have a hunch someone will show up that needs the comfort of a warm belly.

When the kitchen had been cleaned up, she gathered the ingredients for a hearty, butternut squash soup. As she began to peel the skin around the squash, her heart felt light as she recalled memories of cooking for her family, and she began to hum a tune that seemed to fill the room with joy.

She chopped some onions, cut the squash into large chunks, and placed everything into a medium sized soup pan half full of chicken broth that she had frozen for such a time as today. All she needed to add for a hearty soup was a bit of cream, butter, and her favorite spices, and then wait for some hungry bellies to show up and partake of the meal.

After the soup was completely prepared, she turned the temperature down and placed the lid on top. Then she made a creamy cornbread, which she put into the preheated oven, and set the timer for sixteen minutes.

"Speaking of food, better see what's available for Tom," she said as she looked in the refrigerator. "He will probably show up soon; he's been gone for several days, so no doubt his belly will be empty!"

She combined several small dishes of leftovers for Tom, and cleaned up the kitchen again. When she was finished, she removed her apron and hung it back on its usual hook.

I think everything is in place; now I'd better get myself in order.

She went into the bedroom to get dressed. Within ten minutes or so she emerged, dressed in a pair of brown cargo pants with several pockets, an off-white turtleneck, and a purple sweater vest that was zipped halfway up the front. As usual, she had braided her hair, applied a bit of blush to her cheeks, and put a light pink gloss on her lips that added a splash of color. She was ready for whatever the day would bring.

Today might be a good day to check the shed for seeds from last year. It's time to get the garden planted.

She stopped at the stove to check on the soup.

"Mmm, smells good!"

She scooped out a small spoonful and blew on it gently to cool before tasting it.

"Delicious! Now to let it simmer for a bit, and it'll be perfect!"

She had just turned the burner to its lowest setting and the timer buzzed. She pulled the cornbread out of the oven and put it on top of a back burner to let it cool, and placed a piece of aluminum foil over the top. Her tummy rumbled with delight at the smell of the fresh cornbread as she turned to go into the utility room.

She put on her garden jacket and made certain her gloves were in the pockets. Then she slipped on her boots and walked out the door.

Grandfather was now high in the sky, as a warm breeze blew through the trees and the bushes swayed with the wind.

"Ahhh, the warmth of summer will be here soon. Grateful to be getting this done today, and take advantage of the rain predicted for later this week."

Her wooden potting stand was just outside the back door, and she grabbed a rag from a large wooden container to wipe down several Mason jars. One large jar contained several neatly folded white envelopes that she pulled out and carefully examined.

Let's see, we have cucumbers, butternut squash, green beans, snow peas, acorn squash, and beets. That'll be good for right now.

She put the selected envelopes in her pocket and returned the others to the jar, and smiled joyfully.

"I'm ready to get my hands in the dirt!"

The ground had been tilled a week or so earlier by the neighbor that farmed the land behind her. It was something he had done for many years and she was most grateful for his kind assistance!

Sure am grateful for my faithful cohort in gardening!

"What a great smell after a long winter's rest! Fresh, rich soil!"

She closed her eyes and inhaled deeply. "It's so fresh and pure; how it makes my heart sing!"

She exhaled slowly as she reopened her eyes, then headed to the shed. Once inside she retrieved a hoe, black weed control paper, and gathered a few painters' sticks she used each year to identify the placement of the seeds in the garden.

She stood in front of the garden space, pulled a purple bag from her coat pocket, and removed a small amount of tobacco from the bag. She returned the bag to her pocket, then leaned over and mumbled a few words as she sprinkled some tobacco over the area. The wind assisted with the ceremony by scattering the tobacco over the garden.

She pulled the gloves from her other pocket and slipped them on. Then she carefully placed three of the wooden stakes about one foot apart on one side of the garden, and inserted the remaining three stakes into a bottom pocket of her pants.

She picked up the hoe and began on the East side of the garden to carefully make a shallow trough all the way to the other side of the designated planting area. She looked at the line of rich soil that had been parted to make certain the row was fairly straight. It appeared even, so she placed another stake in the ground at that end of the row. She repeated the process two more times, resulting in three parallel rows.

After she surveyed the rows, she carefully dropped a green bean seed into one trough every three inches for the entire length of the row. Then she tore a hole in the bottom of the white envelope labeled green beans and placed it over the stake at the end of the row.

"Well, there's our first row of garden seeds planted for this year!" she exclaimed as she admired the freshly unearthed soil.

The remaining two rows were done in much the same way, but with those seeds randomly scattered within the freshly troughed ground. At the end of each row, she once again slid the appropriately labeled white envelope onto the garden stake.

She was pleased with the neatly planted rows of green beans, beets and snow peas.

"We now have three complete rows of vegetables, so let's get the squash and cucumbers planted and we'll be done for today!"

She grabbed the black weed control paper and went to the opposite end of the garden where three pallets lay on the ground. She dropped to her knees, lifted one of the pallets to carefully lay a sheet of the weed paper under it, and slowly lowered the pallet onto the paper.

She pulled the glove from her right hand and buried her finger into the paper to make a hole, then pulled it open about four inches. She pulled the butternut squash envelope from her pocket, dropped four seeds into the opening, scooped soil on top of the seeds, and gently patted the rich soil over them.

She repeated this process with each of the remaining two pallets for the acorn squash and cucumber seeds.

No need to label those pallets; I certainly know by now what those plants look like.

She stood up slowly, slipped off her gloves and placed them back in her pocket, and surveyed the garden space.

"You look beautiful!" she marveled.

With a huge smile, she pulled more tobacco from her purple bag, and lifted it to the sky.

"Thank you, Father Sky, for the blessings that you offer. May you continue to add your warmth and rain to Earth Mother." She once again lowered herself to her knees and placed the tobacco on the soil as she finished her prayer.

"And to you, sweet Mother, thank you for receiving Father's gifts, and for allowing the richness of life to continue to provide abundant health to my sturdy Body, Mind and Spirit, that I may be a good steward of all that I am given."

She felt the warmth of Grandfather on her back and the coolness of Earth Mother on her knees as she allowed the sweetness of both to fill her heart and body with strength. She knew she had the courage; it was the strength that was most needed at this time in her life.

She carefully stood up again and collected the black paper and hoe. Then she noticed someone walking the path toward her cabin.

Perfect timing. I believe our visitor is here.

She carried her gardening items back to the shed and put them away. Then she entered the back door of the cabin, where she slipped out of her garden boots and into a pair of very worn slippers. She hung up her jacket and stepped out of her work pants, revealing a pair of black leggings with purple and turquoise stripes.

This will have to do.

She hung her pants on a wall peg, straightened her vest, smoothed her hair back on both sides, and glanced down at her clothing.

Looks presentable enough to entertain our visitor. Besides, more than likely the person has something on his or her heart, so what I look like doesn't really matter.

The kitchen smelled wonderful, and her tummy reminded her that it was time to be fed. She washed and dried her hands and peered out the window. A bright purple jacket caught her eye.

"Huh. Not certain who that is, but she does look familiar," she mumbled. "I presume it's a woman. Can't say as I've ever seen a man wear such a brightly colored jacket."

The visitor stepped from the walking path onto the cobblestone path in the yard, and noticed the green stems and leaves of the emerging flowers. Irises, tulips and peonies were abundant with buds, ready to burst forth in their richness of color.

Oh, I remember how magnificent her perennial garden was the last time I visited. Every type, shape and color of flower imaginable filled most of her yard with fragrance, and the beauty of summer. I knew her flowers were a direct reflection of the love and care she gave them.

She moved up onto the porch with lightness in her step, as she approached the front door and knocked.

The old woman opened the door and greeted the young woman.

"Welcome. Come on in, Ruth," she said with an invitational swoop of her hand.

Ruth was shocked that she remembered her, let alone her name. She had only met her once, and that had been about six or seven years ago. She went inside and slipped off her shoes, then removed her jacket and hung it on the deer antlers that served as coat hooks by the door.

Nothing wrong with her memory!

The old woman moved toward the kitchen and motioned for Ruth to join her. The smell of the squash soup filled the air with a fragrance that would make anyone's tummy growl.

"That smells delicious!" Ruth exclaimed. "I certainly don't want to bother you; I can wait outside if you were getting ready to eat."

"Nonsense! Please join me," offered the old woman.

She turned off the burner and lifted the lid toward the back to release the steam. She stirred the soup, placed the lid back on the pot, and retrieved the cornbread from the counter.

She turned to Ruth. "If you would cut this cornbread, I'll grab some bowls and saucers."

Ruth couldn't believe how different the old woman was from the last time she had visited her, when she had barely spoken two words other than those in her story.

The old woman set a knife and a small metal spatula on a large wooden tray that already held napkins, two spoons, a knife and a butter dish. Ruth waited until the old woman gathered two bowls and a soup ladle, then picked up the knife and began to cut the cornbread into three-inch squares.

Nearly everything was in place within five minutes. The old woman reached for two glasses and asked Ruth if she wanted water or tea. Ruth indicated water would be fine and offered to fill the glasses.

"Let's just fill our bowls and take a piece of cornbread with us into the dining room table. I so rarely have guests, and the dining room might enjoy some attention." The old woman smiled.

Ruth nodded and returned her smile, not because of the comment about the dining room table enjoying some attention, but because of the difference she witnessed in the old woman.

She's hardly the same person; wonder what has changed?

They each took a bowl of soup and a glass of water into the dining room. The dining room table was a beautiful, natural oak, and gold and red stones were embedded in the brocade placemats. The silverware appeared to be real silver, and the red stone napkin holders held richly colored gold napkins. Ruth noticed that there were only two placemats on the table; she surmised it was because of the rarity of guests as the old woman had mentioned.

In the center of the table was an off-white lava bowl and pitcher, no doubt one she had had for many years. The chairs matched the oak table and were covered with a plain, light brown woven fabric.

Very simple. Nothing fancy, which isn't surprising.

Ruth asked the old woman if she usually sat in a particular place, to which the old woman shook her head.

"You may sit where you like."

Ruth set down her bowl and glass, then went into the kitchen to retrieve the tray with the remaining items, and brought it to the table. Once they were seated, the old woman bowed her head, placed her hand over the food, and then to her heart.

"Thank you," was all she said.

Ruth suddenly had no appetite whatsoever, and felt instead an overwhelming urge to cry. She was completely baffled by this surge of emotion that seemed to come out of nowhere. She knew it would be impolite to not eat what the old woman was about to share with her, but she could barely control herself. She took a couple of short breaths, swallowed the lump in her throat, and the tears began to flow.

Time seemed to be suspended in space as silence hung in the air. Ruth suddenly felt herself in her bedroom in the house where she had grown up. Memories of the tears she could not control at that time in her life overcame time and space, and she felt as though she had been transported back to the most difficult and confusing time in her life.

Her parents had always seemed to be fighting; at least, that was her perception. It hadn't always been that way, but after her youngest brother had died her mother began to drink. She would open a bottle of wine, which invariably led to popping another cork, until she passed out on the couch in a drunken stupor.

What had hurt her most were her father's tears. He would come into her room to comfort her and try to explain to her that her mother wasn't well. Her father was a physician, so Ruth figured that he, of all people, would know if someone was sick. Yet, her heart hurt from the all too frequent binges she witnessed.

She had never understood why her father couldn't fix her mother. He had helped so many other people during his career, so why couldn't he help her mother? He had been a well-respected doctor who went out of his way to help everyone, despite anyone's ability to pay. Why, then, couldn't he heal her mother?

Oh, he would attempt to assure Ruth that it was not her fault, and that it was because of the pain her mother felt after losing her son. But Ruth hadn't been able to accept that. He, too, had lost a child, and if he had managed to get on with life, why couldn't her mother?

She had ultimately concluded that it must have somehow been her fault. She had helped her mother keep the house clean, did well in school, cared for her younger sibling, and she had hoped that maybe, just maybe, her mother would decide to quit drinking and get well. It never happened. Never!

Her mother had died at the young age of forty-two. Ruth had carried those burdens her whole life and, despite going to therapy several times, the guilt she carried would inevitably resurface and open the old wound.

Now, despite her efforts to pull herself together, tears continued to slide down Ruth's cheeks. She gathered her senses, slowly opened her eyes and batted away the tears, and then remembered where she was. Embarrassed, she glanced over at the old woman, who sat very still with her hands folded in her lap.

Ruth took several deep breaths, and wiped her face with a paper napkin from the tray. After a few more deep breaths, she softly spoke.

"Goodness, I apologize. I believe your soup must be cold by now."

The old woman continued to sit in silence.

"May I warm up your soup?" Ruth offered.

The old woman took a deep breath, scooted her chair back and reached for Ruth's bowl. "Let *me* warm up our soup."

Ruth felt frozen. She had no thoughts, nor words. Her instinct was to just be silent as the old woman picked up both bowls and entered into the kitchen.

She returned within five minutes with two bowls of hot soup. She placed one on each placemat, then sat down in her chair and began to eat. Ruth's stomach rumbled; she picked up her spoon and scooped up some soup to satisfy its call. The two ate in silence until their bowls were empty and they had each devoured a piece of cornbread.

"This is the best cornbread I've ever eaten," said Ruth. "I would love to have your recipe."

The old woman smiled. "I'll be glad to share it with you; it's a very simple recipe." She picked up a fresh piece of cornbread and placed it on her own saucer, then picked up another piece and offered it to Ruth, who received it gladly.

The energy in the air was soon calm, and all that remained of the meal were a few crumbs of cornbread on their saucers. Feeling rejuvenated from the simple, yet delicious meal, Ruth jumped up from her chair and reached for the old woman's bowl and glass. The old woman accepted her offer, knowing that it would help the young woman's heart feel that it had reciprocated her kindness.

Ruth set everything on the large wooden tray, carried it into the kitchen and placed it by the sink. As she ran hot water in the sink, the old woman entered.

"How about I help with that? You wash the dishes, and I'll dry and put them away."

Ruth's heart was warmed by the offer, and she simply smiled and nodded. The old woman put the remaining soup into a smaller container and placed it in her refrigerator. Then she wrapped up the leftover cornbread and set it on the counter next to Ruth. She retrieved an index card from her recipe box, scribbled the cornbread recipe on it, and set it beside the wrapped cornbread.

"You can take what's left of the cornbread home with you," she offered.

"I'll most graciously accept that gift ... thank you!" Ruth gleefully exclaimed.

After the dishes were washed, dried and put away, the counters were wiped clean and the towels hung to dry. The old woman grabbed a jacket and led the way to the front porch. Ruth followed close behind her, cornbread and recipe in hand.

The air was now cool with a slight breeze from the North, as Grandfather began his journey toward the West. Ruth sat down in the willow branch chair as the old woman made her way to the porch swing. She picked up her black bag and removed her tatting tools, and began to make a chain.

The setting was peaceful, and Ruth proceeded to ask her question.

"How can one be supportive of someone with an addiction without enabling him or her?"

The old woman began her story within moments.

"There are places in the heart that can only be understood in silence. When someone is in pain, it is often difficult for that person to describe the depth of hurt that lies within. We may listen as a way to be of help, and offer assistance when asked. We may even accompany them to a therapist, preacher, substance abuse counselor, or a doctor. However, until that person is ready within his or her own heart, nothing will change.

"This is a difficult situation to understand with the human thinking head and feeling heart; yet, until one has experienced first-hand whatever secret hurts lie within another's heart, one cannot truly feel that person's pain. Oh, we may try; however, each of us has our own personal way of dealing with pain.

"Even if one has had *similar* family situations, experienced *similar* abusive behaviors, or made *similar* attempts to help loved ones feel supported and cared for, individual stories can still be very different. Each of us has a lens through which we view life's experiences, and no two person's experiences are the same.

"You see, Ruth, each person's soul is on a unique journey while here. Each person on this planet came with a story within their heart that they agreed to work out during this incarnation. This agreement includes choosing the 'players' within their story. Parents, guardians, and literally every person they encounter during their lifetime, agreed to play their part in that story. In fact, every single experience we have in this life was orchestrated before we came to Earth.

"It is also important to know that the moment we move from the Spiritual dimension to the density of Earth, all prior memory is erased. In essence, we forget those prior agreements to the point that we need to figure things out by using whatever knowledge and understanding we develop as we move through life. From the moment we enter this world, we begin to learn ways to meet the needs we have within our hearts."

She paused her tatting and glanced over at Ruth.

"Would you mind getting us some water?"

"I'd be glad to," Ruth replied as she rose from her chair and proceeded toward the front door. Before entering the cabin, she turned and asked, "Is there anything else I can get for you?"

The old woman shook her head and, with a curious look on her face, turned to look at the Old Oak. Ruth hesitated and looked to see what the old woman was staring at. Then she realized it was probably a personal moment, so she entered into the cabin out of respect for the old woman's privacy.

Stillness hung in the air with only the sound of hummingbirds hovering over the fragrant new blossoms. A faint sound that seemed to beckon to the old woman echoed among the trees in the distance.

I hear your whispers; what is it?

She put down her tatting, stood up, walked toward the edge of the woods, and disappeared among the green.

Meanwhile, inside the cabin, Ruth placed a pitcher of ice water and a couple of glasses and napkins onto the wooden tray on the kitchen counter. She then made a quick scan of the kitchen.

Just what I would suspect: a place for everything, and everything in its place.

Her eyes paused when she noticed the stained-glass turtle lamp.

What a lovely lamp!

She next noticed the three monkeys with red hats.

Oh, I know: "see no evil, hear no evil, speak no evil." Mother always had an affinity for that teaching. She used to say, "If you can't say something nice, say nothing at all."

Her heart was warmed by the thoughts of her mother. Her eyes filled with tears.

She was a good person. She was very caring, always willing to help out others, and very attentive to her children.

"It's good to remember those things about her; she changed so drastically, it's easy for me to forget the good when so many painful memories hurt my heart. I wonder," she pondered, "what life would have been like if my brother hadn't died?"

She quickly wiped her eyes and remembered why she was in the kitchen.

Enough! Let's get back to the moment. She picked up the tray and headed out the front door.

The old woman sat silently on the swing when Ruth arrived with the tray. Her eyes were fixed on the flower garden and her face glowed with peacefulness.

What a lady, thought Ruth. *I don't know if I have ever met anyone so content with life.*

She filled a glass of water and set it on the edge of the tray closest to the old woman.

I know she must have had her share of heartbreaks and hurts; yet, here she sits with a calm and abiding presence all around her.

A cool breeze filled the air as the scent of pine enveloped the two women like the warm embrace of a loved one. The old woman drank half of her water, then picked up her tatting and continued her story.

"The basic need we all have is to be loved, and, while that sounds simple, it is not, as you no doubt have learned. You see, Ruth, emotions manifest in our hearts, and when someone or something causes us to feel unloved, that hurt gets stuck and the pathway to the heart becomes blocked, or even closed.

"Living in Earth's density means learning how to manage these emotions, as they are the key elements in the stories we create about life. In order to maneuver our way through these stuck feelings, the analytical head kicks in. When a situation arises that causes pain to the emotional heart, the rational mind examines the situation, draws conclusions, and tells the heart a story that will help alleviate its pain. Hence, a relationship between the head and the heart is established that will guide every thought, word, and action we express.

"This very personal and individual experience can get in the way of Truth, both within oneself and in relationships with others. Since we are usually unclear about what another person's words or actions might mean, it is easy to make assumptions based strictly on judgments. Conclusions are derived from observation, and from that vantage point a belief system is developed about people and about life in general, all of which become the 'blueprint' that we follow.

"Beliefs, then, become the foundations on which we build future relationships. The basic teachings we learn about people are established at a very young age. As we grow and experience more of life, we attract more people into our lives that support those beliefs, and that repetitive crazy-making brings about the lessons we are to learn. It's a very tricky situation, and we will repeat that cycle until something, or someone, helps us to wake up.

"It is then that we realize we have the power to rewrite, or to eliminate, those old beliefs and understandings of life, and to create what we truly wish for our own lives and for the world. Then the stories within our hearts begin to be corrected, eliminated, rewritten and, hopefully, with a lot of work and awareness, will return the heart to its true, natural state. That is when Spiritual Truths become clear.

"We will then remember what we came here to do, and we will move from being slaves to our beliefs by living on autopilot, to becoming fully engaged creators of our lives. In essence, we become the Masters of our destinies."

The old woman paused her tatting for a moment and pulled the quilt over her lap. The air was beginning to cool as Grandfather approached the treetops in the West.

"What you must learn, Ruth, is that unconditional love is all any of us needs. It is the 'medicine' that cures the ailments of this world. You cannot 'fix' people; you can only love them as they are. That, too, is tricky, because all too often people choose to close their hearts in an attempt to protect that most treasured possession. That's very sad, because the very thing they want and desire most will be unattainable: that is, to give and to receive love.

"And, some people never complete the lessons they came here to learn. In that case, they may choose to leave the planet, and to decide in the afterworld if they want to return and try it again.

"It is very difficult to understand with the practical mind; we want to figure it out, and to help. Yet, how can one figure out what is in another person's head and heart? That is their story, not ours.

"You are only responsible for what is in *your* own head and heart. Therefore, when someone you love has an addiction, and the pain is difficult for you, all you can do is look at the pain you feel and ask your heart what it needs. If it needs that person to be happy, then ask Creator God to guide that person back to his or her own heart.

"The journey to the heart can only be made by the person whose chest it resides in. There is no one who can love you enough if you do not love yourself. And, to judge yourself for somehow failing to make someone you love happy only takes joy out of your own heart. Does it make sense to now have two people feeling unloved?

"Anyone who suffers from an addiction lacks self-love and deeply mistrusts themselves. How can someone receive love and acceptance from another when they cannot give it to themselves? Love them enough to get out of the way, and give them the freedom to find the strength and guidance within that will open the door to their own heart."

She stopped and looked directly into Ruth's eyes.

"The Truth is, a person doesn't have an addiction; rather, the addiction has a grip on that person. It's that cycle we spoke of earlier.

"You spoke of enabling," the old woman concluded. "If you simply love the person unconditionally and get out of the way, you enable them to go within to find their own answers. Their Spirit will take care of the rest. When we trust ourselves, we can surrender that person to the very Source we have within us to guide them to their personal Truths, just as it does for each of us. That is when faith kicks into action."

The old woman bit the thread, tied a knot in the end of the chain and handed it to Ruth.

"Silence is sometimes the most powerful healing tool we have," she said, as she glanced at the top of Ruth's head. "I see you still wear your crown."

Stunned, Ruth's eyes filled with tears.

Good grief, she must have seen that crown before I even felt it on my head the last time I was here ... oh, my gosh!

She looked at the old woman through her tears as she accepted the chain.

"The last time I was here, I promised myself I would remember your story about *The King*, who honored each of the sacred directions every morning. Unfortunately, I forgot about those teachings within a few months after I returned home."

She moved her eyes away from the old woman and focused on the Old Oak. Grandfather had moved further down the sky, and she knew it was time to take action. She turned her eyes back to the old woman.

"This morning I knew I needed to visit you again. I remembered that I had asked God to lead me to the person who could assist me, and I am most grateful that I followed that nudge today. I believe you are that person."

Ruth looked at the beautiful chain. "The last chain you gave me still hangs on my mirror at home." She then handed the chain back to the old woman.

The old woman smiled as she accepted the chain from Ruth.

"You walked the path here facing the East," she said, "the direction of new beginnings. As you walk back to your vehicle, know that you walk into the West, the direction that leads you to your heart. Learn to trust and follow the Divine Light of Love."

She put her tatting tools back into her black bag, then slowly stood up, picked up the tray, and moved toward the front door. Ruth jumped up and opened the door for her. After the old woman entered, she turned again to Ruth.

"These are my words." Then she carried the tray into the kitchen.

Ruth closed the door, turned, and looked straight ahead.

This must be the South direction; if I remember correctly, it has something to do with trust. Hmmm, that makes perfect sense.

She picked up the recipe card and placed it in her jacket pocket, put the cornbread into her purse, and drew out a small, blue-foiled box that she dropped into the twig basket.

I have no idea what's to happen next. That nudge I had in my belly the last time I visited has now brought me back to the old woman to learn what I don't know, I don't know.

She turned and stepped onto the cobblestone path, and paused.

I do remember my question, though.

She closed her eyes, inhaled deeply, and whispered, "I need to know what I can do to satisfy that inner nudge, while continuing to do what I love."

She immediately felt the same peace within her core that she had felt when she simply stated that question the last time. She smiled as she walked toward the West, confident that whatever purpose she brought with her into this lifetime would come to fruition.

Just before she entered the Forest, she paused and looked up.

"I'm going to complete my soul's purpose, Mama, and I hope you are watching. I love you and miss you every day." A breeze moved over her face as a chill went down her spine.

"You know how independent and self-reliant I insisted on being, and how I always resisted letting others help me. Well, Mama, I ask you to walk with me as I do this work. Who knows? Maybe, just maybe, it'll help you decide to return to Earth and complete your own work."

She got into her car and headed toward the main road.

"That wasn't a story the old woman shared," she considered, "it was a teaching! Yep, a very powerful teaching that I'll let settle into my heart. I can only hope it will help my thorn-covered, concrete walls begin to crumble."

Just before she pulled onto the main road, she felt a lightness of heart she had not felt in a very long time. It was a glorious feeling of hope and excitement.

"I want to love completely and unconditionally!" she said, gazing upward toward heaven.

Then she announced to the universe, *"Ruth's Heart* is changing!"

Reflections

HEAD TALK

What part of the story line so far can you
personally relate to?

Was there anything that struck you as "unreal?"

What are you curious about?

What would you like to "think some more about?"

HEART TALK

What stirred your heart the most?

What touched a nerve or a tender part in you?

What memory from your life came to your heart?

What would you like to happen next?

The Time is Now

The mid-day sun streamed through the clouds, as a light breeze cooled the old woman's forehead while she tended her garden. She was dressed in old faded jeans, a tee shirt and long-sleeved light denim shirt, and a colorful scarf secured a large, brimmed straw hat on her head.

She very gently moved the tender vines to encourage their growth within the boundaries of the pallets. She had successfully used this method for years; the simplicity of planting, weeding, and harvesting made the pallets an efficient use of garden space.

The warmth of Grandfather Sun on her back reminded her that summer was just around the corner, and her heart recalled the gifts it would bring.

What a wonderful time to play, and to explore all the colorful displays of nature. It is a time to laugh, and to enjoy the silliness of youth that finds the adventure of life a mystery waiting to be discovered. The innocence of youth is resilient, possessing an innate ability to move from one experience to another, and to get on with life no matter what happens.

She smiled. *I certainly learned that one. If I hadn't, I would have had to play alone, and that wouldn't have been any fun.*

The pallets in the garden, now dotted with green, looked great. She promptly moved to the other rows of emerging vegetables and began to gently remove the weeds. As she moved along the rows she noticed nibble marks on some of the new leaves.

"Now, look there," she whispered. "Those bunnies have found their way into our garden. Hmmm ... I almost forgot that I thought of the need for a fence a few days ago when all those bunnies were in the front yard, so those little fellas will need to look elsewhere for plants to munch!"

She moved on to the next row of vegetables as she continued to reminisce about her childhood.

It was a rich time to just be present with all aspects of life, such as popsicles, my favorite bike, and exploring the woods! Oh, and bugs seemed less plentiful back then; I could actually wear shorts.

"Of course, poison ivy was a routine occurrence when I was very young, and that isn't such a great memory!" she chuckled, as she gathered the weeds into a small pile at the end of the first row.

Some of my most precious treasures of summer were the family get-togethers. How I remember my boy cousins trying to exclude me from the adventures of building forts, riding bikes with no hands, baseball games, and of course, the family game of croquet.

She wiped her brow as she felt the sweetness that emanated from her heart.

What carefree time summer offered our whole family as we gathered for the annual reunion. Nothing compared to my mother's homemade potato salad and deviled eggs. And, of course, my Aunt Pat's baked goods could not be replicated by anyone in the world. Not in our family, anyway! And, most importantly, my abundance of boy cousins had the opportunity to learn that not all girls are "sissies!" We've come a very long way from that belief!

She took a deep breath and straightened her back to relieve her muscles. She then caught sight of Tom, who was sprawled out in the sun for an afternoon siesta. Gracie was curled up under a nearby shade tree.

"She's no fool," the old woman observed. "Grandfather is intense!"

She loved this time of year. The warmth of the quickly approaching summer encouraged growth from the rich soil, and the plants in her garden grew in size every day. Yellow and white blossoms dotted the various plants, promising a good yield at harvest. Some of the vegetables would be canned and others frozen, but all would ensure a healthy pantry for the winter ahead.

It's been a couple of years since I canned. The cupboards will be grateful to be occupied, and my family and visitors will be delighted to receive the abundance from my garden.

She began to hum a frequently used tune. Tom looked up; he seemed happy to hear the tune the old woman sang. He laid his head down again as if to say, "Thanks for the happy tune; I'll make it a lullaby."

After an hour or so of pulling weeds and redirecting the vines, she stood up, gathered the pile of weeds, and placed them in her four-wheeled cart.

"That was relatively easy," she said as she wiped the sweat from her brow. "Especially when compared to a few weeks from now, when things will be in full bloom."

She stretched a bit, then hauled the weeds to the side of the garden to be used as compost. Once there, she placed small amounts of the weeds around the edge of the garden until the cart was empty.

"These weeds remind me of the thoughts, habits, and head chatter that can strangle my happy heart if I allow them to become a source of abundance in my life."

She tilted the empty cart onto the edge of the garden and swept out the rest of the dirt.

"Let this dirt represent those thoughts and, like the remains of the weeds, be of service and add richness to Mother's soil." She smiled. "They are better here in the garden than in my head."

She glanced down at the newly compiled remnants of her day's work.

"Look at those worms; what rich soil we have to work with. It's little wonder the vegetables are so rich and delicious! She lifted her nose in the air and inhaled deeply. "Nothing like the fresh smell of Earth Mother!"

She hummed another tune with a happy heart as she pulled the cart back to the shed. When everything was put away, she glanced back at the garden.

"You all bask in the warmth of Grandfather and multiply your yield. I have lots of uses for the fruits of your labor!"

She entered the back door of the cabin into the utility room, removed her garden boots and gloves, placed her straw hat on a peg, and wiped her forehead.

"Whew! I need a shower!" She stripped off her work clothes and placed them in the washing machine. "What a great morning it has been!"

Her tummy began to rumble. "I hear you, and I'll take care of you when I'm clean!"

She stripped down to her birthday suit, tossed her undergarments into the washing machine, then added detergent and started the machine before scampering off to the shower.

After a warm shower, the old woman slipped into a pair of loose cotton pants, a form-fitted cami that she topped with a bright pink tee shirt, then tucked both shirts into her pants and securely tied the drawstring. She ran her fingers through her hair and tied it behind her head in a ponytail, then slathered cold cream on her face. She stood in front of the mirror and applied her usual swipe of blush and a thin coat of lip-gloss.

"There," she said to her reflection, "I think I'm ready for whatever the afternoon brings."

She scanned the room to make certain everything was in place and exited the bedroom with a happy heart.

"Nothing like spending a morning with your hands in the dirt!"

She moved through the living area and noticed how the sunlight filled the room with warmth, and her tummy once again reminded her that it was past time to eat.

"I'm on my way," she told her belly. "Any preferences?"

As she passed the dining room table, she glanced toward the front window, and noticed Tom staring at her from the front porch. She smiled.

"Yes, I'm certain you're hungry. I'll be with you directly."

"Now that's efficiency," she said to her belly. "I'll get something for you, and something for Tom! You know how I like to be efficient!"

It was easy to retrieve Tom's food; she had a designated container for him that she replenished on a regular basis. Finding something for herself was another story. While she loved good food, cooking for herself was less fulfilling than preparing a meal for someone else. Consequently, she often made a hearty casserole or soup that she would eat for several days.

The old woman chose a package of fresh broccoli for herself, which she prepared and put on the stove to steam. Then she retrieved Tom's container from the refrigerator.

Tom's meal consisted of a bit of leftover turkey burger and, since he liked the green beans she had given him before, she added some of those, along with a small portion of baked sweet potato. She placed the delicacies in his dish and took it to the front porch. One whiff and Tom sat up on his hind legs. He held up his front paws as if to say, "I'll even do a trick for that delicious meal!"

"You're a good boy, my friend!" laughed the old woman. "There's nothing you need to do to gain favor with me. Your presence in my life is the best gift you can offer me!" She set the dish in front of Tom and patted his head.

She returned to the kitchen and lifted the lid on the broccoli pot. Rich, green broccoli was revealed, and her tummy let her know that it was pleased with her choice.

She retrieved a beautiful ornate bowl from the cabinet, placed half of the steamed broccoli into it, and topped it with a generous amount of shredded Parmesan cheese. She put the dish onto her wooden tray, along with a fork, napkin, and a glass of water, and carried everything to the front porch.

She sat on the swing and, with her hands over the food and her head bowed, whispered a few words prior to eating. As her belly began to feel full, she reminded herself that she would have fresh broccoli straight from her garden in another month or so!

That thought made her even more happy. How very grateful she was for her collaboration with Father Sky and Mother Earth, as well as with the seeds from the previous year's harvest that had been planted in the soil with her own hands. This harmonious effort would bring forth this year's abundance.

As in life, nothing exists alone. Everyone and everything is in relationship. One is not more or less than another; each contributes a unique gift that makes the relationship dance along the Sacred Wheel of Life with grace and ease.

The old woman finished her lunch and scanned the front yard. There was a bird's nest in a bush on the East side of the porch that she had watched since early spring. The babies were now big enough that she could see their gray and white heads. She sat very still as she watched their mama and papa bring worm after worm to their offspring. She found it interesting that, when a worm had been dropped in one of the two wide-open mouths, that baby did not open its mouth when the parent returned with more food, thus allowing the other baby to eat. The old woman smiled.

This is the instinctive nature of life. Humans would have fewer problems if they would only pay attention to and learn from nature.

The feeding concluded, and she noticed one of the parents looking in her direction. She smiled and sat very still, while the adult bird quickly flicked its head, and then made direct eye contact with the old woman, as if to acknowledge her presence before it flew off.

Animals are very observant and wise; they know whom they can trust, and I am honored that they allow me to witness the manner in which they tend to their young ones.

She then noticed one of the fledglings standing bravely on the edge of the nest.

"Oh, they have feathers now!" she whispered. "My, my, it won't be long before they take flight. There can't be very many young ones in that small nest."

She sat perfectly still for some time until her old bones told her it was time to get up and move. When the parent that had been doing the feeding left, she carefully stood up and picked up her tray, paused a moment to get her balance, and moved to the front door. Once in the kitchen, she put the remaining cooked broccoli into the refrigerator, then washed the dishes.

The window above the sink faced West, and she could see that Grandfather now appeared well above the treetops.

"It's good to know we will soon have longer days of sunlight. Interesting how everything is in constant motion. Whether we can actually see it or not, we're always moving from one direction to the other."

Washing the dishes took longer to complete than in the winter, probably because there was so much beauty and new growth to observe and enjoy in every moment. The hummingbirds were now plentiful with the onset of warmer temperatures, making it necessary for her to refill the feeder every day.

Her eyes were now fixed on the movement of the clouds, while the treetops moved with the wind, and she thought of the gifts of the West direction.

The place of the heart, where we can hear the whispers of our soul and the deep Truths that come from the wisdom within, and where silence connects us to all that is sacred and true. The West offers us the opportunity to rest, to be still, and to remember! There, Grandfather Sun moves out of view, to allow the beauty and presence of Grandmother Moon to be shared. What a marvelous example of how perfect balance exists when we honor and respect the gifts offered by both the masculine and feminine in all things.

The old woman was deep in thought when she noticed someone walking up the trail. She squinted her eyes for better focus.

"I do believe that's Jim."

She quickly emptied the dishwater, threw a towel over the dishes on the drying rack and wiped her hands. She retrieved two tall drinking glasses from the cabinet, placed them on the wooden tray, then pulled a pitcher of lemonade from the refrigerator and set it on the tray.

Jim knocked on the screen door within moments.

"Anybody home?"

The old woman moved toward the front porch with the tray of drinks, as Jim politely opened the door.

"Why am I not surprised?" he commented. "I had a feeling you'd be serving your yummy lemonade this warm spring day." He promptly closed the screen door and hurried to unfold the small table for the tray of lemonade.

"You must be on the lookout for people; you always seem to be readily prepared to serve visitors."

"Actually," she replied as she set down the tray, "I had just finished washing lunch dishes. Are you hungry?"

Jim shook his head. "No, ma'am, I had a big lunch before heading this direction. I sure won't pass up such a refreshing drink this warm afternoon, though."

The old woman sat down and reached for the pitcher. "If you would like more ice, you know where the refrigerator is."

I love that she's so comfortable with me.

"That I do," he smiled. "May I get you more ice, as well?"

She nodded. Jim promptly entered the cabin, returning shortly with a bowl of ice, and added a few cubes to both glasses.

"I've been thinking about our last visit," he began as he sat down. "You know, it sure helps that I often work nights; it will make daytime visits convenient."

Silence hung in the air as birds darted back and forth across the front yard. A couple of brave rabbits streaked across the side of the porch, while squirrels scampered around collecting nuts.

The old woman's perennial garden displayed an array of colors and shapes of nearly every flower one could imagine, which would no doubt eventually take up most of the East side of her front yard.

"Your beautiful perennial garden makes your front yard so very colorful," Jim observed. "And, there's not much to mow, which must make things easy for you. If I may ask, who mows your grass?"

"Mostly, I do," she managed to say between sips of lemonade. She used her foot to keep the swing gently in motion, as the two of them allowed the flow and ease of the moment to envelope their hearts with peace and tranquility, with only the sounds of nature in the background.

"Jim, there's another potential aspect of this unfolding story that has just come up."

He glanced over at her and watched her facial expressions as she began to speak.

She really does have a lovely face; I can only imagine how beautiful she was as a young woman. And, that's just her physical appearance; look at the energy that surrounds her.

She took a deep breath. "A woman who was here several years ago came to visit me again, just a few days ago."

Jim was still lost in thought about the old woman's presence.

It's like nothing I have ever seen. In fact, I am not certain what to call the presence she carries. Maybe I'll learn more about that as we move along with this project.

His head was in now in full gear.

Hush! Focus on her words.

She continued, "It is my understanding that she will be engaged in this project with us."

The old woman's words abruptly got Jim's attention, and he quickly returned his focus to what she was saying.

Wait! Did she just say someone else is going to be part of our project?

He waited for her to say more about this other person, but only silence filled the air.

"Tell me about this person, or how she might be of assistance with this project." He sipped his lemonade as his mind began to wander.

So, how did someone else get involved? I'm not certain I like this.

Still, he was met with silence.

"Actually," he continued, "tell me whatever you want me to know. This is your story."

That felt much better, as Jim told his ego to get out of the way.

Interesting how old patterns can re-emerge when you least expect it; my issues with trust are coming up again.

He took a deep breath and felt the boards of the porch beneath his feet.

I trust this beautiful old woman; if she feels another person is to be involved, that's all I need to know.

"There's really not much more to say at this point," she responded. "I just wanted you to know that a third person will more than likely be involved."

The silence was broken as a pileated woodpecker diligently and persistently pecked at an unusual knothole in the Old Oak. Both the old woman and Jim watched the amazing creature. Deep black contrasted with pure white, while its brilliant red head drilled away at the tree.

"May I ask if you have a day and time you would like to begin this project? And would you like to have my cell phone number so you can call me when you want me here?"

She sat very still and watched the huge woodpecker hammer away at the wood in search of some juicy insects.

"Such determination and focus," she observed. "There is much we can learn from this red-headed creature of nature."

She turned back to Jim. "I'll call to you like I've always done; your job is to pay attention and listen."

"I'll do my best," smiled Jim.

He then reached into his shirt pocket and cleared his throat.

"I do have a question for you, though. It's about this object you gave me the last time I was here."

She looked at him. "What is it you would like to ask?"

He squirmed in his chair. "Well, why did you give me this marble? I mean, what does it mean?"

Jim suddenly felt silly. Why would he ask her a question to which he knew the answer? He knew when the time was right she would tell him what it was for, or how it would be used, or whatever else this marble was all about.

"On second thought," he said as he put the marble back into his pocket, "I reckon I don't have a question. I guess you'll let me know when it's time for me to know."

The old woman rose from the swing and steadied herself as Jim placed their glasses onto the tray and picked it up.

"That object is a medicine piece," she said. "It carries the Light of the Universe. Allow it to guide you as you learn about the Light within yourself."

Jim felt a pulsation that went from the marble straight to his heart as he steadied the tray in his hands.

Oh, my gosh, pull yourself together!

She brought him back to the moment. "You know, Jim, I need a simple fence put around the vegetable garden."

"Of course," he stammered. "I'd be glad to help. How does this Saturday work for you?"

She smiled and nodded in agreement.

"Is nine Saturday morning good for you? Best we get it done before the heat of the day."

She nodded. "Yes."

"I have plenty of extra chicken wire and metal stakes," added Jim. "Do you need me to pick up any other materials?"

She shook her head and smiled.

"Thank you, Jim; you're a good man."

"Well, thank you. I do the best I can with what I have to work with," he chuckled. "We'll keep those pesky rabbits out of your garden, or whatever other critters attempt to ravage your food supply."

She scanned the flower garden.

"The fence is not about keeping critters out, Jim; it's about protecting the treasure within the perimeters."

Jim scratched his head and shrugged his shoulders.

Now, that's an interesting slant.

"I think we're saying the same thing," he suggested.

She simply said, "The words are different."

A moment of silence ensued, but Jim was not about to get into semantics.

"Okay, I'll be here Saturday at nine with the supplies needed to create a fence that will protect your food supply. Sound good?"

The old woman sat perfectly still and said nothing. Jim didn't know what to say, or why she was silent. What he did know was that his head was still reeling! Then he remembered what she had taught him and he felt the floor beneath his feet.

Ahhh, I feel present in the here and now!

Feeling adventurous, he asked, "How about we seal the deal with a hug?"

The old woman stood up, turned toward Jim and looked directly into his eyes. He took that as a "yes," put down the tray, bent down a bit and reached out his arms. It was an awkward moment; the old woman couldn't remember the last time someone other than her family had asked for a hug. Then she remembered that the last hug she had received was a very welcome embrace from Jim back in early autumn.

For some reason, it felt a bit awkward this time. She wasn't certain why, and it really didn't matter. She hesitated, then bent her arms a bit and allowed him to give her a small hug.

He read her body language and made it a short one, although he really wanted to give her another big bear hug like the last time. However, he was just glad for a small one; she was such a precious soul and he so respected everything about her.

He promptly picked up the tray and turned toward the screen door. The old woman was directly behind him and quickly moved in front of him to open the door.

"Thank you," said Jim as he moved toward the kitchen.

He felt something very magical in that moment, as though he walked on air. Somehow, Jim knew his life was about to change in ways he could not imagine. Once again, he recalled the cabin he had imagined when he was a young boy.

I'll bet it looked exactly like this on the inside. Warm, inviting, peaceful, yet full of magic and mystery.

"I'll be glad to wash up our glasses if you'd like," he offered as he placed the tray by the kitchen sink. He was met with silence, then turned and noticed that she hadn't followed him into the kitchen.

She must have stayed outside. That's good; it won't take but a few moments to get these glasses washed.

He turned on the hot water and reached for the dish soap. The glasses were washed and in the dish rack within five minutes. Jim dried his hands and placed the dishtowel on the handle of the stove. He turned to leave, and then paused; he was absolutely mesmerized by the stunningly beautiful stained-glass turtle lamp that had caught his eye.

What a sweet little light. I've never noticed that before.

He stepped over for a closer look, and noticed a piece of paper with writing on it that lay under the front legs of the turtle. He started to reach for it, and then stopped himself.

Okay, I am not here to snoop.

Still, he couldn't quite leave the kitchen, and his eyes quickly scanned the entire area. He first noticed some stones that had words painted on them: Joy, Love, and Acceptance. Then his eyes rested on a figurine of three monkeys. Starting from the left, one had his eyes covered with his hands, the next his ears, and the third his mouth. The monkeys sat cross-legged and were adjoined at their hips, and each wore a green vest and a red hat.

Hmmm, that looks old; no doubt it means something to her.

He suddenly realized that she was still outside, and probably wondered what was taking him so long.

I need to get out of here!

He promptly headed for the front door, and when he reached the porch he was a bit befuddled to find that the old woman was not in her usual spot on the porch swing.

I wonder if she went to her bedroom? Nah, I would have heard the screen door if she had come in after me.

As Jim stood on the porch, he realized he couldn't call out to her because he didn't even know her name.

Wow! I don't even know her name after all these years!

He smiled as his eyes scanned the front yard.

Such a beautiful place! Those cobblestone steps across the lush green grass are so lovely. She must weed at least once a week. And, I'll bet she pulls the weeds without wearing gloves.

"I'll bet she loves to have her bare hands in the soil," he said softly. "She's the sort of person who would appreciate the tactile contact."

His eyes moved across the yard to the flower garden.

She certainly has a green thumb! That garden is so rich with color, and has no doubt taken years to be so full and lush.

Then he spotted the top of the Atlanta Braves cap she had worn the day they worked on the fire at the Giveaway. He smiled.

There she is, just as I suspected, and she's on her knees 'playing' with her most treasured friends.

He watched the hummingbirds flit from flower to flower as they gathered pollen. The vivid red cardinals hopped about the grass, as yellow and indigo canaries playfully darted along the tops of the flowers like surfers riding the great waves of an ocean. It was a sight to behold, and Jim could feel the life and connection that exists when one is truly a part of all living things. Such connection results in a continual flow of energy that moves through all living things, vibrant and alive with an unyielding presence of unconditional love.

His eyes showed his emotions as he witnessed the purity and innocence of Truth when, even for a moment, everything is in perfect harmony, and no one is higher or lower than another. There is simply a knowing that Heaven and Earth coexist when judgments and prejudices are eliminated, and that absolutely every single living thing is of value, adding beauty, sweetness, and brilliant color to life.

We are, indeed, all equal in the eyes of our Creator.

Jim inhaled deeply as he felt his heart expand in his chest.

"If only we could live that way every day," he whispered as he released his breath. "If only we could realize that we are, indeed, an extension of the Divine, and that absolutely nothing exists outside of ourselves."

A strong breeze rustled the leaves on the trees and the tall flowers swayed with the wind. The old woman adjusted her cap to shade the sunlight as her eyes remained focused on the task in front of her.

Jim knew it was time to leave. Everything that needed to be said and done that day was complete, and the old woman was precisely where she felt most at home: with her flowers and the soil. And, it was time for him to head back to the place where he felt most at home: with his wife, three children and, of course, his dog, Max.

He retrieved a gift from his pocket and dropped it into the twig basket, then slowly and quietly made his way over the cobblestones across her yard. Then he heard a faint sound when he came to the clearing, and paused.

What is that?

He stepped onto the path into the woods, and when he was out of sight from the old woman he stopped to listen more intently. He closed his eyes and heard his heartbeat, along with the sounds of the woods and the inhabitants that danced with delight in the warmth of summer. Then he heard the same faint sound that he had heard on the front porch. His heart beat more intensely.

What is that sound?

"Let me help you hear," the voice said clearly.

Jim felt the hair on the back of his neck stand up as a chill moved down his spine.

"Ahhh, okay, I'm listening," he choked out hesitantly.

"It is time for you to use the 'ears' of your heart," said the voice.

Jim closed his eyes, took a deep breath, and cleared his mind. As he slowly released his breath, the faint humming sound returned. He felt Earth Mother beneath his feet, the rhythm of his heartbeat in the center of his body, and he inhaled and exhaled another deep breath.

Within a few short moments, he identified the sound. It was the old woman humming in her flower garden. Truly, the essence of the entire universe orchestrated a sweet symphony of love and harmony among the inhabitants of that simple piece of ground that was surrounded by the Forest.

The pulsating beats of Jim's heart joined the chorus of energy that was channeled from the heavens, through the top of his head, down through his body, and into the sacred ground beneath his feet, joining with the heartbeat of Mother. He knew he was being fine-tuned for the project before him, and for the transformation that was about to take place in his life. As with the evolution of all things in life, when it is time for something new to emerge, that which no longer serves us must fall away.

He shivered as he opened his eyes, blinked a few times to clear his vision, and then noticed a pair of large, orange eyes that pierced Jim's own, brown eyes. He felt another shiver run up his spine as he held the owl's stare with confidence.

"Are you ready?" asked the owl. *"If you are, I am here to be of assistance. All you need do is call to me."*

Jim had entered a time and space from his youth.

Maybe I've watched too many sci-fi movies!

What Jim did know was that he felt absolutely no fear, but only a steady calm within. Then he remembered to use the "ears" of his heart, and allowed the owl's words to settle within.

He felt the Truth of the owl's words throughout his entire being, and he knew he was ready. In fact, he knew for certain that his life had been spent in preparation for this very moment, although he had no idea exactly how he knew.

With his feet firmly planted on the ground and his breathing steady, he spoke to the owl.

"I am ready; and, yes, I request your assistance."

"Then it is done," responded the owl. *"Trust yourself and, above all, do not think about it with your mind, and do not ask questions to which you know the answers. These are my words,"* said the owl, as he blinked his eyes and flew off into the North.

Jim blinked several times, released his breath, and shook his head.

Oh, my gosh, the old woman said the same words. I'm not even going to try and make sense out of what just happened! Besides, I am not to engage my mind in this.

He tried not to think as he took a few more deep breaths. Grandfather now neared the treetops as he descended into the West, so Jim picked up his pace and was in his truck within five minutes.

I need to get the lead out and get home!

After giving Max a pat on the head, Jim pulled onto the road toward home.

"Max, you really aren't going to believe what just happened, and before I get started let me just say how grateful I am that I have you to talk to!"

Back at the cabin, the old woman had just spread the last pile of weeds from the flower garden along the edge of the woods.

"You'll be absorbed here by Mother; no doubt she's glad to have your presence to enrich her soil," she said with much affection. She wiped her hands on her garden apron, and with the back of one hand wiped the sweat from her brow.

"Reckon I've done enough weeding!" She glanced up at Grandfather. "You've given us a warm one today. I'm ready for another glass of cold lemonade and another good, long shower."

As she approached the porch she caught sight of Jim standing on the path. He seemed to be staring at something.

I wonder who's got his attention? No doubt one of our wise critters has introduced him-or herself. She chuckled. *I'll bet Jim's beginning to wonder what he has gotten himself into!*

She smiled affectionately as she thought of what was about to happen to Jim's life.

"Such a precious man, who has stood in the fire of his shadow side, and has now found the warmth of life that comes from making peace with it. It's going to be an honor to watch both him and Ruth begin new chapters in their lives."

With that thought the old woman made her way to the porch swing. She was as tuckered out as she could be, and the breeze from swinging would help cool her down a bit before heading to the shower. She dropped onto the swing, straightened her back, tilted her head upward and rotated her shoulders in an attempt to loosen her sore muscles.

"Geez, these muscles! That hot shower will help relax them a bit, and tomorrow we're going to take it easy."

Gracie hopped up on the swing and curled up close to the old woman.

"Ahhh, aren't you the healer!" she said to Gracie.

Gracie began to purr, no doubt as a way to say, "Anything I can do to help!"

The old woman stroked Gracie's fur, which intensified her purring.

"Thank you for adding love to my tired body; it makes my heart happy, which directly affects my overall well-being. The least I can do is return the favor!"

She watched the flowers that danced with each other in the warm summer breeze. The harmony displayed a sense of unity that extended well beyond the garden. She sighed happily.

"I feel all of you in my heart. All's well in the world."

She thought of Ruth as she inhaled the fragrance of honeysuckle that filled the air. She closed her eyes and whispered, "It's time, Ruth. *The Time is Now.*"

Fences

Morning rain poured from the heavens as the old woman sat on the porch swing with a notebook in her lap. Gracie sat next to her and purred contentedly.

"Not certain Jim will make it today; the prediction was only for rain this morning, but who knows? Everyone knows the weather is as unpredictable as most men are." She stroked Gracie's soft, orange-striped coat.

She glanced at Tom, who lay near the edge of the porch. He perked up his ears and looked at the old woman.

"I apologize, Tom, that was a rather unkind statement. I know a lot of females who are a whole lot more unpredictable than you males!"

"It's okay, I know you love me!" he seemed to say as he laid his head back down.

"Darned if old beliefs don't sneak out of my mouth from time to time. Words carry powerful energy, and I certainly want to add more positive energy to the environment, rather than the toxicity that comes from negative thoughts and words." She promised herself that she would pay closer attention to her words, in order to keep her current life precisely as she wanted.

She surveyed the sky and noticed that the gray clouds had begun to move northwest as blue skies peeked through.

"Looks like the rain is moving toward our neighbors in the North, Gracie. That's good; their gardens could probably use the moisture as much as our gardens needed it."

Clad in work clothes, the old woman decided that, if Jim didn't make it, she would begin to clean out the old shed in preparation for the fresh coat of paint she had promised it over the winter. That was one of the projects on her "to do" list when spring brought warmth to the Earth.

It'll sure help to get that shed cleared out, and to recycle or give away some of those old jars and tools that I no longer use. I like things simple and uncluttered, and cleaning it out will make it easier for me to move around without tripping over things.

Whether she liked it or not, those sorts of things needed to be considered in order to ensure that she stayed in good physical shape, so she could continue to live on her own.

She mentally visualized everything that occupied space in the shed. She recalled every item that had been gifted to her by someone who planned to relocate, or who had decided to get a newer, more up-to-date version of a product.

"Dad always said to hang onto everything, just in case you might need it. He said, 'You never know when it will come in handy, or when someone else might need it.'"

She pondered his words and considered his rationale. His family had gone through the depression, which had definitely influenced him and his siblings to consider possible scarcity. They were taught to be prepared should another financial crisis befall our country. His words did not come from fear, but were shared as an example of how to take responsibility for one's family. They were teachings about living within one's means, valuing everything one has, and never taking things for granted.

"Those teachings have certainly helped me throughout my life," she mumbled.

The words were barely out of her mouth when she caught sight of Jim coming up the path.

"Hmmm, he doesn't seem to mind the rain; he sure is walking slowly."

He carefully maneuvered around the mud puddles on the path, his arms full with chicken wire and other supplies.

Tom raised his head as though he understood what she had said, and looked toward the path. He promptly got up on all four legs and headed toward Jim, tail wagging.

"I'd say Tom likes Jim," she said to Gracie, who didn't so much as move a muscle. She gave Gracie a pat on the head. "I know you like Jim, too; you just aren't fond of rain. Not to mention, you choose to show affection for someone on your own terms. I guess we're a lot alike in that way!" she snickered.

As Tom approached him, Jim carefully put down his load of supplies, and reached down to scratch Tom behind the ears and give his head a vigorous shake. She couldn't hear what Jim said to Tom; however, between his smile and Tom's wagging tail, she could tell they were words of affection.

The rain turned to a misty shower as Grandfather began to emerge between the parted clouds. Jim smiled as he reached the steps of the front porch.

"Good morning!" he greeted her. "I'll take these things to the garden and then come back; I sure don't want to get your porch all wet and muddy."

The old woman returned his smile and nodded. When Jim walked to the side of the porch, she picked up her journal and pen and took them into the cabin.

Guess I didn't need these today after all, and that's okay. We have a lot to do and I'm ready to get to it! Sure don't want Jim to take up his entire day helping me; no doubt he has plenty of chores at his own house.

She placed the journal and pen in her usual chair inside the cabin, and then moved into the kitchen where she took a pitcher of iced tea and a small dish of sliced lemons from the refrigerator. She pulled two tall glasses from the cabinet and placed everything onto her wooden tray.

She then retrieved a lovely platter with cheese slices, strawberries and cucumber wedges from the refrigerator, and set it on the tray along with some whole-grain crackers and some napkins. Then she carried the pitcher of tea to the porch and placed it on the small table beside Jim.

"The tray is sitting on the counter in the kitchen," she indicated.

"I'll be right back!" he exclaimed as he sprang to his feet, slipped off his boots, and went inside.

Knowing her, I'll bet she's not one for asking for assistance … it warms my heart that she's comfortable enough to ask me.

As they enjoyed their snack, they both noticed that the clouds had disappeared, and Grandfather's brilliant yellow now appeared high in the rich, blue sky. A light breeze blew across the rain-soaked land that had absorbed the moisture, while Grandfather's heat dried the sparkling droplets from the blanket of green.

"I think that rain is going to make putting up the fence quite easy," Jim mumbled through juicy red strawberries. "Excuse me for talking with my mouth full; these strawberries are delicious! And, I gotta tell you, this iced tea is as good an iced tea as I've ever had. How is it that everything you make is outstanding?" he asked as he took another gulp. He placed his glass on the tray.

"That's about all I can eat and still work. If I eat anything more I'll be ready for a nap!" he chuckled.

The old woman smiled as she rose from the swing and covered the tray with napkins.

"Ready for the fence?" she asked.

"Yes, indeed!" Jim exclaimed as he rose from his chair. "But let me take the food back to the refrigerator for safe keeping."

She nodded in agreement, then stepped off the porch and moved toward the garden as Jim took the tray into the cabin.

The old woman surveyed the garden and noted the supplies Jim had brought with him.

Looks like we have more than enough wire and stakes to get this fence built within a couple of hours.

She went to the shed to get the jar of cornmeal, and headed back toward the garden just as Jim rounded the corner of the cabin. "Are you ready to keep those mischievous rabbits out of your garden?" he asked, rubbing his hands together. "I mean, to protect the treasure within your garden?"

The old woman took a handful of cornmeal out of the jar, and acknowledged his words with a slight nod as she looked down at the ground.

Jim hit the pause button on his chatter and held the stillness for whatever ceremony she was about to perform. He had watched her work with cornmeal and tobacco enough times to know that it had something to do with showing reverence for the task she was about to perform. He settled himself by the fencing supplies as he observed her.

I love how she approaches everything with such a sense of purpose and intention. She's so focused. I could use more of that in my own life; I just seem to move from one thing to another without giving thought to anything besides getting something done. Darned if I can't get so distracted that I rarely complete one task before I'm off to another one.

The old woman slowly walked clockwise around the perimeter of the garden, scattering a few sprinkles of the cornmeal onto the ground. When she arrived back to her starting point, she lifted a hand to the sky, then placed both hands on the ground and patted the Earth.

That was it! She pulled her leather gloves from her pants pocket and looked at Jim.

"I'm ready," she said.

Jim slipped on his work gloves and unrolled some of the chicken wire, stepping on it to flatten it a bit. When one side had been stretched out, he picked up a stake and shoved it into the ground.

The old woman picked up a half dozen more stakes and walked to where Jim stood.

"You sure have a keen eye," he smiled.

No doubt this lovely woman knows how to collaborate on projects for which she knows she can be of help.

He reached into his pants pocket and pulled out a dozen or so pieces of six-inch lengths of wire and handed them to her. He reached into his other pocket and pulled out a pair of pliers.

"Hold onto these pliers; I'm going to show you what I'd like for you to do."

He walked again on the chicken wire until he came to his original starting place, then turned to the old woman, who handed him a stake.

"I see you've done this before," he chuckled.

She nodded slightly and waited for him to proceed.

"Okay, now hand me a couple pieces of that cut wire," he said as he extended his hand to her. She placed a piece in his hand while he held the edge of the chicken wire up to the stake. He then wrapped it between the holes of the chicken wire, and twisted the piece of wire to secure it onto the stake. Then he went a third of the way down the stake and repeated the process.

"You'll need to twist the ends of the wires several times to make certain they are secure, and then you'll do the same thing about two-thirds of the way down the stake. Oh, and there are plenty of precut wires in the coffee can by the supplies. But, I have a sense you know how to do this," he smiled.

"The pliers will keep your fingers from getting scratched or too sore from handling all the wires we're going to use. We don't want to harm your hands; they make such delicious treats!" he said with a laugh. "Sorry, I tend to think about food when I'm here!"

She took a wire from her pocket, bent two thirds of the way down the stake and carried out Jim's instructions perfectly.

"Very excellent!" Jim praised her. "Let's get this fence built!"

He walked down the chicken wire about four feet from the stake and shoved another stake securely into the ground. He picked up the chicken wire, pulled it tight from the first stake, and stood aside for the old woman to secure the wires in place. When she had tightened the first piece, Jim walked about another four feet down and drove in another stake.

They repeated the process around the entire perimeter of the garden until they were within about two feet of the beginning stake. Jim drove one last stake into the ground, and the old woman affixed the wires onto the stake and waited to see what Jim was going to do. She had, indeed, made fences around her gardens before; however, never did she leave a two-foot opening.

She pondered Jim's intention for a moment.

Maybe he's going to put up a board that I can just move aside when I'm ready to work. Hmmm, let's see what he does.

Jim then took a piece of chicken wire and cut it two-and-a-half feet long. He placed a piece to the right of the opening and secured it snuggly onto the stake as before. He then extended the other end of the piece to the very first stake, and bent the remaining six inches around the edge.

He's making a door! How creative, and so very functional! She smiled.

Sure enough, Jim took one of the six-inch wires and bent the end into a hook, and affixed the other end securely onto the curved edge.

She knew Jim's heart and mind were at play, which was confirmed by the "voice" of her own heart.

"This is so exciting! How I love the ingenuity that occurs when the creative heart and masterful mind collaborate so beautifully."

"We're all finished!" He looked at his watch. "It only took a little over two hours. I'd say we make a good fence-building team. Wouldn't you agree?"

She nodded and smiled from ear to ear. Then she took a pinch of the cornmeal and placed it on the ground in front of the sweet door.

"With gratitude," she whispered.

At that moment, both of them turned and noticed a young woman rounding the cabin and heading in their direction. She paused and waved.

"Hey, I hope I'm not interrupting anything."

The old woman shook her head and motioned for her to join them. Jim leaned over to the old woman and whispered, "Is that the girl you spoke of?"

"Yes," she said, as the young woman now stood in front of them.

"Ruth, this is Jim; Jim, this is Ruth."

The introductions made, the two smiled and shook hands as the old woman began to pick up some of the leftover materials and place them in a pile.

"Looks like you two have been busy!" Ruth smiled broadly, as she noticed the remnants lying on the ground. "May I help with the clean up?"

"You'll have to ask the boss lady if there's something you can do for her," Jim responded. "I'm just here as a second set of hands." He grinned and joined the old woman with cleaning up.

"On second thought," Jim turned to the old woman, "I can finish this if you want to sit on the porch and visit with Ruth."

She looked at Ruth. "I believe Jim has worked up an appetite! Come with me and we'll fix something to eat."

She turned to Jim. "Thank you for your help; we'll have something special for you on the porch in a bit." She picked up the jar of cornmeal and handed it to him. "I believe you know where this goes in the shed."

"That I do. And, I wasn't hinting for something to eat; we still have some things on the tray to pick at. Although, everything you make is exceptional!" he declared, smiling sheepishly.

He couldn't help himself; he knew she would prepare something else, if only some of her refreshing lemonade. Jim was aware by now that the old woman always seemed to intuitively know when someone was coming for a visit. He had never shown up unannounced when she didn't have something delicious readily available!

Ruth and the old woman went to the cabin while Jim headed to the shed. He placed the cornmeal in its usual place, and returned to the garden area to gather his work supplies, which he rolled up in the remaining chicken wire.

He was about halfway to the front porch when he caught sight of something flying overhead. He stopped and looked up.

"I'll be darned." He craned his neck upward. "Yep, it's an Eagle!" His heart skipped a beat as he marveled at the majestic bird. "What perfect timing!"

Jim knew that an Eagle indicated that it is time to reach higher, and to become more than you think you are capable of becoming. It is an omen from Creator that you are seen, loved, and supported on your current path.

Can't ask for more than that! He patted his pants pocket. *Yep, it's still there. I have a hunch this has something to do with what the Eagle represents.*

He scanned the sky and, sure enough, the Eagle had disappeared.

"Guess only time will tell."

Chatter from the porch brought his attention back to where he was headed before the Eagle had beckoned. He smiled.

"Sounds like those ladies are enjoying their time together."

He rounded the side of the cabin and noticed two chairs angled beside each other, just to the right of the swing. It was obvious they had been strategically placed so that all three of them could see one another.

Now, that's convenient. Women certainly have a knack for creating an environment conducive for socializing. Most men aren't as thoughtful about such things. Guess we feel it's every person for him- or herself. As long as people are having fun, that's all that matters.

He rounded the cabin with an armful of chicken wire and tools.

"Sounds like you two are enjoying each other's company. Mind if I join you?" he asked, as he neatly stacked the extra materials and supplies on the ground beside the porch steps.

"This is waiting for you," smiled Ruth as she patted the empty chair beside her.

Jim stepped onto the porch and sat down. He looked at the small table beside the swing. A bright orange cloth covered something that was no doubt refreshing and delectable.

"My, my, you ladies certainly work together efficiently." He eyeballed the orange covering again, then quickly averted his eyes and changed the subject.

"The weather certainly cooperated with our project today," he commented as he scanned the sky. "It's become a beautiful afternoon."

He glanced again at the table, and then promptly looked toward the flower garden. "No doubt your flowers are being adequately nourished. And," he laughed, "of course, so are your weeds!"

The old woman looked at Ruth and smiled.

"Better remove that cloth before our friend keeps talking about everything except what his eyes are most curious about!"

The three of them laughed as Ruth removed the orange fabric, revealing a colorful assortment of fruit, including the strawberries from earlier. Small sandwiches made from the remaining cucumbers and cheese, with added tomato and mayonnaise, as well as the wheat crackers were also on the tray. Bright purple plates, floral napkins, forks, and three bright yellow glasses were stacked on one side, as well as a glass pitcher painted with bright yellow sunflowers, filled with lemonade and ice cubes. It was a summer display of crisp, fresh color that would entice anyone to partake of the refreshing assortment of goodies.

As if on cue, Jim and Ruth glanced at each other, then looked at the old woman. She bowed her head, placed her hands over the food and mumbled a few words. Then she motioned to Jim to help himself.

"You go first," he said. "You're the elder."

Ruth nodded and looked at her. "May I fix you a plate?"

The old woman smiled at their thoughtfulness. It was difficult for her to accept that she was an elder; in her heart and soul she felt much younger. However, her body reminded her quite often that the regular activities she had enjoyed most of her life were now to be done less frequently, and on a smaller scale. She smiled as she remembered how her children had described her as the "Energizer Bunny." Well, it seemed her batteries were much weaker these days.

She shook her head in response. "Thank you, though."

She picked up a plate and napkin, and selected a few pieces of fruit and a sandwich. Ruth poured a glass of lemonade and handed it to her. The old woman carefully placed her drink beside her on the swing, set the plate on her lap, and waited until the other two had made their selections.

Ruth handed Jim a plate, fork and napkin, and got some for herself. After they had filled their own plates, they all commenced satisfying their taste buds as they enjoyed the warmth of the afternoon air. They watched as critters frolicked in the front yard; it seemed they, too, enjoyed the light-hearted interactions between the two visitors and the woman with whom they shared the land.

The old woman quietly enjoyed her snack, almost as much as she enjoyed watching Ruth and Jim get to know each other. The two of them chatted about where they were from, what each did for a living, and who knew whom from the local area. They were surprised to learn that they had both attended the same high school, although Jim was six years older so they never really knew each other.

"I remember my father speaking of a really nice fella that worked at the sawmill. Was that you?"

Jim blushed. "It may have been; however, all of our employees at the sawmill are really good people, so who knows?" He sipped his lemonade. "Thank your father for me, regardless of whom he was speaking. We've done our best to make it a place where people are able to come and get what they need in a timely, friendly manner."

The air was now humid as Grandfather continued to move across the sky. His warmth continued to help the land absorb and release the moisture from the morning rain. The flowers stood erect, reaching for his warmth as if to say "thank you," while the grass seemed to turn a deeper shade of green before their very eyes.

"This lemonade is most refreshing," Ruth commented as she picked up the pitcher and offered more to the old woman.

She shook her head.

They sat peacefully for a few more minutes, observing the activity of the winged ones that flitted about the flower garden, and the butterflies that hovered over the bright periwinkle flowers of the butterfly bush. Hummingbirds happily drank the nectar of the colorful zinnias and marigolds as their tiny wings filled the air with the soothing hum of joy.

Ruth finally broke the silence.

"I've been thinking about the fence you two put up today," she said as she observed the abundance of rabbits and squirrels that scampered in the yard. "I take it these critters are eager to partake of your bountiful plantings? It's a good thing the bees can still access your broccoli for pollination. You certainly can't build a fence tall enough to keep them out!"

Jim smiled and waited.

I feel a story coming on.

The play on words regarding the fence during his last visit would no doubt become more clear when the old woman responded to Ruth's comments. Somehow, every story she told held a teaching that was so much greater than the actual story itself.

It'll be interesting to watch Ruth, as well. She seems a very kind person. She would have to be; the old woman obviously trusts her.

The old woman returned her plate and eating utensils to the tray, and pulled the tatting shuttle and thread out of the black bag that sat beside her. Then she began her story.

"It was in the early 1800s that thousands of settlers began the movement westward in search of a new beginning and a place they could call home. Men, women, and children traversed the rugged terrain of the Oregon Trail, willing to endure whatever elements they confronted in order to accomplish their dreams.

"The Homestead Act was created in 1862, to provide incentives for those who sought a dream. This Act literally catapulted the mass migration westward, and allowed pioneers over the age of 21 to claim 160 acres of free land, provided they agreed to live on the land for at least five years and make various improvements, such as building a house on the land.

"Such a feat required hundreds of men, women, and children to work together in the spirit of cooperation, commitment, and with a unified effort by all. The physical and mental stamina of each and every member was sustained by the common goal to be free, and to set permanent roots on new lands.

"Each person needed the emotional and spiritual strength necessary to stand on their personal convictions, while remaining open to other perspectives about how that dream might be realized for the entire group. While great dedication, determination, and perseverance were required to endure the often-treacherous terrain and seasonal weather conditions, it was the ability to hold true to one's self, while still respecting each individual's perspective, that allowed the final destination to be realized."

The old woman stopped tatting, glanced at her glass, and set the chain in her lap. Ruth immediately reached for the pitcher and the old woman nodded affirmatively.

Jim slowly stood up. "May I get you some ice for your drink? Seems the heat has melted most of what was in the pitcher. And, I can take the tray back inside while I'm at it if everyone is done nibbling."

"Thank you," she responded.

The two ladies awaited Jim's return in the warmth of the afternoon, and they both welcomed a cool breeze that swept the heat from the porch.

Jim returned with an ice bucket and tongs and set them on the table. He lifted the lid of the ice bucket, then playfully clicked the tongs together several times.

"Ice, anyone?"

Both ladies chuckled and held up their glasses.

"Why, thank you, sir." Ruth smiled at Jim as he plunked several ice cubes into her glass. She liked him.

Such a pleasant spirit, and his willingness to be helpful is, well, refreshing.

When all three glasses had been replenished with ice and lemonade, the old woman once again picked up her tatting and returned to her story.

"Life offers us the opportunity to 'fall asleep;' that is, to forget what gave our life purpose, and what moved us from deep within. Grit and personal fortitude carry us to our destinations, because once we have settled into our dreams, we often allow our visions to fade as we become focused on maintaining what we have attained. What once seemed a profound accomplishment can all too often become buried beneath the responsibilities required to maintain that dream on a day-to-day basis.

"Such was what happened when the settlers neared the end of their five-year commitments. The constant maintenance and resources needed to raise enough food to feed their families, horses, several head of cattle and pigs, or to use to barter for goods and services, now required that fences be built.

"This was done for several reasons. First, to identify the boundaries of the property; second, to protect the crops and farm animals from predators that had resided on the land well before humans arrived. They also served to protect possessions from poachers and thieves."

She looked up and glanced into the surrounding woods.

There she goes, observed Jim.

Ruth pondered the old woman's words.

I never thought about fences protecting what is within the perimeters. I always thought it was to keep predators and intruders away. Hmmm; I guess it's the same thing, but somehow the word 'protect' sounds gentler than keeping something out.

The old woman's fingers once again moved at warp speed as the chain became nearly a foot in length. She continued her story.

"Our hearts guide our lives and let us know what brings us joy and purpose; and, if we are also in good relationship with our head mind, will help us to live in balance. Our human emotions can then either become our friends or our foes. If we do not make friends with our emotions, our lives will be filled with an endless stream of wondering and wandering that eventually puts our heart to sleep, and then we lose our vision.

"When that happens, we become dead within. We lose our passion for life and for our dreams, and allow our disappointments to culminate in a new perspective, always on the lookout for potential problems. We stop listening to our heart's guidance in life's decisions, and rely only on our practical mind. This is where the separation begins. The moment we ignore our heart's guidance and become suspicious and cautious of others, we begin to doubt our own inner knowing, and we start to fall asleep. We 'unfriend' our emotions and make them our foes, making friends instead with our practical mind."

She paused her tatting and carefully examined its length. She smoothed the chain with her fingers, and with a slight pull straightened the carefully crafted loops of the beautiful chain that by now far exceeded eighteen inches. She carefully laid the chain across her lap, bit the end of the thread, and tied a knot in the end.

She put the thread and shuttle back into her black bag and tenderly tucked it close to her left hip. She stroked the chain across her lap a few more times to flatten it before she continued her story.

"When we fall asleep, we lose our sense of purpose. We forget who we are, and life becomes a series of rewinds of past experiences and disappointments. That is when the fence around our heart is complete; that is, when we can only remember the difficult times, and the hurtful words and actions of others as well as ourselves. We begin to 'snore' a warning to others to stay away. Our exterior may be beautiful, as is this chain; however, the delicate loops of our life have become a long chain of knots."

She looked at Ruth and Jim. "Are you ready to fully awaken while your looped chain is still delicate and beautiful? Are you willing to learn what it means to be fully present to life, and to notice the perimeters of your heart that may need some tending? There is no "bogeyman" to keep out; there is only our human self that can easily be drawn away from our true self, and be pulled into a world that is driven by material possessions and judgments that separate us from others.

"These often emotionally charged events keep us locked in the chains of unforgiveness, and we become slaves to our unmet desires. This is when fences become our prisons. Our old beliefs and perceptions were built from a human understanding that created those fences, and that will keep out the very thing we need the most: loving, compassionate, adventurous, and trusting relationships.

"Protective, loving fences help us become Gate Keepers of our tender souls, by providing a safe place to keep a watchful eye on our open, loving hearts, which hold those qualities we need the most. The heart needs to be loved, respected, and listened to, so that it can give us what we need in order to stay fully awake. Therefore, the fence needs to be light, airy, delicate and beautiful, just like this chain."

Silence hung in the air as a cool breeze swept over the porch. It seemed to be nudging the trio to individually choose how they would proceed. A faint chime resounded a tune like background music in a movie, as the stillness of the moment moved within, between and around the three souls. It was a dance to behold, and the old woman sat in perfect stillness with her eyes affixed on the ancestral knothole on the Magnificent Old Oak just beyond the flower garden.

Jim and Ruth sat perfectly still while her words settled into their hearts. Something very profound felt familiar and safe.

Jim allowed the silence to open the "ears" of his heart as he considered what being a Gate Keeper would look like.

Gate Keeper. Interesting. Yet another word to learn more about. Rather, to understand.

"I'm in," he said, as he pulled the cat's eye marble from his pants pocket and clutched it in his hand.

Tears filled Ruth eyes as she pulled a beautiful hair comb from the back of her hair, releasing the French twist and allowing her long hair to fall midway down her back. She held the ornate silver and pearl hair comb in her left hand.

"I have no idea what I'm doing," she managed with a dry mouth. "However, I know that my heart indicates a resounding '*yes!*'"

Birds sang and chirped with delight as they flew above the gently swaying array of color in the magical flower garden. Gracie and Tom emerged from the path in the woods and made their way to the front of the porch as though to witness this moment. Every living thing on her land seemed to acknowledge that a threshold had been crossed, and the emergence of something new had just been birthed. The adventure had begun, and called for joyful celebration!

The old woman slowly stood up and tied both ends of the tatted chain together to form a circle. She stepped off the porch, slipped off her shoes, and felt Earth Mother beneath her feet. Jim then also stepped off the porch and slipped off his boots, stood on her right, and felt the sacred ground beneath his feet. Without a moment's hesitation, a very tearful Ruth did likewise, and stood on the old woman's left with her bare feet on sweet Mother.

The old woman turned and walked toward the Old Oak, with Jim and Ruth directly behind her. She looked to the heavens as she raised the beautiful circle of tatted loops to the sky.

"Receive this as our token of love, and guide us on this journey. Let this circle represent the energy fence that unites our commitment to the task in front of us. May our hearts together create a spiral of love that will ignite the hearts of those we encounter during this journey, and may we remain humble and present, so that we may be clean, hollow bones, through which Spirit may guide our work. Let our physical bodies be instruments through which you may speak to those who are ready and willing to use the 'ears' of their heart, to listen to the song it is ready to sing."

She turned and looked at Jim and Ruth. "Always remember, you are representatives of the Light."

As if on cue, they assumed their positions to the right and left of her.

She held the chain up toward the sky.

"As Above," she said, and then knelt to the ground. Jim and Ruth followed her lead and knelt beside her.

"So Below," she said as she patted the Earth.

Then, with her hand to her heart she concluded, "So Within."

She reached for Jim's hand, and he assisted her to her feet.

She stood on her tiptoes and grabbed a sturdy branch of the Old Oak, onto which she slipped the chain about halfway down.

Ruth's chest shook from uncontrollable sobs that came from deep within her soul. Tears streamed from her eyes, and the old woman pulled a hankie out of her pocket and handed it to her.

The three of them stood side by side for what felt like an eternity, as nature sang a song of abiding love and reuniting joy. The heavens continued to send a steady stream of forgiveness, unconditional love, and blessings for their journey.

Suddenly the singing went silent, and within a few moments the owl that had agreed to guide Jim hooted three times to indicate his commitment to assist. Jim's eyes filled with tears as a smile broadened across his face.

I see you! Thank you!

It was the final signal the old woman had waited for. Jim and Ruth smiled at each other as the old woman let out a shout.

"Aho Mitakuye Oyasin!"

They all laughed as they walked up to the porch.

"It has been a very full day, my friend," said Jim to the old woman. "You must be exhausted. I do have a quick question, though, if you don't mind?"

She nodded.

"You probably told me before, but I've forgotten what that last phrase means. 'Aho' something?"

"*Aho* has several meanings. It can be a greeting, to show agreement or understanding, and is often used at the end of a prayer. *Mitakuye Oyasin* is a Lakota phrase that means, 'All Our Relations.' It is used to respectfully acknowledge that we are all related; humans and nonhumans."

"Thank you," he said. "Hopefully, I will remember, now. I will need to practice saying it, but at least now I know what it means. What a powerful blessing!"

Then the old woman turned to them. "These are my words."

Jim knew this meant she was done talking. He looked at Ruth, then turned back to the old woman.

"Let us help clean things up so you can be about your regular evening routine."

"Indeed!" Ruth agreed.

Within minutes the chairs were in their regular places, the small table was folded and placed behind the porch swing, and anything else that needed to go inside was in the kitchen.

After the dishes had been washed and put away, Ruth and Jim thanked the old woman for an amazing day, and wished her a good night's sleep. There was nothing more to say; it was time for them to return home, and to allow what had been ignited to take whatever action was needed to settle into their hearts. They knew it was not a time to engage in talk, in an attempt to understand the events of the day.

The old woman entered her bedroom and closed the door behind her as Ruth and Jim exited the cabin. Each of them dropped a gift into the twig basket on the porch, and Jim picked up his extra materials and supplies and secured them under his arm. Together they walked the path back to their vehicles in silence.

When they arrived at their vehicles, Ruth turned to Jim and smiled.

"I feel like we're old friends. Maybe I did know you in high school?" She cocked her head and smiled as she stroked her chin.

"Nah, that couldn't be," Jim said with a shake of his head. "I had a very prickly fence around my heart at that time. You wouldn't have gotten within three feet of me without getting repelled."

They both laughed.

"Wait until you meet my wife, Sarah," he said. "You're going to love her. She's an amazing woman, who patiently waited while I peeled away those prickly places in order to allow her close to my heart. Truth is," he continued with a lump in his throat, "she's the reason they got smoothed away. She, and the old woman. I hope you have such a man in your life, Ruth."

"I do," she smiled. "However, my thorn-covered walls have been solidly intact most of my life; that is, until today."

She turned to unlock her car, and looked back at Jim.

"You know, I'll bet he will notice that some of those thorns have thinned out a bit after today. At the very least, my 'no trespassing sign' has been taken down."

They both laughed, and she added, "He's really a pretty amazing guy; I think you'll like him."

"Oh, no doubt I will if he's chosen you," he said with a broad smile. Then he had a thought.

"How about we exchange cell phone numbers?"

"That's an excellent idea!" she replied. They both pulled out their phones and exchanged numbers.

"How about we meet up soon," Ruth suggested, "so we can meet each other's partner and coordinate a date to come back here?"

"That's a great idea!" he responded, pointing to his head. "Great minds!"

They said their goodbyes and got into their respective vehicles to begin their treks home. Jim left first, followed by Ruth.

As she turned onto the main road toward home, she considered the teachings and events of the day. Her heart felt a sense of both excitement and tenderness about the journey that lay ahead.

"I'm ready for the *Giving and Receiving* of my heart to be in balance!"

Joy filled her heart as she deeply and gently breathed in and out the love that had patiently waited for years for her to embrace. There was so much to learn, to experience, and to transform, so that her heart could expand and be allowed to truly breathe.

Carpe diem! She felt the crown upon her head and could sense a sword strapped on her side.

"Oh, this is important; I need to pull over!"

She pulled onto the next side road and stopped, and immediately felt the Goddess of Love stream golden light from above, down through her jeweled crown and into her whole being, as it filled her veins with courage. She was, indeed, ready to move through the beauty of her heart, knowing she would unleash the rich and abundant gift of unconditional love that resided both within and just outside the *Fences* of her heart.

"*I love you, Rick,*" seeped from her heart. She continued her journey home, filled with the lightness of love, and with hope, faith, and trust in her newly unleashed heart.

Turned the Page

Ruth was awakened by a sound just outside her bedroom. She laid very still and listened intently, to determine if the sound was from her dream, or if someone was actually in her apartment.

She glanced at the clock; it was 3:45 in the morning.

Oh, my goodness! Her heart beat faster and her breathing became heavy. *Stay calm; it's probably just another crazy dream.*

Then she heard someone faintly humming.

Or, are they chanting, or maybe singing? She took a couple of deep breaths as quietly as she could.

This is not a dream! Her heart was about to beat out of her chest as she attempted to calm her thoughts.

Okay, don't panic. No one is going to be singing if they mean harm.

She immediately thought of the old woman.

This is something she would know about … let's see, what to do?

Try as she may to quiet her fearful mind, her body tensed up in fight or flight reaction. Then her heart spoke.

"You have got to stay calm. We just made a commitment to begin a new journey, and you need to work with me; we must work as a team."

Suddenly the sound ceased, which caused her to engage in all sorts of terrifying thoughts.

You'd better call 9-1-1, just in case someone is in the next room.

Ruth sat up in bed immediately.

Oh, no, we are not doing that. The only way to find out if someone is here is to grab the bat beside the door and take a peek. We have enough nightlights on in the rest of the house to see whomever may be out there.

She took several deep breaths to calm herself, then slowly and gently pulled back the covers and swung her feet to the floor. She sat perfectly still and listened intently. Nothing. There was only a deafening stillness.

Her heartbeat had settled a bit, and a peaceful calm filled the air. Even her head no longer warned her of impending doom. Rather, it was as though her sacred knowing self stood outside of her and observed the moment.

"Thank you," she whispered. "Let's remember our strength. Now, what would *The King* do in this situation?" She felt the jeweled crown that sat upon her head and, after a couple of calm, centering breaths, she slowly stood up and called to her heart.

Guide and protect me as this journey begins.

Then she remembered the prayer she had learned as a child:

The Lord is my shepherd; I shall not want.

He maketh me to lie down in green pastures: he leadeth me beside the still waters.

He restoreth my soul: he leadeth me in the paths of righteousness for his name's sake.

A calm abiding surrounded her and she felt the warmth of love. She tiptoed to the bedroom door and grabbed the bat, then cracked the door open ever so slightly and peeked out. Everything looked normal. She stepped back a bit and closed her eyes as she silently continued to pray.

Yea, though I walk through the valley of the shadow of death, I will fear no evil: for thou art with me; thy rod and thy staff they comfort me.

She paused.

Okay, I don't remember the next part, and it doesn't matter. Let's go!

She opened the door very carefully, placed the bat against the wall and walked into the living room.

"Hello?" she whispered as she scanned the room. Absolutely nothing was out of place. She walked to the sliding doors that led to the patio, and slowly parted the blinds. She sighed with relief to see that everything was in order.

Surely goodness and mercy shall follow me all the days of my life: and I will dwell in the house of the Lord forever.

"Oh, good, we're fine. Whew! That was an interesting morning wakeup call!"

She pulled open the blinds, allowing the lights from the street to filter into her apartment.

"Well, I'm awake; might as well make a cup of coffee and enjoy the starry sky until the sun comes up."

"*That's another couple of hours,*" her head responded. "*You'll be tired if you get up now.*"

"Always looking out for me!" Ruth chuckled, with great affection for her ever serious, thinking mind. "Let me get that cup of coffee and then we'll chat."

She glanced at the sky and surveyed the stars.

"I rarely pay attention to you," she said tenderly. "Certainly not like I did when I was young. I'm going to do something about that, though; it's certainly no accident that I've been awakened so early."

Ruth gasped as a whitish, red streak pierced the sky, and her eyes filled with tears of joy.

"Oh, I haven't seen a shooting star in years! Or, maybe it's a meteor? Whichever it is, it is such a gift! I believe this is the southeast sky," she mused, and then recalled that the morning sunlight always appeared to the left of the building across from her patio.

"Yep, that's it, the East is to the left of my patio. But, enough; I need to make that coffee and bring it out here to enjoy while I have some contemplation time."

Ruth's heart felt light as she headed to the kitchen.

"Oh, such an amazing time! I am so very ready to turn the next page in the book of my life."

She dropped a pod into the coffeemaker, grabbed a cup and placed it below the dispenser, and hit the brew button. She yawned as she stretched her arms up and out, bent over and touched the floor, then twisted her body to the left and right.

"Oh, my!" she exclaimed with a smile, as her back popped and cracked. "I can't be so old that my body is making such noises!"

It has nothing to do with age; it's lack of exercise. It's time to get this body into a routine. We used to do yoga on a regular basis. What happened to that?

She shook her head, "Be kind my over conscientious mind; it doesn't matter! It's just time to get that back into our daily routine."

She sniffed the air.

"Mmm, the coffee smells delicious! This will help get my brain focused on a new day, rather than dwelling on the crazy thoughts of what happened a bit ago! What a morning!"

Ruth took her coffee to the patio and sat down in her favorite lounge chair. The streetlights hummed, cars began to dot the streets, and the stop-and-go of trash trucks added to the early morning noises. Blackbirds and pigeons scurried about the landscape of buildings, bringing a bit of nature to the city, and the fullness of strategically placed trees bordered the streets with rich color.

"This is a far cry from the peacefulness of the old woman's cabin," she mused. "I can only imagine what it must be like to wake up in her place. It must be amazing to observe the critters of the Forest awaken in their natural habitat with only the backdrop of the wide-open skies." Her heart expanded and warmth filled her whole being as she sipped her coffee.

"Oh, and the tall trees. What does she call them?" She scratched her head, "Oh, yes, the Standing Ones! What a perfect name for them, they are always reaching for the heavens! And, what grand teachers they are, reminding us to stay deeply rooted in order to bend and sway with the changes life brings."

Her curious mind prompted her to recall the sound that had awakened her at 3:45. *I wonder what that was? It sounded like someone singing.*

"It really doesn't matter. It will become clear if it's some sort of message, or signal, or whatever else may be introduced through the work Jim and I will be doing with the old woman."

Then, just when she began to feel calm and comfortable, she heard a whisper.

"Thou preparest a table before me in the presence of mine enemies: thou anointest my head with oil; my cup runneth over."

Her heartbeat quickened and tears began to fill her eyes as she recognized her mother's voice. She sat very still and allowed the tears to flow as the voice continued.

"You remembered more of the prayer than I thought you would; you were so very young when we began to recite that prayer together each night before bed."

Silence hung in the air as a cloud of mist swept across her patio, and the sky began to lighten with the ascending sun. Then, like the mist off a body of water, a dense fog rolled in, obliterating everything beyond Ruth's patio.

Memories of her childhood and the fondness she had once felt for her mother flooded her heart. Those were the times before her mother began to lose herself in alcohol in order to bury the sorrow within her heart.

She felt her mother's breath on her cheek as she whispered into Ruth's ear. *"I'm sorry; please forgive me."*

That did it. Ruth buried her face in her hands and wept uncontrollably. Deep groans came from the very depths of her soul as she felt the presence of Jesus standing with her, as he had done her whole life. For Ruth, he was the Divine connection between Heaven and Earth.

She had not thought about those early teachings in years. Somehow, the painful memories of her youth had overshadowed the sweetness of her childhood.

And then she felt the presence of a small child; it was her little brother.

Sorrow overcame her like giant waves of the ocean during a storm. They swelled in size until they peaked with whitecaps of foam, and then descended into the turbulent waters to become one with the ocean. The next wave then appeared as the storm of tears continued to tear down the walls around her hardened heart. Ruth sobbed for what felt like an eternity, as the waves of her emotions became a tsunami that swept through her entire being.

She felt as though she would never emerge from the thralls of sorrow and bitterness; yet, she knew that this was a long overdue release of that which no longer served her. She had carried those burdens long enough! If she was going to turn the page in the book of her life, those bitter memories needed to be released so that she could once again remember the sweetness of her childhood. It was time for her to lighten her load and to let go of the past, in order to make room for what would unfold in the next chapter of her life.

The dense fog surrounded and caressed her trembling body. Ruth allowed the release of pent up emotions that had been waiting for such a time as *This Moment. And, yet, those emotions deserved to be honored for the gifts they had given her. She knew she would not be the strong person she was now had she not had the experience of the tragedy that had brought about loss and pain. This was indeed a sacred moment.

The fog became a thin veil as it lifted upward toward the heavens. Ruth wiped her tears and her breathing slowed. She felt her mother's presence beside her, as well as the presence on her mother's lap of the toddler they had lost so many years ago. Her mother seemed to want to reassure Ruth that she had healed her own heart. And, that she and Ruth's brother were now together, and that both of them would always be with her.

With focused intention, she inhaled the Light of Love that emanated from her mother and brother, and exhaled her love to them in return. A cycle of loving energy flowed with grace and ease as forgiveness healed old wounds.

Orange rays of sunlight filtered through the mist as Grandfather began his ascent in the eastern sky, bringing light to the darkened sky of the South in front of her patio. She was reminded that the teachings of the South were about the gifts of innocence and of the purity of Spirit we bring with us. Faith, trust, resiliency, and unconditional love are all qualities necessary to open the door to forgiveness. They offered Ruth and her mother the opportunity to pierce the veil of bitterness and hurt, and to restore the ebb and flow of love between them. At that very moment, Ruth and the spirit of her mother were cradled in the arms of the Divine.

Ruth felt the cool mist of the fog on her face. She slowly opened her eyes and watched the mist lift upward. The circle of love between her and her mother was no longer broken; the chain of harmony and deep connection had been restored.

"I forgive you, Mama, and I love you forever." While Ruth could not see her mother, she felt her smile.

Then a picture of her little brother's face flashed before her eyes. It was the photo that had been published in the local newspaper following the tragic accident that had taken his life. Tears once again burned her eyes when she saw his sweet face, and she realized she had never fully grieved his loss. She had been too young to understand exactly what had happened. All she knew was that he was no longer around, and that life had dramatically changed for her family.

The floodgates opened once again as she recalled his sweet spirit. He had been a quiet little boy of three when he passed from this world, and she yearned to hold him. In that moment she understood how her mother must have felt when she lost that precious, innocent soul that had been a part of her. Ruth had never borne a child, and she could only imagine the depth of sorrow a mother would feel after such a loss.

The sun was now three-quarters visible on the horizon, and the sounds of the city reminded her that a new day had begun. She batted away her tears and inhaled a few deep, cleansing breaths through her nose. She held each breath for a few seconds, then slowly exhaled through her mouth. Her chest relaxed more with each breath, clearing the way to her heart.

She felt her feet on the floor and pulled energy from the Earth upward through her body, which brought her back to the present. She then felt the spirits of her mother and little brother begin their ascent back to the heavens.

Like the calm after a storm, the air felt fresh and clean with the crispness of something new. A siren sounded in the distance, and when a church bell began to toll, Ruth counted the chimes: one … two … three … four … five … six …

"Oh, my goodness, it's 6 o'clock!" She stood up and picked up her coffee cup, and glanced toward the southeast.

"Okay, we've crossed the threshold of a new day. We have turned the page, and a new chapter lies before us. Let's see what we will learn about faith and trust now that forgiveness has been granted between us." A long yawn, followed by another, reminded her that she'd been up since 3:45 in the morning.

"Boy, am I grateful that I don't have to work today!"

She stretched and yawned again, and noticed the lights flick on in the donut shop directly across the street from her. She looked more closely and observed that patrons already stood in line for their morning delicacies.

"Nothing like the comfort of something special in our bellies when we've accomplished a task. Reckon I'll think about a gift I could give myself for this morning's work."

"Really?" Her head chimed in. *"You feel you need a reward?"*

"You're good!" she chuckled. "Of course you would ask me a question like that, you…" She searched for a kind word. "You beautiful, practical mind. You're right: the freedom I feel right now is all the reward I need," she said as she tossed back her head and inhaled deeply.

"Thank you, thank you, thank you," she sighed, and walked through the patio doors toward the kitchen. As she passed through the living room, she had a sudden thought.

"I need to call Jim this morning! He would be very interested in this turn of events. No, wait … maybe it would be best to first call and ask to meet with both him and his wife. Yes, I need to meet his wife before meeting with him alone. Heaven knows, we need to get things off on the right foot when it comes to a strange woman calling her husband." That felt right in her gut. She felt butterflies in her tummy, which she had come to learn was a message of affirmation from her Sacred Self.

She glanced down at the remaining half cup of coffee.

My brain is foggy; I need another cup of coffee before making any decisions. She walked into the kitchen and made herself a fresh cup. Then she took her coffee back to the porch and returned to her lounge chair.

After a few sips she remembered, "I need to find my notes from my first visit with the old woman, when she told me the story of *The King and how he managed his kingdom. That was such an impactful story. No, it was more than a story;" she reflected, "It was a teaching about how to live life in relationship with all things."

"I think I know where I put those notes." Then she chuckled. "Who am I kidding? I know exactly where there are! It pays to be organized!" Her instinct was to get up immediately and find them.

"No, there's no hurry. Stay here and finish at least this cup of coffee, and watch the birds play, work, and do whatever they do to be happy and present to life."

Of course, her practical mind began to think about where the notes were.

"Please," she implored, "let's enjoy the moment; we'll get 'em later. Such a funny human being! It's so easy to get into habits and go mindlessly about life without noticing the beautiful beings." She glanced upward, "That's changing right now!"

At that precise moment she felt someone or something staring at her. She instinctively looked down at the street below and spotted the source.

"Hey, there, little buddy," she said to the white and gray French bulldog that stared up at her. His ears stood straight up as both he and his owner sat on a bench in front of the drugstore. She waved at the little critter and smiled.

"I see you, little fella."

With a surprised look on his face, his ears perked up even more, and his tail wagged as if to say, "Hello! You see me!"

An "open" sign was placed in the drugstore window, and the dog's owner promptly stood up, tied the dog's leash around the back of the bench, and entered the store. The puppy was very attentive to the owner's words, then looked back up at Ruth.

Her smile widened. "What an obedient puppy!"

Wonder why I've never had a puppy?

"Probably because I've always preferred cats," she mused aloud. "I love all critters; however, cats seem to be more independent and less needy than dogs. At least, that's been my experience."

She continued to wave at the puppy, and giggled when he wagged his tail each time.

"Who says animals don't communicate?" she pondered, as flashes of a small cabin outside of town ran across the movie screen of her heart.

"I'd love to have both a dog and a cat, like the old woman does. Her critters live outside; in my opinion, that would be the perfect scenario." A rush of excitement moved through her heart at the very thought of such an idea.

"That would be a fabulous beginning to my next chapter!" Her heart felt happy and her tummy flipped at the very thought of it. She grinned from ear to ear as she brought her attention back to the puppy across the street.

"He's gone! For heaven's sake, I missed that whole goodbye. Well, back to reality. I can dream all I want, but if changes are going to happen, I need to take some sort of action." She picked up her cup, headed to the kitchen, and glanced at the clock.

"Goodness, it's nearly 7:30! I need to get something in my belly and get ready for the day. No," she paused, "first I need those notes."

She placed the cup in the sink and went directly to her second bedroom, which had been turned into an office. The pale apricot walls were warm and inviting, and she smiled at the brass daybed, piled with colorful satin pillows on a turquoise duvet. A large window above the bed overlooked the city park, and from her second-floor apartment she had a full view of the park's rich display of nature. Various hues of green leaves of many sizes and shapes adorned brown branches, along with a bounty of birds that made their homes among the richly colored foliage. From the vantage point of the doorway, it looked like she lived in a tree house.

Ruth carefully opened the folding doors of the closet, revealing an antique wooden file cabinet. She pulled a purple file folder from the bottom drawer and peeked inside.

"Yep, there it is."

She lifted a thick leather journal from the folder, and returned the folder to the file drawer. The journal was very well worn from use. On the cover was a very large tree with colorful, red heart-shaped leaves that now appeared as old as the branches from which they hung. She smiled as she gently touched the front cover.

Oh, such memories you carry within your pages.

"Interesting, the fondness and affection I feel for you," she addressed the treasure in her hands. "You held my heart for many years."

She went to her desk across the room from the closet, a desk that looked like she had probably had it when she was a young girl, and was now an antique. It had three drawers on each side of the center space that was for a matching wooden chair. Above the desk hung a large painting of a modern rendition of a castle, and a sign below it read, "The Merlin's Home." Deep blues filled the sky and mist filled the air surrounding the castle. The frame was jet black, which further emphasized the magnificence of the painting, and the apricot colored wall on which it hung brought even more focus to this most unusual and intriguing picture.

Ruth grabbed a pen and pad of paper from the bottom drawer on the right, and exited the room.

"Enough sentiment," she mumbled. "Let's find the entries about *The King* and get busy."

She returned to the kitchen, placed a piece of bread in the toaster, and retrieved a saucer, a knife and some honey. She yawned again and glanced at the clock.

"It's still only 9 o'clock; I'll see what I can get done and take a nap afterwards."

She seemed to be speaking to her body, which now felt like half the day had been spent in heavy contemplation.

"I know this has been a very important and emotional morning. I promise to get some shut-eye by eleven," she informed her body. "In the meantime, I believe I'm going to have one more cup of coffee; I didn't even get a quarter of my first cup and half of the second consumed."

She dropped a pod into the coffee maker and hit the brew button. As she retrieved a clean cup from the cabinet, the toast popped up, and her stomach growled.

"I gotcha; you've been very patient." She quickly spread the toast with honey and put it on a saucer. She took her toast and coffee to the patio and placed them on the table next to her lounge chair.

She went back inside to retrieve the journal, pen, and paper, and returned to the patio. As she settled comfortably into her chair, she felt even warmer air coming in from the South.

"It's going to be hot today; it's really good that we're doing this so early. And," she chuckled, "why do I always say 'we' or 'us,' when it is only me?" She grinned as she felt a flutter in her belly, and acknowledged her intuitive gifts.

"I know. You've been talking to me my whole life; that's why I use those words."

Ruth took a big bite of toast and washed it down with a sip of coffee. She smiled with a peace and contentment in her heart that she had not known in many years.

The toast that satisfied her hungry tummy was quickly consumed. She dusted the crumbs from her hands, sipped a bit more coffee, then set the cup on the plate and picked up the journal.

I remember going to meet the old woman in hopes of better understanding the nudge I felt in my belly.

She placed the journal in her lap and untied the red cord that held it closed, then closed her eyes long enough to fumble with the pages until she felt something. She opened the journal and smiled broadly. Stuck between the pages was the tatted chain from her very first meeting with the old woman.

"What are you doing here?" she asked in disbelief. "I distinctly remember hanging you on the mirror in my bathroom!"

Why does anything surprise me when it comes to this aspect of my life?

"That's a very good question," she whispered. "You are absolutely correct!"

The phone rang, bringing her back to the moment. She pulled her phone out of her robe pocket, and saw Jim's name.

Why am I not surprised?

"Well, good morning, Jim, how are you?"

"And, a good morning to you, Ruth. I'm very good; just checking in to see how things are moving along in your life." He cleared his throat. "Actually, I was wondering if you and your fella would like to get together with Sarah and me."

"You know, Jim, that's an excellent idea! What did you have in mind?"

"Sarah and I were thinking of having you over for a cookout. It's early August, and summer will be over before you can shake a stick. We might as well take advantage of the short time we have left."

"That sounds like a great idea, Jim. I'll check with Rick, but I'm certain he'd love to meet you and your wife. Actually, I was thinking about giving you a call to suggest that we get together to meet each other's partner. Did you have a particular day and time in mind?"

"Great minds!" he chuckled. "It must be in the tea leaves. How about this Saturday around 5 or 6 o'clock?"

"Sounds perfect! Rick and I usually get together over the weekend, so I'll check with him and get back with you."

"Terrific. And, I do text, so if texting works best for you just get back with me that way."

"Oh, yes, texting seems to be the most useful form of communication for me. I can text while things are fresh on my mind." She giggled. "I'm not that old, but my brain is so full of thoughts and ideas, it's easy for things to slip through the cracks. Know what I mean?"

"Oh, I certainly do!"

"Now, what can we bring?"

"Before I answer that, are you and Rick vegetarians, or do you eat poultry, meat and fish?"

"Oh, we eat everything!" she responded. "And, I insist on bringing something. How about I make my mother's famous potato salad or deviled eggs ... or, both?"

"Actually, Sarah makes a mean potato salad, but it might be nice to try someone else's recipe. Sure, bring the potato salad. Sarah will want to make the deviled eggs and baked beans; she'll feel it's her duty to make the bulk of the food. Know what I mean?"

"That I do!" laughed Ruth. "I'll also bring my favorite summer dessert; it's cool and refreshing. Sound good?"

"If you haven't already noticed, I love good food. You witnessed that the day we met at the old woman's cabin. You know, the day I helped her build the fence around her garden."

"I do remember that! Okay, I'll text to confirm the time after I speak to Rick."

"Fabulous!" he exclaimed. "Do you have a couple of minutes? I also wanted to see how you are doing, and what, if anything, has happened these past several weeks." He knew the answer to his question, but he asked, anyway.

"Huh," smiled Ruth. "That's a timely question and, actually, Jim, part of the reason I wanted to reach out to you was to share a few things that happened just this morning." She chuckled. "However, it would take more time than I have right now to elaborate. Besides, I would prefer to talk about it face-to-face."

Jim laughed. "I had a feeling things were stirring up for you. And, you are correct; face-to-face meetings are definitely better than phone chats. Truth is, that's why Sarah and I decided we should all meet in person. Our partners need to get to know the person with whom we will be spending time. As I've said, Sarah is my very best friend; we trust each other, and that's what makes our relationship work. And, I treasure that relationship over everything in my life. I couldn't have become who I am today without her love and support."

Tears burned in Ruth's eyes as he spoke.

Oh, to have that sort of relationship! That's exactly what I've held out for. What a grand opportunity to witness that in real life!

"What's up, Ruth?" asked Jim, after a few moments of silence.

"Oh, nothing. Just listening to your words about your relationship." She took a deep breath and quickly changed the subject.

"I'd better let you go. I'm actually still in my pajamas and robe."

"Sounds like you had a very early wakeup call," he chuckled. He knew she was shifting gears, and that was perfectly fine with him.

It takes time to develop trust.

"I'll let you go and get ready for your day. Thank you for taking my call and accepting our invitation. If Rick can't make it, you plan on coming, anyway. Sarah's looking forward to meeting you."

Ruth gathered her wits about her; she knew her emotions had been intensified by the events of the morning, not to mention her lack of sleep.

"And, I'm looking forward to meeting her, and for you two to meet Rick; you'll like him. You have a great day, and I'll text you by the end of today about Saturday evening."

"That sounds perfect, Ruth. Get some rest and take care of yourself. If you ever need to chat, do not hesitate to call or text. Remember, we're in this together!" He knew she would understand that he knew first-hand what she was experiencing.

"Thank you, Jim. Tell Sarah I'm eager to meet her."

The call left Ruth with a heavy heart.

"I'm not sad; this is a wonderful turn of the page for me. I know it is my responsibility to be clear, intentional, and committed to creating the life I truly desire. The universe waits to assist me."

"I just need to get some sleep," she yawned, as she put the phone back in her robe pocket. She left the tatted chain in the page where she found it, then closed the journal and tied the cord. Then she picked up her plate and headed indoors.

Just before closing the patio door, she turned and gazed at the blue skies that were dotted with white, puffy clouds.

I wonder who's watching all the stuff that is going on at this time on Earth? I wonder ... well, I wonder all sorts of things. However, I need to get some sleep, in order to comprehend what I wonder!

She fell into bed with a smile on her face, pulled up the covers, and off she went to dreamland.

Ruth's cell phone rang several times as she drowsily opened her eyes.

"Who's calling so early?" she wondered.

"Oh, my goodness, I feel like I've been run over by a Mack truck! What did I do yesterday that my body feels so tired?" She glanced at the clock.

"One o'clock!" She bolted up in bed. "Did I really sleep that long?" She stretched her arms with a big yawn and looked out the bedroom window, then grabbed her cell phone and noticed four missed calls and one text from Rick. She knew he must be concerned, as she always returned calls and texts promptly.

"Oh, my gosh, I must have been dead to the world!" Then she remembered her early morning wake-up call. She yawned a couple more times and reached for her robe, only to discover that she still had it on.

"My goodness, I *was* tired!" She let her feet hit the floor as they searched for her slippers.

She went into the bathroom, brushed her teeth and splashed water on her face. Then she slowly moved to the kitchen and brewed a cup of chamomile tea, which she took to the patio and returned Rick's calls.

He answered immediately. "Hey, it's good to hear from you! Are you okay?"

She smiled. He was such a good human being.

"Yes, and I apologize for not responding earlier. It's been quite a morning."

"No need to apologize. As long as you're okay, that's all that matters."

"What are you doing today?" she asked as she sipped her tea.

"Oh, you know me, just working! Do you need anything?"

"Well, no, I don't need anything. I just wanted to see you if you have some time." *He's such a caring man, and always willing to help.*

Her question was met with silence. She knew what she had asked was out of the norm.

He's probably fainted! She smiled as she waited for him to recuperate.

"Huh, sure, I have some time," he stammered after a few moments. "I always have time for you!"

She held back her laughter. They had dated for nearly five years and, while they were exclusive, she had not fully opened her heart to him. The wall of protection around it had undoubtedly scarred Rick from trying to scale it. Yet, he had continued to respect where she was as he patiently waited.

Okay, Ruth, stop this! I think the page has turned, and I'm going to trust what my heart calls forth, regardless of how scared I may feel.

"What time are you available today? I'm free all day." She giggled. "That is, what's left of it!"

Rick laughed. "It is unusual for you to sleep so late. I guess that's what you've been doing, unless you have a project you've been working on. I can be available whenever you need. Technically, I'm off the clock today."

He smiled broadly. How he loved that woman! However, he wasn't about to pressure her in any way.

"Actually," he said, "I do have some projects I'm working on here at the house, what about you? Are you working on any projects?"

What a silly thing to ask! He knew her well enough to know that she didn't just sit around and relax unless she was sick.

"No. Well, yes, I do have a project, and that's part of what I need to chat with you about." She glanced at the clock again. "How's 4 o'clock? Or, I can make dinner around six? Whatever works best for you."

Rick could barely stay focused on the conversation; he wondered what was going on with Ruth.

It's not like her to sleep in, and she rarely wants to see me just to talk.

"Let's split the difference," he responded. "How about 5 o'clock? I'll bring dinner, though. You just enjoy your day off."

"I do love that man," Ruth's heart resounded.

"I know," responded her head. *"Just stay focused; we have things to get clear about before the conversation this evening."*

Of course, she communicated through her thoughts.

"Five is good, and thanks, Rick, I'll let you take care of that. I have a bottle of Malbec; select whatever goes well with that."

"Oh, and I'll be out of my PJ's by then; that is, unless you want me to stay in them," she teased.

Rick's heart quickened. As unpredictable as she was, he knew she was "the one," and he would wait for her, however long it took.

"There you go again, getting frisky!" he laughed. "Hey, you know me; it's fine with me if you don't wear anything at all! Okay, I need to let you go, or I'll be over within thirty minutes!" He felt as though his heart would pound out of his chest as he felt a surge of passion.

"You'd better not offer that again or I'll take you up on it!" she playfully responded.

Touché. She had him. That was precisely why he loved her so much. Being with Ruth was like living a mystery; he never knew what she would say or do next. Just when he thought he'd figured her out, she'd do something completely out of the norm. While it was often quite frustrating, it was also unpredictable, and that wasn't always bad. It certainly made life darned interesting.

"You little vixen," he teased. "I'm heading out the door."

"You are not," she giggled. "I'll see you at five," and she hung up.

There was no doubt about it; her heart was the new chapter that was being rewritten. And, both she and Rick were ready for whatever showed up!

Rick went about the rest of his day in a curious daze, wondering what she wanted to talk about.

Maybe she's finally come to her senses and decided she can trust me with that beautiful heart of hers. Whatever it was, he knew he'd meet her somewhere in the middle. And if he had to, he'd go the extra mile … or two.

"Actually, I'll do whatever it takes," he mumbled. "There aren't many ladies like my Ruthie."

He picked up his toolbox and level and headed to the spare room to hang shelving. He eyed the wall carefully, then pulled out his metal tape measure and held the small level over it. Then he carefully marked several lines on the wall, and stepped back to check them.

"Yep, those look pretty even." He drilled and affixed one shelf securely to the wall, and stood back to examine it.

"It looks level, but I'll double check," he said as he held the level on the flat shelf.

"Perfect! Now I can put the others in place and we'll have this project done."

As he finished the final shelf his mind began to wander again.

"Not many women can measure up to Ruthie. Oh, she's not perfect, but neither am I. It's a good thing people don't put levels on humans; many of us are off kilter!" He gathered his tools and wondered what life would be like if he and Ruthie were married.

"There would never be a dull moment!" he noted with a smile, as he moved on to the next unfinished project.

Hmmm, that's what Ruthie and I are: an unfinished project. But, I'll definitely see this one to completion!

Wonder what she's up to now?

Ruth made her bed, showered, and pondered what to wear.

"I feel like this is going to be a special evening, and I want to look exceptionally nice." She stood in front of her closet and remembered something she had purchased a month or so ago, but had never worn.

"That's it, I'm going for it!"

She quickly dressed, made-up her face and did her hair, tidied up a few things, and glanced in the mirror.

Well, I may be a bit overdone for staying home; however, it seems the perfect look for this evening.

She made her way back to the patio.

Geez, I've been a lazy one today. It's good, though.

She glanced down at her outfit again, and straightened her hair a bit.

I need to be out of character more often, in all areas of my life!

She returned to her lounge chair, picked up her journal, and sat down. The sun hung in the western sky and she felt a breeze sweep across her patio.

Sure am glad that intense heat is blocked by my neighbor's apartment. I'm not going to complain, though; it'll be autumn soon enough.

"It's 4:22," she noticed on her phone. Then she looked at her journal.

"I need to get the table set for dinner," she said, "so we're going to have to wait to recapture everything. If I could just go directly to what I want to read, we'd be done. You know me, though, something else can always get my attention!"

Then her head spoke.

"What are you going to tell Rick this evening?"

"I have no idea and, you know, I just need you to remember whatever you witness tonight. This evening is about … well, it's about letting the 'voice' of my heart speak."

Her heart immediately began to thump harder, and her head jumped in again.

"We got this, and I'll be still. Just know I've always got your back. I'm the Queen of options, and there's nothing we might confront that doesn't have a ton of potential alternatives."

"Well, thank you!" responded her heart. *"I can certainly use your forthright courage. We're on foreign territory, here; words have been held back by you as a way to keep me from getting hurt."*

"This is true," admitted her head. *"I'm guilty as charged!"*

Ruth laughed. It was like witnessing a couple who were learning how to understand each other, and how to work together in a spirit of loving cooperation and respect.

"Oh, make no mistake about how grateful I am for you. No doubt even more teachings would have been put in front of me if you hadn't interceded. I have learned what I have because you helped me to step back from emotions and pain, gather my wits, and look at a situation from a thoughtful, rather than judgmental, perspective."

She glanced at her phone again. "Yikes, 4:45!"

She jumped up, set her journal back on the table, and headed indoors to prepare things for Rick's arrival.

Rick knocked on the door at 5 o'clock sharp, slowly opened it, and stuck his head inside.

"Anyone home?"

"I'm in the kitchen!" Ruth shouted.

Rick walked into the kitchen with a sack of take-out for dinner, and a bouquet of daisies.

There stood Ruth, in a bright blue, v-neck jumpsuit that revealed a subtle hint of cleavage. Diamond studded gold earrings dangled from her ears, drawing attention to her beautiful pale skin that was made up to perfection. A pale, pink color adorned her lips, and her hair was tied up on her head and clipped with a jeweled hair comb.

Rick's jaw dropped. "Wow! You look amazing!"

She blushed. This was not her standard attire, and she was not used to drawing attention to herself. She had always been most comfortable in baggie, neutral-colored clothing.

He looked her up and down, and then noticed her bare feet.

Now, that's my Ruthie!

He quickly set down the dinner and daisies, and grabbed her with strong, loving arms. She didn't even have time to say anything before he pressed his lips passionately on hers. Ruth melted like butter on a hot biscuit, and fell into his embrace as she returned his passionate kiss.

They held each other and absorbed the love that was so evident between them. Rick had never known her to be so receptive in the five years they had known each other, and she felt a deep need to be close to him. The walls around her heart were now crumbling around her bare feet.

"Oh, Ruthie," Rick finally said, "I am so grateful for whatever happened this morning. I love you so very much."

Ruth's head was spinning. She felt like she was observing this loving exchange from outside her body, between two people who respected and cherished each other so very deeply. She had had glimpses of this with him before, although she had always managed to hit the pause button and get her wits about her. She had always known how to control her passion, and this was a different scenario than she had ever experienced.

She suddenly felt her feet beneath her, and she stepped back to collect herself.

"Oh, my goodness, Rick," she smiled. "What happened?"

He didn't want to let her go, but he knew her well enough to know that he needed to honor what she needed in that moment. He grinned and took a deep breath.

"I don't know, but I like it!"

"Well, I'm starved, and…"

Rick gave her a teasing smile, but knew this was Ruth's call.

"I know that look," she giggled as she wrapped her arms around his neck. "We have all night, you know. What do you say, let's get some food in our bellies, I'll put those gorgeous daisies in a vase, and we'll go from there."

Rick kissed her passionately again.

"That's a wonderful idea," he said as he released her. "I'd really prefer there was nothing between us but flesh, anyway."

They laughed heartily, hugged, and Ruth put the daisies in a lovely green vase.

"I love that vase," Rick commented. "There's something very compelling about that color."

"It belonged to my great-grandmother. Mama always said there was something very special about it. My heart was happy when my dad gave it to me when I left home."

"Well, it's beautiful. Not as beautiful as you, of course!" He leaned over and gave Ruth a kiss on the cheek, then proceeded to fill their wine glasses.

They filled their plates with a variety of Chinese food, and turned to leave the kitchen.

"Patio or dining room table?" she asked.

"Let's sit at the table," he suggested. "You look dressed for an evening out … of course, without shoes." They giggled.

The evening was a playful and light beginning to a new chapter in both their lives. Conversation was light and informative as they caught up on the events of the three days they had not seen each other. Rick reached over for her hand a couple of times and gently rubbed his fingers on her soft skin.

"I have missed you. It's only been three days, but I've missed you."

"I understand, Rick," she smiled. "I see you differently, as well. Actually, I see my life more clearly than I think I ever have, and that's why I wanted to talk to you tonight."

She proceeded to tell him a bit about the old woman she had met a couple of years before he entered her life. No details, simply a few highlights. Then she told him she had recently felt a nudge to revisit this woman. She told him about meeting Jim, and how he had developed a close relationship with the old woman.

Rick was attentive to her every word. He could hardly believe how different she was, not only in her appearance, but more importantly in her embrace, in the look on her face, and in the manner in which she had held him. Her whole demeanor was different, and even the feel of her home had changed. Everything felt authentic and something he wanted to know more about, not for himself, but to support this woman he so deeply loved. Anything that could help her feel affirmed was something he was willing to learn more about; that is, when she felt led to share it with him.

Ruth concluded the conversation by telling him about the work she and Jim would be doing with the old woman.

"I have no idea what any of that means, Rick. Yet, I know it is important, not only for myself and for Jim, but for those we love and know, who, like us, are seeking something else — something with meaning, and something that can set us free."

She laughed. "Again, I don't know what it means. I just know that within my soul there's been a nudge, and I'm ready to get about the work necessary to satisfy that nudge."

Rick smiled and reached for her hand.

"Ruth, I'm all in. Whatever you need, I want to support you. And, I'm not being grandiose; I have a hunch there's something very important for me to learn as well."

She couldn't respond immediately, and tried to hold back her tears, but to no avail. She took a few deep breaths.

Rick wanted to reach for her hand, but something in his heart told him to wait.

"Jim and his wife, Sarah, have invited us over for a cookout Saturday evening," she finally continued. "He and I both feel it is important that our significant others get to know the person with whom we will be spending time."

Significant other. Rick liked that. While he knew how Ruth felt about him, it touched his heart to hear her refer to him as her "significant other."

"You got it; I'm in. What time?"

Ruth felt overwhelmed. It had been such a full day, and she wore her emotions on her sleeve. A long pause ensued.

"Come on, Ruth," her head spoke up. *"We only have a few more minutes to keep our wits about us, and then we'll get some sleep."*

Then she asked her heart what she needed. Within a split second she released her tears, got up and stood by Rick's chair, and said nothing.

He read her body language and scooted the chair back to make room for her. She allowed the tears to flow as she sat down in his lap.

"Oh, Rick," she hugged his neck. "Thank you for not asking any more questions. I'm feeling a bit overwhelmed."

He held her in his arms as she wept, as one might hold a child who needed comfort and assurance. After a few moments, Ruth sniffled and wiped her eyes with her napkin.

"I'm sorry; I seem to have crashed our amazing evening."

Tears filled Rick's eyes as he pulled her closer.

"This is a perfect evening, my darling."

His heart filled with a warmth he had never experienced. He had a surge of confident knowing, about which he neither could, nor would speak at that time. This was about Ruth, and the unwinding of her heart.

He smoothed her hair with his hand as he continued to hold her close.

There is nothing I want more in my life than this very moment.

Ruth composed herself within a few moments and gave Rick a kiss on the cheek.

"Jim and Sarah want us there around five or six."

"You got it!" He looked at her with a tenderness neither of them had ever experienced. "Ruth, do you need me to give you some time alone tonight?"

She laughed. Her nose was red from tears, and mascara smeared her face.

"Do I look that bad?" she giggled.

"Gracious, no! I have never seen you more beautiful!"

"I want you with me tonight, Rick," she said as she buried her head on his chest.

They took a few deep breaths, cleaned up the kitchen, and held hands on their way to the bedroom. Ruth washed her mascara-stained face, brushed her teeth, slipped out of her clothes, and wrapped a robe around herself. When she returned, Rick smiled, kissed her, and took his turn in the bathroom to clean up. Then Ruth texted Jim to let him know they would both be there Saturday evening around five.

When Rick came out of the bathroom he slipped into bed beside her. To his surprise, she was completely naked.

"I do pay attention to what you say, and you said you'd be okay if I had nothing on," she whispered.

He held her close and kissed her tenderly.

She smiled. "I have *Turned the page.*"

He held her even more closely; somehow he knew what she meant.

"And, I am eager to be a part of the next chapter!" he exclaimed.

Follow the Snake

Summer quickly moved along, and more than a month had passed since Jim or Ruth had visited the old woman, who by now, was no doubt busy harvesting and canning her vegetables. The yield had surely been abundant this year with the protection her sturdy new fence had provided.

The dog days of summer would soon come to an end, and families scurried about the city in an attempt to fit in their remaining summer activities. The streets were filled with cars, trucks, motorcycles and city buses, as commuters explored festivals, fairs, and outdoor dining venues during the warm days of early August.

"This will probably be my one and only batch of potato salad this summer," Ruth mumbled through a mouthful of the decadent treat. "Mmm, there's nothing like my mother's recipe to complete the menu for a summer cookout. I don't even care how many calories are in this dish; summer just isn't complete until Mother's potato salad is served," she said as she savored the last tasty morsel. "Yes, I do believe it is perfect!"

She sprinkled paprika across the top and carefully placed the lid snuggly on the large, turquoise Tupperware bowl.

"Now to get this chilled for tonight's cookout." She opened the refrigerator and looked in. "Geez, how did my refrigerator get so crowded? I'm the only one who lives here!" She finally managed to make room for the potato salad, and then she noticed the coconut cream dessert she had made the night before. Just looking at two of her favorite summer dishes made her stomach growl.

"Okay, I hear you," she said to her tummy. "Let's get something in you besides samples of Mom's potato salad." She looked around her very full fridge for something quick and nourishing to eat.

"Aha! There's some yogurt and blueberries from yesterday; that ought to hold you over until dinner," she assured her hungry belly as she took out the bowl of leftovers.

She grabbed a spoon from the utensil drawer and placed it beside the yogurt. Then she sprinkled a bit of granola over the yogurt, and filled a glass with water.

"I think we're ready!" She went to the patio with food and water in hand, and sat on the lounge chair.

"Ahhh, it feels good to put up my feet; I feel like I've been cooking for hours." She watched the traffic below while she ate her yogurt.-

Goodness, everyone's going somewhere. It's already a busy Saturday, and it's only noon.

Ruth finished her yogurt, and felt great satisfaction that she had not only balanced her diet with the yogurt and fruit, but she had also completed her contributions to the evening cookout before noon. Her mind then began to wonder and wander.

I wonder what Sarah's like, and if their children will be there? Her heart felt tenderness at the thought of children.

I don't know why I haven't chosen to have children yet. Heck, I'll be thirty-four in a couple of months; I'd better disassemble that protective fence around my heart if I do want to have any.

Her eyes fixed on a Father walking behind a stroller across the street in front of the drugstore. He appeared to be around Rick's age.

Of course, Fathers can have children when they are older. It's the Mamas who need to be under the age of forty.

"At least, that's how it used to be. Nowadays it doesn't much matter." She took a deep breath and smiled. "So, I'm good; I have at least six years to decide."

Who am I kidding? Rick has asked me many times if I wanted children, and I've managed to redirect the question.

"I don't know why I've avoided answering him; I do want children and, after nearly five years with Rick, I certainly know he would be an excellent Father."

Her thoughts were interrupted when her cell phone rang. Sure enough, it was Rick.

"Hello, Rick, you're right on time." She smiled as her heart quickened.

"On time? It's only noon, what do you mean? As I recall, we're heading to the cookout about 4:30, or has that changed?"

She smiled; he was such a conscientious soul.

"That's correct. I was just thinking about you, that's all," she chuckled.

"Whew! I was a bit nervous! You know me, always on time!"

"Indeed, I do!"

"I was just checking to see if there is anything you need me to pick up on my way over this afternoon."

"Nope, I just finished the potato salad, and it's chillin' in the fridge. Made the dessert last night, so everything's ready."

Rick smiled. Although he was still a bit cautious about the changes he'd experienced in Ruth the last time they had been together, he knew her well. Of course, she was prepared. That was her old Girl Scout training! He had spent several years as a Boy Scout, so between the two of them things were fairly organized and efficient. What she didn't think of, he did.

"I'm not surprised!" he responded. "Now, is there a special wine I can pick up?"

"You know, I don't have an answer for that. I haven't spent enough time with Jim to know if they drink wine or beer, or just iced tea. How about you pick up what we like and, if they don't drink, we'll bring it home."

She paused and cleared her throat. "I mean, to my house."

Rick snickered at that comment. *That woman drives me crazy!*

"So, what's so funny?" asked Ruth.

"Oh, nothing. I just love how you think."

Oh, go ahead, Rick, just say it…

"I love you, Ruthie; you're so organized and thoughtful." He was met with silence, so he continued, "I'll pick up a bottle of Malbec. How about flowers, shall I pick up some of those as well?"

Ruth's stomach flipped and her body tingled.

What the heck is this? I feel like a 16-year-old kid!

Her stomach didn't care about her words; her whole being was on fire with excitement. Adrenaline pumped through her veins and, for the first time in many years, she felt full of hope with the possibilities that lay in front of her … and Rick.

"That would be a very nice gesture. You know how much we women love flowers; they speak to our hearts." The yogurt in her belly felt unsettled as her solar plexus chakra reminded her that she was alive with passion.

"Oh dear, I think I'm in trouble," spewed out of her mouth.

Rick shook his head. "Uh, what does that mean, that you're in trouble?"

Ruth laughed as she stumbled for words.

"Ahhh, that wasn't supposed to come out of my mouth. I was just connecting the comment about flowers and a woman's heart, and the word 'love' popped into my head."

Rick was over-the-top with excitement. He didn't quite know what to say.

"Uhhh, okay, but *What's Love got to do with it?"

She was trapped! As quick-witted as she was, she had nothing to say!

Quick, she implored her head, *help me out, here!*

"Oh, love has everything to do with flowers," came out of her mouth. Then she quickly clammed up.

Jiminy Christmas, you need to stop talking, right now.

Rick read the silence, and he knew that whomever had taken over his Ruthie was completely in charge now. He couldn't help but grin like a Cheshire Cat as his heart thumped in his chest.

Geez, we could skip the cookout and I'd be happy.

He calmed his racing heart and took a deep breath. He knew his lady well enough to know she was in unfamiliar territory. She must feel possessed! He decided to help her out.

"Okay, I think we have everything under control. Text me if you need anything else. I'll be over around 4:15."

"Thank you, Rick, I appreciate you. Have a wonderful afternoon and I'll see you in a bit." She paused, and then said, "I love you!"

There it was. She'd said it. Not that she hadn't from time to time, but this time was different … she meant it!

The yard had been freshly mowed and the deck swept clean of debris from the surrounding trees. Sarah was busy in the kitchen and the kids were playing in the backyard. Jim had just begun to clean the grill for the cookout when his phone rang. It was Ruth.

"Hello, Ruth, how are you today?"

"I'm great," responded Ruth, "and a good morning to you. Oh, I mean, good afternoon. My goodness, how quickly time goes by when you're busy cooking!"

"Tell me about it, although Sarah's the one who has been cooking this morning, I've been busy getting this place cleaned up and ready for you and Rick."

"Hey, you guys," he called to his boys, "take that somewhere else to play with. I'm talking on the phone. Please and thank you!"

"Sorry about that, Ruth. We got them a new battery-operated racecar, which seemed like a good idea at the time. It's bright red, so we can easily keep an eye on 'em. However, now that we have it home and have discovered how noisy it is, we've had second thoughts about that purchase!" he laughed.

Ruth heard the boys giggling in the background. "It sounds like they're having fun. How old are they?"

"Oh, they are definitely having fun! Let's see, Larry's nearly twelve, Randy is nine, and Cindy, our princess, is five. She's inside helping her mama. Remind me, do you have children?"

She cleared her throat. "No, I don't have children. At least, not at this time." Just saying those words brought a sense of sadness to her heart.

Come on, we're good; we have plenty of time.

"Okay, where were we?" Jim interjected. "What can I do for you?"

She had to smile. "Rick just called and asked if he could bring something to drink tonight. Just wondered what would you recommend?"

Still carefully watching the boys, he refocused his thoughts on what Ruth said.

"Sorry, I'm a bit distracted by keeping an eye on the boys. Did you ask what you could bring for us to drink?"

"I did."

"You're bringing plenty, and Sarah has made iced tea and lemonade. If Rick would like to bring a bottle of red wine, we drink Malbec on occasion." He paused. "Hang on a minute, Ruth."

Once again, Jim had been distracted by the boys. He motioned for them to turn off the new toy, to which they promptly obliged.

"Okay, now I can hear myself think and give you a sound answer," he laughed.

"Oh, no problem, Jim. I completely understand. Rick is planning to pick up a bottle of Malbec; that's what we drink." She smiled; yet another thing she and Jim had in common.

"Sounds perfect. We look forward to seeing you this evening and meeting your beau."

Beau. Ruth had to laugh. She hadn't heard that word in years.

"Okay, my beau and I will be there at five sharp! If you need us to pick up anything, just text me and we'll get it for you."

"Sounds good. Thank you, Ruth; I think Sarah has everything under control. "She's the organized person," he snickered, "and I'm the planner. Not to mention, the boys are with me, and that keeps me on my toes!"

"Oh, I'm certain they do. Take care and have a great afternoon. See you in a few hours."

"You have a good one, too. Oh, I do have one thing to ask you before we get together." He cleared his throat. "Have you ever heard the old woman use the phrase, 'Follow the Snake?'"

What a strange saying. Whatever would that mean? Ruth pondered.

"No, can't say that she has. What an interesting phrase. 'Follow the Snake,' huh? Guess we'll find out about that in time. You've given me something to think about!"

"Well, try not to think about it too much," chuckled Jim. "The old woman has told me that on several occasions. I think we're in for an interesting ride! See you soon."

Ruth laughed. "I've always loved living on the edge!"

Who am I kidding? I've always played by the "rules!" But, who cares? This is the new me!

The sound of the battery racecar roared in the background. She raised her voice in order to be heard over the noise.

"Have a delightful afternoon with your boys; I am eager to meeting them."

She smiled at the thought of the adrenalin racing through the two brothers from the excitement of their new prize.

Oh, how I remember those days when my brother and I got something new. We didn't even care if we had to share. It was especially exciting when we had saved our allowance to help buy it.

Her thoughts went to her younger brother, Doug. She hadn't talked to him in some time. "I wonder what he's up to these days? I really need to get in touch with him, but not today. I need to get back to the journal I pulled out several days ago."

She got a glass of water and moved to the patio. She had just picked up the journal from the lounge chair and sat down, and opened the journal to where the tatted chain was, when her phone rang.

Oh, my gosh, it's Doug! Go figure!

"Speak of the devil!" she exclaimed when she answered his call. "How's my little brother?"

He let out a belly laugh. "How did you know the devil and I are good friends?"

They both laughed joyfully.

"But, you haven't seen me lately," he continued. "I certainly am not your 'little' brother! Younger, yes, but not little!"

"Okay, it's good to hear from my *big* younger brother! And, I'm glad to know you're still among the living!" she added affectionately. "I've missed you!"

"As a matter of fact, I'm doing quite well. You have been on my mind a lot deal lately, too. Thought I'd better get in touch with you before you disown me!"

Doug sounded good; however, there was something different in his voice she couldn't quite put her finger on.

"Oh, I'd never do that, but I would probably cry myself to sleep if I thought you had forgotten your favorite sister."

"Fat chance of that. Even if you weren't my only sister, you'd be my favorite."

Something was up with Doug; she felt it in her gut. He never just randomly called.

"Seriously, Doug, how are you? Is everything okay with you and the family? The kids doing well?"

When he didn't respond immediately, she simply waited. She knew her brother well enough to know that he would tell her why he had called when he was ready, and not a minute before.

Doug cleared his throat. "Listen, Sis, don't be worried. Sue and the kids are all healthy and happy. I've just had a few things surface that I knew only you would understand." He paused. "We lived in the same home and had the same parents, so if anyone knows my heart, it's you."

Ruth swallowed the lump in her throat and took a deep breath.

"When can we get together, Doug? I have plans tonight, but I'll free up any time to see you."

Silence. A deafening silence that made a knot in her stomach.

Oh, dear God, he's probably dealing with our childhood stuff. We always were so in tune with each other.

"Do you have time tomorrow morning?" Doug asked. "Say, 10 o'clock?"

"I do. How about I make a big pot of coffee and some of those cinnamon rolls you like so well?" she suggested. "You do remember where I live, don't you?"

Though he was silent, she felt strong. She had pulled her energy from within rather than reacting to whatever might be going on with her brother. For what felt like five minutes, she held a place of strength and calm for both of them.

"You know," he finally responded, sounding a bit more grounded. "I sure don't need the calories, but I'd love some of your cinnamon rolls! And, just hearing your voice helps, Ruthie. I look forward to seeing you tomorrow at ten."

Pictures of her brother at various ages flashed across the screen of her mind as her heart remembered his mischievous, yet sweet spirit.

"Me, too, Dougie." She smiled; she knew she was the only person who could get away with calling him that.

"Seriously, it'll be good to see you. And," she chuckled, "I can't wait to see how much rounder you've gotten!"

They both laughed.

She shook her head as she hung up.

"Wow, I sure didn't expect that call. Everything in my world is certainly getting stirred up!" Her mind wanted to speculate about what Doug was remembering, but her heart changed the subject.

"What are you going to wear tonight? Let's wear something bright and pretty ... something that will bring the same look to Rick's face as the v-neck turquoise jumpsuit brought."

Butterflies stirred in her stomach at the very thought of his face.

"Whatever is happening to me?" she wondered. "Well, whatever it is, bring it on!"

Oh, you know what is happening! You've unleashed a part of your heart that has yearned to be free!

Ruth grinned as the flutters continued, and she could feel her blood bringing brightness to her cheeks.

"I could get used to this!" she giggled.

Her rational, practical head piped up. *"Just remember, you need to get up and make cinnamon rolls in the morning."*

"Hush, I know how to multi-task," she responded, wrinkling her brow.

She immediately visualized what she would wear to the cookout.

"Perfect! Thanks for redirecting the energy! I am so ready to be free!"

Rick knocked on the door promptly at 4:15, opened it and peeked in. "Anyone home?"

Ruth appeared within seconds, clad in a soft, flowing, brightly colored summer dress. Her hair was scrunched into a messy bun on top of her head, while tiny daisy pins placed on both sides of the bun held it in place. Pearl teardrop earrings hung from her ears, and her makeup was exquisitely applied, with her lips painted a soft coral.

Her appearance took Rick's breath away! He immediately placed the flowers and wine on the floor, and wrapped her into his arms with a tender, yet firm embrace. He held her close and smiled.

"Wow, Ruthie, did you get one of those girly makeovers or something? What are you trying to do to me? And, your lipstick looks great, but do you mind if you need to reapply it?"

She smiled and responded with a loving, passionate kiss that might have ignited a fire. Within a few moments, Rick pulled back and looked her in the eyes.

"Whatever has happened, I'm in!" He kissed her again.

"We're going to be late," said Ruth as she opened her eyes. "Can we pick this up later?"

"Indeed, we can! Whew! I need to splash cold water on my face!" He chuckled, his smiling face flushed.

Ruth loved it; this was what she had always wanted. Finally, she was free!

"Go take care of yourself," she tenderly responded. "I'll send Jim a quick text to let him know we're running a bit behind, and that we're on our way." She gave him a last peck on the cheek.

Then Rick did something he had always wanted to do, but didn't know how she would feel about it. He gave her a pat on the butt on his way to the bathroom.

Ruth grinned from ear to ear as she watched him walk to the bathroom.

"Hey, Rick, you certainly have a nice booty."

Rick was in shock; he had no words, and she took advantage of his speechlessness.

"There, I said it. I've always wanted to, but I didn't know how you'd feel about that."

He shook his head. "I love it, almost as much as I love you. Now, let's get to Jim's before we have to call and cancel!"

Jim's house was a lovely old brick home located outside of town, about twenty miles from Ruth's. When they pulled into the driveway, two very excited young boys ran to meet them. Rick turned off the car, and the youngest boy walked up to his window, while the oldest appeared on Ruth's side, and each introduced himself.

"Come on, we'll take you to the backyard," said the older boy.

Just then Jim appeared. "Hey guys," he said to the boys, "let 'em at least get out of the car." He walked over to Ruth's window. "Guess you can tell my boys aren't shy! They get that from their mama!" he laughed.

Ruth and Rick got out of the car, and Ruth gave Jim a quick hug before she introduced him to Rick. Jim walked around to Rick's side of the car and the two men shook hands. Sarah came out of the house holding the hand of a little girl in pigtails and waved to them.

"Welcome to our home," she greeted them as she hurried to the car. "May I help you carry anything to the back yard?"

The little girl let go of her mama's hand and hurried over to her daddy. Ruth smiled and watched Rick to see his reaction to this exuberant little girl, then turned to Sarah.

"Hi, Sarah, I'm Ruth. It's good to finally meet you." Then they walked over to the side of the car where Jim and Rick stood.

"For heaven's sake," Jim said with embarrassment. "I didn't get a chance to properly introduce you two."

He turned to Rick. "This is my wife, Sarah; Sarah, this is Ruth's beau, Rick."

There he goes again, thought Ruth. *Well, Rick wouldn't care; at least I don't think so.*

"And this," said Jim, gesturing to the little girl, "is our precious princess, Cindy."

The little girl gave them a beautiful smile as she held her daddy's hand and leaned her head on his leg.

"She's shy, like her daddy!" he laughed.

Ruth leaned over to be at eye level with Cindy. "Hello, Princess Cindy, we're very glad to meet you."

"Indeed, it's a delight to meet a princess!" agreed Rick as he also leaned toward her. Cindy buried her face in her daddy's leg.

"It's good to meet you, Sarah," said Rick as he stood up. "And, you have a great welcoming team!"

"Hey, Rick," said Ruth, "let me have the pan with the yellow top; it needs to be refrigerated."

Rick retrieved the pan from the car and handed it to Ruth.

"I'll take it," offered Sarah.

He smiled and handed the pan to Sarah, who looked straight into his eyes. He felt a bit strange; he couldn't remember the last time someone other than Ruth had looked him directly in the eyes.

Then she noticed the bouquet of daisies.

"I can take those, too, and put them in some water," she suggested.

Rick smiled and handed her the flowers. "Thank you."

"No, thank *you*, Rick! Daisies are my favorite flower. Well, actually, I've never met a flower I didn't love!"

"Yeah, Ruthie told me women really love flowers," he smiled. "I like them, too, but apparently not as much as women do." Then Sarah walked back toward Ruth, and they headed toward the house.

"I like your guy," said Sarah. "He feels like a really good soul."

Ruth blushed. "Well, thank you," she stammered. "I sorta like him too!" she grinned.

I like her, too, thought Sarah. *They feel really good together. I have a hunch they'll be married by the end of this year!*

The boys led Rick and Jim to the back yard, while Cindy held her daddy's hand. The back yard was handsomely groomed and well maintained.

A very old looking, furry dog slept lazily on the edge of the deck.

"Oh, this is our faithful friend, Max," said Jim, as he leaned over to pat the dog's belly. Max rolled over and welcomed Jim's affection. He's an old fella who's been with us since shortly after Sarah and I married. I had a dog, Shiloh, when we first met, and after he passed, Max entered our lives. Don't know what we'll do when he decides to join Shiloh in that great dog heaven in the sky."

Jim stood up, "Yeah I do, Sarah and I love dogs, we'll get another one!"

Everything was set up and ready for the evening, with the smell of burgers and hot dogs in the air. The younger boy grabbed Rick's hand and pulled him toward the bright red racecar.

"Look what Mom and Dad got for us!"

"Only for a few minutes, Randy," interjected Jim. "We're about ready to eat."

Randy plopped excitedly into the seat of the racecar, strapped himself in, and off he went. Rick smiled from ear to ear as he watched the little fella proudly zoom across the back yard.

One day, I'll have a son, or daughter, who loves being adventurous. He glanced over toward Ruth, who smiled at the interaction between the two of them.

He's going to be a fabulous Father, just like my father, except that he's going to have an emotionally healthy wife to stand with him. Ruth glanced upward.

No disrespect, Mama; I know you did the best you could. And, I promise to remember the importance of leaning into my pain rather than pulling away from it, in order to heal any wounds that I experience.

As Ruth carried a dish to the picnic table, her eyes moved toward Rick and the young boy who proudly showed off his skills. She smiled at him.

I have never been so ready to step into this new adventure in my life.

Rick looked in her direction and returned her smile.

As Ruth and Sarah brought out the remaining food, the boys hurried over to pick their seats. Randy wanted to sit by Rick, while the oldest, Larry, chose to sit by Ruth. Cindy sat between her mama and daddy. Once everyone was gathered around the large picnic table, Jim and his family reached for the hands of the person on either side of them.

"I'll say the prayer!" Larry proudly announced. Ruth smiled at Rick again as they bowed their heads.

The evening was filled with the sound of laughter, and the youthful exuberance of two young boys very willing to entertain the grown-ups.

After about an hour, Sarah announced that it was time for the kids to get ready for bed so the grown-ups could have some "big people" time. The boys grumbled a bit, but didn't resist. All the excitement had clearly worn them out.

"It's time for me to go to bed," said Cindy to Max as she hugged his neck. "You sleep good, too. I love you!"

She kissed her daddy and smiled at Rick and Ruth, then ran to catch up with her mama and her brothers. Just before she entered the house, she turned and waved goodnight, then went inside.

Rick, Ruth, and Jim cleaned everything up while Sarah settled in the kids for the night, and then Jim brought out four wine glasses and the bottle of Malbec that Rick and Ruth had brought.

Ruth stood up. "Hey, we haven't had the coconut dessert that I brought! You two must taste it; it's a summer family favorite." Just then Sarah came out of the house, dessert in hand.

"You two talk," said Jim as he gave his wife a peck on the cheek. "I'll get plates and forks."

Rick promptly stood up. "I'll go with you; looks like you could use an extra set of hands." He also gave Ruth a peck on the cheek and whispered, "Can't wait to get you home!"

Ruth blushed and looked at Sarah, who simply smiled and looked away. Once Rick was inside the house, she leaned toward Ruth.

"I really, really like your guy. He so reminds me of my Jim."

"I like him too, thank you," responded Ruth, still blushing. She wanted to say 'love;' however, she didn't know Sarah well enough to share such a deep emotion.

"I'm just telling you, Ruth, I can tell that he's a very good guy. Not to mention, you two just seem to be a good fit for each other!" She paused. "I don't mean to overstep my bounds; I know I just met you. However, you two really look and feel good together."

Ruth wasn't used to being so transparent, and she felt a warmth within herself.

Wow, that was bold! She is clearly very self-confident, that she's so willing to just say what she feels without censoring herself. Now, that's something I certainly would like to be able to do more freely!

"Oh, no problem," said Ruth. "Thank you for being so direct. I've never done well with beating around the bush. Truth is, I've had to learn to hold my tongue in order to keep things peaceful." She looked directly at Sarah. "Thank you for being real; that's a rarity these days."

"I think Jim is correct," smiled Sarah. "We're going to become good friends."

Then Jim and Rick came out from the kitchen.

"You two look like you're having a rather serious conversation," remarked Jim.

"Oh, we are," giggled Sarah. "But now I guess we need to be proper and let you men take over the conversation."

They all had a good belly laugh over that comment.

Rick leaned over to Ruth. "I do love you!" he whispered, as he set the plates and wine glasses beside the dessert in front of her.

Ruth's heart raced as blood rushed to her face.

Hush, my beating heart. My God, this is overwhelming!

She wanted to grab him and hold on like she had never done with another soul in her life. She did, however, manage to control herself, and simply smiled.

"Would you like to serve your yummy dessert?" asked Jim as he handed Ruth the serving knife.

She stood and proceeded to cut the dessert, placing a piece on the plates and passing them to her right. Rick popped the cork on the wine and filled each glass, also passing each to his right.

When all were served, Jim reached for Sarah's hand, and Rick reached for Ruth's hand. Jim then lifted his glass in a toast.

"May this be the first of many visits. And, while this may be our first get-together, it feels like we've done this many times." He smiled. "Maybe in a former life?" They all laughed as they lifted their glasses.

"To old friends," chimed in Sarah, and they clinked their glasses together.

Ruth knew Jim literally believed his statement about a former life. She may have only known him a brief time; however, it was apparent the two of them held similar beliefs.

Tears came to Ruth's eyes, and she pleaded with her heart.

What is happening to me? Please don't cry, please!

Jim noticed her tears and smiled in reassurance.

Somehow that helped her, and the tears quickly disappeared. Sarah leaned over and kissed his cheek.

Oh, how well he understands what Ruth is feeling.

She, too, smiled at Ruth, then looked at Rick and offered another toast. "To you and Ruth, our new friends!"

And, to you, Rick – hang in there. Her love is worth waiting for!

After second helpings of the dessert and a refill of wine, Sarah leaned back and said, "Oh, my gosh, I have completely overindulged!" Then she looked over at Jim and smiled. "Ready to be a Fire Keeper?"

Jim was taken aback! It was such a brazen thing for Sarah to say in front of people she had just met. His eyes sparkled and his heart thumped as he grinned.

"Ab-so-lutely! You've started the fire!" he declared with a hearty laugh, then leaned over and kissed her on the lips.

Rick looked at Ruth and grinned. Nothing needed to be said; it was an intimate moment between two people who obviously had a deep and abiding love for each other, and who were unhindered by anyone else around them.

Sarah finally stood up.

"Speaking of hot, are you two ready for a cup of coffee? I have decaf."

"I'll have a regular coffee," responded Jim as he winked at his wife. "Seems like I may need the caffeine!"

Rick stood up with a huge grin "I'll help you take in the dishes and dessert, Sarah, so these two can chat a bit."

Ruth glanced at him appreciatively and stayed put, which was very unusual for her. She always felt lazy if she let others do all the work. But, everything else was changing, and she and Jim really could use a few moments to check in with each other.

"So, how is it going for you?" Jim began. "As I recall, you were going to share with me something that happened the other morning. Would you like to expand on that?"

"The other morning…" She paused. "That feels like a couple of weeks ago, so much has been happened. How do I make this short?"

"Well," she continued, "first I had a visit from my deceased mother and brother. Then I found myself feeling a depth of love for Rick I have never felt for anyone. And, just today, I had a call from my youngest brother, whom I have not seen in about a year. He'll be coming by tomorrow morning for coffee and homemade cinnamon rolls."

She looked directly into Jim's eyes as she waited for his reaction, but was met only with silence.

"Hmmm, I've never seen you speechless!" she laughed.

Jim smiled. "It's just such a delight to have the opportunity to get to know you, and your beau."

"Seriously, Ruth," he continued as he leaned toward her, "it's just the beginning of the end of life as you've known it. And, this new life will forever engage your heart. It is such an opportunity to learn to trust what has never made sense, and then to discover that it makes more sense than anything else that has happened in your life."

"I don't quite know what that means," she snickered.

"Oxymoron, huh? Guess it's something you just need to experience." Jim leaned closer. "You will begin to understand these unexplainable events only when you experience them."

She remained silent, but kept her eyes fixed on Jim. Finally, she leaned back in her chair and crossed her arms.

"Interesting. While I can't wrap my mind around that concept, my heart seems to understand. And, it's really very exciting!" she said with a grin.

"This," she said, tapping her finger on her temple, "has always wanted to make sense out of things before I could embrace them. But, you know, Jim, my heart pushes me forward, and then the flow of adrenalin is absolutely unstoppable."

"You got this, Ruth, trust me, you got this!" declared Jim as he leaned back in his chair.

"Indeed!" she agreed, as she caught a glimpse of Rick and Sarah in the kitchen.

"You know, Jim, we need to find an afternoon to really talk. Maybe it needs to be at the old woman's cabin. Or, maybe I just need to spend more time with her. It's time for me to show up and ask the questions my heart has wondered about most of my life."

Sarah held the door open for Rick as he brought out a tray of mugs and a thermos of coffee.

"Absolutely! And, trust yourself, Ruth! Now, I have a question for you. But first," he said as he turned to Rick and Sarah, "let's move to the lounge chairs, where we can get a better view of the sky."

They scooted four lounge chairs close together, poured coffee into their mugs, and settled into the chairs to enjoy the fullness of Grandmother Moon's face, while stars adorned the beauty that radiated from her onto the inhabitants of Earth Mother. They all silently gazed upward and absorbed the rich beauty of the night sky, and the occasional streak of a falling star.

"Now," said Ruth, "about that question, Jim."

He inhaled deeply and sipped his coffee.

"What do you know about the saying that I mentioned earlier, 'Follow the Snake?'" he asked.

Ruth scanned the stars. "You know, there is a constellation in the shape of a serpent, or snake, whichever word you choose. I'm not certain where it is, but I understand that the Serpent head is toward the West and the Serpent tail is toward the East. The brightest star in the Serpent is the giant red star, Alpha Serpent."

Rick looked at her; he hadn't realized that she even knew such things. He wanted to say that, but felt it best to be silent and see what else he might learn about her.

"What little I know from what the old woman has mentioned to me," she continued, "is that the West is the place of the heart, and the East is the portal to new beginnings and opportunities." As she spoke, she felt life surge through her entire being from the depths of her soul.

"Perhaps," she continued, "to 'Follow the Snake' means to become aware of what is in your heart, and to allow the flow of all that is unknown to guide you toward your heart's desire."

Perfect stillness. Only the sounds of nature, the wisp of the wind, and the sway of the trees were audible. In that very moment, everything was in alignment, and even those things neither understood nor spoken waited to be revealed.

"My goodness, Ruth," Jim finally said, "that is a wonderful story. And, you know, it's much like the stories the old woman tells. There are profound Truths within your words."

He glanced at Rick. "I don't know what Ruth has told you about this old woman we know; however, I hope you realize that your support is immeasurable for the work Ruth is doing."

He looked at Sarah, then back at Rick. "I would not be as successful with what I'm doing without Sarah's understanding and love. And, trust me, it sometimes takes a great deal of work. Just know this: I'm a different man than I was before I started working with the old woman. Sarah can attest to that!"

"That I can," Sarah agreed, "and it's worth the sweetness, strength, and peace that I have seen Jim grow into as a result of whatever work he does with her.

I've met the old woman, and have had the privilege of sitting with her and Jim at the cabin. There really are no words to describe that experience."

The air cooled as clouds began to move across the sky and darken the night.

Rick looked at Sarah. "It sounds like you and I are the 'Gate Keepers' for our partners."

They all sat in complete silence. Stillness hung in the air as though the world had stopped, suspended in time and space.

"Geez," Jim interjected, "I have no words for what you just said, Rick. That's a very powerful statement." He looked at Ruth. "I think your Rick knows some things we might want to find out more about."

They continued to enjoy the peaceful contentment of the night for a few more minutes, until the youngest son peeked out the door. Sarah noticed him and got up.

"I'd better go see what's up with Randy."

Ruth stood up. "We need to be going home; it's been a very long day, and I have a 10 o'clock appointment tomorrow morning."

Jim and Rick moved the chairs back in place, and carried the tray of mugs and coffee back into the house.

"Thank you for a perfectly lovely evening," said Ruth as she hugged Sarah. "I am so very glad we got to meet. Next time you'll have to come to my place."

She then hugged Jim. "And, I'll see you real soon. Thank you for a sweet evening."

"Oh, thank you for the delicious potato salad, decadent dessert, and your insightful words. You've given me something to consider."

She smiled. "Oh, I've given myself something to consider!"

Rick hugged Sarah and shook Jim's hand. "Thank you both for your hospitality and for your words. Obviously, I leave with a lot of things to consider as well! Tell your kids I look forward to seeing them again soon. I have a few acres, so the boys could bring that fancy red racecar and wear themselves out!" he laughed.

Jim indicated a thumbs up.

They got into the car, buckled their seat belts, and Rick started the engine. He looked over at Ruth and reached for her hand.

"Whatever it is we are doing," he declared, "I'm going to '*Follow the Snake!*'"

Reflections

HEAD TALK

*What part of the story line so far can you
personally relate to?*

Was there anything that struck you as "unreal?"

What are you curious about?

What would you like to "think some more about?"

HEART TALK

What stirred your heart the most?

What touched a nerve or a tender part in you?

What memory from your life came to your heart?

What would you like to happen next?

This intricate, beautiful spiral is known as a

Vegvisir

It is an ancient Magic Navigation Compass.
Vikings used many symbols in accordance with Norse mythology,
widely used in Viking society.

Ties that Bind

Grandfather Sun's light filtered through the sheer curtains in Ruth's bedroom, onto the snuggled couple. Rick burrowed his head in the nape of Ruth's neck.

"Good morning, sleepyhead!"

She wiggled with delight.

"Good morning, my fellow sleepyhead," she giggled, as she sat up in bed and glanced at the clock. It was 8:23.

"Oh, my goodness, we are sleepyheads!" she exclaimed. "Doug's going to be here at ten, and I promised him cinnamon rolls."

Rick yawned and stretched as he propped himself up and reached over for her.

"I do remember you told Jim something about an appointment at ten." He sat up and rubbed the sleep from his eyes, and noticed her silk gown lying on his leg. He held it up and smiled playfully.

"I believe this is yours?"

"So, I didn't hear you complain about that last night!" she teased.

"No, ma'am, not for one moment!" He leaned over and gave her a tender kiss on the neck.

"Okay, we need to get moving," said Ruth. "I apologize for sending you out of here so early. It's just not like Doug to call and want to see me. I don't have time to tell you about it, but he sounded rather … distressed? I don't know, I'll find out when he gets here." She scooted out of bed, slipped on her robe, and leaned over to give him a quick kiss. "Want to get together this afternoon?"

"Sure," he smiled broadly, "just let me know a good time after you complete your business with your brother. I can always work on small projects that I can easily walk away from," he said with a yawn.

"I hope you don't say that about me," she said with a curious frown.

"What!" He threw himself back on the bed, reached for her and brought her down next to him. "Let me assure you, my love, that is not a possibility. As long as you want me around, I'll be here. And, I hope you feel the same way."

After a quick hug, they both got up. Rick threw on some clothes and they headed to the kitchen.

"How about a quick cup of coffee?" she offered.

"That would be great, if you have time."

She dropped a pod into the coffee brewer, and within a few moments she handed Rick a cup of hot coffee.

"Mmm!" he said with a big whiff.

She smiled as she pulled her recipe box out of a kitchen cabinet.

"Hey, Ruthie, I know your brother loves your cinnamon rolls, but what if I zip by the bakery and just buy a dozen? It would save you time and, from what you just said, I'll bet he's more interested in talking to you about what's on his mind than whether you actually made the cinnamon rolls or purchased them. At least the ones from the bakery aren't just refrigerator rolls."

She thought for a moment as she made herself a cup of coffee.

"You know, you're right, that's actually a fabulous idea. I'll promise him that I will make my recipe the next time he comes for a visit." She sipped her coffee. "Hmmm, that *is* good."

"Maybe offering to make them on his next visit will entice him to return more frequently." She looked at Rick. "You have never met him, have you?"

Rick shook his head. "Sure haven't, and you know I'd be glad to."

"I know you would, and I really want you to get to know him. He was always such a polite and thoughtful boy. I don't like that we've grown apart." She glanced at the clock.

"Yikes, it's 9 o'clock. I need to get cleaned up."

He quickly sipped a bit more coffee in response.

"Don't burn your tongue!" she said. "Take the cup with you."

"Thanks, I'll do that." He kissed her, then turned and walked to the door.

"I'll be back in twenty minutes, tops. Oh, and thank you for an absolutely amazing evening with your friends. Maybe we can chat about that later this evening." He smiled on his way out.

She shook her head. "He's such a fabulous man. Why has it taken me so long to accept that?"

"Who cares, as long as you finally realize it?" she heard her mother say.

"You are absolutely correct, Mama! Now let's see what we can do for Dougie."

I'd better keep it Doug; it used to pester him to death when I called him Dougie.

"Nah," she smiled mischievously, "maybe that's precisely what he needs: a nudge from his sister to help him remember the playful moments from our childhood."

She zipped in and took a quick shower, and threw on the first pair of leggings she grabbed from the drawer. Then she quickly pulled out the first sports bra and tee shirt available.

Goodness, slow down, girl! You have plenty of time.

"You're absolutely correct," she sighed.

She went back into the bathroom, wiped off the mirror, and grabbed her make-up case. She applied a thin layer of moisturizer to her face, then whisked a bit of blush onto her cheeks, and finished with a swipe of lip-gloss.

As she began to run the comb through her wet hair, she took a couple more slow, deep breaths, and felt the floor beneath her feet.

"Okay, I'm steady and in the present moment." She felt her mother's presence enter the room.

"*It's time for Doug to heal his own childhood wounds, just as you are doing,*" she heard her mother say. "*I trust you to know how to do this. Now, trust yourself.*"

Ruth thought of the last visit she had had with the old woman, and recalled a few snippets of the valuable teaching that she could apply to the current situation.

"*You can help others but just remember, it's not your job to do their work. All you need do is listen with your heart, and offer unconditional love. The rest is up to them.*"

She sighed deeply as she twisted her hair and clipped it on top of her head. She moved into the living room, pulled out a smudge stick from the side table next to the couch, and lit it. Slowly, she closed her eyes and asked for guidance, in order to help her brother find his way to whatever he needed to confront.

Just then, Rick knocked on the door and let himself in. The delicious smell of fresh baked cinnamon rolls filled the air, and Ruth promptly extinguished the smudge stick.

"Hope I'm not interrupting anything," said Rick.

She ran a drop of water over the tip of the smudge stick and placed it back in the drawer.

"Oh, no, you aren't. It's always good to see your handsome face," she said as she gave him a quick kiss. "You know, I love those luscious lips of yours."

Rick smiled. "I'm glad of that, because these luscious lips love those beautiful lips of yours!" He gave her a sweet kiss.

"Okay, where do you want these rolls? Your brother will be here in a few minutes, so I need to get out of here."

"You are welcome to hang around for a bit, if you would like to meet him," she offered.

"You know, my love," he smiled, "whatever has happened with you has made my heart most happy! Now, where do you want these rolls, on the dining room table or on the kitchen counter?"

"Let's put them on the kitchen counter," she said, returning his smile. "I'm going to make a full pot of coffee for us to share. We'll see whether or not Doug wants complete privacy after he arrives."

He set the rolls on the counter and Ruth prepared the coffee pot.

"You know, Ruthie, as a man, my hunch is that he'll want some privacy with you. Let's not put him on the spot. You can introduce us and then I'll make my exit."

He put his arms around her waist. "You look as hot as those cinnamon rolls, and you look even more delicious than they do," he teased.

"Now you're just being silly," she replied. "I literally threw on the first thing I could find."

"You still look fabulous. Throw them on or throw them off, either way you're beautiful!"

Her heart fluttered as those darned butterflies woke up from their night's slumber. She returned his hug and glanced at the clock.

"It's 9:50; could you pull out some coffee mugs while I get some saucers and forks?"

He nodded his head, which was still spinning from their newly emerged love.

Within five minutes there was a knock on the door. Ruth hurried to the door and playfully knocked back from the inside.

"Who is it?"

"It's the boogey man," Doug laughed in a deep voice. "Now, open the door and let your younger brother in!"

She opened the door and giggled excitedly.

"Oh, my sweet brother," she said as she hugged his neck. "What a wonderful sight you are!"

Doug smiled. It felt good to see and feel her youthful exuberance. He had almost forgotten how absolutely full of life she had always been.

"Do come in; it's so great to have you in my home." She gave him another hug, then took his coat and hung it by the door.

Doug caught sight of Rick as he loosened his sister's hug.

"And, who might this be, Ruthie? Have you gone and gotten married?"

"This is Rick," she giggled as she stepped aside. "And, no, he's not my husband," she stammered. "He's my very good friend."

She turned to Rick. "Rick, this is my brother, Doug."

Ruth's heart nearly beat out of her chest as the two men shook hands. She couldn't believe how long it had been since she had felt such complete joy in her life. Here she was, with both her precious brother and the love of her life standing in front of her.

Why did I introduce Rick as my very good friend? I sure hope that didn't offend him!

"I'm very glad to meet you, Doug. Ruth has spoken quite highly of you."

"And, I'm glad to meet you, Rick," said Doug as he glanced toward his sister. "No doubt my sister keeps you on your toes. She always kept all of us in line; she tried her best, anyway!" he laughed.

"Okay, enough about me," said Ruth. "Come on into the kitchen. Your cinnamon rolls and hot coffee await your indulgence."

Rick spoke up as he headed toward the door. "It was good to meet you, Doug, and I look forward to getting to know you."

"You don't need to run off on my account," Doug responded. "Stay and have some coffee and rolls with us."

Doug immediately liked Rick. He sized up people well, as it was a part of what his job required, and Rick seemed very solid.

Rick looked at Ruth, sweetly smiled. She was so happy; how could he leave?

"What do you think, Ruth?"

"I think I have two of my favorite men in front of me. Who could ask for anything more?"

"In that case, I have a few minutes, and I'll be darned if those rolls don't smell delicious!"

"Good!" Doug replied. "I have a hunch you've had my sister's homemade cinnamon rolls before." He winked at her.

She blushed and bit her lip to keep from embarrassing herself and Rick, and quickly turned away.

"Let's get our stuff from the kitchen and take it out to the patio. Does that sound good to you two?"

Doug's heart was already happy. He grinned from ear to ear, just thinking about his sister finally finding a really good man. She had had her fair share of quirky guys, and a long stretch of no dates. It was time for her to settle down with a good man, and to bring some babies into the world that would call him "Uncle Doug!"

Once in the kitchen, Ruth looked at Doug. "To be Truthful, Doug, these are not my homemade cinnamon rolls," she admitted as she glanced over at Rick. "Rick bought them at the bakery early this morning, so they're at least freshly baked."

Doug smiled at Rick. "She's always been so frank and honest," he chuckled. "Sometimes it's a curse, but mostly it's refreshing. You always know where she stands, and she's very trustworthy."

"Thank you for your forthright and honest words," said Rick. He looked at Ruth and took her hand. "I couldn't agree with you more."

"Whoa, this is so fabulous, I … I have no words." Doug laughed with great joy as he reached for his sister and gave her a big bear hug, and then extended his hand to Rick. "You've got a good one, and she'll give you a run for your money!"

He hugged his sister again. "You have no idea how happy I am for you." Tears filled his eyes as he shook with laughter. He bit his lip and batted his eyes a few times to compose himself. Then he patted his belly.

"Let's get those cinnamon rolls into our bellies! We have a lot to celebrate!"

Ruth's ears perked up. "Oh, we're celebrating? You came here to celebrate something with your big sis?"

"That's a silly question!" he said, as he poured himself a cup of coffee, then gently pulled a roll from the pan and placed it on a plate. He grabbed a fork and headed toward the patio.

Rick kissed Ruth. "I guess he approves of me? I mean, *us.*" He grinned as he got coffee and a roll for himself, then moved toward the patio with Ruth directly behind him.

Just before they exited onto the patio, she leaned forward and whispered in his ear, "That tush of yours drives me crazy!"

Rick felt blood rush to his face. "Behave yourself!" he grinned as he sat down in the chair opposite Doug, while Ruth headed for her lounge chair between them. Then she noticed her journal.

"Oops," she extended her mug to Doug. "Hold onto this for a moment, please."

"Oh, certainly." Doug placed his own mug on the floor and reached for hers.

She placed the journal under the lounge chair, then sat down and got comfortable. She retrieved her coffee from her brother and glanced at both men.

"Man, this is a dream come true!" she said with a big smile. "My two favorite men on either side of me. Life is good!"

The men returned her smile, as the three of them enjoyed the early morning fresh air and the sounds of nature that Sunday mornings offer.

Doug spoke first. "Got to tell you, Ruthie, your cinnamon rolls are every bit as good, if not better, than these bakery ones."

"Thank you, I'll accept that as compliment."

"Whoa, that's another big change!" said Doug. "You have always been your own worst critic, and have shied away from compliments."

Her heart felt joyful! *This Moment* was something she had only dreamed about and, now, at this precise moment, she was living it in real time!

"I know, but what the heck, I'll be thirty-four soon. It's about time I made some drastic changes, don't you think?"

Doug wiped his mouth, poured a bit more coffee, and offered to refill Ruth and Rick's mugs. Ruth accepted, while Rick declined.

"I've had plenty, thank you," said Rick as he stood up. "I'm going to head out and leave you two to catch up with each other."

Doug smiled. "It certainly was nice to meet you, Rick. Let's do this again soon, only next time I'll bring my beautiful wife, Sue. She's a peach! Just ask Ruthie, she'll tell you."

He stood and extended his hand to Rick. Rick gave him a strong handshake and looked him in the eyes.

"Thank you for allowing me to share in your morning coffee and rolls with your sister. I'm certain I'll see you again soon."

"Oh, you can count on that! Have a good day and enjoy your Sunday."

Rick leaned down and gave Ruth a quick kiss. "I'll see you later!"

She started to get up. "I'll walk you to the door."

"Oh, no, just enjoy your visit. I think I know where the front door is!"

She watched him walk to the door, gave him a wave, and blew him a kiss. Rick smiled as he turned and closed the door behind him.

My God, now I'm blowing him a kiss. What am I, twelve? She chuckled inside, then turned back to Doug, who stared at her with a heartfelt, happy grin.

"Gotta tell you, Ruthie, I've never seen you like this. I think you've found the one!"

"I know!" she said as a single tear ran down her cheek. "Give me a minute." She shook her head.

"I seem to be in a place I've never been before. And," she smiled, "I welcome all of it!" She quickly regrouped and turned her focus to Doug.

"Now, my precious brother, tell me what's on your heart; that is, whatever you came here to chat with me about." She touched her ears and smiled. "And, in addition to these ears, the 'ears' of my heart are open."

The energy around Doug shifted, and he adjusted himself in the chair.

"The 'ears' of your heart, huh? I've never heard that expression." His eyes moved to the street across from the patio as he refocused on what *was* on his heart.

"I like it, though," he nodded. "The 'ears' of my heart. Well, what I want to talk about probably requires those ears over the ones on your head." He chuckled, and then took a few moments to collect his thoughts.

"To be honest, Sis, my heart feels so happy to see your life so together, I think my itch has been scratched." He shook his head and smiled. "I couldn't get you off my mind. And, my mind's crazy wanderings led to a whole host of different scenarios that were so ridiculous, I decided to just call and see how things were going."

Ruth smiled as she watched and listened to her brother.

It's interesting how our creative minds can lead us into places of concern that kick our hearts into a host of emotions, emotions that then lead us to feel either hope or despair.

How she loved her brother, and how joyful her heart felt to see his face and to have him sitting beside her. She promised herself she would make certain their lives stayed connected.

"I have missed you, Doug. How in the world did we get so involved in our own lives that we lost touch?" She reached for his hand. "Promise me we'll do better!"

"You got it, Sis!" He grinned and squeezed her hand, then gave her a peck on the cheek. "There, it's sealed with a kiss!" he laughed.

Doug stretched in his chair as his eyes scanned the sky.

"You have a lovely place here. I'm really surprised that you don't live somewhere in the woods, though; that was always your favorite place to be when we were growing up."

"You've got that right. I guess because I work so many 12-hour swing shifts at the hospital, there really isn't time to keep up with all the maintenance required by owning a house. Not to mention the driving that would have been involved by living in the country.

"And, what about you, Doug, what have you been up to? You told me Sue and the kids are healthy and happy." She looked him directly in the eyes. "I want to know how *you* are."

He sat very still for a few moments.

What do I say? She's so happy; I don't want to disrupt that. He cleared his throat and squirmed in his chair.

"I'm good."

She looked at him skeptically. "Hey, look at me."

"I'm okay, honest," he said as he fumbled with the buttons on his shirt.

"Doug, look me in the eyes and tell me that."

He straightened his pant legs, smoothed his hair and glanced in her direction. "You can't even look me in the eyes." She reached over and affectionately touched the bend of his arm. "Remember me? I'm your big sister. You can tell me anything. We've always been that way until the past few years. I know when you're okay and when you're not," she said, rubbing his arm. "Now, tell me what's going on."

Doug took a deep breath, let out a sigh, and looked her directly in the eyes.

"I knew I couldn't fool you. Guess that's why I put off seeing you."

She felt a flutter in her stomach that pushed an alarm button and she quickly but silently acknowledged her belly.

No fear; we've had enough practice to know how to manage whatever is going on. Stay calm and listen.

"I've been experiencing some really weird things," he continued. "I mean, Ruthie, it's really hard to even describe."

She listened attentively as she waited for him to share whatever he needed to express.

"Don't get me wrong," he said after another deep breath, "I'm not seriously ill or anything; it's just that I've felt the presence of something, or someone, hanging around."

There, he'd said it, and it felt good to get the words out.

"Remember when Mom used to talk about seeing things, or having a sense that someone was trying to tell her something?"

Ruth nodded.

"Well, that's how this is, Ruthie, except that I'm not drinking. We always felt Mom was hallucinating when she talked about seeing deceased family members, because she was so intoxicated."

Ruth nodded as her thoughts immediately went to the old woman.

"This feels important, Sis; it feels like someone is trying to tell me something." He shook his head. "Darnedest thing I've experienced since Mom's episodes. Sure makes me feel like I'm losing my mind; however, I know that's not true."

He looked Ruth straight in the eyes and wondered if she thought he needed mental help. When his words were met with a smile, he was confused.

"Why are you smiling?"

"I know someone you need to meet," she responded with a broad grin. "First, though, the only problem you have is in understanding what all of this means. The Truth is, it's an opportunity to bring some stored memories to the surface for cleaning and clearing."

Though still a bit confused, Doug immediately felt peace in his belly.

Very interesting. Very interesting, indeed. He thoughtfully rubbed his chin with his hand.

"So, what am I to do with this situation?" he asked. "And, who is this person you think I need to meet?"

Ruth thought for a moment. *Should I open that Pandora's box?*

Her gut seemed to indicate that she should wait, while her head gave her no response. When she went into her heart she felt a deep warmth that seemed to indicate that she and her brother were more alike than different.

"You know, Doug, the changes you see and feel in me are a result of a nudge I felt in my belly. Yours is more a sense of someone or something around you. Both are the same. I've learned that it's an innate sense of something we've suppressed, something that is now ready to be noticed."

That felt perfect! She was very content with how she had responded to his question, although she knew it would open the door to many other questions.

Doug kept his eyes intently on his sister, while his mind went into high gear. He opened his mouth and let his thoughts flow.

"Noticed? Are you saying that something that happened many years ago still lingers in my body? That what we witnessed with Mom was repressed until we could handle dealing with it? That the crazy-making that completely transformed our mother into someone we didn't recognize is asking for our attention?"

He looked away from Ruth for a moment, and she simply waited for him to voice everything in his head that had been buried in his heart. Her years of working with patients had trained her to simply be a *witness* to their words, and to observe without judgment.

She had learned that people found their way through a maze of confused feelings from past hurts, to discover what lay beneath them. She had learned to not interject her observations or ideas, because every person has an interpretation of their experience. For her to interject her take on it would stop the flow of energy released by their words, their sacred points of view, and the uniquely personal experiences that were based on the beliefs they had developed from their parents and caregivers, followed by their own life experiences.

Once again, Ruth recalled her last visit to the old woman, and the teachings she had taken away regarding her question about enabling another person.

"*You are only responsible for your own actions,*" the old woman had said. "*To interject your thoughts is to disrespect that person's soul work and stand between that person and Creator. Everyone must find his or her way in order for true change to happen. Our business is to treat people the way we want to be treated, to stand with them, and to hold the light of unconditional love.*"

Ruth's heart silently thanked the old woman for her forthright and honest words.

Doug felt a flutter in his belly and took a few deep breaths.

"Pay attention!" the flutter seemed to tell him. He knew her words were of the most high and powerful Truth; he could feel it in every cell of his body.

"How did you get to be so wise?" he asked. "I always knew you were smart, but those words didn't come from a book. You've obviously learned a thing or two from someone. Does that wisdom come from the person you referenced a minute ago?"

"First, thank you for noticing," she said with a grin. "And, yes, she's a very wise woman. She doesn't give answers to questions; she simply tells stories that help you to find your own way to the answers." She wanted to say more, but once again waited to see if Doug had more to say.

He sat perfectly still as he looked off into the sky behind Ruth. He felt as though he had gone to another place. She observed that his breathing had slowed, and that the tension in his face and body had lessened.

That look can only mean he's visiting his past or his future; he's certainly not in the present moment.

Time felt suspended in mid-air as she brought her focus back into her own body. She felt the arms of the lounge chair, and became mindful of her breath, as she instructed her heart to observe her brother while he absorbed the energy around them.

*Let's emanate as much love as we can to my precious brother, as he
discovers what he seeks.*

A flame ignited within her heart, and peace swept through her body like
a warm summer breeze. She closed her eyes and focused on the love she had
invited into her heart, and allowed the coolness of contentment to bring her
entire being into balance.

"*The duality of life,*" whispered her heart. "*That is what is required to live
on Earth. Rather than seeing the differences between black and white, good and
bad, this or that, view them as contrasts rather than contradictions. Consider
the ways in which these dualities actually expand our understanding and allow
us to float on calm waters, and life will take us places we have only imagined.*"

Ruth took a deep breath and opened her eyes. She glanced at Doug, who
sat very still while in his place of reflection. He finally took a deep breath as
he made his way back to the present moment. She looked away from him out
of respect for the sacredness of the moment.

Doug took another deep breath, exhaled, opened his eyes, and shook his
head. He looked at Ruth.

"Good grief, I seemed to have forgotten where I was! Such a daydreamer."
He smiled at his sister. "We've both been daydreamers, haven't we?"

She returned his smile. "Indeed, we have been. Actually, I need to use
the present tense. I'm still a daydreamer; always have been, always will be.
And, I never want that to change!"

Doug shook his head, stretched out his arms, and slowly stood up.

"I've been sitting too long! Time to get this body moving."

"I've missed you," said Ruth as she observed her brother affectionately.

"And, I have missed you, my precious and, now, very wise sister. I think
we have a lot to share with each other. I know you work crazy hours, so how
about we schedule another time to meet up? You say when, and I'll be here."

A tear slid down her cheek; she felt overwhelmed with love for her
brother. She looked up at him tenderly as she extended her hand to him.

"I'm in; now, help me up!"

Doug helped her to her feet, and then extended his arms to her.

"How about another hug for your ol' brother?"

"Now," said Ruth as they released their embrace. "let's talk about seeing things, and having a sense that someone is trying to tell you something. Do you have a sense who this someone is, and what it is they want to tell you?"

He thought a moment.

"Honestly, sometimes I do and other times I haven't a clue. Yet, I have questioned whether it is my doubt that leads me to not knowing." He took a deep breath. "Do you have time to talk about this now, or shall we save it for another time?"

"I have as much time as you need." Ruth sat back down in her lounge chair and tapped the seat of the chair Doug had been sitting in.

"Give me a minute," said Doug as he pulled out his cell phone. "I need to give Sue a call and let her know what's going on." As he waited for her to pick up the call he whispered, "She won't care; Truth be told, she's been after me to take the time to reconnect with you."

"Hey, Honey," he said into the phone. "I just wanted to let you know that I'll be home a bit later than I expected. You were correct; my sis and I definitely needed to reconnect." After a brief silence, "Okay, will do, and thanks for understanding." Another pause. "Yes, I'll be sure to let her know you said 'Hi.' If you need me to pick up anything, just send a text and I'll get it on my way home. Thanks again, Hon. I love you." He ended the call and returned the phone to his pocket.

"Okay, we're set. Now, Ruthie, I know you're a busy lady …"

"Just talk," Ruth interrupted him. "This is our time together, for whatever is on your mind that you want to share. I certainly don't have your answers; however, I have learned that if we just say what's on our hearts, those answers will appear."

Doug's smiled broadly. He simply could not believe how wise his older sister had become.

"I know you are older than me," he said, "but your words come from a wisdom that has nothing to do with age."

"That was a good save, Doug, and I forgive you for reminding me that I'm older than you!" She smiled and patted his hand.

He sat in the silence for a few moments, and then tuned into his heart.

Okay, I'm turning on the 'ears;' what is it that you want to tell me?

Almost immediately he heard the voice of his younger self.

"What is it that you want me to do, Mama? How can I help? What have I done wrong?"

It was a sad voice, and one he knew all too well. And yet, somehow he felt anger for the voice that seemed to be pleading to his irrational, unpredictable, and unloving Mother.

"Why even try?" he asked his whiny, resentful, broken heart. *"Nothing I do will ever make this miserable woman happy."*

He knew the answer. He loved this poor, broken woman who had shown him tremendous love and tenderness until he turned seven. Then, the day his baby brother had died, life had made a complete 180-degree turn.

Pain pierced Doug's chest and his breath became heavy and shallow. Waves of confusion and grief swept through him as he recalled his mother's last few breaths before her soul left her body. She had rested on a bed with pink flowered sheets that were covered with a faded wedding ring quilt. Her face was sullen and pale from the loss of energy needed to stay alive.

Doug once again felt the rage he had felt as a thirteen-year-old boy, who hadn't understood why his mother was dying. He was angry and confused as to why his mother had given up on life. Bitterness welled up in his chest, and he felt an urge to scream at her.

At that point he summoned the strength to pull back from those memories and return to reality. He quickly opened his eyes, leaned back in his chair, and took a very deep breath. He felt the air around him, took another deep breath, and slowly exhaled. He shook his head and then noticed Ruth beside him.

"Geez, Ruthie, I apologize; I wandered back to our childhood."

He continued to shake his head as he rubbed life back into his face with his hands.

"That's what I'm talking about, Sis. Mom seems to be haunting me." He looked at Ruth and smiled tenderly.

"I'm telling you, it's been years since those memories even crossed my mind; however, about a year ago they began to enter my dreams. Then they began to also fly in from nowhere during the daytime."

Ruth sat very still as her brother shared what he'd experienced. She observed his face and body language as he recounted other snippets of his experiences during the past year, and noticed how solemn he became between the bouts of anger that appeared as he spoke of the events. What she felt most of all was his intense sadness at losing his mother for reasons he still could not understand, even as a grown man.

"When Dad was alive," she asked during a pause, "did you ever talk to him about any of these accounts, or any other memories you have from your childhood? Did you ask him why Mother died?"

Doug looked deeply into his sister's eyes. He was speechless, exhausted, and beyond any words. He only felt a depth of sadness and love that seemed to melt together into a sense of calm.

She held his look and allowed him to reach into her heart for whatever he needed at that moment. Her heart felt compassion for his confusion, knowing full well that it would lead him to the answers he sought. She again felt deep gratitude for the many patients and their families for whom she had held space as they unraveled the twisted emotions that occur during such times of great sorrow.

Doug blinked away his tears and Ruth reached for his hand. The floodgates opened, and he allowed his emotions to flow. The dam that had held back the waters of a river finally cracked open, giving way for the overflow to release into a larger body of water. The power of the release was strong and intense, until the overflow expanded into a holding place that allowed the waters to calm.

The chill of the late afternoon air brought them both to a calm holding place on Ruth's patio. Doug pulled a handkerchief from his pants pocket to dry his eyes and blow his nose. He looked at his sister and shook his head.

"You're something else, you know that?" He grinned and took a deep breath. "I had forgotten what a responsible, loving person you were. I mean, that you are!"

"Well, I do the best I can with what I have to work with," she said with a shy smile, and they both laughed. "I know I keep saying this, but it's true; I've missed my brother, and I love you beyond words!"

She squeezed his hand, released it, and held out her pinky finger.

"Pinky swear we'll make these visits a priority?"

With a broad smile, he, too, lifted his pinky finger and hooked it around his sister's.

"You got it! And I love you more!"

The crispness of the air, and the growl of two empty bellies broke the seriousness of the moment. Doug glanced at his watch.

"Oh, my gosh, it's 3 o'clock! Where has the time gone? I sure didn't mean to take up your entire Sunday."

"Oh, don't be silly, I've loved every minute of our time! From the sounds of our stomachs, though, we probably need some nutritious food. Do you have time to eat a little something with me before you go?"

He stood up and stretched his arms, then patted his belly. "I always have time for food. Let me touch base with Sue first, though. I want to make certain we don't have plans I have forgotten about."

Ruth also stood up and stretched her arms in the air.

"Goodness, I feel stiff; I need to take a walk! You're welcome to join me if you have no other plans." She picked up her journal and turned to enter the apartment. "I'll let you talk to Sue; come on in when you're done."

Ruth went inside and took her journal into the bedroom. She placed it on the nightstand next to her bed and gave it a gentle pat.

Now I'll remember to take the time to read the section about The King!

She went into the kitchen and looked in the refrigerator to see what she could put together quickly for a healthy snack. She took out a container of lettuce, a tomato, a yellow pepper and a bit of leftover chicken, and began to make a vegetable salad. She cut the chicken into bite-sized pieces and placed them in a small dish, then covered it with a lid.

There we go. If Doug needs to leave, there's plenty of salad ready for me to take to work this week.

She liked being prepared; it gave her a sense of structure. Having things in place somehow helped her mind to feel a sense of order.

One less thing to think about! Sure need to keep my monkey mind from taking charge!

A sense of order not only helped keep her mind from taking over, but also gave her heart a chance to utilize its creativity and spontaneity. If her thinking mind was always "on," there was no time to just enjoy a given moment, and she might miss the hummingbird flitting at the feeder.

Doug walked into the kitchen and smiled. "Would you look at that delicious healthy meal! I'll gladly help you eat some of that. Now, where are your bowls and silverware? The least I can do is get those ready."

"Thank you, I'll gladly accept your help," she said as she pointed him in the right direction. "Get a couple of dinner plates for us to set our bowls on, and we'll eat outside, unless you'd prefer eating inside. You might be tired of all the fresh air."

"You know me, I'll take the fresh air! I would rather be outside than stuck in the house! Remember how seldom we were in the house as kids?"

"Sure do, and I'm still the outdoor girl."

"So," she continued, "no commitments this afternoon, and Sue's good with you staying?"

He nodded. "I've got the best wife anyone could have! I'm one lucky man," he said as he pulled two bowls, dinner plates, glasses and forks from their respective places.

"And, I have time to take that walk afterward if you'd like. Did you call Rick and clear things with him? I remember that you mentioned something about seeing him this afternoon."

"Geez, thank you," she smiled. "I certainly don't want to leave him waiting." She grabbed her phone and sent him a text.

She pulled a box of crackers from the cabinet and set them on the counter. Then she uncovered the chicken and retrieved a pitcher of water from the refrigerator.

"This is a self-serve meal, so help yourself to as much as you want!"

Her cell phone sounded; it was a text from Rick. "We're doing great," she responded. "Doug and I are going for a walk. Thank you for being patient. I'll let you know when Doug has left. xo" She smiled.

"I'm so happy for you, Ruth," said Doug. "It's an answer to prayer that you've found someone to love. And, you know, he's crazy about you."

Her smile broadened. "Yes, I do know that. Thank you for confirming it, though. If my brother recognizes that, it must be true. Until recently, I doubted what men said to me. They seemed to start out all loving, and then things would die down. I guess I've always had a fear I'd end up like Mom and Dad, and I never wanted that."

The thought gave her deep sadness that she felt in her belly.

Oh, please don't do that. That's old stuff, and its Mom and Dad's stuff, not mine. Why, just look at Doug and Sue! That's what is possible, and that's what I choose to focus on bringing into my own life!

Her belly immediately settled down.

They ate in silence on the patio, with only the sounds of the streets below, then took their eating utensils back into the kitchen and set them in the sink.

"Just leave them, Doug, I can do them later. Let's get that walk in before it gets too late. I've taken up your entire Sunday, and I know your kids and Sue would like to have some of your time today."

"You're probably correct, my thoughtful sister." He reached over and gave her a hug. "Now, get your jacket; it's probably a bit cool by now."

He walked to the door and put on his own jacket. "I'm ready!"

As they sauntered down the walking path behind her apartment, they spoke very little. They seemed to simply enjoy being with each other.

It was Ruth who broke the silence.

"Ties that Bind!"

He waited for her to continue. He knew her well enough to know she was going somewhere with that. Ruth's words were purposeful; they were rarely just idle talk.

She grabbed his hand and held it as they walked.

"Remember when we were kids and life would get so confusing that we would take walks in the woods and agree to always stay close to each other?"

He nodded.

"Then, Dougie, trust me, and go with me to meet that special friend of mine." She looked over at him and observed the calm that surrounded him.

"You didn't respond when I asked if you had shared your experiences and questions with Dad. That let me know that you probably didn't."

Doug was silent.

"The things you spoke of have surfaced for a reason," continued Ruth, "and my hunch is that it's time for you to confront the old hurts that created them, and to find answers to your questions.

"My experience has shown that forgiveness is the healing salve for those old wounds. I'm not a therapist; however, I've learned so much from the patients and family members that I've been privileged to work with over the years. Of course, my old wounds surfaced as a result of those experiences, so I, too, needed to find ways to deal with those painful, unanswered questions, and to forgive all those involved, including myself. It's the only way to truly be free."

She suddenly slowed their walk to a stop directly in front of a very large and ancient oak tree. The abrupt stop brought Doug's eyes up and he noticed the old tree. Ruth could feel his energy surge. She knew her brother better than anyone. They had spent many hours among the trees of the Forest around their home in search of answers to the unspoken questions around their mother's illness.

As they stood in silence in front of the Ancient One, Doug finally spoke.

"I trust you implicitly; I'll meet whomever you feel can help." He turned to Ruth and gave her a bear hug.

"Ties that Bind!" he said. "Now, Let's get back to your place. You have your man to meet and I need to get to my family. Just say when, and I'll go with you to meet your special friend."

Once they had returned to her home, Ruth went into her office and came out with a piece of paper that she handed to Doug.

"It's the old woman's address, in case you would prefer to go alone. Trust yourself. And, crazy as it may seem, I do not know her name."

He looked puzzled. "You don't know her name? That does seem odd, but apparently it works." He gave her one more hug.

"Thanks again, Sis, for seeing me on the fly, and for spending your entire Sunday catching up." He smiled and shoved the paper into his coat pocket.

"Ditto, my sweet little brother!" said Ruth, returning his smile. "I'll be in touch with you in a few weeks."

Ruth gave Rick a call after Doug had left. He answered on the third ring.

"Hey, Babe, how are you doing?"

"It's been one of the best days of my life, Rick, and it started with you. And," she added with lightness in her voice, "I'd like it to end with you."

"I'll be right over," he said, his heart about to burst.

Within twenty minutes he knocked on the door, and Ruth greeted him with a tight hug. She didn't want to let go, and he held her as long as she wanted. He had waited a very long time for this moment.

She loosened her hug and pulled back just enough to see his face and still have him in her arms.

"Ties that Bind, Rick, *Ties that Bind!*"

The Compass

The morning was picture perfect. A crisp, cool breeze filled the air with the scent of autumn, and blue skies provided a backdrop for the yellow, orange and brown leaves that adorned the trees along the street in front of Ruth's apartment. She went out to the patio with a mug of coffee and her red journal and placed them on the small table next to her lounge chair.

Several weeks had passed since the flurry of visits that had brought many changes to her life. She seemed to experience transitions every day, and barely had time to take a deep breath and to simply be in the moment.

It's been well over a month since I've heard from either Doug or Jim.

She picked up a light blanket from the lounge chair and wrapped it snuggly around her shoulders, then sat down to enjoy the sounds of early morning. She sighed as she wiggled into a comfortable position, and she smiled a heartfelt smile.

"Ahhh, fall is my very favorite time of the year." She gazed across the skyline.

It's wonderful to have an abundance of love in my life; my heart is very happy! And, it's also good to have a day to myself to absorb it all.

After a few sips of coffee, she retrieved the journal and opened it to the tatted chain. She touched the delicate chain tenderly as she recalled the first day she had met the old woman.

My life felt so uncertain then; I had no idea what the unrelenting nudge in my belly was trying to tell me. All I knew was that things felt out of sorts, like something was missing.

She thought a bit more. "No, not missing, but simply getting my attention. That nudge let me know that it was time for a change in my life."

That was it; that perfectly described what that unnerving feeling had been nudging her toward. It was time for something new to come into her life, and something old needed to be released to make room for the new. A visit to the old woman had helped her open the door to a deeper understanding.

She admired the scenery in front of her. The rich, vibrant colors of fall brought life to everything. Nature provided her a different perspective on literally everything in her life, and it always brought comforting guidance to her heart.

"This crazy head of mine can find more ways to waste my precious time than to actually find a manageable solution. Just thinking about it wears me out!" She sighed, picked up her journal, and began to read some of her scribbling.

Geez, I must have been writing by candlelight. I can barely read my own words.

Her eyes quickly scanned the first page. Nothing grabbed her attention, so she proceeded to the next page.

"There it is, *The King*."

This is where the old woman described each of the directions.

She flipped through the pages of the journal, and stopped.

Oh, I just had a great idea!

She got up and went to her office to retrieve a bright yellow spiral notebook and a purple pen from her desk. As she closed the drawers, her eyes caught movement in the picture window that faced northwest.

"Wait; maybe this is the room I need to be in while I take down a few notes? No, I think I'll take advantage of the outdoors and use the patio until it's too cold to sit out there." Brilliant gold and red leaves on the tree outside the window began to sway with the rhythm of the morning breeze. The Standing Ones seemed to indicate that they would appreciate her presence, and would reciprocate by supporting her work in whatever way they could.

Ruth stared at the magnificent display and smiled.

Thank you; I hear you and accept your offer.

"Such a sweet life; how in the world have I lived almost thirty-four years and not truly seen the beauty that is right in front of me?" She shook her head as she picked up her notebook and pen and headed back to the patio.

"Oh, I must be kind to myself!" Her eyes surveyed the beauty around her. "Ever since I was a small girl I have loved the abundant rich colors of fall, the massive mounds of leaves, and the crispness of the air. Reckon I am just learning about the depth of their beauty."

She opened the notebook, picked up the pen, and began her journey. She drew a large circle on the page, then drew two straight diagonal lines inside the circle that crossed in the center.

"That looks good, like four large pieces of a pie."

She wrote "East" just outside the piece of the pie on the right. She then moved clockwise around the circle and wrote "South, West, and North" respectively, until all four sections had been labeled.

She began to fill in the open pieces with notes she had taken that pertained to each of the directions. After about an hour and a half, she had transferred into the circle as much information from her journal as she had about each direction.

"I think that's enough for today."

I must get back to see the old woman.

The air was beginning to warm up, and her tummy was letting her know that it was time to feed it. Her head was taken care of for awhile, so she put the notebook and journal on the side table.

"Oh, my body is ready to move!"

She stood up, stretched, and glanced down at the busy street.

"It's good to see humans moving around. And, yet, I need to be in the silence of the woods, very soon."

She pulled out her cell phone and called Jim as she entered into the kitchen to feed her belly. Jim picked up after three rings.

"Hey, Ruth, Sarah and I were just talking about you and Rick."

"Oh, is that right? That must be why my ears were burning!" she giggled. "I'll get to the point. Are you interested in making a trip to the cabin with me?"

"Interesting, Sarah and I were talking about that as well! I'm very ready to accompany you to our Teacher's cabin."

She smiled. *Teacher! That's precisely what she is!*

"Great! Is today too soon, or do you need a couple of days?"

Why do I always leave decisions to the other person? Why do I try to fit into another person's schedule over my own? Enough!

"Before you answer that, Jim, I work 12-hour shifts the next two days, so my next opportunity would be Saturday or Sunday."

"Thanks, that's good to know; hang on a minute." Jim turned to Sarah and Ruth heard only the sound of muffled voices.

"I can make today happen," said Jim. "What time works for you, and do you want me to pick you up?"

She glanced at the time on her phone. "I can be ready in about forty-five minutes, and how about I drive this time? I can be at your house around noonish."

"Perfect! I'll see you about noonish. I like that word," he laughed. "It makes being late an option!"

"Hey, you men do that, too," she teased.

"Oh, I know that. My, my, we're a bit sensitive this morning!" he snickered. "I wouldn't begin to say anything about a woman that wasn't kind.

I've certainly learned to appreciate a good woman. They're like good men, few and far between! So, does that make everything good?"

She chuckled. "Hey, I've worked in a hospital for a very long time, and I've learned to simply let people talk and not take any of their words personally. But, enough; I need to get ready. I look forward to catching up with you. Give Sarah my best."

"Sounds good! I'll see you in a bit."

Ruth placed half an English muffin in the toaster, and pulled a saucer from the cabinet. When the muffin was done, she spread it with honey, and took it to the bedroom to eat while she dressed.

I've actually missed seeing the old woman. She's changed so much since the first time I met her. Somehow, I have a hunch she's needed some visitors. She never talks about her family; however, I know she must have family.

Her thoughts began to weave a story about her Teacher's life.

I know she was raised in an old-fashioned Christian home, that she was in education for many years, and that she has grandchildren. That means she has, or had, children. In any case, her past has certainly made her one wise woman.

Ruth grabbed a heavy jacket, stocking cap and gloves, and set them on the bed. She quickly brushed her hair as she continued to speculate.

She picked up her pace, grabbed her purse, and double-checked that everything was in place.

Let's see, am I forgetting anything?

Then she had a sudden intuitive hit.

For some reason, I feel compelled to take my hair comb with me!

Baffled that the thought had come out of nowhere, she nonetheless trusted her instincts and retrieved the comb from her bedroom.

She felt tenderness for her grandmother as she held the comb in her hand for a moment before twisting up her hair and securing it in place with the comb.

Don't know why my grandmother is still such a vital piece of my heart.

"And, it doesn't matter. I'm just very grateful to have had such a wonderful, wise woman to show me what unconditional love looked and felt like!"

I'll bet the old woman's grandchildren feel that way about her, too.

She zipped down the stairs, unlocked her car, buckled up and started the engine.

"Oh, yeah, the old woman had a very powerful and wise teacher. That is for certain. Guess I know more about her than I realized."

The conversation in the car was lively as the two new friends shared all that had happened since they had last seen each other nearly a month ago. Jim asked how Rick was doing, and told Ruth how much both he and his wife felt that she and Rick were a good match.

He also shared how their children liked both of them. Then he told her that all three kids had said the two of them would be great parents.

The innocent observation of three young children that she and Rick would be good parents gave her a lump in her throat. She caught her breath.

Oh, out of the mouth of babes! Such honest and Truthful words spoken from the purity of young hearts.

As they rounded the last leg of the road to the old woman's cabin, Ruth slowed down, then turned into the parking area that led to the walking path to the cabin. They got out of the car, and Ruth paused at the entrance to the path.

"What a magnificent sight. How I love this place!" She deeply inhaled the smell of the Forest. The crisp autumn air was filled with the scent of harvested corn, soybeans, and freshly baled hay. The leaves on the trees were abundantly rich in color, which further added to the fullness and warmth of the harvest experience.

Not a word was spoken as Jim led the way along the meandering path through the beauty of the Forest, and toward the clearing to the old woman's cabin. Then Jim turned to Ruth.

"There she is, waiting for us to appear. What do you want to bet she already knew we were on our way?"

Ruth smiled. "Oh, I'm confident of that!"

She moved around Jim and picked up the pace, and within a few moments they stood at the steps of the front porch. The old woman didn't look up; she was focused on tie knotting a quilt on her lap.

"It's good to see you, my friend," said Jim. "It appears you're busy making something to keep you or someone you know warm this winter."

She grinned. "You're welcome to join me."

Ruth and Jim moved to the willow chairs, and absorbed the beauty of the surrounding trees. They watched critters hurriedly scamper around the front yard with grace and speed, their cheeks bulging with acorns, hickory nuts and walnuts. They were clearly focused on their tasks; that is, to ensure that their winter stocks were safely and securely stored before the first snowfall.

Ruth glanced over at the old woman and broke the silence.

"It's good to be here. You look well."

The old woman nodded and placed the quilt beside her on the swing.

"I've been very well, thank you. Would you two like to share some hot cocoa and whatever else I can muster up in the kitchen?"

"Why, certainly," Jim piped up. "What can I do to help?"

Ruth's eyes sparkled as she shook her head and grinned at him as if to say, "Always thinking of food, aren't you?"

Jim returned her smile and stood up to extend his hand to their Teacher. She received his hand and carefully got up from the swing.

"Thank you. These old bones have been sitting too long!"

"What can I do to help?" asked Ruth.

"You can relax and enjoy the scenery," responded Jim. "We'll be right back." Then he and the old woman entered the cabin.

Ruth imagined what it would be like to raise children in such an amazing place. She could picture two, maybe three children running about the yard, chasing each other until they fell onto the ground from exhaustion and laughter.

I wonder what our children will look like? Wonder how many children Rick would like to have?

"*I'm very happy with your thoughts,*" her heart seemed to say, which brought an even broader smile to her face.

"*Usually you're giving me the devil for thinking too much! I'm grateful that happy thoughts seem to be in the forefront these days, and that it pleases you, my faithful heart.*"

She stared straight ahead and thought of her notes from earlier in the morning.

This is the South direction, the place of childlike innocence, forgiveness, and not taking life too seriously. Hmmm, little wonder I'm thinking of children.

Her heart was so full that she didn't want the moment to end when Jim and the old woman returned. Her natural instinct was to stand up and help in some way, but she seemed to be fused to the seat of her chair.

Okay, I understand. Things are changing, and I need to cooperate. New ways are welcome!

That's what she told herself, despite how uncomfortable she felt.

"Sugar cookies," Jim whispered to Ruth. "Wait until you taste these! I already sampled one in the kitchen." He pressed his lips together with childlike anticipation and delight, thrilled to let her know what delicious treats awaited their indulgence.

She chuckled to herself as she watched Jim allow the "little boy within" to be so excited.

No doubt Rick would be just as thrilled. Oh, how very much I love that man!

As the three of them enjoyed hot cocoa and absolutely delicious sugar cookies, Ruth glanced to her left, just past the old woman.

Speaking of changes, that's the East, the direction of new beginnings and new opportunities. I'm ready ... bring it on!

Ruth looked at the old woman, and broke the silence.

"I retrieved my journal yesterday, and read through my feelings about the significant teachings you shared the first time I visited you. I'd intended to learn more about the four sacred directions *The King honored each day, only to let that intention fall along the wayside."

Jim sat back in his chair and listened intently. He had never chatted with Ruth about her first experience with the old woman. After she mentioned the four directions she had his full attention. Although he had made many visits to the cabin over the years, and had heard the old woman mention the directions countless times, he had never asked her to elaborate. Ruth had now opened that door.

The old woman placed her cup and saucer on the small table beside her and picked up the black bag that held her tatting. She carefully removed the shuttle and ball of thread and began to create a series of the fancy loops that made up her chains.

"I am curious," said Ruth, "if you would be willing to share what you know about the key elements *The King called to each morning? I believe it was the four directions, but whatever it was that helped him to keep peace and harmony in his community."

The old woman paused her tatting and looked at Ruth for a few moments before responding.

"My experience has shown that the best way to learn is first-hand."

She carefully placed the very small beginnings of a chain back into the black bag and carefully stood up. She then noticed that Jim had finished his snack.

Looks like Jim's ready.

"To be clear," she continued, "there are actually seven sacred directions. Let's start where life begins."

She stepped off the front porch and moved to her left, which was the East side of the yard. They walked around and behind the perennial garden that had by now been prepared for the cold months ahead.

The old woman led the way into the Forest, and stepped onto a well-trodden footpath. Within about five feet they stood in front of a reddish boulder that glistened from the light filtering through the Standing Ones behind them in the West.

Jim and Ruth stared wide-eyed at the massive stone. It was an absolutely amazing rock that was obviously foreign to their region. It looked like something one would find in Colorado or Utah, or someplace where massive, red-hued stones existed. It looked completely out of place here, and they wondered how in the world the old woman had managed to get it onto her land. They both hoped to learn more about many such mysteries that were a part of this woman.

Do I ask? Jim wondered.

"No, it's time to simply listen," responded his heart.

You got it; the "ears" of my heart are open!

The old woman walked up to the boulder and placed her hand directly over the top, then bent over and touched the Earth for a few moments. She straightened up, touched her heart, and lifted her hands to the sky in the East.

"Welcome, Spirits of the East. We stand before you and request your teachings of new beginnings, new choices, and new ways of being. We know that you offer us the gift to choose something new, and that in order to receive that gift we must release what no longer serves us. We know if we pay attention you will show us new options for moving through life and new ways to see and live in Truth.

"We thank you, Eagle and Condor, for offering your backs for us to ride on high in the sky, so that we may see the big picture and not get caught up in the details about how to figure things out with our human minds." She placed her hands back on her heart.

"We stand before you, prepared to listen with the 'ears' of our hearts, in order to learn and to experience the sacredness of life. I call to you and ask for assistance in guiding Jim and Ruth as they learn what it means to walk the Sacred Wheel of Life. May my hands and my heart always be of service for the greater good of Earth Mother and all of her inhabitants."

She took a pinch of tobacco from a pouch around her neck, leaned over and touched the Earth again. "Thank you, Spirits of the East. Thank you!"

The ceremony felt like an initiation of sorts to the teachings of the sacred directions, and Jim and Ruth felt completely humbled by their Teacher's words. She turned toward them.

"This sacred stone was a gift from my Teacher. 'Let this be your anchor to the East,' he said, 'and a reminder that we have many beginnings and endings throughout our lives. When we begin with a solid and sturdy foundation, that energy will carry us forward. The teachings of the East assist us with those cycles of beginnings and endings, until we return to the stars.'"

Jim and Ruth followed her back into the yard, to the Magnificent Old Oak that towered in the South. When she was directly in front of the Old Oak, she placed her hand over an unusually shaped knothole.

Using the pointer finger of her right hand, she touched an indentation at the top of the knothole. She slowly moved her finger around the knothole until she returned back to the top, and repeated this action six times. By the end of the seventh time around, the knothole was clearly heart-shaped. She then brought her finger from the top center of the heart straight down to the center of her own heart, and tapped it seven times.

"Spirits of the South, with grateful hearts we call to you to guide us through this journey. We ask for your teachings about how to reclaim the gifts of faith, trust, and unconditional love that we knew as children. Help us to have the resilience of a youthful spirit that offers forgiveness to others, and to ourselves, so that we learn to take responsibility for our lives.

"Help us to reclaim the playfulness of youth and to not take life too seriously. May we regain the ability to laugh at the silliness of some of our choices. May we be gentle and kind to others as well as to ourselves.

"We call to the Dolphin that moves through the waters with grace and ease, and ask that we learn how to move through our emotions in such a loving and gentle manner. And, to Mouse, we ask for assistance in noticing the details of our lives, while not getting trapped into the intricacies of our thinking minds that can confine us to our human understanding. She took another pinch of tobacco from her pouch, leaned over and placed the tobacco on the ground. She concluded, 'We thank you for these gifts, Spirits of the South.'"

The air became brisk as leaves quickly fell to the ground as though the Sky Nation had showered them with the colorful beauty of fall to acknowledge that their prayers had been heard.

Jim and Ruth stood in respectful silence and waited for their Teacher to make the next move. Within a few moments, the old woman took a few deep breaths and sighed. Then she stepped back into the Forest and moved toward the West side of the cabin, just past the cobblestone walking path, and they stepped through the thick foliage of the Forest, hearing only the crunching sounds of fallen leaves.

Suddenly, much to Jim's and Ruth's surprise, a tarp that covered something mysteriously appeared out of nowhere. Jim was amazed that in all the visits he had made over the years he had never noticed this. While it was a bit off the path to the cabin, it would have been hard to miss, especially during the winter months when the trees were barren.

The old woman stood directly in front of the tarp, then lowered herself to her knees and placed her forehead on the ground.

"Welcome, Spirits of the West," she said softly. "We humbly acknowledge your presence on this land, and ask that you hear the prayers of our hearts."

She raised her head and carefully pulled the front of the tarp back to reveal a very small lean-to. She brushed away a few leaves from the piece of plastic that served as a floor, then turned around and crawled backwards into the makeshift cave. It was a tiny structure, but a perfect size for her to face out to the Forest in prayer.

"You already know our hearts, and we know that you offer a place for us to come when it is time to truly understand and listen to the 'voices' of our hearts. We honor the feminine energies of knowing that come from the West, and we acknowledge those gifts that will guide us through this Earthly experience.

"We thank you, Bear, for showing us the importance of taking time to hibernate from the busyness of human life, and to listen to what the silence has to share from the quiet spaces of our hearts. We thank you for showing us how to make ourselves big, and yet to remain gentle. And, to remember that no matter what is happening in our lives, Mother's womb is always available, for it is from there we will find our connection to all that is true and real."

She leaned forward and moved out of the makeshift cave on her hands and knees, then leaned forward and kissed the ground. She retrieved tobacco from her pouch, and lifted the tobacco and her face to the heavens.

"We offer this tobacco as a token of our respect for Grandfather Sun, as he holds the masculine energy of action during the day, and disappears into the West at night. We know he does this out of respect for the feminine gifts of intuition, knowing, and deep emotions that Grandmother Moon offers. Her presence reminds us that everything in life is in transition from one phase to another." She then placed the tobacco on the ground in front of the makeshift cave.

"We thank you, Buffalo, for the gift of abundance and prayers." She looked upward. "Thank you, Spirits of the West, thank you."

Jim and Ruth silently stepped together over to their Teacher and stood on each side of her. Jim extended his hand to his Teacher, and the old woman looked up, smiled, and firmly grasped his hand. Ruth reached down and gently held the old woman's forearm and elbow, and together they helped their Teacher get to her feet.

"Thank you!" She turned toward the North and led the way through the Forest to a large Cedar tree behind the wooden shed in her back yard. As they approached the Tall Standing One, Ruth noticed something shiny halfway up the tree.

What is that? She squinted her eyes to get a clear view of the object. *I have no idea!*

Jim followed Ruth's gaze, and almost immediately, the old woman turned and looked at both of them.

They both glanced down at her, as though they were in trouble. The old woman smiled; she knew they had discovered the hidden treasure on the Cedar and were probably wondering what it was. However, she continued her ritual, as she held up her hands and raised her eyes toward the heavens.

"Spirits of the North, we call to you Wisdom Keepers, to those of you who have walked this Sacred Path and learned how to be sacred human beings. We thank you for sharing the ancient ceremonies and traditions that helped communities before us live in harmony with All Their Relations. May we strengthen our own communities by honoring these ancient ways, so that we, too, may respect and live in harmony with All Our Relations.

"We call to the white furry ones and the white feathered ones, and we thank you for freely sharing the stories of our ancestors to those of us that call to you for guidance along this Sacred Walk. Hear the prayers of our hearts as we present ourselves as instruments through whom the mysteries of life may be shared here on Earth Mother.

"It is with gratitude that we acknowledge the wisdom you so freely share, and ask that you help us to connect to the North Star that guides our lives. We thank you for your unrelenting faith and trust in us as we move along this Sacred Wheel of Life.

"We bless our Ancestors, the seven generations behind us, and the seven generations that will follow us, that we may be strong links in the ancestral chain. May we be good stewards of the rich abundance given to us every single day. We thank you, Spirits of the North, we thank you!"

The old woman lowered her eyes and walked about six feet from the Cedar tree, and past the woodshed. She stopped in front of a copper disk about three feet in diameter that was secured by a large stone.

Jim and Ruth followed behind her while keeping a respectful distance from their Teacher, so as not to intrude on her personal space. They knew this was sacred work; she was the Teacher and they were the students.

The old woman once again pulled tobacco from the pouch around her neck and sprinkled a small amount on the ground as she walked clockwise around the disk. When she had completed the circle, she removed the stone, revealing a small handle that was snuggly tucked within the copper.

She placed the stone on the ground and pulled up on the handle to lift off the copper top, and set it to the side. Buried about four inches within the ground was a small, primitive, stone fire ring.

Jim and Ruth felt they stood at a threshold in time and space, as though the very land they stood on was electrified by a mystical, magical sense of reality. They knew that what they witnessed was real; yet, they felt as though they were in a time warp. The stones around the fire ring were aged from the elements of nature, and the inside edges of the stones were blackened from the many fires it had held.

I wonder, thought Ruth, *how many people have held ceremony around this fire ring?*

Jim was having similar thoughts.

How have I not noticed that copper cap before? Or, for that matter, that good sized stone?

Then a brilliant orange reflected from the copper piece as Grandfather Sun moved further down the western sky.

It's as though the flames from many fires have embedded various hues of orange into the cap, he thought.

The old woman stepped into the center of the fire ring; the fit was perfect! She turned and looked up at the shiny object affixed to the Cedar tree. From where Jim and Ruth stood, the shiny piece now looked like an oval mirror, or some sort of reflecting metal. As Grandfather Sun moved further down in the West, the object appeared to become more muted.

Ahhh, thought Jim, *it was the reflection from the sun that made it look so shiny. I wonder what that is all about?*

The old woman again took a pinch of tobacco out of her pouch, looked upward, and raised her hand toward the sky.

"We call to you, White Buffalo Calf Woman; we thank you for listening to Great Spirit, and for courageously bringing forth the teaching of the Sacred Pipe to the community."

She slowly lowered her hand in a diagonal line from the object in the Cedar tree to where she stood in the center of the fire ring, and placed the tobacco at her feet.

Jim gasped. *Oh my gosh! She's standing in the bowl of the Sacred Pipe!*

Then she stepped out of the fire ring and very methodically walked around it seven times.

After the seventh round, she bent down and touched the Earth, brought her hands to her heart, and again raised her hands to the sky.

"We call to the great Above, and we thank you, Sky Nation, for witnessing our ceremony today. We thank you for your steadfast presence and constant reminder that we are part of something so much bigger than we can imagine. And, that while we are very small and insignificant, what we do is of great importance here on Earth Mother.

"As Above," she said with her hands still raised, "so Below," as she bent over to touch the Earth, then dropped to her knees.

Ruth sensed what they were to do, and lowered herself to her knees beside her Teacher. Jim followed suit as the ceremony concluded.

"We humbly acknowledge that which is Below, and we thank you, Earth Mother, for the abundant riches that you provide. We ask that you guide us as we tend to the needs of humans and nonhumans that reside on your body. May our hearts be ever present to the love from which we came, and to which we will return. We honor your gifts of unconditional love, forgiveness, and resilience, to all that we confront while in human form. May we stay awake and live our lives with clear intention and purpose and, to consciously choose to be of service to All Our Relations."

She touched her heart. "We respectfully acknowledge the beauty Within; the place of our hearts.

"We ask that these gifts from all of the sacred directions, along with our constant guidance, help us to re-member that we are all part of the same family, and that we are all birthed from the Eternal Flame of Love. May we see our reflections in all human and nonhumans who reside here, Earth Mother.

"May we courageously look within the Great Smoking mirror at the illusions of our own personal myths. Help us to remove the smoke screen that hides our natural talents and our worth, and to develop those areas, that we may be of service to All Our Relations. May we stop cowering before our potential and live into our Truth."

The old woman paused.

"In lak'ech AlaK'in!"

What does that mean? Jim wondered.

The old woman glanced at Jim, then moved her eyes toward the heavens.

"We thank you, our Mayan brothers and sisters, for that simple phrase that reminds us to see our own reflections in every set of eyes that we look into and, with a spirit of love, to honor the Sacred Walk of each person we encounter. Help us to fully realize that we are more alike than different and that, in Truth, we are not separate from each other."

"Ask and it shall be given." Jim's heart whispered as joy filled his entire being.

She continued, "We thank you, dragonfly, for helping us to break the illusions we humans have created and, like the winged ones, to take flight into the world of possibilities. And, like the butterfly, may we transform outwardly into that which is already within us."

The old woman tapped Jim on the leg; he opened his eyes and she reached for his hand. Ruth then opened her eyes and straightened herself as she reached over to take the old woman's other arm. Together she and Jim helped their Teacher get to her feet and, once she was up, she looked upward and raised her right hand to the sky and made a complete circle above her head.

"Like the Standing Ones, may our roots grow deep into you, Earth Mother, that we might have a sturdy base from which we can always reach for the heavens. May we weather the actions of unaware humans, and do as you and all the nonhumans do: hold steady, be flexible, and trust All Our Relations to guide and support us.

"*Aho, Mitakuye Oyasin*, it is with tremendous gratitude that we thank the sacredness of these teachers within our hearts, that we may embody them in everything we think, say and do."

In that moment, only the sounds of the wind and the nonhumans could be heard. A flock of geese appeared from the North, and flew overhead toward the South in perfect V formation, as a sign that all the creature teachers had heard the old woman's prayers. Life at that moment was in perfect harmony.

The old woman brought her hand down and placed it on her heart. The three of them stood in the stillness of the moment and simply allowed the flow of the seven sacred directions to envelope their presence, to bless the land, and to carry the songs of their hearts back into the world of the Great Mystery.

The air had cooled with Grandfather Sun's descent toward the horizon just above the tops of the tall Standing Ones. The stillness of the Forest was now alive as squirrels, rabbits, and a flurry of chipmunks hurried to their homes before the air became cold. The old woman looked at Ruth on her right and Jim on her left.

"I think we're about done here," she said. "There's just one thing left to do."

She reached for the copper lid and gingerly placed it back on top of the fire ring. She replaced the stone on top, then looked at Jim and smiled.

"What do you say we get something to eat?"

"Just lead the way!" exclaimed Jim with a broad smile.

Ruth giggled. *That man is one eating machine. I can only imagine what their grocery bill is like! I wonder if Rick's that way when he's not around me?*

The thoughts were no more out of her head when her belly flipped.

Oops, those butterflies she spoke of just took flight in my belly! Looking forward to seeing my fella this evening … hopefully!

They entered into the old woman's cabin through the utility room, where the old woman retrieved an abalone shell, sage, and matches from a cabinet just above the dryer. She proceeded to light the sage and placed it into the abalone shell.

"We need to smudge ourselves to rebalance, cleanse, and purify our energy. This we do to show respect and gratitude for the sacredness of all things, including the space within our homes."

She drew the smoke toward her with both hands until she felt enveloped in love. She then picked up the shell and moved toward Ruth, who also moved the smoke over her head and down her body with her hands, as though she had performed this ceremony all her life. She joined her hands in prayer position and made a quick bow to her Teacher to show respect, then moved aside for Jim to step forward.

The old woman looked up at Jim with a tender smile and nodded to him; he knew it was his turn to participate. He repeated the ritual he had observed from Ruth and his Teacher, then placed his hands over the shell, closed his eyes and bowed his head.

May my heart be completely cleansed of all impurities, and may my hands be evidence of my commitment to learning these ways.

Tears filled the old woman's eyes, and her heart felt alive. This was something she had not shared with anyone in many years. Once again, she felt the love of a community in which Truth reigned. Her heart was warmed.

The abalone shell now held only a small amount of smoke, and the old woman took it into the kitchen and placed it on the stove to smudge the room as it smoldered out.

She turned to Jim. "How does chamomile tea and pumpkin bread sound?" she asked. "Or, do you need something more substantial?"

"Pumpkin bread sounds very appropriate for this time of year." He glanced over at Ruth. "Does that sound good to you?"

"Oh, heck, yeah, I love pumpkin pie, cookies, cake, and bread!" She looked at the old woman. "How can I help?"

"You can get saucers and cups out of the cabinet," she said, and then turned to Jim. "And, you can put napkins, forks, and a butter dish from the fridge on the wooden tray, while I take care of the tea and bread."

Within fifteen minutes, Jim held the very full tray.

"Where are we going to devour this treat?"

She nodded toward the front door.

"The porch it is!" he exclaimed.

Once everyone was seated, the old woman placed her hands over the tray and whispered, "Thank you for our abundance; may we be instruments through which love flows."

Colorful leaves began to fall to the Earth as the cool winds of the North reminded them that the meetings on the porch were numbered.

"We're certainly fortunate to have such a lovely day to enjoy one of the last few days on the porch," said Ruth. "And, I have a question about the ceremony today; is now a good time?"

"Now is always a good time. We'll need to be brief, though, since Grandfather is descending in the western sky."

Ruth considered her question for a moment.

"Just to be certain, Above, Below, and Within are the three additional directions of which you spoke earlier. Is that correct?"

The old woman nodded.

"I would also like to ask if I have your permission to bring my brother to meet you?" added Ruth.

The old woman looked up from her cup. "Your brother is welcome to visit; however, it's best that he makes his first trip alone."

Of course, that makes sense; it takes courage to make the trip by one's self.

She had to smile; somehow, she had known to give her brother the old woman's address.

"Thank you." She thought about asking for a good date and time, and then realized that she hadn't had an appointment the first time she had come. For that matter, she and Jim just dropped in today.

Jim offered both ladies more tea, and filled their cups when they nodded affirmatively.

"I, too, have several questions," he said. "However, I've learned that if I wait, you'll answer them without my need to ask." With a grin, "You did that a few moments ago."

The old woman nodded, then pulled a small black bag from her shirt pocket. She carefully untied the string, opened the pouch, and pulled out her gold Compass.

Jim and Ruth observed her reverence for this beautiful gold object, and eagerly waited to see what it was. Jim then reached into his own pocket and retrieved the cat's eye marble he had received from the old woman.

Ruth felt a nudge, and she knew it was her turn. She had no idea why, but she reached behind her head and pulled out the comb, allowing her hair to fall around her shoulders. She held the silver and pearl hair comb in her hand.

"We all have our sacred reminders," said the old woman. "Generally, they are gifts from someone who may not have even realized just how precious the gift would become.

"Nonetheless, the gift was a token that represented a piece of that person's heart. Something that said 'I see you!' It is in those moments and through those random acts of kindness that we are given the nudge we need, to trust, to move forward, and to 'Follow the Snake' until we find whatever it is time for us to discover."

She looked at Jim. "The red line that runs through your gift represents the Love that entwines all things in the universe. It was given to me by my Teacher, and it is now ready to work with you."

She flipped the gold stem at the top of the object in her hand, and revealed the face of the Compass.

"Remember what moved you today. Take the time to recall what you can of the gifts of each of the seven sacred directions, and know this for certain: they *will* guide you throughout your life, *if* you stay awake."

She stood up, closed the front of the Compass, placed it back into its bag and returned it to her shirt pocket.

"These are my words."

Jim returned his cat's eye marble to his pocket, then stood and picked up the tray. He held it out to Ruth, who placed her cup on the tray, then pulled her hair behind her head, twisted it, and carefully reinserted the comb.

Jim turned and held the tray in front of his Teacher. She carefully rearranged a few items on the tray before securely adding her own cup.

She slowly rose from the swing and led the way to the front door, and held it open for Jim. Once in the kitchen he set the tray on the countertop next to the sink, and began to run hot water to wash the dishes. Ruth and the old woman entered behind him, and within ten minutes all the dishes were washed and put away, and the tray cleaned up and stored.

Jim was the first to ask if he could hug the old woman, and as she reached up to hug him, Ruth waited her turn. Then she hugged her and said, "Thank you for another glorious day. I have much to remember and to reflect upon."

"I second that," said Jim. "I also have much to consider. Thank you! And, are you certain there is nothing else we can do for you before we leave?"

She shook her head. "No, thank you. However, be gentle with yourselves; you heard a lot of information today." She smiled. "Now it's time for me to soak these old bones!"

They exited the kitchen, and the old woman retired to her bedroom. Jim and Ruth went out the front door, closed it snuggly behind them, and each dropped a gift into the twig basket.

Jim led the way down the cobblestone path to the footpath through the Forest. For the first five minutes they walked in silence.

Then Ruth spoke up. "I don't know about you, but it's hard for me to leave. And, yet, I need to be home where I can really let all this settle in."

"I hear that!" exclaimed Jim. "Sometimes I have no idea what to think, let alone what to say. I feel speechless."

"Indeed!" agreed Ruth.

When they were in the car, Ruth pulled out her cell phone.

"Pardon me, Jim, but I need to speak with my brother for just a minute."

"Oh, certainly!"

Doug answered the phone after two rings.

"Hey, Doug, I only have a few minutes, but I wanted to let you know the old woman said it is fine for you to visit her. However, she said it is best that you come by yourself the first time."

"Oh, no problem. You know me, I'm friendly with everyone." He chuckled.

"For sure you are! Do you still have her address or do I need to text it to you again?"

"Nope, I still have the address."

"Oh, and there's a twig basket on her porch that is used for gifts one might bring to show respect for her time. If it's cold, the basket will be just inside the cabin. Anything you feel led to bring she'll appreciate. She's a simple person and not one for knick-knack things, so just something useful. Of course, money is always useful. Or, you might just ask if she needs anything done in exchange for her time.

"Call me tomorrow if you have any questions. I need to get back to my conversation with Jim. We just spent the day with her."

"I understand. I know my big sis, she's always fast-trackin'," he laughed. "You guys have a safe trip home. Thanks for asking. I love you!"

"And, I love you. I'm so excited that you're going to meet her. Oh, and one last thing. You are only allowed to ask her one question. Take care, and give Sue and the kids my best. We must make plans to get together soon!"

"You got it; but wait, what do you mean about one question?" When he was met with silence, he continued, "Never mind, your silence speaks volumes. I'll figure it out. Say 'hi' to your beau for me!"

She ended the call and looked at Jim. "Okay, we're ready to roll! Oh, and Doug called Rick my 'beau,' like you do," she said with a sheepish grin. "I think that's so cute, although it makes me feel old!"

They buckled up for the ride and, after Ruth had pulled onto the main road, Jim let out a robust laugh. "Well, if the shoe fits!"

They both laughed heartily, and then settled in for the drive home. Grandfather was now low in the western sky, adding a brilliant orange and red glow to the horizon.

"Would you look at that sky?" exclaimed Ruth. "It's going to be a beautiful sunset tonight. Maybe we'll be home in time to see it actually set."

"Oh, we will. You don't drive like a Grandma!"

"Glad you like my driving!" she laughed.

Then she glanced at him. "I'm puzzled by the old woman's comment about not asking questions to which we know the answers. Whatever does that mean?"

"It must be a woman thing," responded Jim. "Sarah will make comments seemingly out of nowhere, and it can be quite confusing. Maybe we guys take longer to comprehend.

"You know, Ruth, I'm beginning to understand that comment a little better, and what I know is that you will need to find the meaning of that for yourself. If I tell you, I would be robbing you of your gifts."

She smiled. "Hmmm."

She pulled the car over at the first access road. She looked at Jim, then removed the comb from her hair and held it in her hand.

"Our Teacher had that amazing gold Compass; I wonder...?"

She felt the texture of the ornate shapes of the silver, and the smooth roundness of the pearls on the hair comb. When she stopped moving her fingers, she began to feel the comb almost pulsate in her hand.

"My grandmother gave me this hair comb when I turned thirteen. I wonder if somehow this is *The Compass* for my life?"

A smile spread across Jim's face. "I understand precisely what you are saying." He withdrew the cat's eye marble from his pocket and held it up for Ruth to see.

"I have my Compass right here!"

The Boomerang

"Good grief!" the old woman exclaimed. "I'd nearly forgotten about taking care of the shed out back! Well, I've remembered it now."

She was snuggled up on the porch swing in a warm burgundy sweater, enjoying the crisp, fragrant fall air. She looked at Gracie, who was curled up on the edge of the porch, serenely soaking up the mid-day sun.

"You have the right idea, my friend. Better enjoy the warmth of Grandfather Sun while we still have him. He'll soon be spending a great deal of time behind the clouds during the cold winter months."

She picked up the journal on her lap and flipped through the pages until she found a blank sheet.

"Better put a new journal on my shopping list; this one's almost full." She thought about what else she needed to add to her list.

"Let's see, I need coffee, cat food, and a few extra cans of soup for backups when I feel lazy." She smiled, and said to her practical head, "Yeah, right, I'm lazy!"

She had to chuckle. She had been a go-getter her entire life. She could pack more into a day than anyone in his or her right mind! It was how she managed life. For some reason, she had decided as a very young girl that it was best to do things herself rather than to rely on anyone else to do them for her.

I really don't recall when, or why that started. It just sort of became a way of not feeling beholden to anyone.

"Perhaps I heard my parents talk about that," she mused. "I just remember becoming very determined that no one would ever tell me that I wouldn't be where I am now if it hadn't been for them."

Just then, Tom appeared from the back of the cabin, wagging his tail like a hungry puppy.

"Well, look at you, my skinny friend," said the old woman as she leaned over to pet him. "Where have you been? I guess you've shown up because you're getting yourself ready for winter, too. Yes, we do need to get some meat on those bones before the weather turns cold!"

He closed his eyes happily as she continued to pet his head, and then he headed toward the front door in eager anticipation of a delicious forthcoming meal.

"Just look at you! Are you trying to let me know it's time to get serious and gather you some grub?" She laughed as she stood up and followed close behind him.

"Okay, now you need to scoot aside so I can go inside and get it!"

He seemed to understand her, as he obediently stepped aside. She gave him another pat on the head, then went inside and pulled the leftovers container from the refrigerator.

Tom excitedly licked the drool from his mouth as he waited patiently for her to return. Within five minutes, the old woman was headed toward the door with a dish of leftovers.

Tom stepped back when the old woman returned. Then she placed the dish on the porch, and stood back to give him room to enjoy his feast, which he promptly began to devour.

As she watched Tom nearly inhale the food, she was distracted by the sound of crunching leaves. She looked in the direction of the sound, but couldn't see anyone. However, she knew someone was on the way, so she went into the cabin to brew a fresh pot of coffee.

The coffee was ready within minutes, and a few muffins had been gathered from the breadbox. She looked out the kitchen window and saw that a man of large build, wearing jeans and a bright red hooded sweatshirt, had emerged from the Forest and onto the cobblestone path. She stood on her tiptoes to get a closer look.

He doesn't look familiar, but he'll be here in a few minutes. I'd better set up the tray.

As Doug approached the porch, he spotted the gifting basket that Ruth had mentioned. Then he turned to check out the scenery before stepping up onto the porch.

The sky was clear and the blue backdrop complemented the colorful leaves of the trees that stood tall, reaching for the heavens. He took a few deep breaths to take in the peace and serenity that surrounded the land, and turned when he heard the screen door open.

The old woman pushed open the door with a very large tray. He quickly grabbed the door and held it open with his foot as he reached for the tray.

"Oh, my, let me help you. That tray looks heavy."

He was a very tall, large man, and had a ruddy complexion. She guessed him to be about thirty.

But, I'm no judge of people's ages; everyone looks young to me!

She looked up at him. His eyes sparkled with life, and he had an infectious smile. She extended the tray in acceptance of his offer, then pulled the small table from behind the swing, opened it, and placed it securely between the willow chair and the swing. The gentleman gingerly set the tray on the table and waited for her to take a seat.

The old woman moved the quilt on the swing to one side, and sat down next to the table. She poured a large mug of coffee and extended it to the man, which he received with gusto.

"Thank you!" He blew on it and took a sip. "Mmm, that's good coffee, and hits the spot on this cool morning! Thank you."

She removed the fabric from the top of a basket, revealing blueberry muffins. "Help yourself," she indicated.

His eyes widened. "Those look delicious!"

He placed a muffin on a saucer and carefully balanced it on his lap as he sliced off a generous portion of butter with the butter knife. He smeared the butter on his muffin and took a big bite. His eyes nearly rolled to the back of his head.

"Oh, my goodness! Ruthie never told me I'd be treated to a homemade goodie!"

So, this is Ruth's brother … he didn't waste any time coming here, so he must have something he is ready to find out more about!

She felt warmth in her belly; she loved when people came to sit and chat. And, to observe the looks on their faces as they ate something she had made was the *pièce de résistance*.

The old woman finished her coffee and half a muffin, then pulled her tatting bag out from under the quilt. She wound the thread around her fingers, and a delicate looped chain began to magically appear as she moved the shuttle.

Okay, so I can only ask one question, thought Doug as he watched her. *I'm taking the old woman's silence and busy hands to mean that she's waiting for it.*

The ruminations in his busy head made him chuckle. He was actually glad his mind was wandering; it allowed his senses to take in the beauty within his peripheral vision. From the various types of birds that flew about the sky, to the four-legged critters and magnificent trees and bushes, *everything* was alive!

Peacefulness. Nature shows us first-hand how it looks, feels, and even smells! I love it! He sat back in his chair.

When Gracie saw the man in the red sweatshirt sitting next to her "friend," she sensed the man was kind. Carefully, and very methodically, she moved closer to him. When she was directly in front of him, he placed his saucer and mug on the table, which she took as an invitation. She obliged him and leaped onto his open lap.

The old woman looked up and grinned.

I'll be darned, how unlike Miss Gracie! He's okay, or she wouldn't be in his lap.

She returned to her tatting as Gracie began to purr. Ruth's brother felt comfortable, and knew now was the time to ask his question. He adjusted himself in the chair and looked at the old woman.

"Reckon I'd better get to the reason I'm here."

Gracie jumped down when he squirmed in his chair.

"Oh, I didn't mean to scare you, little friend."

He bent over and patted her on her head. She looked up at him, hesitated, and then hurried over to the porch swing and jumped up onto the quilt next to her dearest friend. She licked her paws and looked over at the visitor before resting her head on the quilt.

"Looks like she's decided she's better off with someone she knows rather than someone she's uncertain about." He remarked.

Can't say as I blame the little cat; better to be safe than sorry.

Clearly, he felt deep concern about the effects his actions had on the lives of others, including Gracie. He watched as the old woman worked on her project. She seemed oblivious to anything else around her. He sat back in his chair again.

A breeze brought a chill, and he reached for the thermos of coffee.

"I'm going to have more coffee. Would you like more?"

She nodded as she put down the tatting and held out her mug. He filled their mugs, and then took a sip.

"You have a fabulous thermos; the coffee's still hot!

She sipped a bit of coffee and wrapped both her hands around the mug as warmth filled her belly.

"Someone gave me this old thermos many years ago, and it has served me well. Thank you for the refill."

Leaves whirled in spirals across the front yard like children scampering around a playground, while others were lifted into the sky and then scattered out like pollen across the yard. It was a colorful display of autumn in its fullest beauty.

Doug wanted to talk about what his heart felt just from observing the rich view. He had not taken time to witness nature at its finest in many years. He always seemed to be too busy; and, whenever he was outside, he was there to fix something or to tend to the yard. It was always about action. Rarely was he outdoors for a time of stillness or silent observation.

He took in a deep breath. "When I'm thinking of others, am I losing, or scattering, my own energy? Are my thoughts or concerns interfering in their lives? Am I snooping into their business?"

Darn, that sounds weird; I didn't say that very well. I sure hope she understands what I'm asking.

"That was really three questions, and they sound a bit confusing. Do you want me to condense them into one question?"

He noticed the white lace chain that had begun to emerge as the old woman quickly moved her fingers. He basked in the energy that filled the air, from the critters who busily prepared for the winter months ahead. Then he looked down at his arm.

It's electrifying! My hair is literally standing on end, and it's not from being cold. It's this absolutely supercharged energy emitted by nature. Just look at those swirling leaves! Simply amazing!

In response to Doug's question, she began her story:

"I recall when my children learned that there is no Santa Claus, and that he is simply a myth. Something of their childlike innocence ceased to exist from that point on. Oh, they enjoyed getting gifts and decorating the house;

however, the excitement they had felt from the belief that someone watched their every move all year, and still found them worthy of gifts, had abated. The realization of that untruth resulted in the first loss of innocence from losing the belief that someone outside the family loved them unconditionally. It opened the door to mistrust, which led to questions and doubts about other stories they had been told.

"The belief in Santa Claus is a family tradition for many families that continues to be passed on. Regardless of a person's age, that childhood belief in a magical, mysterious Santa Claus, peeks through when colorful lights are strung throughout the house, and brightly wrapped gifts are neatly placed under the Christmas tree. And, as the stories behind each of the homemade tree ornaments are retold each year, one can feel a bit of that innocence from childhood seep through; it is proof that those early feelings of generosity, unconditional love and kindness, remain in their hearts."

Doug was mesmerized by the beautiful chain of white thread that emerged from the old woman's hands. He felt frozen in time as bits and pieces of his childhood passed across the movie screen of his mind. Every word she spoke brought forth a picture from his past that offered yet another piece of his unfinished puzzle.

For some reason, I've not been able to remember much from my childhood; maybe because it wasn't that great? At least, that's what I've always surmised.

Gracie jumped off the swing and leaped back into Doug's lap. He smiled and began to pet her as the old woman continued her story.

"Everything that exists is energy and, while it is often difficult to understand, that *is* the very essence of life. What we hold in our hearts to be true is demonstrated in our words and deeds.

"I heard a saying many years ago that has always stuck in my brain: 'it's not about what you do, but about the energy with which you do it.' In essence, it is evidence of what you hold to be true. It is the belief we hold that is important.

"Most of that energy is invisible to our eyes and ears, but we can feel it. All too often we go through our daily routines and chores never thinking about how our thoughts, words, or actions may affect our own lives, let alone someone else's. Or, for that matter, what other energies are emitted around us that influence our lives."

She looked at Doug. "Is this making sense, Ruth's brother?"

He blushed. "I guess I didn't tell you my name. I'm Doug."

"Nice to meet you, Doug," she said as she resumed her tatting.

"I can tell you're a kind person. Not just because you thoughtfully offered me coffee; or, because you are wearing a bright red sweatshirt, which indicates that you are a bold person; or, that you smiled and looked me directly in the eyes when you spoke. I know it because Gracie jumped into your lap. She's picky, very intuitive, and has a keen sense of awareness.

"Animals have a natural sense about humans; they can tell whether or not someone is kind, and they have an innate ability to *feel* someone out. Animals use all of their senses. They can smell emotions, danger, or forthcoming weather, for example, and they trust what their senses tell them. They do not question, doubt, or second-guess what they sense. And, that innate, natural ability is present in every human, as well.

"If you judge someone or talk behind their back, that toxic energy will boomerang back to you at some time and place, either through another person or through your own critical, self-doubting voice. When someone comes into your thoughts, check in with your gut to see if a phone call or text might be appropriate. If you are uncertain, simply send a prayer their way. Just make certain that it is a prayer from your heart and not from your head, which often worries and frets.

"Heart energy is sent through the ethers as love, and the natural world knows how to send it to the recipient in a more powerful way than we can! It's that voice of doubt in our head that keeps us trapped!"

She glanced up from her tatting. "Seems we have an abundance of judges, jurors, psychiatrists and psychologists, who analyze, label, and find guilt, without even knowing the Truth. That, Doug, is *Meddling* in someone else's life, and it will boomerang back to us. It's best we mind our own business, and take whatever we notice about someone else into the quiet space of our heart.

"A Christmas movie years ago had a line that best describes the differences in how people view life. An adult commented, 'Seeing is believing,' to which the young child responded, 'No, believing is seeing.'

"Humans need to recapture the childlike innocence of trust we had as children, and to remember that something bigger, more powerful, loving and kind, can deliver the treasures of our hearts in Divine timing. We must merely hold the space of knowing, then stay out of the way and trust!"

She scanned the Forest and settled her eyes on the Old Oak.

"Trust. Those Standing Ones know how to trust. They stay rooted in the Earth, reach for the sky, and move with the flow of the wind. Whatever the natural order of life brings to the Standing Ones, they remain flexible. They live in the moment, and have a natural confidence in their innate ability to move with all of life.

"Just as important, they live in relationship with the other trees around them, as well as with the critters that inhabit their environment. They do not judge, criticize, or compare; they simply live in the moment with All Their Relations."

She looked at Doug and smiled sweetly.

"Can you imagine what the world would be like if we very important humans lived that way? What a different life we would have if we regained the spirit of Christmas and lived from that Truth. I dream of that, Doug, I dream of that."

She tied a knot at the end of her thread, and bit the thread to detach it from the shuttle.

"Pay attention to your instincts, trust your gut, listen to the 'voice' of your heart, and cease the chatter in your head." She rose from the swing and handed the tatted chain to Doug.

"Remember that boomerang! Love every single moment of your life. Trust yourself, and know that whatever happens is what you have chosen. If it doesn't bring you joy, change it. The Truth is, only *you* are responsible for everything in your life. No one can offend you unless you allow it."

Doug looked at the old woman. "How can I allow someone to offend me? I certainly wouldn't give someone permission to be mean or disrespectful; that's on them."

She looked directly into Doug's eyes. "Precisely! However, when someone has been unkind, or has been distant, or has seemingly disengaged from your life to the point that it seems they care nothing about you, does that not hurt your heart?"

Doug took a deep breath. That question hit a nerve.

"Wow, that's a Truth; I can feel it in my heart."

"My point is, Doug, only you are responsible for what you do. If someone is unkind, it is up to you to address it. If they continue to be unkind, it might be time to detach from them.

"You are only responsible for the energy with which you deliver a message through your words or actions. You are not responsible for how that person receives the message."

Whew! That was profound. I need to take this in; it's almost overwhelming.

He inhaled deeply, then exhaled slowly. He felt as though the porch was spinning, and shapes and colors began to gently swirl around him as warmth embraced him.

He smiled broadly as his mother immediately came into his thoughts. He knew it was her, and with tears he remembered her tenderness and love. Truth spoke to his heart, even through the veil of confusion, hurt and disappointment.

Thank you, Mama! I love you!

He took a couple of deep breaths and looked down at Gracie, who remained content in his lap, and appeared oblivious to what he had experienced.

She's probably used to this energy. He smiled, and felt the floor beneath his feet as calmness began to bring him back to reality.

Okay, I'm good.

He looked at the old woman, who stared straight ahead at the Old Oak.

"Every soul has a journey," she said, "a contract of sorts, about what they want to experience and to learn while they are on Earth. You cannot know another person's soul agreements, and it is not your business. Your only task is to discover your own journey, and to live it as impeccably as you can."

She looked at Doug. "Respect these agreements, Doug, and you will discover the purity of Truth. Begin by taking responsibility for clearing out the 'shoulds' of your mind!"

She patted his hand. "You are a very good man, Doug, and your soul is waiting for you to notice that. Time to clear out the clutter of old wounds, get out the 'polish' to spruce up those treasures within, and bring them out to be used!"

Doug held the chain tightly, and then placed it in his shirt pocket. He stood up as the old woman began to carefully put their dishes on the tray.

"These are my words. And, speaking of clearing clutter," she continued, "are you ready to get busy right now?"

Wow! She shifted gears quickly, and, what did she mean by that? Did she mean right this moment?

"Yes, right this moment," she chuckled, as though reading his mind. "If you'll carry the tray into the house for me, we need to clean out the shed behind the house."

Doug laughed heartily.

I sure didn't see this one coming!

"Sure! I'll be more than glad to help you!"

"Let's see, the laundry is nearly done; all I have left to do is mop the bathroom floors. Then I'll cook a big pot of soup to have over the next couple of days."

Ruth hung the broom on its hook in the utility room, then retrieved the mop, bucket and Pine Sol cleaner, and headed toward the first bathroom.

Wonder when Doug's going to visit the old woman?

"I hope it's soon; knowing Doug, he'll drag his feet. But, that's his decision; it's really none of my business."

She added the Pine Sol to the water in the bucket and stirred it with her hand. She caught a glimpse of herself in the mirror above the sink, and her head began again to chatter away.

Now, aren't you the negative person! Who made you the judge of your brother?

She stared at her reflection. "I am not judging my brother! I love him, and whatever he chooses to do is fine with me. I trust he'll do what he needs to do in his own time." There. That was as direct as she could be with that irritating head chatter.

"Look," she continued, "I know you mean well, but we have gone over this dozens of times and you know whatever you say will boomerang back to us! If you want to tell me about something," she stopped and looked into her eyes, "use smooth, round words, not words that are sharp and pointy!" she finished, as tenderly as she could.

Whoa, where did that description come from? I don't recall ever hearing that!

She took a deep breath and stared straight into the mirror.

"Mirror, mirror on the wall, make certain I'm the kindest and most loving soul of all!"

Warmth filled the air as love embraced her. Her head was spinning and she felt the floor beneath her feet, as a vibrating energy streamed down through the top of her head and all the way to the floor. Suddenly, she felt a love so strong that it brought tears to her eyes.

Once again, she felt a crown on her head. This time, however, she felt herself cloaked in a soft, pale yellow fabric. Her mother stood before her.

"*It is time for you to claim the richness of your soul; it is everyone's birthright!*"

Then, as quickly as she appeared, she disappeared.

Ruth was draped in a haze of yellow light, and the mop in her hand became a sword strapped to her side. She felt the coldness of the metal handle and the roughness of its leather sheath. Slowly, she closed her eyes. Tears of strength flowed and began to moisten the hard places in her heart.

"*This is who you are; remember this when the world presents you with seemingly important decisions. Everything on this Earth wishes only to work with you; it is the human reconstruction of Truth that has complicated the Divine design of creation. Use your sword to cut through the illusions you believed in the past.*"

She suddenly felt the sword become a very tall staff. Energy flowed from the heavens, down through the staff and into the Earth, while the unknown, yet familiar voice continued,

"*Let your heart be your guide, and allow compassion and love to permeate every aspect of your life. You are a Sentinel Warrior, a Bringer of Light.*"

The energy began to move upward toward the place from which it came. She once again felt the floor beneath her feet as she batted her eyes open. She glanced at the mop in her hand and burst into laughter.

"Goodness, can't say as I've ever had *that* kind of experience while I mopped the floor!"

Still laughing, she looked into the mirror. "What? No crown?

"Okay, I've shared a lot of things with Rick, but I'm not certain he's ready to hear this story!"

Dear Heaven!

She smiled as she dipped the mop into the bucket and began to clean the floor. It was clean in no time and she went directly to the second bathroom.

"I wonder if Cinderella ever felt like this? I don't have a pair of glass slippers or two mean stepsisters, but I do have a warrior's outfit, a crown, and a sword that can become a staff. Oh, and a very handsome Prince who is in love with me!" She smiled.

Suddenly, the floor became a mosaic patchwork of pictures from her life that flashed before her eyes, and each picture randomly fell into place like pieces of a puzzle. She stopped.

"Wait; I need to be still and focus on these pictures so I can understand this."

"You most certainly do not need to do that," she heard in her heart. *"The last thing you need is to take charge of what's occurring. Simply stay with the task in front of you, and listen with the 'ears' of your heart. Disengage your head, and allow your eyes to observe how your life has unfolded, and where it offers to take you."*

She took a deep breath, then dipped the mop in clean water, squeezed out the excess, and continued to slowly move it across the floor. She noticed the shine that appeared where she had mopped, in contrast to the dullness of the areas she hadn't yet cleaned.

I suppose that's how my life looks. What is yet to be cleared and cleaned away looks dull beside the areas just cleaned. I'm a good housekeeper, so it's not like my floors are filthy; they just need to be tended to in order to bring out their natural beauty.

"Good gracious!" she exclaimed as she stood up straight. She quickly glanced back down at the floor and pushed her mop across the remaining areas.

"I'm not going to think about this. It's a waste of my time and energy!"

The floor looked spic and span! Then she noticed that the picture puzzle had no real sense of order.

"I guess it doesn't need to make sense or to be in any particular order. I just need to remember what pictures I see here." She returned the mop to the bucket and glanced across the floor.

She had to laugh at several of the pictures; they were such memories of her youth: her first car, first boyfriend, first breakup, and first job. She even saw her high school graduation diploma, and then her cap and gown from nursing school graduation. She saw the small church that she and her family had attended for most of her life, until they stopped attending at all.

Then she saw her mother hanging out clothes and, from behind two blankets that she had pinned together, Ruth could hear the voices of herself and Doug, laughing about what they were going to do to their younger brother, Steve.

"Shhh!" She put her finger to her lips as they snickered. "*He's going to hear us, Dougie, and he'll know something's up!*"

Then she heard her mother's voice. "*I'm sorry, and I am grateful that we have forgiven each other for the past.*"

Her father then appeared next to her mother. "*We are so very proud of what you have done with your life. We are grateful to be witnessing the reopening of your heart, and we look forward to watching your children fill your home with the warmth of unconditional love. We always did the best we knew how to do, and please know that our sadness was never your fault or your responsibility.*"

She then saw herself sitting at a desk, typing away.

"*Whatever am I doing?*" Her head had kicked in. "*Oh, never mind that question,*" her head quickly acknowledged to her heart. "*You have the reins of this moment.*"

She then realized that her practical head had spoken to her heart out of respect and support.

Now, that's a perfect union!

She pulled the mop from the water bucket and squeezed out the excess water.

"Thank you," she said looking upward, "whoever you are!"

At that moment, she heard the unknown, yet familiar voice.

"*We are called by different names: Guardian Angels, Holy Spirit, Creator God, Teachers and Guides are but a few. In essence, we are your Allies that agreed to support you during your Earthly experience. We will continue to be with you until you return 'home.'"*

"Allies; I love that word, and I absolutely remember your voices from my childhood."

Tears of joy came as a smile spread across her face. The mosaic puzzle began to make sense.

"Thank you, and I will pay closer attention!"

Suddenly she had an epiphany.

"Aha! I know what happened! I had stopped listening!"

That's changed as of this moment! Now, back to the worldly tasks in front of me.

After wiping down the basin, faucet and handles, she picked up the bucket and mop and looked directly into the mirror.

"Nope, no crown!" she laughed. "None that is visible, anyway. I feel it on my head, though, and that's all that matters!"

She stared in the mirror and held up the handle of her mop. "This is my sword." Then she lifted her bucket. "And this is my challis! I accept the opportunity to be a Bringer of Light, and I ask my sacred Allies to work with and through me."

Within a few moments, Ruth felt fully present in her body, hair scrunched into a bun on top of her head, bucket and mop still in hand.

"Whew!" she laughed. "That was one heck of an experience cleaning the bathrooms!"

Three boxes sat outside the old woman's work shed. One was half full of glass jars of every size and shape, old flower vases, and empty milk bottles. Another held broken down cardboard boxes, old paper sacks, biodegradable seedling holders, newspapers, magazines, and miscellaneous junk mail. A large third box held several old farm implements and a box of quart canning jars, with old flannel shirts and used sweatshirts neatly stacked on top. A few grocery bags filled with gloves, hats, socks, and a pair of old coveralls secured the items for safe travel to the local thrift store.

Doug stood beside the old woman and surveyed the goods left in the shed.

"She needs to be painted next," the old woman commented, nodding toward the shed.

He looked down at her. "It's late in the day, or I'd be glad to paint her for you."

"Thank you for the offer, and I may take you up on that another time. For now, I would imagine you're pretty hungry. We've done a lot of work today."

"Just say when, and I'll be here. And, no need to feed me; I could stand to burn a few calories and skip a couple of meals!" he chuckled.

She shook her head. No one was going to leave her house hungry, but he would learn that soon enough.

"Would you mind taking these boxes back to town for me? You know which go to the recycle center and which go to the thrift store."

"Not at all!"

She pointed to the four-wheeled cart. "Use that cart to take the boxes to your vehicle while I sweep the shed."

"You got it!" He then pulled the cart from the shed.

"I'll meet you back on the front porch," said the old woman.

Doug placed two of the medium sized boxes on the cart and headed toward his truck.

"Somehow, I knew I needed to drive my truck today. Now I know why."

As he pulled the cart back to the shed he noticed something shiny on the ground behind the cabin.

What is that?

He didn't want to appear nosey, so he slowed his pace in an attempt to get a better look at it.

Hmmm, that's odd. It looks like a copper cap of some sort.

He looked up and noticed that the old woman was no longer around the shed. He stacked the last large box into the cart and peeked into the shed. It was spotless!

He shook his head. "She's something else!"

He paused and scanned the woods behind the cabin. He noticed that most of the fields beyond her back yard still awaited preparation for the winter.

Doug inhaled deeply, taking in the fresh air and the fragrance of the surrounding pine trees in the Forest.

Gosh, I really need to get the kids out in the country. How I remember these smells from my childhood. My kids only breathe city air. It's all good, though; I'm grateful for this reminder while they are still young.

He thought about Ruth.

"She'd be more than glad to share the country experience with her niece and nephew." He felt tenderness in his heart at the thought.

Ruthie; what a special woman. She's always been so aware of the natural world. And, there wasn't anything I did that she couldn't keep up with.

He smiled. "In fact, it was all I could do to keep up with her!"

Okay, back to the task at hand. He headed toward his truck.

Twenty minutes later Doug stepped onto the porch and took a seat while he waited for the old woman.

I'll bet she's pooped. She may be small, but she's certainly a spry little thing. I know most women couldn't keep up with her!

"Except Ruthie, of course!" Then he thought of his wife, Sue, and smiled.

"She's in good shape, but I'm not so sure she could work at that little woman's pace!"

He scanned the front yard and observed the lay of the land. He looked to his left and noticed how well-groomed the area was.

I'll bet that's her flower garden. The loving care she has put into it really shows. I wonder if she has someone who helps her?

His thoughts were interrupted by the sound of the screen door opening. The old woman carried a very large tray that was draped with an orange fabric.

"Oh, please, let me help you!" He jumped up from his chair and relieved her of the tray.

She then moved around him, and set up the small table.

"What in the world do you have on this tray? It's certainly heavy! I hope you didn't go to any trouble on my account."

"I didn't; *I* was hungry!"

He tried not to laugh. *She's something else!* Then he set the tray on the table and asked where he could wash up a bit.

She nodded. "Follow me."

They entered the cabin and she showed him to the small bathroom in the utility room.

She returned to the front porch and took her seat on the swing while she waited for Doug. When he returned and took his seat, she pulled the orange fabric off the tray, revealing a plate of small sandwiches and a platter of vegetables and fruit. Doug's mouth watered and his stomach growled in anticipation.

Doug waited for the old woman to begin. After she had made her selections, he lifted the thermos toward her mug. She nodded, and he filled both mugs with hot tea.

The air was a bit chilly. "The days of eating on the porch are limited," observed the old woman.

That was all she said; she had simply stated a fact. Doug found it entertaining that she was a woman of few idle words. When she spoke, her words had purpose.

That's a rarity these days. Everyone seems to have an opinion about literally every topic. And, they are more than willing to share it, even when not asked.

The only audible sounds were from the squirrels and rabbits that scurried about the yard gathering goodies for the winter, a woodpecker drilling away in the distance, and an occasional rustle of leaves, indicating that some critter was scavenging the Forest for prey.

Doug broke the silence. "May I ask another question?"

The old woman nodded.

He repositioned himself in his seat as he began to formulate the question in his mind.

"I'd like to know your thoughts about how to deal with regrets."

She finished the last bite of her sandwich and placed her saucer on the tray. Then she reached for the thermos and offered Doug more tea.

"Sure," he nodded.

She filled both mugs, then wrapped both hands around her own steaming mug and gently blew on the tea before taking a sip. She certainly didn't mind the tea being a bit hot as the breeze from the North began to pick up speed.

"Regrets are a waste of time, and time is precious," she finally responded. "Mulling over an occurrence for days, weeks, or even years, shows disrespect for the gifts you've received from the choices you've made."

Silence. Not one word was spoken for what felt like ten minutes. Doug began to feel uncomfortable, and wondered whether he should ask questions about her comment or give a rebuttal to her response. Or, was he to ask another question? He wasn't certain what was appropriate. What he *was* certain about, however, was that he felt irritated and annoyed, but he knew from her earlier teachings that only he was responsible for what he felt.

"What regrets do you carry in your heart, Doug?"

He was flabbergasted by her question.

I thought I was supposed to ask the questions! I don't know this woman well enough to share my feelings with her.

His face became flushed and the inside of his mouth felt like cotton, as she patiently awaited his response.

Okay, Doug, stay calm; if you can ask questions of her, she certainly has a right to ask you some questions, too.

"I'm not really certain," he finally responded. "I do have regrets; however, to pinpoint what I carry in my heart, I suppose the first thing that comes to my mind is that I wish I would have talked more to my mother while she was still alive. I have so many unanswered questions."

"Which of those questions would you most like to have answered?" asked the old woman.

He scratched his head and sipped his tea.

"The first thing that pops into my head is, what could she tell me about the voices she heard? Were they real, or just a consequence of her overindulgence of alcohol?"

That was his knee jerk response, although he wasn't certain it was the most important question. However, if the old woman could at least help him understand that, it would be helpful.

"Why is the answer to that question important?" she inquired.

He leaned forward in his chair. "I suppose because it would help me understand why she detached herself from the family."

That was it. It wasn't really about the voices; it was about why she had disconnected herself from the family and isolated herself. He pondered that thought for a few moments.

"She withdrew her love," he continued, "from two little kids who didn't understand why their youngest brother was no longer around, and then they were also losing their mother."

The old woman sat in silence as she used the "ears" of her heart to understand what Doug was really asking. His heart was bleeding, and she knew that he needed to be able to express that buried pain.

"I regret not letting my mother know that I needed her; for that matter, we all did. Dad placated her as much as he could, but he was hurting as well." His eyes burned with tears.

"Truth is, no one said anything. We were just left to feel the absence of both our younger brother and our mother, without so much as a word about what had happened."

He sighed deeply, sipped his tea and sat back in his chair.

"I've forgiven my mother and my father. Now that I'm a father I can imagine how difficult it must have been for both of them to lose a child. Their silence about what had happened was intended to protect us, but it only hurt us. However, they made the choice they thought was best for us, and now, as a parent, I understand that it was to protect their own broken hearts as well."

The old woman unfolded the quilt that lay beside her on the swing and draped it around her shoulders, as Gracie moved up to the porch and leaped into Doug's lap. He smiled and welcomed her, and she immediately began to purr.

"I reckon this regret I've carried most of my life has taught me to open my mouth and ask tough questions," he continued, "without thinking about not hurting the person I'm asking. If I don't ask those questions, the chasm between us will widen, which will make the building of a bridge a lot more difficult."

It felt so good to say that!

"I thank you for your words. I want my children to grow up in a home where they feel free to ask anything they want, and to know their mom and dad will be honest and tell them the Truth."

He felt a lump in his throat as he leaned his head back in his chair.

Dear God, this feels good. That weight on my shoulders has been lifted. I know Mother loved us.

The old woman looked at Doug, then looked in the direction of a woodpecker's hammering.

"That woodpecker demonstrates that despite how difficult things may be, if you are persistent and steady, you will find your hidden treasure. You know, you have set yourself *and* your children free. At this very moment the stars are realigning, and the birds are heading South for the winter. That's how life works; we are all connected."

"And," he promptly responded, "if I would not have let go of that regret, the sun wouldn't come up in the morning?"

"I'm afraid you're not that important!" she laughed. "And, yet, Doug, how you respond to life does affect everyone around you. You saw that with Gracie this morning. She jumped into your lap when she sensed you needed some lovin' and jumped off again when the energy from your unpleasant memories returned. That's the flow of energy we spoke of this morning, and that boomerang always comes flying back to us. Regrets are bitter, and they keep our energy low and dense, whereas forgiveness and release free our energy to become light and take flight. Regrets come from our human mind, that head chatter that keeps us from hearing the 'voice' of our heart."

Gracie perked up and looked directly at Doug. "I see you!" she seemed to say.

Doug's heart began to pound as tears rolled down his cheeks. He wiped them away with the sleeve of his sweatshirt.

"You know, as I reflect on your story, I want to restore my innocence and faith so that I can truly *see*. And, I want my children to grow up, '*believing so they can see!*' what's real and true." He paused in thought.

"Well, I reckon I've done all the work I can do today," he continued. He looked at the old woman. "And, you must be tuckered out as well."

She nodded as she stood up, folded the quilt, and set it back on the swing.

"If you'll get the door, I'll carry your tray into the house for you," he offered.

She smiled. "Thank you; you and Ruth are very much alike."

She held the door open as Doug carried the tray into the house. The old woman moved around him and entered the kitchen, then pointed to the counter beside the sink.

"Would you like for me to help you wash the dishes?" he asked.

She shook her head. "No, you'd better skedaddle along home before the sun sets."

"Are you certain?"

"Yes."

"Okay, and thank you again for a most interesting day. I'll make certain your boxes get to their proper places tomorrow."

"Thank you!"

Doug found his way out the front door, then took some cash from his pocket and dropped it into the twig basket.

"What a day!" he exclaimed as he walked briskly back to his truck. "I can hardly wait to talk to Ruthie. Geez, how did she find this woman?"

Oh, let's not go there! I'm going to watch that needless head chatter. I want to make certain when that boomerang comes back it'll be with much love and compassion.

He thought of Sue. "Yes, love and compassion!"

Speaking of boomerang…

He grabbed his phone, put in his ear buds and found his sister's cell number. Ruth answered after one ring.

"Hey, my little brother, I was just thinking about you."

"I'll bet you were!"

"What's up?"

"Well, let's see, the answer to that requires that we get together again."

She gasped. "Oh, my gosh, you visited the old woman!"

"Indeed, I did! And, Sis, I've got to tell you, it has already changed my life!"

She sat in silence; it was her brother's turn to let the "voice" of his heart speak whatever he was ready to share. She knew that experience all too well.

"Sis, are you still there?"

She smiled as tears began to flow. She could feel her heart expand, and was tremendously grateful to bear witness to her brother's rediscovery of his own heart. For the first time in their adult lives, each of their hearts had the freedom to speak from a place of innocence. She covered her mouth so he wouldn't hear her cry, but to no avail.

"I'm so grateful for you, Doug," she sobbed. "Whatever would I have done without your presence in my life?"

And then her tears turned to laughter. "Hey, wait a minute, I'm the oldest, here; it was *you* who relied on *me* the most!"

They both laughed, as the release of pent up hurt and pain began to transform into something new, fresh and, above all, innocent.

"Boomerang!" Doug laughed.

Oh, my gosh, I just said that word a few moments ago.

"I love that word!" she responded. "And, when we get together you'll have to explain why you used it. Right now, I'm heading out the door for work, and I have 12-hour shifts the next two days. Check your schedule and text me some possible dates and times when you're available after that."

"You got it! I know you're in a hurry, Sis, so I'll simply reiterate again how grateful I am that you told me about the old woman. She's quite a lady, and I helped her clean out her shed today. Truth is, I have three boxes of her giveaways in the back of my truck that I'll be taking to the shelter and to the recycle center."

"*What?* She actually asked you to help her?"

"Yes ma'am, and it surprised me as well. You said she didn't talk much, but I found her quite talkative!"

Ruth laughed. "I guess it's true that, when you change, others around you change, too." Her heart felt joyful.

That little woman deserves to be surrounded by people who love and respect her. I had a hunch she was a bit lonely.

A call clicked in on the other line; she looked at her phone and saw that it was Jim.

"Listen, Doug, I need to catch this call. I look forward to getting together and hearing every detail of your day at the 'magical' cabin in the woods."

"You got it. Love you, Sis."

"Hello, Jim," she said as she picked up his call. "Why am I not surprised to hear from you?"

"I don't know, but you should know by now that nothing is ever by coincidence. Do you have time for a chat?"

"I'd love to chat, Jim; however, I need to get out the door within the next ten minutes and head to the hospital. My next opportunity for a good chat would be late Sunday evening or Monday afternoon. Text me a time and date that works for you and I'll make certain I'm rested and clear-headed."

"That's fine, Ruth. I'll check my schedule next week and text you a couple of dates and times and we'll go from there. You take care and give Rick my best."

"I'll do that, and thanks for understanding." She paused. "And, I'll boomerang a confirmation back to you," she giggled.

Jim roared with laughter.

"What the heck? I haven't heard that word in years! I guess you getting back with me is a boomerang, though?" he cackled. "Oh, my gosh, you're something else, Ruth! Stay safe and don't work too hard."

Rick called her just as she ended Jim's call.

Oh, my gosh, I haven't had one call this morning, and they're all coming in now.

She clicked to the other line.

"Hey, Rick, it's good to hear from you, but I have got to get out the door for work. Let me call you back when I get in my car, okay?"

"Sure, no hurry, though, I just wanted to do a quick check-in. Drive carefully; you have precious cargo!"

She smiled and hung up. *That man says exactly what a woman wants to hear.* Only she knew he meant it.

She grabbed her coat and bag and glanced around the room.

"I have everything. That's one nice thing about being organized; I can head out the door in a few minutes and know that everything I need is packed and ready for takeoff!" She smiled.

At least that's what I tell myself when people laugh about how organized I am!

When she was in her car she turned on her headset and called Rick.

"Hey, you weren't kidding when you said you were ready to walk out the door, were you?"

"Indeed! It's funny, though; I hadn't had a call all day until about twenty minutes ago. First Doug called, and then Jim, and now you!"

"How are they both doing?"

"Jim's well, and we're going to chat later this weekend. Doug? Well," she smiled broadly, "he visited the old woman today. What does that tell you?"

"I'll bet he was full of things he wanted to share!"

"He was; unfortunately, however, I had to get out the door, so he and I need to get together soon. Rick, he's so precious; I really can't wait for you two to get to know each other better."

"Well, he didn't waste any time going to see the old woman! Sounds like he's just like his conscientious sister who doesn't let any grass grow under her feet." His heart quickened.

"Well, that's not true; he's always been quite the opposite from me. It used to drive him crazy that I'd jump right into whatever I said I was going to do. He's always been one who wanted to ponder things before rushing into anything. Of course, that meant he often didn't accomplish what he had claimed was of importance."

"You sure can't say that about yourself. I've never met anyone who jumped into things with both feet as quickly as you do." He paused. "Well, maybe not *everything*."

She caught that one. "I know what you are referencing, and you are absolutely correct about that."

"I understand, and I am not complaining; that's not something to rush into. Anyway, your willingness to take action is one of the many admirable traits you possess."

Another plus for Rick! She grinned.

"Well, I won't keep you, Ruth. You work 12-hour shifts the next two nights, is that correct?"

"Yes, and thanks for remembering."

"I remember a lot when it comes to you. In particular, I remember that turquoise jump suit, and that flowing, flowered dress. Yep, I can picture you in those outfits right this moment, and the thought makes me smile!" He was filled with warmth as he thought of those two beautiful evenings.

She blushed. "Nice to know that you think of me in such a ... well ... new and adventurous way!"

"Adventurous?" he chuckled. "Yeah, let's say adventurous!

"And, speaking of adventurous, did your brother find the old woman as enchanting as you and Jim do?"

"That's really nifty how you quickly you changed the subject!"

They both laughed.

"Actually," she continued, "I believe he did. We didn't talk very long, but he seemed to have enjoyed his time with her. He even helped her clean out her shed, and he described her as quite talkative."

Rick was puzzled. "I don't know all that much about her, but didn't you say she doesn't talk a lot?"

"That's correct. That's why it is most interesting. I told Doug that, when a person changes, other people in their life change as well.

"I guess it's like a boomerang," she continued awkwardly. "That is, whatever you put out into the world, however you treat others, will come back to you ... sorta like a reflection."

Rick let out a roaring laugh. "Boomerang? Now, that's an interesting way to describe what you just said. Ruth, you are undoubtedly the more interesting person I have ever met!"

"I wasn't certain that made sense," she laughed, "so I'll take that as a compliment. Thank you!"

"You are certainly welcome," he fired back. "Take care of yourself and be safe. I look forward to your return in a couple of days, my most beautiful Boomerang."

Ruth's heart expanded as she smiled broadly. She knew the love she felt for him was a reflection of the love he felt for her. The warm glow of the courageous, adventurous, and bold journey they shared, was *The Boomerang* that reflected the healing occurring in her heart.

Reflections

HEAD TALK

What part of the story line so far can you personally relate to?

Was there anything that struck you as "unreal?"

What are you curious about?

What would you like to "think some more about?"

HEART TALK

What stirred your heart the most?

What touched a nerve or a tender part in you?

What memory from your life came to your heart?

What would you like to happen next?

The Gathering

"Well, for heaven's sake!" declared the old woman. She stared out the front window as light snow mixed with the gentle rain. "Mid-October is very early for snow!" Her face pressed against the window, she could feel the cold air that had produced the first visible snowflakes of the season, and she noticed Gracie cuddled up in the willow chair her last visitor had occupied just a few short weeks ago.

"She's cozied up! She really did like Doug; she rarely lies in that chair."

She scanned the front yard and porch to see if Tom was following his "sister's" lead.

"He's nowhere in sight! He's probably off preparing a place for the two of them to cuddle up when the weather really turns cold." She glanced back at Gracie.

"Guess she's noticed the changing weather, too, so she's practicing her 'snuggling up' position for the winter ahead." She tapped on the window, but her furry friend didn't budge.

"Okay, play hard of hearing!" She smiled and went to the kitchen.

I need to get out the winter drapes, so maybe I'll do that today.

"I'll let 'em air out a bit while I do a few other things this morning.

She put on the teakettle, and placed a mug and tea bag on the tray by the stove. She patted her tummy as it rumbled when she took a muffin from the breadbox.

"You know I do the best I can to take care of you. After all, you take such great care of me, it's the least I can do."

She poured hot water over the tea bag, covered the mug with a ceramic lid and placed it on the tray beside the muffin, then moved to the living room and set the tray on the walnut table beside her chair in front of the fireplace.

She looked at the hearth, and within a few moments kindling, wadded newspaper, and a couple of medium-sized twigs eagerly awaited a fire. She lit a match and held it beneath the iron stand, and the twigs and paper immediately caught fire. As small flames spread across the twigs, she gingerly angled three split logs over the dancing flames.

"This will do for a bit." She held her hands over the small flames.

"Thank you for your warmth," she whispered. Then she moved her hands to her heart as she addressed the fire.

"May our relationship, and the warmth you provide, also ignite a 'fire' in those who come here, that will burn away whatever our visitors need to release."

In her mind's eye she saw an extraordinarily colorful and beautiful Phoenix begin to rise. After several deep breaths, she felt compassion and love ascend from the flames, while the prayers of those seeking a new vision burned away old paradigms, leaving room for answers to emerge from within the embers.

She exhaled slowly, and asked that the answers to prayers throughout the world return tenfold to the hearts of those making the requests. And, in a moment, she felt the veil of illusions that had been created by humankind throughout the centuries, now pierced by humanity, and fall into ashes beneath the fire.

"Thank you," she whispered. "The power of prayer far surpasses anything anyone can do to help another soul. Each of us must look within our own heart and carefully examine what it is time to bring forth in our life in order to help heal the planet."

She opened her eyes, and the flames appeared to dance with joy. She smiled, then placed another large log on the now well-established fire, and again held her open hands in front of the fire and bowed her head.

"Thank you! Just as the bear hibernates, we, too, go within our hearts with the rhythms of the cold season, so that we may be shown what is waiting to be birthed. Within the womb of Mother, we will be given the opportunity to seed those dreams deep within our hearts."

She closed her eyes and took a deep breath.

"We will bring forth those young seedlings when the warmth of spring returns, and plant them in the richness of Earth Mother."

She lifted her hands to the heavens.

"And so, the new cycle on the Sacred Wheel of Life will begin. Thank you, Sky Nation, for your guidance and unconditional love."

She bent over and touched the floor.

"As Above, so Below. Thank you, sweet Mother, for receiving our dreams and guiding our feet as we walk yet another cycle on the Sacred Path of Life. Help us to walk gently upon you, always grateful for all that we are given. You are so very loved."

She stood up and placed her hands on her heart.

"So Within," she whispered. "May my thoughts, words and actions be impeccable, and in alignment with Truth."

In that moment, she recalled an old, familiar song: *Amazing Grace*. The "voice" of her heart began to hum the tune she had first heard as a child. Somehow, the song always connected her to all that was good, despite whatever else might be happening in her life. While she heard the tune with her physical ears, it was the "ears" of her heart that reminded her that something greater always had her back. And, that "something" resided within her like a constant companion that waited to be noticed and called upon whenever she needed anything. Like a warm, comfy blanket, or an embrace from a loved one, it provided unconditional love at all times!

She opened her eyes and smiled as she watched the flames embrace the large log.

"What a gift; what an amazing life! How I wish all humans knew these Truths!"

She returned to her chair and set the tray on her lap. She smiled in anticipation of her snack. "Okay, belly, it's your turn!"

With a fresh cup of coffee in one hand, Ruth slid the porch door open. She barely got a toe out the door before the cold air got her attention.

"Good grief! It's cold out here!"

She noticed that the blanket she had used the morning before was still lying across her lounge chair.

"That thing has to be frozen, and I sure don't want to be its warming unit!"

She zipped over to the chair, grabbed the blanket, and hurried back inside.

"Brrr, you *are* nearly frozen!"

She hung one end of the blanket over the couch and the other end over the swivel rocker before comfortably nestling into her chair.

"This will do! In fact, this is great," she chuckled. "You, my faithful chair, are indeed a comfortable, cozy place to nestle into!"

She had taken just a few sips of coffee when she got a text from Jim.

"Hey, Ruth, hope you're getting some good rest. Does Monday morning around ten work to visit our friend? And, it's my turn to drive."

What a fabulous time in my life! Rick is in my bedroom, sleeping like a baby; Doug's heart is sorting through his past; and, Jim and I are on an amazing journey together.

"Sounds good," she responded. "See you then, and thank you for driving. Have a fabulous Sunday!"

There. Short, sweet, and to the point! I am indeed changing my ways!

Two strong arms slid down her shoulders as she hit "send." The scent of Rick's hair preceded his lips on her neck, igniting a fire within her whole being.

She turned her head and kissed the side of his face. When their lips met, the message was clear.

"To heck with coffee," she said. "There's something hotter I'd prefer to have."

"You won't hear any complaints from me!" Rick said softly. "I have all day, and I'm all yours!"

"Then let's do a full circle and return to where we started last evening!" Ruth whispered.

The old woman rummaged through an antique trunk at the foot of her bed and found several pairs of heavy drapes.

"Whew, those are heavy; and, that's why they help conserve energy. No sense wasting precious resources when these old drapes are still very eager to be of service."

She carried a pair into the dining room and draped them over a dining room chair. Thoughts of her grandmother stirred her heart on her way back to the trunk, where she carefully and affectionately removed another pair. She carried those into the dining room and smoothed them over another chair, and did the same with the remaining two pairs. Then she stood back and admired the beauty and durability of the impeccably sewn drapes.

This will help you breathe a bit before I hang you over the windows.

She paused and caught the scent of "White Shoulders," which had been her grandmother's favorite perfume. She closed her eyes.

She was such an amazing woman!

A breeze flew through the room, and she knew.

"Okay, okay," she giggled. "What an amazing woman you *are!*"

"Not too many people realize we can still communicate with those we love even after they've crossed over. I reckon such thoughts scare them."

306 ～ゐ～ *Walking a Sacred Path*

She felt warmth in her heart as she entered the kitchen for a cup of coffee, and looked upward.

"You are welcome to join me; let's enjoy a cup together!"

She pulled out a small thermos as the coffee brewed.

"I'll put the coffee in this so it stays hot. Nothing worse than lukewarm coffee. Well, yes, there are worse things. I've just learned to accept only what makes my heart happy. Simple things, like hot coffee!" She smiled.

When the coffee was ready, she moved to her chair in the living room and set her mug and thermos on the walnut table. She stoked the fire, then pulled out the basket of goodies that held all her memories, and set it on the chair.

I know I'll find what I need among these treasures.

She glanced at the exquisite drapes that hung over her dining room chairs. "How I remember my grandmother's hands. Always busy creating something."

Immediately she recalled when her grandmother had taught her to make lined, pinch pleat drapes.

She was so frustrated that I couldn't make those pinch pleats more quickly, while keeping them precisely spaced.

"Granny, I'm grateful you still look over me to keep me in line!"

Both her mama and her granny had had a gift for sewing. There wasn't anything in a store window they couldn't replicate perfectly! Tenderness swept through her heart.

"What amazing women I had as examples of how to be dedicated and of service to one's family."

She pulled herself back to the moment with a full heart, and settled into her chair with her basket of memories on her lap.

Reckon I'd better get busy! Enough reminiscing; the past is past, and I have done my best to practice what I was shown. I'll look over my shoulder and remember only to bring those gifts to the here and now!

She closed her eyes, felt the floor beneath her feet, and rested her hands over the top of the basket.

"Feel my heart's request. May all that is to be told be made clear. Guide me as I share from my heart those Truths that it is time for Jim and Ruth to learn. Rather, to re-member!"

She lifted the top of the basket and carefully held her hand over the top to ensure that every precious item stayed intact. Each piece in the basket was infused with an abundance of love, heartache, or pure joy. All who are willing to receive their own gifts will also find treasures within. Each gift offers the curious seeker an adventure if they have the courage to look deep within.

The warmth of early afternoon offered Ruth and Rick the opportunity to venture out onto the patio. Grandfather Sun was high in the azure sky, while white, billowy clouds shape-shifted and floated above the tall city buildings.

Rick stared up at the sky and reached for Ruth's hand.

"Reckon we'd better enjoy this warmth, and the blue hues of the heavens."

Ruth was mesmerized by the beauty of the moment. She felt contentment in every cell of her body, and couldn't be happier. She closed her eyes and allowed the warm breeze to clear away any old residue of doubt that had lingered in her body for most of her life. This was what she wanted.

She looked at Rick. *He* was what she wanted, and she was grateful to welcome the love he had so freely offered, and had so patiently waited for her to accept. She felt safe as he held her hand. Never in her life had she felt so safe, so loved, and so sure of the love they shared.

As Rick held her hand, he felt his own hand tingle.

Wonder what that is?

"Does it matter?" He smiled at his heart's response. Of course it didn't matter; what was important was that he felt the pulsing energy that transferred from her hand to his.

"Ruth, what would you like to do for your birthday this year?"

His question was met with silence; Ruth was somewhere else.

She's probably in one of her magical places, or in some exotic dreamscape she's created in that beautiful heart of hers.

He stared at the contours of her face. She was a beautiful woman. He loved her upturned nose, the fullness of her lips, the almost porcelain-like skin, and the dark brown hair that hung down around her shoulders.

She is beautiful; however, it's the radiance that emanates from deep within her soul that is beyond words. I know precisely what I want to give her as a birthday gift.

He grinned as Ruth turned to look at him.

"What are you smiling about?"

"You!"

She blushed. "Okay, are you talking about my disheveled hair? Or, maybe this gorgeous bathrobe that's been my best bud for more years than I care to admit?"

He laughed and squeezed her hand. "Oh, my gosh, now you are psychic, too! I can't hide anything from you!" He feigned a shiver, and they both laughed.

Ruth leaned toward him, closed her eyes and puckered up. He responded with a warm, juicy, passionate kiss, then opened his eyes and leaned back.

"It's nearly one in the afternoon! What do you say we get some lunch in our bellies?"

"That sounds great," she agreed. "I'm starved. We can scavenge through the refrigerator; I know we can muster up something healthy."

"Sounds like a plan," he responded, "although I'll gladly place a phone order and pick up something for us, or have it delivered. You did just finish two 12-hour work days."

"That's very kind of you; however, I probably have food that needs to be eaten before it spoils. Let's just use whatever I have in the refrigerator."

"I see," he laughed. "The garbage disposal is here, so let's pawn off some questionable food!"

She giggled, then headed to the kitchen.

She found several ingredients to make a hearty soup, and after she got it going on the stove she returned to her lounge chair and flipped through the pages of her journal. Rick was in the shower, and Ruth wanted to review her notes before she and Jim went to visit the old woman.

"Goodness, I have been negligent about reading through my entries. It's amazing how information flies in and then is quickly forgotten. I'm grateful that I've always kept track of things in a journal of some sort."

As she reviewed her scribbled words she immediately felt herself in the Forest around the old woman's cabin. She could even smell the pine, hear the birds as they flitted from tree to tree, see squirrels scamper about the land and the white tails of rabbits as they hopped through the thick foliage.

She turned several pages and came upon the circle with the pie-shaped sections that represented the first four sacred directions. Scribbled within each section were words that described her recollection. As she read the "shorthand" she had used, she recalled the last visit she and Jim had made.

"I have not even recorded what we witnessed in the woods around her cabin." She quickly took her pencil and drew a small picture of the significant objects that represented each direction.

"Let's see; the first direction we visited was the East, which holds a very large stone, and then we went to the Old Oak in the South."

She moved on to the West and sketched the tiny lean-to that resided there. Finally, the North revealed a copper lid, beneath which a small fire pit was nestled within the ground. She recalled how when the old woman drew a line in the air from the shiny object in the Cedar tree to where she stood in the fire pit, Jim quickly recognized that it symbolized the Sacred Pipe.

She heard Rick move through the apartment.

I need to hurry; I'm not quite ready to talk about all of this with him or anyone else but Jim at this point.

The sliding glass door opened and Rick peeked out.

"Hey, the soup looks like it's ready. Can I bring you a bowl?"

"Actually," she responded as she continued to sketch, "it's chilly out here, so I'll come in." She looked up at his handsome face and smiled. "Give me five more minutes, please."

Rick put bowls, saucers, some bread and butter, and two glasses of water on the counter. He heard the glass door slide open and closed, and Ruth walked into the kitchen.

"Brrr, it's getting cold." She rubbed the sides of her arms. "Thanks for getting everything ready. I needed to review some things before tomorrow. Jim and I are going to visit the old woman, and I need to see if I have any questions for her that need clarification."

"Let me help warm you up a bit," he said as he gave her a bear hug and rubbed her back. "It's been a great day; thank you for fitting me into your busy schedule."

Ruth felt horrible; she didn't want him to feel as though she had "fit him into her schedule." She stood back and looked up at him.

"Rick, I never want you to feel that way! I hope you know I'm happy to have a day with you." She hugged him. "Maybe it's time to reassess our routines and ensure that each of us is content with the time we have together."

He loved her so very much. He returned her hug and stood back with a wide smile, and looked her in the eyes.

"You are a mind reader!"

"No," she said, returning his smile. "I just know you, as you know me! Now, let's get some food in our bellies. That soup smells delicious!"

The old woman held the basket of treasures in her lap and lifted the lid. "Okay, let's do this."

The very first objects to fall out were the black bag with the gold compass and the large wooden ring that her Uncle had carved. They landed smack dab into her lap. She glanced at the fire.

"Now, that's obvious! I like when things are clear! My brain doesn't have time to 'mull' things over."

Then she felt a nudge in her heart and she responded.

I gotcha!

She returned the lid securely onto the basket and put the basket back in its place. Then she slipped the wooden ring onto one of her fingers, held the compass in her hand, and took a deep breath.

The image of a beautiful Mandala she had been gifted by a friend appeared before her. She smiled as she reminisced about their sweet relationship. He, too, was a Seeker of Spiritual Truths, and when they had first met, the deep spiritual energy and communication between them was almost immediate.

We all have that ability; it is an innate gift with which we are born. It's just a matter of uncluttering the beliefs we learn from our culture, and to make room for our natural instincts. It's not about either/or; it's about honoring both aspects.

The vision dissolved, and she glanced over at the sailboat painting.

"Destiny happens, if we pay attention. And, it *can* bring love into our lives." She held the black bag and the wooden ring to her heart.

"Love comes in many ways, and I am grateful to experience the different relationships that it brings."

The fire began to crackle and pop as flames danced with the burning logs, and another vision began to emerge as she was lifted up to the Sky Nation. She was nudged to look downward and, as she did, she saw the unique pieces that sat in the sacred directions and around her cabin.

Looking down from Above, her eyes were drawn to the East direction, where the giant stone glistened and pulsed. She moved her eyes toward the South, to the Magnificent Old Oak, and the wonder of nature that created such natural beauty stirred her heart.

Most humans cannot imagine such natural wonders!

She inhaled deeply as her eyes continued to the West, and a feeling of sweet quietness filled her heart as the lean-to came into view. Her heart fluttered.

Ahhh, my place of prayer!

Another deep exhale, and she moved to the North. Her heart was filled with joy as she felt the warmth of the many fires that had burned in the fire pit within Earth Mother, while the reflector in the tree hung directly over the copper cover. She smiled. "The Sacred Pipe!" She touched her heart, and looked with gratitude upon this symbol of unity and balance, and how it so beautifully represents the masculine and feminine within each of us.

She felt a nudge to look up. A group of Elders sat around a glowing fire and watched her as they had for many years. They had called her to that land, and had guided her to her Teacher on Earth. They were a brother and sisterhood of friends that sat together around the fire on the "other side" for more years than can be imagined. They held the fire for those who sought clarity, understanding, and a path to Truth. While they all acknowledged her presence with a familiar nod, one of them encouraged her to look down.

She turned her eyes downward and noticed something she had never realized. The sacred pieces on her land that represented the sacred directions formed a perfect circle, with her cabin strategically placed in the center.

"A Mandala!" she stammered. "It's a Mandala!"

As she inhaled deeply, she felt the cushion of her chair and her feet on the floor, as well as the ring on her finger and the black bag with the compass in her hand. She exhaled slowly, allowing her "light body" to fully integrate with her physical body. After several more rhythmic breaths she was completely present in the here and now. She slowly opened her eyes and focused on the fire in front of her. She smelled the scent of the logs, and felt the warmth of the fire and the comfort of her sweet home.

It is wonderful to visit the other side, and when I return to the coziness and comfort of my physical home I am also more aware and appreciative of my Earthly gifts, so often taken for granted.

The sound of the fire seemed to welcome her back as it crackled and popped with the joy of her return.

"Okay, we know what's next. Let's do it!"

She slipped off the ring and held it in her hands along with the black bag, and then rose from her chair and approached the fire. She gently dropped to her knees and held her treasures close to the fire as she began to pray.

"Infuse these gifts with the sweetness and innocence of the hearts that gave them to me. May the beauty of love burn brightly within these treasures." She held them to her heart.

"I hold these objects to my heart to multiply the love within my heart, that I may have an abundance of love to share with the Seekers of Truth who find their way here." She opened her eyes and addressed the fire.

"Eternal Flame of Love, help me to stay in the moment, to listen to my heart, and to speak Truth to every individual who comes to me." The entire room filled with the energy of her prayers, and joy filled her heart as she spoke to her Allies.

"It has been many moons since we gathered with others to celebrate life, to renew our relationships with the Divine, and to connect as a community to share our lives." She smiled and stood up.

"I feel like dancing! Let this be the beginning of something transformative for the entire world! Indeed, I know that whatever we do for ourselves also assists others with doing the same." She giggled as she moved about the room in a playful dance. She was grateful to be a witness to the birthing of a new chapter for the planet.

Not to mention, I love to dance, and I am a very willing dance partner!

The dishes were washed and put away, and Ruth had just put the remaining soup into the refrigerator.

"Hey, Ruth, I have a question for you," stammered Rick.

Ruth closed the refrigerator door.

His voice sure sounds different; wonder what's up?

She looked at him. "You look sorta serious. Actually, I don't think I've ever seen that look." She hugged him and then stood back. "Ask away!"

"Well," he hesitated, "ahhh, this is weird; I never feel awkward asking you anything. Cautious, yes, but not awkward. But, what the heck," he grinned, "I'll just spit it out!"

"By all means, do! I can hardly wait to hear your question."

"I know you are going with Jim tomorrow to see your Teacher," he said, shifting uncomfortably. "I was just wondering if it would be okay for me to go with you two?" He took a gulp of his water. "Now, if you think it is best for me to go with just you, I certainly can wait, I was just thinking ..."

Ruth gave him a big smile as she put her finger across his lips to interrupt him.

"You are so darned cute I can hardly stand it!" She grabbed him and gave him a kiss.

"Well, I..."

"This is so out of the blue," she laughed, "and, Sweetheart, it makes my heart so happy that I cannot even find the words."

He stood in front of her, feeling relieved that the question had been asked.

"This wasn't planned," he admitted. "I'll assure you of that."

Ruth smiled. "I do want you to meet her, and the sooner the better. I feel as though I need to check with Jim, though, to see if he's comfortable with the three of us going together."

"Of course, and I understand that. Whatever you and Jim decide works for me. Now, do you need me to get out of your hair for a while? I've taken up a lot of your time these past twelve hours."

She grabbed both of his hands. "I love you, Rick. There is no one else in the world like you, and I want you to know that."

They embraced tightly as though to confirm their commitment to each other. Something organic and very powerful had just transpired between them.

She glanced at the clock.

"It's 2:15; would you mind giving me a few hours to sit with all of this? I'd love for you to come back, or I can come to your house … say, about 6:30?"

"You got it. I definitely need to take care of laundry that is piled sky high, or I'll be going to work in my birthday suit!" he laughed.

"I know you're a lot like me. You always have something you can work on, and laundry is definitely one thing that can only wait so long. Besides," she said, blushing, "I'd prefer to be the only one who sees you in your birthday suit!"

He, too, blushed, "Then I'll be back around 6:15 or so. How about I pick up a pizza on my way here?"

He knew she loved pizza, and did her best to not eat it often. But, this was a special occasion. At least, in his book it was. He was about to enter into foreign territory that he knew absolutely nothing about, but he loved her enough that if it was important to her, he wanted to support her as much as he could. Or, as much as she would let him!

Her eyes widened. "Pizza!! You know my weaknesses." She reached out and gave him a bear hug. "That, and you!" They both laughed.

Rick had never felt happier in his life. He put on his jacket and hat and gave her another hug before he left.

She just stood there for a few moments after the door had closed.

"I have no idea what just happened!" She looked upward. "But, whatever it was is long overdue!" Then she called Jim.

"Hey, Ruth, what brings a call from you? Are we still on for tomorrow?"

"Yes, I'm ready to visit our Teacher. Something has come up, however, that I would like to run by you. Do you have a few minutes?"

"Actually, I'm at work; however, I can stop by on my way home if you need to chat."

"You know, that would terrific, if Sarah and the boys aren't eagerly awaiting your arrival."

He laughed. "Yes, they are generally glad to see me after a long day at work, and I won't complain about that! I'll text Sarah and let her know I'll be home about forty-five minutes later than usual. That often happens since I'm the 'boss man' and need to take care of things that sometimes don't get completed on time. So, how about I drop by about three, give or take a few minutes?"

"That would be great if it isn't an inconvenience. Would you like some tea or a cup of coffee?"

"You know me, coffee would be great," he responded. "Thank you! I'll see you in a bit."

"Sounds good, and I'll get that coffee brewing so it'll be fresh and hot when you arrive."

"Perfect! Is there anything I can pick up for you on my way?"

"No, thank you. I'm good!"

"Okay! See ya soon!"

Ruth went out to the patio and brought in her journal and blanket.

"I'm not certain I'm ready for winter. But, I guess I don't need to be just yet. We still have more than a month or so before we will officially have to contend with those steady cold temps." She set the journal and blanket on the couch and headed into the kitchen.

I'd better see if I have something to offer Jim; I know he loves snacks.

"Let's see, I have some leftover peanut butter cookies that I made for Rick … that's it! Jim will love those!"

She gathered the necessary items and placed them on the kitchen counter. *Guess I'll make a half pot of coffee; I could use a bit myself.*

Everything was ready for Jim when he rang the doorbell. She opened the door, smiled, and swept her arm toward the living room as a grand welcome.

"This way, my friend."

"First things first," he said as he grinned and gave her a hug.

He hung his jacket and hat on the coat pegs and followed her into the kitchen. As he moved through the entryway into the living area, he noticed how impeccable her home was. Everything was color coordinated, items were perfectly arranged on the coffee table, and accent pillows were thrown across the couch. He couldn't help but notice two large stones on a coffee table that was made from three chunks of an exquisite wood that had been sanded and shellacked.

I'll bet Rick made that table for her. I believe he's quite the handyman.

"You have a very nice home, Ruth. And, your directions were perfect, so it was easy to find." He followed her into the kitchen.

"Thank you. I'm glad you didn't have any trouble."

She motioned to the counter. "Help yourself to whatever you'd like, and let's take our snack into the living room. I don't want to take up much of your time."

"Look at those cookies! You know me … already!" They both laughed.

She threw the blanket over the rocker and pointed to the couch. "Have a seat, and please feel free to use the coffee table as you need it. That's what it's here for."

She scooted her journal and blanket to one side of the rocker and sat down before getting straight to her question.

She cleared her throat. "Here's the thing, Jim. Rick asked if he could accompany us tomorrow. I was wondering…"

Jim nearly choked on his coffee. "Geez, that fella doesn't waste any time! My, my." He wiped his mouth. "Pardon me for interrupting; were you about to ask how I felt about that?"

She responded with a sheepish grin.

"Let me help you out. I can tell from the look on your face that you are both surprised and pleased."

She nodded. "I really don't know what to think, and I told Rick I needed to ask you how you felt about it. I did tell him that I want him to meet her, and that it meant so much for him to ask. It's just that we do … well, you know…"

"Unusual work?" he suggested.

"Yes."

She eagerly awaited his response.

"Ruth, if you're waiting for me to decide for you, you'll be waiting awhile. You're a smart woman; you know what you want to do, and what you feel is best."

She stared at him, and he could almost hear her brain analyze, contemplate, and consider the best choice.

"Trust yourself. Trust your gut!" he said as he patted his belly.

She sipped her coffee and took a deep breath.

"Jim, I really want to honor his request. In my wildest dreams I would have never believed a man could see me so clearly and still want me." Tears appeared in her eyes.

"These are happy tears!" she exclaimed. "No doubts, no second guesses; this man is the man I've waited for my whole life, and if he wants to know what touches my heart and feeds my soul, I'm not going to hesitate. He's going to meet the old woman." She returned Jim's smile. "I simply wanted to respect what you and I had planned, because I can take Rick with me another time!"

She grabbed a tissue from the Kleenex box and giggled.

"How do you like my red nose?"

"Ruth, I'm good with whatever *you* decide is best. I'll be here at ten in the morning to pick up whoever is ready to go."

"And, speaking of ready to go, I really need to skedaddle along. I am taking a cookie with me, though. They are delicious!"

He finished his coffee and wrapped a cookie in a napkin.

"If I'm not mistaken, you've never met a cookie you didn't love!" she teased. "Take the rest of them; Rick has some at his place, so he's good. Besides, I'm certain the kids will be glad to help you out with them!"

They both got up and took everything to the kitchen sink.

"I'll take care of these things," said Ruth. "You get going."

She put the remaining cookies into a small bag.

"Here you go. Enjoy your family this evening."

Jim put on his jacket and hat and turned to Ruth.

"I will see you at ten tomorrow morning." He gave her a hug. "And, you have a delightful evening too. I'm certain Rick will be along soon," he said with a wink. "Oh, and I think you look quite lovely with a red nose!"

They both laughed.

"Well, thank you, Jim!" Ruth grinned. "Give Sarah and the kids my best. I'll be ready at 10 o'clock sharp!"

When the door had closed, she went back into the living room, picked up her journal, and wrapped the blanket around her.

"Now, where was I?"

I say that a lot when it comes to this journal. I really need to make this a priority.

She nestled into the blanket, flipped through the journal to where she had left off earlier, and looked at her drawings.

"Hmmm, I wonder?"

She turned to the page with the circle and flipped forward to the pages with her drawings of the objects that represented each of the directions the old woman had shown them when she and Jim had last visited. Then she had an idea.

"Brilliant!" She quickly got up to get scissors and Scotch Tape from the kitchen drawer, and headed back to her comfy "nest."

Within half an hour she paused and smiled. "There it is!"

She had carefully cut around each of the drawings and taped them within the sections that represented the direction in which they were located around the old woman's cabin.

Why is this familiar, and where have I seen something similar to this?

Time passed as she sat deep in thought.

"What is it? I need to reboot the 'computer' in my head, so to speak. So much has happened in the last several months, and there's a lot of 'stuff' stored there!"

The sun was low in the western sky and the orange glow streamed through the hall directly across from where she sat.

"Oh, my gosh, what time is it?"

A text appeared from Doug. "Hey, work just got crazy. Any chance we can chat on the phone this evening?"

"Rick is coming over in a bit; can you chat now?"

Doug responded, "Now is perfect!"

His phone rang within two seconds.

"Wow, that was fast!" he said as he picked up her call. "Thanks for being so flexible."

"Now, talk away, I'm eager to hear anything you want to share."

"I can't really tell you everything; I'm still sorting through it all. What I can say is that my heart feels more peaceful than it ever has. And, my life is taking new directions, which is partly why I can't get together with you for a while. My career just took a giant leap! It's all good, though; Sue's very supportive and feels it's a long overdue promotion.

"I didn't want to leave you hanging, though, so let me just say that I owe you big time for connecting me to that incredible woman in the woods! I know I have a lot to learn, and even more work to do; however, I'm committed to being the best version of myself that I can be. And, who knows? Maybe one day I'll be as wise as you are!" he laughed.

Ruth's heart quickened as a smile spread across her face.

"I'm so happy for you, Doug. When you find your new rhythm at work, let's do have a face-to-face conversation. In the meantime, we can text. Just know this, Doug, we're in this together! Now, get back to what you need to take care of, and know how much I love and respect the man and the brother you are!"

"Thank you, Ruthie," he said with a shaky voice. "That means a lot to me, and you can bet we'll stay connected. Sorry to have to make this so short, and thanks for understanding! I love you, Sis, and give Rick my best."

Doug hung up and Ruth glanced at her phone.

"Oh my, it's nearly six! Rick will be here any time. I need to put this stuff away and shift gears."

She closed the journal and stood up just as Rick knocked on the door and opened it a tad.

"Is there a beautiful woman in here who is waiting for me?"

She greeted him with a smile and a hug. "I'm not used to showing such affection to the pizza delivery person, but you sure are cute!"

"I hope you're hungry, because I got a large one with everything you like."

"Just put it on the coffee table, and I'll get us some wine. We'll have a party in the living room."

"Clothes or no clothes?" he teased.

"Goodness, you read my mind!" she said, blushing. "I'm leaving my clothes on, at least for now. You know me," she laughed. "I tend to be a bit sloppy, and that pizza's probably hot!"

"It is, but not as hot as you are!" he snickered.

He took the pizza to the coffee table, grabbed a few pillows off the couch and set them on the floor in front of the table. Meanwhile, Ruth retrieved two wine glasses and popped the cork on the wine.

"That's my girl!" he grinned.

He patted the pillow beside him, and she promptly placed the wine bottle and glasses on the coffee table before sitting down next to him. Then she poured a generous amount of wine into each glass as Rick lifted the top of the pizza box.

Suddenly, she gasped! Rick was confused by the shocked look on her face.

"What is it?"

She stared at the pizza as though she had never seen one. Her heart began to pound as her pulse raced.

"What, Ruth, what's up? You look like you have never seen a pizza!"

She shook her head and opened her mouth, but nothing came out. All she could see was a giant circle divided into pie-shaped pieces. She was speechless.

I mean, what in the world?

"It's ... it's nothing, really; I just can't explain it right now."

She lifted her wine glass. Rick picked up his glass, though still bewildered by her reaction to the pizza.

"To magic, miracles, and mysteries," she toasted, looking into his eyes. "And, I would be most grateful for you to accompany Jim and me to the old woman's cabin tomorrow."

His eyes widened as he returned her toast, filled with the humor of it all. *This is going to be a wild ride!*

"And, to many more mysterious happenings! I'm most excited to share the journey with you, my beautiful lady!"

Another clink of their glasses sealed the deal.

Rick and Ruth were cloaked in warm attire by 9:45 the next morning, ready to embark on the next chapter of their lives.

"Come on down, the car's warm!" Jim texted her.

She responded, "We'll be right there."

They exited the apartment building and hurried to Jim's car, and Ruth noticed someone else in the car.

Who is that?

Then she saw that it was Sarah, and smiled.

Rick opened the door for Ruth, then went around the car and got into the back seat beside her.

"Glad you could join us today, Sarah!" said Ruth.

"You never know what to expect," Sarah said as she turned to look at Ruth. "I'm glad to be accompanying you and Rick. I hope the old woman is as glad to see the group of us show up unannounced!"

"You know she won't be surprised," responded Jim. "She's probably already preparing food for a larger-than-usual group of visitors!"

Rick reached for Ruth's hand. He was both nervous and excited.

"We'll be received with much love," she assured him as she squeezed his hand. "You can bet on that!"

Jim looked at her through the rearview mirror and winked. This was going to be a day all of them would remember.

"How was the pizza last night?"

Ruth was puzzled; she hadn't mentioned the pizza to Jim. Then she got her wits about her. Of course, he knew; that's how this works.

"I'll tell you about that one of these days. But, for now," she paused, "to the cabin, James!"

They all laughed heartily as they headed out of the city into the country, and to *The Gathering* at the old woman's cabin.

The Mandala

The "get acquainted" drive was lovely. Sarah spent most of her time turned to the back seat as she and Rick exchanged lively conversation. They chatted about everything from living in the country versus the city to politics.

Ruth was lost in thought as she stared out the window at the landscape.

I wonder what Rick will think of my friend? Wonder if he'll have the same impression I did the first time I met her? The circumstances are different, of course; I was seeking to resolve an internal nudge, and he's coming now to support me. But, he'll still have some sort of impression. She's such a unique individual. Still…

"Hey, where are you?" Rick whispered as he gently touched her hand. She seemed to be in another world, and he didn't want to scare her.

She quickly returned to the moment.

"Why, I'm here with you!" She softly kissed his cheek.

"I meant to tell you how beautiful you look today," he whispered. "Is that pearl hair comb new? I don't believe I've ever seen it."

She blushed. "Why, thank you, and it's actually very old. I don't wear it often, but there's a story behind it that I'll share with you sometime."

He smiled as he softly moved his hand down her hair.

"I look forward to hearing it."

"Well, we're almost there. How ya feeling, Rick?" Jim interjected as he looked in the rearview mirror at the two lovebirds.

Sarah grinned at Jim. She felt so grateful for the amazing transformation in both their lives since he had met the old woman.

"I'm doin' good, thanks," said Rick as he cleared his throat. "If I'm to be completely honest, I'm a bit nervous, but I'm good!"

Ruth felt excited to be sharing this experience with him. Doug now knew her special friend, and to be sharing it today with Rick was the icing on the cake!

They pulled into the parking spot and retrieved their personal items. Ruth noticed that Sarah had flowers.

"Those flowers are gorgeous, and I'm certain our friend will be more than delighted to receive them. That was very thoughtful of you, Sarah."

"Well, thank you," smiled Sarah. "You know how we women love flowers." She looked at Rick.

"So I've been told," smiled Rick.

Jim led the way as they meandered along the path through the Forest, while Rick brought up the rear. Though it was only mid-October, the air was brisk, signaling an early winter.

"I see smoke coming from the chimney," Jim observed, as he turned to Rick.

"We might need to carry some wood to her porch. I try to make certain she has plenty of kindling and wood for the winter by mid-November." He looked at the gray skies, dotted with peeks of blue. "But, from the look and feel of things, it may be really cold before then."

"I'd love to help," offered Rick. "My *gramps and grams* live in the woods, and I always enjoy the looks on their faces when the porch has been stacked with wood and kindling." His heart fluttered at the thought.

"Actually, I need to get over to their place and make certain they're ready for the coming cold weather, as well. If I don't, Gramps will be trying to do it himself, and at eighty he has no business doing anything but pointing to where he wants it stacked."

Ruth hadn't heard Rick speak of his grandparents for some time, and she could hear the tenderness in his voice as he spoke of them now.

Rick took in the beauty of the Forest, the thickness of the woods, the various sizes of trees that were nearly bare, and the richness of the land now covered with leaves. The fresh scent of pine filled the air with an intoxicating fragrance, as the various critters that lived on the land scurried about preparing for winter.

Rick felt a rush of emotions as they approached the clearing to the cabin, and then steadied himself.

It's more than my memories; there's something in the air that's ... well, mysterious.

He felt a thrill as the cabin became visible. He felt as though they had entered an enchanted land, filled with an intense energy beyond words.

It feels like something from a storybook! I remember this place! But ... that's not possible ... is it? I have never been here; and, yet, it feels very familiar.

He suddenly smelled chocolate chip cookies, hot cocoa, and the scent of his gramps' pipe.

Wait a minute, what's happening?

Ruth turned around. "Rick?"

That brought him back to the moment. He saw how far he had fallen behind the others and picked up his pace.

"Wow!" he responded. "Sorry about that; this place is enchanting!"

"No need to apologize," she grinned. "That's what happens on this land."

Jim stepped onto the porch, opened the screen door and knocked on the interior door.

"Your visitors are here," he warned the old woman. Within seconds the door opened and the old woman moved aside to let them in.

"Hurry on in!" she said. "It's cold outside!"

They all went in, removed their boots, and hung up their coats. Jim was the first one in and, after he had hung up his coat, he walked over to the old woman. He wanted to hug her, but he thought she might need to adjust to having four people visit at one time. And, she hadn't yet met Rick.

Not that she doesn't know him; she has a way of "knowing" everyone that comes onto her land, even before she officially meets them.

"It's good to see you, my friend, and I hope you're ready for some visitors." Jim glanced at the fireplace and noticed that three additional chairs had been added beside the usual visitor's chair.

"It appears you were expecting us!" he whispered with a grin.

She grinned back and whispered, "Tell your friends where to sit, then come into the kitchen and help me."

"You got it!" He directed the others where to sit, then followed her into the kitchen. They soon came out with two trays and placed them on the fireplace ledge.

"I got this," he said. "You can take your seat and I'll pass the trays around."

She nodded and sat down in her chair.

Ruth stood up. "May I help you, Jim?"

"Certainly!"

Jim handed out mugs and napkins, while Ruth followed behind him and poured the cocoa. He then brought around a tray of chocolate chip cookies, and everyone took what they wanted. Jim and Ruth then poured hot cocoa for themselves, as Sarah stood up and offered to get cookies and napkins for the two of them.

The five of them enjoyed the warmth of the fire and the peacefulness of the room as they indulged in their snack. The crackling and popping of the fire invited them to sit in the quietness of the moment.

Rick's mind whirled.

Oh, my goodness, hot cocoa and chocolate chip cookies ... I smelled 'em on the trail! I suppose the scent of Gramps' pipe will be filling the air next!

Ruth leaned toward the old woman.

"This is my friend, Rick. Rick, this is my friend and Teacher, whom I have mentioned many times."

The old woman and Rick acknowledged one another with a nod.

"I apologize for not using your name," Ruth said to her Teacher. "However, I've never heard you mention it!"

"You've never asked," she responded.

"Neither have I!" laughed Jim.

Sarah and Rick joined in the laughter, while the old woman merely sipped her cocoa.

Jim shook his head. "Please, accept my apologies for not asking, either. But, nothing like the present moment," he said, clearing his throat. "What is your name ... or, maybe it is best to ask what you would like us to call you?"

The old woman set her mug on the small table, grabbed her tatting bag, and pulled out the shuttle and thread. She wove the thread between her fingers, moved the shuttle through the thread, and began to tat.

"Just call me the old woman," she smiled.

The four of them looked at each other and Jim broke the silence with a hearty laugh! The laughter spread across the room with a playfulness that put a smile on the old woman's face. Her heart was very happy; it had been many moons since she had known such lightness.

As the laughter began to subside, Rick spoke up.

"May I stoke the fire?"

She nodded, and he rose from his chair and stood in front of the fire with open palms facing the warmth of the flames. Then he carefully moved the long pieces of wood to the side with the poker and stirred the coals. Mindful of the fragile logs, he slid them back over the hot burning coals and added a couple of medium sized logs diagonally on top of them. He finished by adding a slightly larger log directly on top, then placed the poker back in it's holder and returned to his chair.

As the others watched Rick, the old woman paused her tatting to observe how he worked with the fire. Ruth, with tearful eyes, couldn't remember ever watching him tend a fire.

Wash the windows of my soul; it's time I see clearly everything about Rick, so that he may see everything about me.

Rick leaned over and gave her a soft kiss as he squeezed her hand.

Sarah shared Ruth's tears, as she reached for Jim's hand and whispered, "I love you!"

He leaned over and kissed her on the cheek.

"Back atcha!"

Flames danced across the logs and warmth filled the air as the old woman resumed her tatting and began her story.

"Many years ago, our ancestors sat before a fire such as this one. A fire was a sacred place for all in the community to bring their concerns to Great Spirit. All indigenous tribes knew the importance of living in right relationship with all the inhabitants that shared the land, which resulted in a peaceful, harmonious way of life. They understood life to be a Sacred Walk."

She put her tatting aside and went into her bedroom. The visitors looked at each other in silence, but Jim and Ruth knew that whatever she was doing had purpose.

The old woman emerged from her bedroom within a few moments, holding a large, circular, tanned piece of leather strung onto a metal ring that had been wrapped with strips of the tanned leather. It was beautiful, mysterious, and magical, with drawings, feathers, bones, and a host of other tokens affixed to the front. The back had only some sort of writing.

Rick held his breath.

My God, it's a Mandala!

The hair on the back of his neck stood up as he exhaled. He had to compose himself, although he had no idea why. The Mandala just seemed so familiar, and he felt a deep reverence for it.

Ruth glanced at him; she reached over and tenderly patted his hand. Then she put her hand back in her lap; it was his work, and only he could move through whatever he was experiencing. She was merely there to be a witness, and to stay strong within herself in order to support him.

The old woman walked past the four of them, who looked on in amazement, but tried not to stare. She held the object up in front of the fire for a moment, then sat down in her chair and held it in her lap.

She put her finger on the top of the circle.

"Wherever you start on a circle," she said as she slowly moved her finger clockwise around the outside of the leather-bound ring, "you will always return to where you started. When you continue this rotation, it is always about moving forward. If you turn around, you will go backwards, but to get to your destination, you must always walk forward."

When she had returned to the top of the circle, she stood and placed the object on the fireplace ledge and returned to her chair.

"Our lives are like that. If we are to grow and evolve, we must move forward with intention and purpose; we must know where we want to go. Life will present us with a few curves, but they are merely bumps in the road if we remain focused on our destination and do not allow distractions to interfere.

"Let me be clear, however; those side roads can offer us many valuable teachings. It is important to stay awake, and to consciously choose which path to take. More importantly, we must be willing to accept responsibility for the consequences of our actions. If we find the results of our choices are not what we thought or hoped they would be, we can choose again."

She stared at the fire and gently shook her head.

"It seems the word 'responsibility' has been deleted by the masses. Few still remember the spiritual significance of that word, and it seems most folks these days would rather blame their choices on someone else when things don't go as they had hoped or planned. But, I digress.

"Circles," she continued, "have a very powerful significance in countless religions and traditions. While the verbiage may be different, their meaning is universal. The circle was thought to be an outer manifestation of an inner understanding of Life. The word to describe this geometric design originates from the Sanskrit word for circle, which is Mandala."

"Whether in Hinduism, Buddhism, Christianity, Native American, or the beliefs of any other indigenous tribes, the Mandala symbolizes that life is never-ending, and that everything is interconnected. It holds the energy of life that represents the wholeness of self, and is based on respect for Elders and traditions.

"Just as important, the Mandala encompasses the spiritual journey within an individual, and is used as a way to connect the Earthly and Spiritual realms. It is also a way to contemplate the self in connection with the Divine, for it is that world Within that is most important in order to intimately know how to truly *be* our Divine, authentic Self.

"We must understand the basic teachings that we were indoctrinated with through societal norms and other beliefs, in order to be able to unravel some of those traditions that do not reflect Truth. We must look to our ancestors for Truth. My bloodline, like most of yours, is a blend of several cultures. However, the ways of the Native Americans of this land taught me most about who I am as a Seeker of Truth, and it is those teachings that I want to share with you today.

"Let us begin in the East, where all creation is birthed. It is through this portal that all beings emerge from the Spirit world and into physical form. Spring resides in the East, where new endeavors and dreams are planted into the richness of sweet Mother.

"All seasons are Divinely orchestrated and heralded in through the rhythms of nature, which are based on the laws of the Universe. Humans may try to explain, rearrange, and redefine those laws; however, they will not succeed, because humans come and go, as do the laws they live by.

"*Because* the universe shifts and changes, nature is always the orchestrator of life. We must honor and move with that flow, and with what we feel in our hearts to be true and real. In order to do this, we must understand the core of our inner being."

She paused a moment.

"Each direction is also represented by animal totems that represent the energy of that direction. These totems serve as teachers and guides, and assist those who enter the perimeters of each respective direction. They may be called Gatekeepers, Protectors, or Guardians of the Divine gifts offered by each direction.

"The animal totems I share today were taught by my Cherokee Teacher, although other tribes may speak of different animals. Always remain respectful, and listen to the teachings that others share to describe the 'medicine' or energy of the animals they hold sacred for each direction. Use the 'ears' of your heart, and tell your ever-curious mind that its only task is to respect and to remember what is spoken, rather than to judge or analyze.

"The Eagle and the Condor are the totems of the East. We begin our Sacred Walk on Earth as pure Spirit, and these winged ones are the overseers of our souls.

"During childhood, our caregivers tend to our basic physiological needs of food and shelter, and provide a sense of security and safety in order for us to thrive and survive this Earthly experience. This very early stage from Birth to Childhood sets the tone by which we will move through life. Spring is a time of growth, and each year we begin the next round on the Sacred Wheel of Life.

"We, like all of creation, grow and expand, and then move on to the next stage of life, where we will experience new teachings. After we have walked the Sacred Wheel approximately twelve times, we leave the comfort of our 'nest,' as we carry the innocence of childhood into the next stage of life, known as Adolescence."

She glanced at the fire.

"May I take care of the fire?" asked Rick, as if on cue.

She nodded, and Rick got up and stoked the fire. The old woman "recognized" him, and was pleased. She knew he was familiar with these ways, even if he had not yet consciously become aware of these Truths.

He's definitely in tune with the natural world!

When Rick had returned to his seat, the old woman continued.

"The South represents the season of summer, offering us the gifts of play, adventure, and the opportunity to feel the warmth of relationships outside of our families. During this stage of Adolescence we begin to question what we were taught during our childhood by our families, churches, and teachers. As we maneuver our way through these years of exploration, we learn about trust, resiliency, forgiveness, and how to not take ourselves, or life, too seriously. These years may be exciting, but also may be fraught with confusion and uncertainty as we struggle to find our sense of identity and purpose.

"In the South we learn about love and belonging, and about the powerful emotions that come with being human, as we strive to find our place in this new territory. Our search for identity will open the door for us to take a closer look at the beliefs, perceptions, judgments and prejudices that we internalized as a child. We will explore more deeply what feels true for us as young adults, what we wish to leave behind with our childhood, and what we will carry into the next stage of life. We will also begin to seek a partner as we discover the burning passion of love.

"The totems of the South are Dolphin and Mouse. Dolphin will teach us how to breathe, in order to move with grace and ease through the currents of emotions. Dolphin will also help us learn how to dive deeply into emotions, rather than to hold our breath and wait for them to subside.

"Mouse offers to help us learn how to pay attention to what is in front of us, so that we do not get trapped by the details of life.

"After we have walked the Sacred path approximately forty rounds, or years, we enter the next stage, which is Mid-Life. The midpoint of life beckons us to seek an answer to two questions: 'What have I done with my life?' and, 'What do I want to accomplish in the second half of my life?'

"The West gives us the opportunity to closely examine what we have learned and experienced throughout the year, and during our cumulative rounds. The West represents fall, a time of harvest, and during the years of Mid-Life we will metaphorically 'separate the wheat from the chaff' in our lives.

"The Standing Ones drop their leaves in the fall; likewise, all the illusions and secrets we have hidden away will drop at our feet. Just as the trees become fully bare and exposed, we, too, will feel more vulnerable than we ever thought possible. The nudges we ignored over the years will now beckon our attention.

"Bear and Buffalo are the two totems for the West. Just as the Bear gathers what is needed to prepare for winter, we will determine what of our 'harvest' needs to be recycled or kept for the winter months ahead. Bear teaches us to be gentle with ourselves, while remaining strong within.

"Buffalo helps us to notice, and to be grateful for, the abundance in our lives, and to value the life-supporting gifts of prayer. Just as the Buffalo gifted the Native Americans with every part of its body to sustain the community, so we are asked to look at the gifts it is time for us to offer to others. We will uncover the things that we've squirreled away, and make decisions to either ignore them or to deal with them, which will help us to truly feel a sense of self-esteem and self-confidence.

"After approximately sixty rounds on our Sacred Walk around the Wheel, we will enter the North, and the final stage of our life: Old Age. Here we accept our place as an Elder in our family and in our community. We are offered a place to present the gifts that we came here to leave as a legacy for our families and communities, and ultimately for our world.

"The totems for the North are all the white critters, who represent the purity of life; and, the Wisdom Keepers, who once walked this Earth, and who now sit on the Other Side to assist those in the physical world. Like all totems, they are ready and willing to guide us on our Earthly journey, *if we ask*. They will not interfere in our choices; it is up to *us* to make the request, and then listen for their guidance, which they will provide in our hearts. We will become familiar with the 'voice' of our heart if we pay attention. This gives us the confidence and trust to develop the gift of discernment when our heart speaks.

"Hopefully, with each round we experience in the North, we learn more clearly how to connect with these Wisdom Keepers throughout each season, stage, and round of our Walk. Then we will enter Old Age with these totems as our most precious Allies, who will ultimately assist us with our move from Earth back home to Spirit."

With the long chain still attached to the spool, she stood up and carried it to the fire.

"Lastly, I wish to honor White Buffalo Calf Woman, who resides in the North. She honored the voice of Creator and offered those in her community the Sacred Pipe ceremony as a means to carry their prayers to the Great Mystery. Her courage is an example of what each of us carries within our heart. As in all matters, what we do with these gifts is our choice."

At that very moment, Rick caught a whiff of his Gramps' tobacco.

There it is ... dear heaven!

The old woman turned and looked at her visitors. All were solemn, and tears streamed from Ruth's and Sarah's eyes.

"She still offers the Sacred Pipe to anyone who feels the call to pray in such a way."

She turned back to the fire and placed the tatted chain and thread across the mantle, waved her hand over them, touched her heart, then turned to her visitors.

"Let's feed our hungry bellies!"

They were startled; it felt a bit anti-climactic for her to shift gears so quickly! Yet, Jim and Ruth knew that it was simply another of the old woman's ways.

"The soup is in the crockpot," she said to Jim and Sarah, "and there's a plate of cold cuts and cheese in the fridge. If you'd get the flatware and dishes ready, I'll be back directly." Then she disappeared into her bedroom.

Jim turned to Ruth and Rick. "We can take care of things if you two would like to just sit and chat a bit."

"Thank you," responded Ruth. "We just need a few minutes and then we'll be in to help."

She then turned to Rick as Jim and Sarah headed into the kitchen.

"How are things for you?"

He nodded his head. "I'm good. Reckon my body's a bit stiff from sitting, not to mention the tension it feels just from me trying to absorb all those teachings. I'm telling you," he said as he reached for her hand, "something has happened today that I cannot begin to put into words."

She listened quietly to his heart's attempt to absorb and put into words all the information he had received. How well she knew his dilemma; there was just so much energy, and so much purity and Truth in the words that were shared. As she examined his face, she saw him in a way she had never seen him before. He was so strong, so confident, so sure of things; yet, here he sat, so…

Vulnerable! That's it; he's vulnerable!

"Would you like to sit by yourself for a bit?" she offered.

"No; what I really need is to step outside for a few minutes." He leaned over and gave her a kiss. "You do know how much I love you … right?"

"Indeed, I do!" she smiled. "Take all the time you need."

Rick put on his hat and coat and stepped outside, and walked down the steps to the land.

Let's see…

He looked up at the sky and noticed the sun was past the mid-way point, then looked to his left.

"So, this must be the East," he whispered as he began to walk toward the Forest.

Ruth watched him from the front window as he headed into the East.

He's moving toward the huge, sparkling boulder; I wonder if he'll go far enough into the woods to see it?

Then she had an epiphany! The drawings she had cut and pasted into the pie-shaped sections representing the directions of the old woman's yard revealed a Mandala when viewed from Above!

She returned her focus to Rick, and then realized what he was doing was his business, not hers, so she went into the kitchen to help Jim and Sarah. The old woman entered shortly thereafter, and pulled from the oven a pan covered with aluminum foil.

Ruth's tummy growled.

She's made those delicious corn muffins! Yum!

Everything was on the table within ten minutes, ready for everyone to fill their bellies. Rick returned as if on cue, and sniffed the air.

"I knew it; everything's ready to eat. I timed that perfectly!" he grinned.

Everyone laughed as they took their places at the beautiful oak table. The old woman sat at the head of the table and extended her hands to the person on each side of her. They all followed her lead until everyone was connected, and then she bowed her head.

"We are grateful for the food of which we are about to partake," she prayed. "We thank you, Mother, for providing the rich soil that brought the seeds into the fullness of their bounty. May these gifts fill our bellies and our hearts with the richness of your love, and renew the cells within our bodies with good health, so that we may be of service to those we meet. As Above, so Below, we thank you!"

The hearty lunch was eaten mostly in silence, as though all the information that had been shared by the old woman was being processed along with the food in their bellies.

"These corn muffins are delicious," said Sarah, breaking the silence. "I'd love to have your recipe."

"I have it and will gladly share it with you," offered Ruth. "That is," she addressed the old woman, "if it is alright with you?"

The old woman nodded her approval.

Sarah continued, "I'll bet everything in this delicious vegetable soup came from your garden?"

"Yes," responded the old woman. "Your husband greatly helped the bounty this year, by building a fence around the perimeters. Those rabbits were no competition for his creativity!"

"That's my Jim!" Sarah said, patting her husband on the shoulder. "He's good with keeping things in order; all you need do is tell him what you need, and if he can't figure it out, he'll find someone who can!"

Jim put his hand in a fist, blew on it and rubbed it on his chest, as if to brag about himself.

"Oh, I love how humble he is!" chimed in Ruth.

The old woman smiled as they laughed. She didn't say what was in her heart; however, the tears in her eyes said it for her. In that moment, her solitude was extinguished and her heart was happy.

When everything had been cleaned up and put away, the old woman offered, "I have a light dessert; would anyone like some coffee as well?"

"Dessert? Did someone say dessert?" piped up Jim.

Sarah shook her head. "He's like this all the time, and wonders why he can't lose a pound!"

"Hey, at least I keep my weight steady," he chuckled as he patted his belly.

"Besides, I want to continue making kids happy by playing Santa at Christmas. Can you imagine how disappointed the kids at the mall would be if the same Santa didn't show up every year?"

"Yeah, right, it's all about the kids," smiled Sarah. "What a sacrifice you have to make!"

The old woman prepared the coffee while the others exchanged teasing comments, then joined them while the coffee brewed.

"I do have three more directions I would like to share with you, if you all have time," she interjected.

Rick looked at Jim.

"I didn't drive," he responded, "but I would love to hear your teachings."

Jim glanced at Sarah, who nodded her affirmation. He turned to the old woman.

"The kids are with their grandparents, so if you're sure you're up to it, we're in!"

"If you'll get the large wooden tray and put some cups and napkins on it, I'll get the dessert," she said to Jim.

Sarah jumped in. "I'll do that for you. Jim can show me where things are if you need to take a few moments for yourself."

The old woman reached into the cabinet and pulled out a large thermos.

"Pour the coffee into this thermos when it's done, and it'll stay hot for some time."

She then pulled a platter covered with an orange cloth from the refrigerator, and set it on the counter next to the tray. As she turned to leave the kitchen, Rick followed behind her.

"With your permission, I'd be honored to stoke the fire."

She looked him directly in the eyes and held his gaze for a few moments. He felt a bit uneasy until she smiled.

"Thank you, Rick. I 'see' you," she said.

With that, she turned and went into her bedroom.

His spine tingled; he had never felt so transparent in his entire life. Who *was* this woman? Was she of this Earth, or a messenger sent by the Spirit world? It was a mystery he looked forward to finding out more about.

Ruth knew something had been spoken between Rick and the old woman, and her heart was filled with joy.

Whoever would have guessed?

Sarah picked up the thermos of coffee and held the kitchen door open for Jim, as he carried a tray full of cups, napkins, sugar and cream, and a mysterious orange covered platter. He set the tray on the fireplace ledge, and Sarah set the thermos beside the tray, mindful to keep a good distance from the Mandala.

Sarah sat down beside Ruth and Rick, and the old woman approached the fire behind Jim. He stepped aside and took his seat as the old woman picked up the abalone shell filled with sage, took a match from the wooden box, and moved in front of the fire. She lit the match and held it to the sage, and when it was well lit she waved the sage around herself, then turned and smudged the others, as well as the tray.

I've seen Jim do that many times, thought Sarah.

When the room felt completely cleansed, the old woman placed the remains of the sage back in the shell. She picked up the tatted chain and thread from the fireplace ledge, took her seat, and returned to her tatting.

"While we experience life on Earth, we will make many walks around the Sacred Wheel of Life. Each year we move through the wheel as one season ends and another begins. Whether we view that walk as a yearly cycle or as a lifetime, each direction offers us the same basic teaching, regardless of the stage of life we occupy."

She looked at Jim and Ruth.

"Do you remember the last three directions?"

"I believe it is Above, Below, and Within," offered Ruth after a few moments. "Is that correct?"

"That is correct, Ruth. Everything Above is part of the Great Mystery; it is the home of the Spirit World, where countless galaxies exist beyond this galaxy. It is what is referred to as the Sky Nation.

"Some refer to Above as the place where angels exist; the residence of our Creator God. It does not matter what name we call to; what matters is that we acknowledge the place from which we came, and to which we will return.

"Our ancestors reside in the Sky Nation, and it has been said that the night stars are the eyes of our ancestors watching over us. These Star

Beings also communicate with us through constellations, and through the movement of the planets. They send these messages from the heavens, to let us know they *see us*! The planets play an intricate part in all life on Mother, and most humans aren't even aware of their influence. Astrology is a very interesting study that will certainly open your eyes to the deep connection between this world and the great beyond.

"Father Sky and Grandfather Sun are pivotal occupants of the great Above. They are the masculine counterparts to the feminine Earth Mother and Grandmother Moon. It is said that the light of Grandfather Sun heralds in each day as Grandmother Moon rests; and, when night falls on Earth, he steps aside as she shares the beauty of her light, and teaches those on Earth how to honor the different phases within themselves. She is a reminder to us that we go through many phases throughout our lives. Thus, anything that troubles or concerns us is a waste of our precious time and resources.

"Together, all of these Teachers offer us a deeper understanding of the importance of both the masculine and the feminine. One is not greater or lesser than the other; rather, each shares its own unique gifts with the inhabitants of Earth Mother.

"It is interesting how little humans know of the powerful influence that both Divine masculine and feminine offer to all living things on this Earth. For example, the gifts of Grandfather and Grandmother directly influence the ocean tides, the weather that transforms the landscape of Mother and enriches her soil, and the changing seasons.

"This is yet another example of what we can learn about our heritage if we will take the time to talk with our parents and grandparents. We need to know our history in order to understand how and why we are the way we are. It doesn't matter whether our families are biological or adoptive; the adults who were our caretakers taught us about life.

"With all those amazing teachers Above, we could say the winged ones are the totems for *both* the Above and Below, because they move fluidly between the two directions."

She paused her tatting and leaned over to touch the floor.

"Below represents the Earth beneath our feet, as well as the living organisms that reside in the depths of the ocean and deep within the core of Earth.

"The totems for Below are the creepy crawlies that move upon Mother on their bellies, the finned ones that swim within her oceans, and all of the microorganisms who live within her. When your human mind is confused, it is always helpful to lie down on the Earth, sit with your back against a tree, feel your bare feet on sweet Mother, or simply pay attention to any animal that crosses your path. A single leaf, a stone, or a shell on the beach, can all be totems attempting to offer you guidance or healing, so pay attention and trust what you see and hear in the natural world.

"Many will deny what they see or hear, but sometimes messages can come through a thought, a phrase, or a dream. Why, even a knothole on a tree can be a message."

Ruth and Jim looked at each other as they remembered the perfect heart-shaped knothole on the Magnificent Old Oak that stood in the South. He pulled an object from his vest pocket and held it to his heart. Sarah noticed and, with a curious look on her face, cleared her throat to get his attention.

He looked at her and opened his hand, revealing the large cat's eye marble, then quickly placed it back in his pocket. She stared at him; she had never seen it before, and was curious to hear more about it when they got home.

"The last direction is the most important connection," continued the old woman. "That is the place Within, which resides in your heart. The totems for this direction vary according to what animal, shape or color you feel drawn to when you think of your heart. While the other directions may also carry a shape and color for you, it is the heart that often takes on a different shape or color as a form of recognition."

She nodded in the direction of the Mandala.

"Within is the most important direction to stay connected to while in physical form, for it is the balance point between the heavens Above and the Earth Below.

"Notice the heart in the center of this Mandala," she continued. "Within it is a Yin and Yang symbol, which represents unity and balance. The white represents the feminine, while the black represents the masculine. Together, they pay homage to the many gifts within my heart. They remind me to stay in balance, and to see the best in all of creation. When I look at this symbol, I see the Great Smoking Mirror that teaches me to see my own reflection in all of creation.

"Within is where, if we allow our hearts to stay open, we will become like the Standing Ones; that is, an anchor between the Spirit world and the physical world. Sadly, few humans allow their hearts to be truly open."

She sighed deeply, looked down at the very long chain, detached it from the spool and tied a knot at the end. Her eyes returned to the fire.

"Any questions?"

The four guests looked at each other, and Jim, Sarah and Rick shook their heads. Ruth, however, spoke up.

"If I understand correctly," she said, "each spring we begin another round on our walk around the Wheel, and that after so many rounds we grow and move on to another stage of Life." She sat back in her chair and gathered her thoughts.

"So, the *East* is about *growth*; the *South* is about *adventure* and discovering what is true for us; the *West* is where we *pause and examine* all that has happened during the year; and from there we move to the *North*, to *be silent, and to reflect* upon what the year has been for us. Then, when spring returns, we're back in the *East*, we *act on* what we learned during the winter, and then the cycle repeats."

"And, that's what *The King did every day in the story you told Ruth?" Jim asked the old woman. She smiled and nodded.

"Yes," responded Ruth, "he honored each direction every single morning. I'll be darned; I finally understand the big picture. Is there anything else you wish to add?" she asked the old woman.

Her teacher shook her head as she placed the spool of thread and shuttle back into the black bag. She stood up and walked to the Mandala, and placed her finger on the East.

"Here's a simple way to remember," she said, as she began to move her finger around the Mandala.

"The *East* represents the *physical*, the *South* represents our *emotions*, the West our *intellect*, and the *North* our *spirituality*. Those are the four core aspects of being human. Stephen Covey offers a very simple summary from a psychological perspective, of the four core aspects of living life with purpose: *to Live, to Love, to Learn, and to Leave a Legacy,*" she said as she repeated the cycle with her finger.

Rick and Sarah looked overwhelmed, but the old woman was confident that Jim and Ruth would help them come to understand the teachings.

"These are my words," she said as she went to Rick and reached for his hand. He felt breathless as the old woman took his left hand and placed the tatted chain into it, then closed his fingers around it.

"It is time to wake up, and time to re-member what you came here to do," she said as she looked directly into his eyes. "You know these ways, so pay attention, and the natural world will direct your path." She patted his hand. "Pay attention!"

She returned to the slowly burning fire, lowered herself to her knees, and bowed her head. Silence hung in the air as the flames began to diminish, and an orange glow danced the length of the well-burned logs. The embers sparkled beneath the logs as if to say, "*Well done, my good and faithful servant.*"

She raised her head and, with a smile, whispered to the fire. She reached for a metal can, lifted the lid, and took out some tobacco. She brought it to her lips and then sprinkled it over the fire. She did the same with some cedar from another can. When she sprinkled the cedar over the fire it danced and crackled with delight.

The others were mesmerized by what they had just witnessed. Jim was attentive to the old woman's cues, so when she turned and looked at him, he immediately stood up and helped her to her feet.

"Are you ready for some coffee and dessert?" offered the old woman.

Jim wanted to respond with "Does a bear poop in the woods?" However, he held his tongue. Sarah read his thoughts and smiled.

"My handsome husband has a phrase he normally uses in response to such an obvious question. I'm grateful he's learned to hold his tongue … well, most of the time, anyway!"

They all laughed heartily, which shifted the seriousness of the moment.

"I don't know about anyone else," interjected Ruth, "but I need to stand for a few moments. I'll step out and see how the temperature feels. Maybe we could have our dessert and coffee on the front porch?"

"That sounds good to me," agreed Rick. "I'll come with you; I could use some fresh air."

The old woman stepped into her bedroom, while Jim and Sarah moved to the fire. They observed the slowly burning embers, and tenderly embraced.

"It's been quite a day!" whispered Jim. "And, if I have not told you lately, I love you to the moon and back."

Sarah smiled. "You have, and I never get tired of hearing you say those words." She looked into Jim's eyes. "Your actions speak what is in your heart and, Sweetheart, I couldn't possibly love you any more than I do at this very moment!"

They exchanged a sweet kiss as Rick and Ruth walked back into the cabin.

"It's downright cold outside," said Rick. "Maybe we should stay in front of the fireplace."

Ruth nodded. "I agree; we certainly don't want our friend to get a cold."

Jim and Sarah sat holding hands. Ruth and Rick sat down beside them, as the old woman emerged from the bedroom with some papers and returned to her seat.

"Would you like the fire stoked or do you want it to burn out?" asked Jim.

"Please stoke it, thank you."

Ruth and Sarah simultaneously got up from their chairs, and both smiled at the synchronicity.

"We're in tune!" observed Sarah.

"Are we ready for the coffee and dessert?" Ruth asked. She looked at the old woman and Rick. She knew Jim would certainly agree with anything that had to do with food.

The old woman smiled. "You might want saucers and forks for the dessert."

Sarah promptly went into the kitchen. Within a few moments she came back with five saucers and forks.

"Thank you; I presumed we would be eating your delicious cookies from this morning. You certainly have gone to a lot of trouble."

"It makes my heart happy to feed those who show up," she replied.

Ruth and Sarah filled two coffee cups and handed them to the old woman and Rick. Ruth lifted the orange cloth and her eyes widened.

"Cheesecake squares! Yummy!"

Jim glanced over as he placed the fire poker back in its place, brushed his hands, and excused himself to go clean up. He passed by Rick and the old woman and saw the cheesecake squares in their laps.

"Mmm, mmm!" he moaned.

Ruth and Sarah were in their seats when he returned, holding their desserts and coffee. He saw his dessert sitting on his chair and went to get himself some coffee.

Sarah jumped up. "Your cup is under your chair; have a seat and I'll pour your coffee."

"I have the best wife in the world!" he proudly announced.

Sarah blushed and smiled. "I do the best I can with what I have to work with!"

They all laughed; everyone seemed to use that phrase rather frequently.

Warmth filled the air, with only the sounds of the fire as it crackled and popped. It was a moment of sweet contentment, as the joy of happy hearts, good food, warm coffee, and the smell of burning wood filled the cabin with abounding love.

Rick had been silent from the moment he had sat down. No words or buzzing thoughts ran through his head; he just had the sweet feeling that comes when one knows everything is as it is supposed to be.

"Except when I'm with Ruthie," he finally said, "I can't say as I have ever felt so peaceful." He looked at the old woman. "Thank you for being so generous with your wisdom, and I have many more questions. Perhaps on my next visit I'll be able to articulate what my heart wishes to know." He glanced at the other three.

"I believe I speak for the others when I ask how we can repay you?" he continued. "Is there anything we can do for you, other than stack firewood?"

Sarah and Jim nodded in agreement as Ruth stood and spoke up.

"I noticed you have drapes over the back of the chairs in the dining room. May Sarah and I help put those up while the guys are busy?"

"Yes, we're eager to help!" added Sarah.

Ruth and Sarah looked at the old woman, but it was Jim who noticed tears in her eyes. He took a deep breath and leaned forward in his chair to look her in the eyes, with great respect and love for her willingness to share her wisdom. It was obvious that it had been a long time since such a large group had gathered in her home. He could feel the joy in her heart as she looked into the fire and stood up.

"It appears we have some work to do … I'm ready!" she agreed.

They all laughed as Jim and Rick rose from their chairs to join the ladies.

"Okay!" Jim said as he rubbed his hands together. "I believe your ladder is in the shed out back? And, your tool box is in the utility room?"

The old woman simply smiled and nodded.

The men put on their coats, as the ladies moved the tray filled with dishes and leftover cheesecake into the kitchen. Jim headed out the back door, while Rick went out the front door to begin clearing a space for wood to be stacked. It was a joyful, yet serene moment, in which five human hearts busied themselves with the tasks at hand.

Busy hands, happy hearts, thought the old woman as she instructed the ladies where to put the curtains they had taken down from the windows, to be cleaned before being stored.

Jim entered the cabin through the utility room, grabbed the toolbox and headed into the main room. As he passed through the kitchen he leaned over and gave Sarah a kiss as she carefully wrapped a small box with foil.

"Your friend felt you would enjoy the leftover cheesecake and cookies. Of course," she smiled, "she claims they are for the kids, but you and I know she has great affection for you. As do I!" she said as she stood on her toes and returned his kiss.

Within an hour, everything had been cleaned up and put away, and the five of them again stood in front of the fire. The old woman took a few small pieces of the newly stacked wood and fed the fire.

"Thanks to all of you for your help. All the beautiful ones that live within and around the boundaries of this home appreciate your strong hands and wide open hearts."

She took a pinch of tobacco from the can on the fireplace ledge, touched the floor, held it to her lips and scattered it onto the reignited fire. The flames danced with delight as she held her hands before it. Then she turned to her guests with her hands on her chest.

"Before you leave, I have something that might be helpful to you." She retrieved the papers from under her chair and handed them to Jim.

"These are old; however, they might be of use to help you remember the various teachings of the Mandala. They were handouts I used many years ago." She rose from her chair and picked up the Mandala.

"Before we go, where would you like these other two chairs to be returned?" inquired Jim.

"Place them on each side of the West window in the dining room. Thank you." Then she turned and disappeared into her bedroom.

Rick and Sarah looked concerned.

"Is she alright, or do we need to see if she needs anything?" asked Rick.

Ruth and Jim shook their heads and smiled.

"No; it's just time for us to leave," Jim whispered.

They all donned their coats and hats and slipped on their boots. Ruth took one last look at the fireplace before they left the cabin, and Rick and Jim each dropped a gift into the twig basket by the door.

"She gave us notes!" exclaimed Ruth through joyful tears. "I love it! Now we can really understand the Sacred Walk, the endless circle of life, the *Mandala.*"

The Awakening

Cold air blew in from the North as Rick walked out the front door onto his porch. He smiled as he scanned the sky and smelled the fresh scent of autumn from the Standing Ones that surrounded his country home.

"Won't be long and the cold winds of winter will keep us inside our homes. Time to get over to Gramps' and Grams' and help them prepare for winter."

He loved *Gramps and Grams;* they had what he aspired for in a relationship. He looked up and closed his eyes.

"That's what our relationship will be like, Ruthie, I promise!"

Clad in several layers of clothing, he was ready for another busy day at work. *I have so many things for which to be grateful.*

"One of which is my occupation. I get to build homes for people to enjoy, and where they can make lifelong memories." He took a deep breath and smiled. "Makes my heart happy!"

He put the tools he needed into his truck and headed to the worksite. He considered the tasks that needed to be completed before the subcontractors could begin their work.

His thoughts shifted to Ruthie, the visit with the old woman, and the anticipation of new mysteries that lay before him. Then he returned his focus to the present.

Okay, I need to see the jeweler today and order the ring. Geez, life has suddenly become very busy!

Warmth swept through his heart. "And, I couldn't be more pleased!"

Rick pulled up his gramps' number and pushed the call button. His gramps answered after only a couple of rings.

"Hello, Rick, your grams and I were just talking about you the other day. We wondered what you've been up to. How are you?"

"Actually, I have been busy, and that's not an excuse for letting so much time go by without seeing you two. And, that's why I'm calling. Are you and Grams going to be home this evening?"

"We sure are! We don't go many places these days, but then I guess neither do your mom and dad, because we haven't seen them in at least a month."

Rick heard his grandmother in the background.

"What is Grams saying?"

"Oh, she's just reminding me that we saw your dad last week. What do I know? Every day seems to be the same."

"I'm sure!" laughed Rick. "If it's okay, I'll drop by after work. It'll be about 5:30. Does that work for you and Grams?"

"It sure does. We have plenty of food, and you know your grams; she's happiest when she's feeding someone! That's why your gramps gets rounder every year!" he laughed.

"Then by all means, I'll be there shortly after five. I wouldn't miss one of Grams' meals! Tell her I look forward to seeing you both! Have a great day, Gramps, and I'll see you later."

"You have a good one, too, and don't work too hard."

Gramps hung up the phone and hollered to Grams.

"Set another place for dinner tonight; Rick's comin' by!"

Grams was thrilled. "Oh, Lord Jesus, thank you! Now, what to make for dinner?" She scurried about the kitchen looking in all the cabinets.

"Mama, how can you fret about what to make when you cook enough for an army every evening? You know our Ricky; he'll eat whatever you put in front of him, as long as it's something you made."

Gramps got up from the kitchen table and put on his hat and coat.

"I'm going outside for a bit to take in some of that fresh, fall air. Have you looked outside, yet, and noticed those trees shakin' off their leaves? There's hardly any left on 'em."

"Now, you know that's a silly question," she chuckled. "I noticed 'em before the sun was even up." She turned to her husband. "Make sure you have on enough clothes to stay warm. Don't want you catchin' a cold!"

He smiled and gave her a peck on the cheek.

"Love ya, Mama. I reckon after fifty years I know what makes you happy."

Sarah opened the Super Heroes notebook she had "borrowed" from Larry, and flipped to the page where she had made a drawing of a large circle divided into four pie-shaped sections. She had then recorded her recollection of the teachings of the Mandala into each section.

Let's see, where was I?

She scanned the drawing and reread the descriptors. Ruth had taken the handout sheets home, so Sarah did her best to fill in everything she could from memory.

She put on a heavy sweater, slipped on her *Red Boots*, and headed out to sit on the back deck.

"Brrr, it's a bit chilly."

She felt warmth on her back and turned to see Max stretched out "sun bathing." She leaned over and patted him.

"You're nice and warm; aren't you the wise one!" She scooted her chair beside him and glanced up at the sun.

Now, this is inspiring!

As she flipped through the notebook, her eyes fixed on her *Red Boots. She had to laugh.

I don't know what inspired me to buy these boots, but there's something about them that makes me feel … free! Yep, that's it, lighthearted and free!

She tapped her heels together three times.

There's no place like home!

"Okay, back to the task at hand."

She spent about an hour sketching a few small pictures beside her notes, then flipped the page and jotted down random questions and ideas as they popped into her head.

Then something stirred within her heart, and she felt guided to look up at the large red maple tree directly in front of her. She squinted her eyes to check out something near the top of the beautiful tree.

"What is that?"

The words were no more out of her mouth when large wings lifted the creature to the very top of the tree.

It looks like a Christmas tree with an angel on the top, only it's a bird!

The huge bird was snow white.

I know birds; what is that?

Then the bird turned its head, and she recognized what it was.

"It's a snowy owl!" she gasped. She sat as perfectly still as she could while her heart raced.

I don't want to scare you away!

The owl just stared at her. Sarah's gut sensed it was trying to communicate with her.

Good grief, what do I do? What would the old woman do?

Then she knew. She kept her eyes on the beautiful owl and inhaled slowly.

Hello, beautiful one; is there something you wish to tell me?

When she was met with silence, she remembered the old woman's words the first time she met her.

"You have a steadfast and patient heart. Treasure it, keep it open, and always appreciate the love you receive."

Then she recalled the most recent teachings the old woman had shared with the four of them.

"Use the 'ears' of your heart," she had said, *"and tell your ever-curious mind that its only task is to remember what you hear. Its task is not to judge or to analyze, but simply to listen and to remember."*

Sarah slowly moved her hands to her heart and silently spoke to the owl.

What is it you wish to share with me, beautiful one?

Immediately she heard, *"Listen with your heart."*

Her heart pounded as she opened her eyes and looked up at the owl.

Are you talking to me?

As the giant wings of the bird unfurled and opened wide, she received the message, *"Trust what you hear."*

Then the majestic wings carried the owl off into the direction of the North. It was a magical moment and, despite her attempts to blink away tears, they continued to fall. When the bird was out of sight, she pulled out her phone and searched for the spiritual meaning of the snowy owl. This is what she found:

"They bring the message of seeing through illusion and fantasy with eyes of clarity. They tell us to open our eyes and pay attention, so we are better able to see things in Truth, and to be open to valuable insights that are offered. They travel between the Spirit world and the world of the living."

The air was now cold, and Sarah stood up, stretched, and looked down at Max. She leaned over and patted his head.

"Hey, you're used to being outside, but I need to get back to the warmth of our home. You enjoy the sunshine!"

Max opened his eyes and then immediately closed them, as if to say, "Okay, take care of yourself!"

Sarah smiled. How they loved their wise old friend. He had seen Jim and her through many experiences. She picked up the notebook and moved her chair back to its regular place.

"I love you!" she said to Max. "You keep taking care of yourself, too!"

She went into the house and found a comfortable spot where she could look out at her precious Max, and in view of the red maple tree, just in case the owl returned. She opened her notebook and began to write down precisely what she had just witnessed.

I can't wait to tell Jim!

"It's simply amazing! This must be the sort of thing that Jim and Ruth experience on a regular basis."

She felt her heart quicken as the room suddenly seemed to move. She sat straight up in her chair, placed her feet flat on the floor, and closed her eyes. She began to take deep breaths, and within a few moments she felt steadiness return.

"I'm grounded, and I feel fully present. Still a bit fearful, but I welcome this awakening."

Interesting, she thought as she opened her eyes, *that I would use the word 'awakening' … very interesting. Perhaps it's not fear; maybe it's excitement? I'm not certain; maybe it's both. What to do? Let's see…*

"Jim burns some sort of incense every morning and every evening," she recalled. "Maybe that would a good thing to do right now." She went into their bedroom where Jim kept the shell he uses. She had watched him do it enough times to know that it was important to wave the incense around herself and over her head, and then place it back into the shell.

She inhaled deeply several times, slowly releasing each breath until she felt steady.

"Good grief, I had no idea this ritual would have such a powerful effect! No wonder Jim does it every day!"

She went to the kitchen and got a big glass of water. She drank it immediately, refilled the glass, then went back to her chair and returned to where she left off.

"Okay, now to get caught up with what is really important. This is, indeed, an awakening," she smiled, "and I couldn't ask for a better person than Jim to guide me through this. How I love that man!"

Sack lunch in hand, Rick told his coworkers that he was using his lunchtime to go to town, and that he'd be back directly.

"Does anyone need anything? I'll be glad to pick it for you."

One young worker promptly responded, "Yeah, make certain she's a blonde with long legs and big..."

"Stop right there," interrupted Rick. "We do not tolerate disrespectful remarks about women. What you say off the job is your business, but while you're here none of us cares to hear your sexist remarks!"

"Oooh, touched a nerve, did I?" smirked the young man as he glanced toward the other workers.

"Let me ask you this," Rick sternly replied. "How would you feel if someone described your sister or your mother that way?"

The young man shook his head and rolled his eyes.

"I was only joking around."

"Well, you might as well learn early, that sort of talk is not funny, and is completely inappropriate and unacceptable on my crew. It will not be tolerated, period. Have I made myself perfectly clear?" He stared the young man directly in the eyes and briefly held a stare. Then he turned and walked straight to his truck before the young man could respond.

The young man snickered and shrugged his shoulders, then glanced at the men who had witnessed the interaction.

"Do you all agree with him?"

"He means what he says," responded one of the workers, "and he's the boss. Take a few moments and consider his question, though. How *would* you feel if someone talked that way about your sister or your mother? You don't need to answer that; just think about it."

Meanwhile, Rick had pulled into a parking space in front of the jewelry store, hurried in, and was greeted by the man behind the counter.

"Hey, Rick, glad to see you; we were just talking about you yesterday. Still wanting to have that engagement ring made?"

"Sure am, and I have a very unique design in mind. Is your jeweler here, or do I need to make an appointment to go over my ideas?"

"She sure is. Let me go and get her, and we'll get you ready to be a married man!"

Rick looked around the store a bit, but he knew that what he wanted wouldn't be in just any jewelry store display case.

My Ruthie deserves the very best — something as unique and beautiful as she is!

An elderly lady walked out from the back room.

"Are you Rick?"

"Yes ma'am!"

"I'm Priscilla," she said as she extended her hand. "I understand you have a unique design in mind for an engagement ring?"

"That is correct, and I hope you're the one that can take it from my mind and make it a reality!"

"I'll do my best! Let's step over to the desk and start by putting it on paper."

"Oh, I have a sketch." Rick reached into his shirt pocket, pulled out the folded sketch and carefully smoothed it out on the desktop. Priscilla examined it for several moments, then looked up at him.

"You've given this some serious thought! It's an amazing design, and the stones you have indicated for each area are certainly diverse. You clearly know what you want."

"That I do. My lady's very special; it took me a long time to find her, and I want her to know this is a lifetime commitment."

She raised an eyebrow, smiled and nodded. "I can tell there's a story behind this design and, from the look of this, it's an interesting one. Do you want a price range?"

"Nope, it doesn't matter. Do you think it's something you can do?"

"I can," she nodded. "I've never seen a piece of jewelry designed from someone's heart that I couldn't create. And, this is clearly from your heart. I suppose you need it as soon as possible?"

He cleared his throat. "I would love to have it fairly quickly, although the quality of the craftsmanship is what's most important." He leaned back in his chair and smiled. "I can give her a cigar band as a token if necessary, and she'd be okay with that."

"Do you have a preference for white gold, yellow gold, or platinum?"

"Yellow gold, to match her brilliantly bright essence!"

"You sure do have a special lady," she chuckled. "And, you know, *your* essence is also bright. That's what love does to someone who lives with a wide-open heart."

"Thank you," was all he could muster with the sudden lump in his throat.

Priscilla stood up; Rick followed her lead, and extended his hand.

"Then I'll wait to hear from you," he said. "Thank you for being willing to put my vision into form."

"It's my pleasure. I'll be in touch within a few days. I'd like for you to see what the setting will look like before we actually put in the stones. I want this to be precisely like the 'eyes' of your heart have seen it."

Rick was taken aback by her words.

The "eyes" of your heart ... hmmm, never thought about that!

Priscilla picked up on his expression.

"What struck you about my words?"

"Actually," he said hesitatingly, "your reference to the 'eyes' of my heart. I've heard about the 'ears' of one's heart, and the 'voice' of one's heart, but the 'eyes' of one's heart is new to me."

"There are many facets of the heart you might consider," she smiled.

"And, by the way," she continued after a brief pause, "your design looks very much like a Mandala." She began to walk away.

"Wait! What do you mean?" His heart began to race.

She turned back and looked him in the eyes as she unfolded the drawing and showed it to him.

"Your mounting is circular, and you have indicated four stones around a sizeable diamond. You indicate a garnet on the right," she said, strategically pointing to each stone, "a topaz at the bottom, onyx on the left, and a pearl at the top. And, with the braided gold band, I immediately thought of a Mandala." She glanced again at Rick.

He didn't know what to say; her observation literally took his breath away. He had drawn the sketch months before he even knew about Mandalas.

A coincidence?

"It's fascinating, and I'll do my best to make it precisely as your heart envisioned."

"And, there are no coincidences," she continued. "You might want to consider that one also." She turned and walked away, leaving Rick standing alone in a daze.

"What's happening?" he whispered to himself.

No time to think about this now … this is my new life!

He went to the cashier, made a down payment, and headed back to his truck. Bewildered, he got into the truck, grabbed the sandwich from his lunch bag, and headed back to work.

As he drove through town his eyes were drawn to a giant billboard.

"Awaken to the Truth," it read, "and become the person you were meant to be." He nearly ran a stoplight as he attempted to read all the words. He looked in his rearview mirror, tapped his brakes as a warning, and quickly stopped.

"That's it … that's the word. I am experiencing some sort of awakening!"

The sign was an advertisement for a new church in town; yet, it stated precisely what was happening to Rick.

"I'm waking up to something else. Geez, another coincidence?"

The light turned green and he proceeded through the intersection.

"It's happened to Ruth and to Jim, and now Sarah is waking up, too, as is Doug. Maybe the whole world is! Now, that would be a wonderful thing to witness!"

The rest of the workday went smoothly after Rick returned. The young man who had made the crude remark earlier was quiet, and spent the rest of the afternoon on task.

Rick put the last of his tools into his truck at 5 o'clock sharp, and headed to his grandparents' house. His gramps was sitting on the porch whittling away on a piece of wood when he pulled up, and seemed oblivious to his arrival, so Rick took the opportunity to send a quick text to Ruth.

"Hey, Babe, hope your night goes well and that things are fairly calm. Just pulled up at Gramps' and Grams' for dinner with them. I love you and miss you."

"Whatcha doing?" Gramps shouted. Rick nearly jumped out of his skin and his cell phone fell to the floorboard. He looked up.

"Good grief, Gramps, are your trying to give me a heart attack?"

The white-haired man stood by the truck, laughing uncontrollably. He was quite proud of himself!

"Gotcha, didn't I?"

He and Rick were always playing tricks on each other, and this time he scared the bejesus out of his grandson.

"Yes, you did, you old fart! Stand back so I can open the door and kick your butt!" he bellowed back. They hugged each other and laughed as they walked up to the porch.

"Let's get in the house," said Gramps. "Your grams has been cooking all day. She's so excited you're here for dinner. I hope you're hungry; she's made enough food for an army!"

Rick's heart was happy. How he loved his grandparents, and it had been too long since he had last visited.

Rick reached for the screen door as the inside door opened, and there stood Grams with a wide smile, a bib apron wrapped around her, and her hair twisted in a bun.

"For the love of God, it's our Ricky! I thought you'd forgotten about us!" She laughed and opened her arms to receive a big hug. Rick obliged her with a big embrace.

"Oh, Grams," he stood back to get a good look at her, "you're as lovely as ever! How do you stay looking so young while Gramps just keeps lookin' older?"

"Hey, I resemble that statement," his gramps interjected. "Now come on in and let's fill our bellies!"

Rick put his arm around Grams, and they followed Gramps to the kitchen. A table was heaped with beautiful blue willow dishes, glass goblets, silverware, and red-checkered cloth napkins. Two wooden candlesticks held burning white candles in the center of the table that was topped with a lacy white tablecloth. It was a heartwarming sight.

"Goodness, Grams, you've gone to a lot of trouble."

"Hey, it's no trouble. It's not often we have a guest for dinner, let alone one of our favorite grandsons. Now, sit down, and I'll get the food on the table."

Gramps took his place at the head of the table and patted the chair on his right.

"Here, Ricky, this is your seat. Grams will sit in front of you so we can all see each other. Gosh, it's really nice to have such a surprise!"

"Let me wash up a bit and then I'll help Grams."

"Nonsense, your grams wants to pamper you tonight! Go and wash up, and we'll be ready to eat by the time you get back."

When Rick returned, the table was full of covered dishes, along with a basket covered with a red-checkered cloth.

"Wow, Gramps, you weren't wrong about dinner! I guess Grams has set a few meals on the table, and she doesn't need any help."

They connected their hands, Gramps said a prayer, and they began to enjoy the delicious homemade meal.

"What brings you here, Ricky?" asked Grams. "Are you still seeing the same girl you had been seeing for the past couple of years? Or, are you already married?"

"Gracious, Mama, it sounds like you're interrogating the boy. Let him eat!"

"I love your questions, Grams," smiled Rick. "I'm here because it's been too long since I've made a visit, and I apologize for that. It's also time to get some wood on your porch before the cold weather is here to stay."

He buttered another biscuit.

"And, to the next questions, yes, I'm still seeing Ruth; and, no, we're not married … *yet*."

Grams' eyes widened as Gramps continued to devour a piece of fried chicken.

"Yet? I heard 'yet!' Are you here to tell us something?" She eagerly awaited Rick's response. He cleared his throat and wiped his mouth.

"Actually, you two are the first to know that I put a down payment on an engagement ring today."

"Oh, Ricky, I'm so happy for you!" Grams was so excited that she got up, went over to Rick, and hugged his back.

"Thanks, Grams, I couldn't be happier!" He squeezed her hand on his shoulder.

"Congratulations, Ricky, it's about time!" said Gramps as he extended his hand to Rick.

"Now, Daddy, don't say that. These kids today don't just rush into getting married; they have careers to work on."

"Phooey! That's nonsense! A good woman is more important than a career! Heaven knows, they are harder to find than a job, or a 'career' as you say!"

Grams went over to the counter and picked up a pie, and brought it over to Rick.

"Here's our celebration pie, Ricky; I just knew something important was going on for you to just 'drop by!'"

She held it in front of him to examine.

"Oh, Grams, is that a blueberry pie?"

"It is! I know it's your favorite." She set it down beside him.

"When we're done eating, I'll make some fresh coffee and we'll celebrate with dessert." She hugged his back again, kissed him on the cheek and went back to her seat.

"When are you going to tell your mom and dad?"

"I'm not certain. I wanted to talk to you two first. Reckon I'll see Mom and Dad in another day or two." He looked at them. "Now, don't you tell them before I get a chance! It's certainly not a secret, but I think they'd rather hear it from me."

Gramps took two fingers to his lips and turned them to indicate that his lips were sealed. He then looked at his wife.

"What about you, Mama? Can you keep from saying anything to our son?"

"Of course, I can!" she responded indignantly. "I've kept many a secret throughout my life."

"Now, Mama, I didn't mean to insult you. I just know how you women are when it comes to love, marriage, and babies!"

"Yeah, you're probably right about that!" She sighed. "Ricky, of course it's your news to tell your parents. Just let us know when it's safe to share our excitement about it!"

When they had all finished the meal, Gramps leaned back in his chair.

"That was a mighty fine meal, Mama, and I've saved room for our celebration pie!"

When the only thing left of dessert was a purple smear on each saucer, and the coffee cups were empty, Rick and his Grams washed and dried the dishes while Gramps looked through the obituary page of the newspaper.

"You know, there aren't many from our generation left, Mama. I suppose our names will be there sooner rather than later."

"Would you quit reading that page? Gracious!" Grams looked at Rick. "You'd think he's waiting for the day he sees his own name there!" They both laughed.

"Gramps, I promise I'll let you know when you're no longer on the planet," teased Rick.

"Well that would be right nice of you," said Gramps, looking up over his glasses. "However, reckon I'll know I'm not here when I'm there."

Grams and Rick looked at each other with affection for this silly old man that had a heart of gold. She pointed her head toward Gramps and rolled her eyes in his direction in an attempt to indicate to Rick to take him outside and chat with him a bit. Rick kissed her on the cheek, and walked over to his Gramps.

"Come on outside," he said. "I need some advice."

Gramps looked up from his paper.

"About what? Do you need me to tell you about the birds and the bees?"

They all burst into laughter.

"How did you know?" laughed Rick. "Come on, Gramps, let's sit on the porch and have a man-to-man talk."

As they walked out of the kitchen Grams overheard Rick say, "Good grief, Gramps, you told me about sex when I was twelve!"

Gramps gasped. "Don't use that word; Grams is in the other room, and she might hear you!"

"Okay, the birds and the bees," smiled Rick.

When they had settled into the porch chairs, Gramps picked up his knife and the piece of wood he'd been working with earlier, and began to whittle away.

"What are you making?"

"Oh, I don't know. Thought I'd make something for your grams, but she's got all sorts of things sitting around. Hey, would your lady friend like something? You know I can whittle all sorts of things."

"She'd love something handmade! Thanks, Gramps, that's very thoughtful of you."

"Okay, now what did you want to talk man-to-man about?" asked Gramps as he continued to whittle.

Rick scanned the land around his Gramps' house, and began to recall many experiences he had had in this place in his youth. He and his sister had spent endless days traversing the land, swinging and climbing in the trees, helping in the garden, raking leaves in the fall, and helping with any chores their grandparents needed done. Rick first learned to drive on his gramps' tractor, and his sister, Katie, kept up with everything Rick did. As he thought of her, he realized that he hadn't seen her in some time, either.

How quickly time can pass. I need to make time to visit her, too. I think Ruth has only met her a time or two, and they're soon going to be related!

"Where are you, Rick?" Gramps asked as he held up his whittling.

Rick shook his head. "Geez, I was right here, but much younger."

Gramps looked over his glasses and smiled. "I was remembering the hours Katie and I spent here with you and Grams."

He glanced at the whittled piece of wood that Gramps held up and handed to him.

"It's a snake! I had forgotten how good you are with a knife and a piece of wood. My goodness, that's fabulous!"

Rick handed it back to him, but Gramps shook his head.

"You give that to your woman. I was thinking about her as I whittled. I hope she'll like it."

"Are you kidding? She'll love it!"

He carefully examined the intricate details on the body and the tiny tongue that stuck out from its mouth. He looked up at Gramps.

"You have no idea how perfect this is for Ruth. Thank you!"

"Oh, maybe I don't, and maybe I do. You might be surprised!"

Rick looked puzzled. "What do you mean, I might be surprised?"

After a long moment of silence, Gramps simply changed the subject.

"Now, what did you want to talk to me about before you started time traveling?"

"Time traveling; what do you know about time traveling?" asked Rick, a bit shocked.

"Plenty. I've been a daydreamer my whole life, and I have visited all sorts of places across the world while I whittled away."

Rick was fascinated. He had never thought of daydreaming as time traveling, and the way Gramps described it made it seem "normal."

Gramps' suggestion that he might know what the snake would mean to Ruth puzzled Rick. However, rather than to open that "can of worms," he returned to his initial question.

"I wanted to ask you where you would be when you are listed in the obituaries. You said you'd know you weren't here when you were 'there.' What, precisely, were you saying? I mean, where is 'there?'"

Gramps stared at Rick. "You know, not here, but there. I suppose it's heaven. You know, up there," he said, pointing his finger toward the sky. "You were brought up in church, so you know what I'm talking about."

Rick was silent. Somehow, he felt it was best to just give his gramps a chance to talk.

"What is it you want me to say?" asked Gramps. He wasn't sure what Rick wanted to hear, and felt a bit awkward.

"I want you to say whatever you want to say. This is your 'story,'" smiled Rick.

"'Story?' If it's *my* story, it'll be a place where people practice the Golden Rule," said Gramps. "You know, where people treat others the way they want to be treated. It will be a place where there is no pain or sorrow, and where people care about each other and take responsibility for their own actions and their own lives. It will be a place where people listen to each other when there is conflict, and search for a compromise that makes everyone happy."

He had more to say but he wasn't certain Rick would agree with him. Nor did he think his son would be happy that he was telling Rick such things.

"Go ahead, Gramps, say what you want. I'm all ears! This is between you and me, and no one else."

"Then, Rick, I want to tell you that I'm not so certain about Hell. I've experienced and observed many events in my life that I'd describe as Hell. War is one of those. It makes no sense to kill people in another country, only to later become friends and exchange goods and services with them. I mean, if that can happen, why didn't we try it before we started killing people? And, think about all those who lost people they loved. I tell you, Rick, that's Hell!"

He stopped for a moment and looked across the yard.

"See those squirrels? They know how to work together, to gather what they need for themselves and for their neighbors. We could learn a lot from the natural world. When people are inconsiderate, mean-spirited, and have no respect for each other, let alone for this beautiful planet, it makes me sick. Humans completely discount the value of anything other than money and material things. That's *not* how this world used to work."

Feeling a bit frustrated, he picked up another piece of wood and began to whittle again.

"If you want to know where 'there' is, I'd add that people who don't believe there is life on other planets are not very bright. In this huge universe, how can anyone think we're the only humanlike species out there?"

Rick was shocked, but he didn't want to show that to his gramps.

I want him to say anything and everything he believes to be true.

He listened from his heart, and his mind soaked up Gramps' words like a sponge. He wanted to remember every detail.

"Reckon not many people talk to you about such things. I know your dad probably hasn't. Truth be told, I didn't give it much thought while I was working and raising a family. I didn't have time for such thoughts. I was too focused on doing: providing for a family, getting along at work, trying to teach my kids how to get along in the world. That, and keeping your grams happy."

He stopped whittling, looked up and scanned the yard. "Reckon I did okay with that, although if I had it to do over again, I would have treated her a lot nicer.

"Rick," he said as he returned to his whittling, "always see the woman in your life as a gift. Women have many special talents; it is important to recognize that and not be so busy thinking only of yourself. Do you know what I mean?"

Rick nodded.

"I'm telling you, Rick, there's more to a woman than what we are taught when we're young. They have special powers..." He looked at Rick.

"I'm going to tell you something I wish I had known at your age. Women have a sixth sense. I believe it is called mental telepathy, intuitive hunch, or something like that. They know things, and can sense when things are, well, 'out of sorts.' You know, when something's not right. You have to learn to trust them, and to ask for their insights and their help when you need it. That's something men of my generation were taught was a weakness. In my day, men were considered the smart ones, and women were merely their 'helpmates.'"

Rick shook his head.

I just knew Gramps had some wisdom to share with me. I'm so glad I trusted my own intuition today.

"I know back in the '70s with the women's livers, or libbers, or whatever they were called, things changed, and my generation didn't much like it.

"And, Rick," he said, looking up, "I'll admit that I didn't like it one bit, either. Your poor grams sure had her hands full with me. Good thing she loved me enough to overlook my crazy behavior.

"It took about twenty years for me to truly come to my senses and understand what it was all about. I now realize that women need to feel a sense of sovereignty. They need to feel a sense of independence, like they can take care of themselves no matter what happens in life. When I understood this, I saw your grams differently. I started to really appreciate the fine human being she was; hell, she still is. And, my love and respect for her deepens with every year we're together."

After a moment of silence, Gramps returned to his whittling.

"Sorry for my rambling, Rick, but every man who is about to ask a woman to marry him needs to hear this. You're a good man, just like your father, and you know about commitment and dedication to marriage. I'm certain if you're asking your lady to marry you, you've already thought about these things."

Rick smiled and nodded.

"I'm glad you haven't fallen asleep from our man-to-man talk!" laughed Gramps.

"Not in a million years!" laughed Rick. "This is exactly what I needed to know about." He touched his forehead. "Hey, maybe men have that mental telepathy, intuitive thing, too!"

They were both laughing when Grams came through the door.

"Is it safe to come out, or is this still a man-to-man talk?"

Gramps motioned her to come out and pulled a chair close to him.

"Have a seat, Mama."

She sat down and pulled a shawl tightly around her shoulders.

"You can feel the fall air blowing in the cold temperatures," she remarked.

"Do you need a blanket, Mama?" Gramps inquired attentively.

"No, thanks; this is one of my warmer shawls. In fact, I think you bought it for me several Christmases ago."

"Shhh," he smiled and put a finger to his lips. "Rick doesn't need to know I do such things!"

Rick jumped in. "Oh, I was sharing with Gramps my memories of Katie and me playing in your front yard. I want you both to know how much you have influenced my life, and how you taught me what love is all about. I think I'm going to be an excellent husband to my Ruth."

"I couldn't remember her name, but I'll remember it now," said Grams. "The biblical name, 'Ruth,' symbolizes loyalty and devotion, and she is known for being a good friend and companion." She looked at Rick. "Your Ruth will make you a good wife. You've chosen well!"

"Thank you, Grams. It's good to know that what I love about her are all qualities her name carries."

"You know," Gramps pointed to the front yard and changed the subject, "speaking of new things, that's the East direction. Mama and I chose the front of our house to face the East, because it is the place where all things begin. We figured that to step out each day and face the rising sun would be a good omen."

He pointed to a small gazebo just to the left of the porch.

"We placed that gazebo in the North, so we could sit and talk to the powers-that-be ... to God."

Rick's mouth fell open. What else did his gramps and grams know? How did he not know these things about them?

"These are important things to know, Rick," interjected Grams. "It'll help you to be in harmony with the natural world. A relationship with nature is crucial to a good life. Reckon we've survived this crazy world because we have lived in good standing with nature. Humans can be very puzzling. And, our government ... well, we won't even go there!"

Rick's heart quickened. He hardly had words to respond, so he decided to just let his grandparents talk.

"Use the 'ears' of your heart to help your relationship grow," said Grams. "Your gramps and I learned that a long time ago, and it keeps each of us in check. By reminding ourselves and each other to listen from our hearts, it helps us to ignore the head chatter about why we're right, and the other person wrong, which doesn't give us time to really listen."

"And," interjected Gramps, "to use the 'voice' of our heart to speak."

"Right!" Grams looked at Rick. "Always remember these two things, and your communication will be strong, which will strengthen your love for each other. And, in the end, you will also like yourself a lot more."

"It just plain feels better when you know you've helped someone feel good about themselves and about life." Gramps added.

"We've said what we've learned as simply as we could," Grams concluded. "After fifty years of marriage, we've learned that too many words get in the way. Our actions are much more important for showing who we are and how we feel."

Gramps pointed again to the gazebo.

"It was the North Star that led the wise men to the birthplace of Jesus. That same North Star still guides wise men and women." He looked Rick directly in the eyes. "Your task, Rick, is to *pay attention*."

Rick felt a bit overwhelmed, and took a few breaths.

"Can I ask where you learned about these things? I mean, the importance of the directions, and the 'voice' and 'ears' of your heart?"

Grams looked at her husband, and he nodded his approval.

"Well, we're 'Seekers,' Rick," said Grams. "We've always been curious about things 'outside the box,' so to speak, even as children. Why do you ask?"

"Because I met a woman about your age a few days ago, and she used the same words. In fact, the jeweler that's making Ruth's ring used some of the same words. That doesn't seem a coincidence. And, she spoke about a Mandala. What do you know about Mandalas?"

Gramps and Grams just looked at each other. They knew everything that needed to be said at that moment was sufficient.

"It's getting late, Rick," said Gramps. "We're more than glad to share what we know, so maybe when Ruth comes out with you we can pick up this conversation."

"You bet we can! In fact, it was Ruth who first introduced me to this whole new way of thinking … rather," he corrected himself, "this new way of *being*."

The sun had begun to set and the air was getting chilly. Rick stood up and looked at his grandparents.

"Thank you both for sharing your wisdom so freely. I look forward to our next chat." Try as he may, he couldn't control his tears.

Gramps stood up, set his whittling on the chair and moved over to his wife's chair.

"Let me help you up, Mama. Rick needs to get home, and we need to get in the house before one of us catches a cold." He knew Rick needed to get home to absorb everything he'd heard.

They all exchanged hugs, and Rick shook his gramps' hand.

"Thanks for the man-to-man talk."

He hugged his grams again.

"And, thank you for a delicious meal, your words, and mostly for being such a tremendous human being! Ruth and I will come by soon and get some wood stacked on your porch for the winter, and listen to whatever else you are willing to share."

"Wait, Rick," said Grams as she moved toward the door. Then she looked at her husband. "Could you help me with something, Papa?"

Gramps followed her into the house. They returned within a few moments, and Gramps carried a box.

"Take these leftovers from dinner," smiled Grams, "and share them with Ruth. I can give her the recipes if she so desires."

She then pulled a folded hankie from her apron pocket and handed it to Rick.

"Give this to Ruth as a 'welcome to the family' gift. It's been in my family for generations." Tears fell from her eyes as she extended the hankie to Rick.

"This hankie belonged to my great-grandmother. Such treasures will add richness to your relationship if you'll use your heart to listen to the voices of your ancestors."

Rick hardly knew what to say; he slipped the hankie into his coat pocket and gave her a big hug.

"I have no words, and I know you both understand what my heart feels."

Gramps handed the box to Rick, and Rick peeked inside.

"Goodness, you've given me all the leftovers!"

Grams smiled. "Enjoy them, Honey; there's enough to share with Ruth."

"Hey, wait a couple of minutes," Gramps spoke up. "I have something else for you. I'll be right back."

Rick and Grams walked across the yard that faced the West.

"Look at that sunset!" gasped Rick. "It's breathtaking!"

"And, you know, Rick, we have that big window at the back of the house so we can enjoy it, whatever the weather may be. We can feel that sun setting even when the sky is overcast, and we know everything is right with the world."

Rick heard the screen door open, and Gramps walked directly over to Rick and stuck something into his coat pocket.

"That's so you never lose your direction. My gramps gave it to me, so I'm passing it on. And, Rick, remember that there are no coincidences in life."

"Thank you again. Now, you two get in the house; it's getting cold! I'll call in a few days and let you know when Ruth and I can come out. Love you both!"

Rick drove home feeling so much joy and love that he thought his heart would burst. He hung up his coat when he got home, then put the leftovers into the refrigerator. He poured a glass of wine and sat down to read his texts.

Much to his surprise, Katie had texted that she wanted to see him soon. His mother's text said they missed him and hoped to see him soon, and a text from Ruth said, "I love and miss you."

"Yikes, I nearly forgot!" he exclaimed as he jumped up from his chair. He hurried to the coat rack and pulled out the object his Gramps had shoved into his pocket, and the hankie his grams had sent with him for Ruth. He felt something within the hankie, unfolded it and a stunningly beautiful brooch was revealed. Its beauty took his breath away.

"Oh my gosh! I love you, Grams, you have such a beautiful soul. Ruth will be over-the-moon."

He set the hankie aside to give to Ruth the next time he saw her, then carefully opened the gift from his gramps.

He gasped at what was a well-worn and scratched silver compass. Tears welled up in his eyes.

Dear God, for a grown man, I certainly have a lot of tears these days!

And, all he could say was, "There are no coincidences."

Jim, Sarah and the kids arrived home from Randy's ball game, subdued and quiet after yet another loss.

"I'm about ready to quit the team," Randy voiced. "I mean, they don't put me in the game, so why even be involved in it?"

Jim and Sarah knew that his words only reflected his disappointment. Randy certainly was not a quitter. He'd been on enough losing ball teams and had never quit, so they felt sure he would not quit now.

"You look good in that uniform, Randy; it matches your blue eyes," Cindy tried to console him.

He rolled his eyes. "Thanks for trying, Sis, but it doesn't help. I'll be alright after a good night's sleep."

"Quite frankly, though, it does suck!" interjected Larry. "I don't know how you keep playing. But, then, you're nicer than I am. I'd quit."

"The subject is closed," Sarah said as she pulled their SUV into the garage. "I'll make a light supper while you all take your showers and put on your pajamas."

Within forty-five minutes everyone was around the table, quietly eating soup and a sandwich until Jim spoke up.

"I want you to know that I'm real proud of all of you. Each of you has determination and dedication to whatever you do. And, I know it's late; does anyone have any homework?"

They all shook their heads.

"That's good. Only another week and football will be over. Then we can break out the board games for the winter," smiled Jim.

"Oh," Larry spoke up, "I'm trying out for the basketball team this year. That's okay, isn't it?"

Sarah looked at Jim and smiled.

"Sure, it is, Larry, but let's talk about it tomorrow. You all need to get some rest so you're refreshed for school in the morning."

They each hugged their parents and headed into their bedrooms.

"One of us will be in to hear your prayers in just a few minutes," Sarah reminded them.

After the kids were tucked in and Jim had showered, he went into his and Sarah's bedroom. Sarah sat in bed in her pajamas with the Super Heroes notebook in her lap.

"Super Heroes, huh? Now, that looks like an invitation!" He snuggled in beside her and kissed her neck. "Which one do you want me to be tonight? Superman, Ironman, or another one?"

"You're my Fire Keeper," she grinned. "None of these Super Heroes can top that!" she teased. "And, I will welcome that in about thirty minutes. First, though, I want to ask you something, and then tell you about today."

He sat up next to her. "Alright, but you've already started that Fire just by sitting there holding that notebook. You have thirty minutes."

"Hmmm, I was wondering if what we learned about the Mandala and the stages of Life yesterday would help us to be better parents. I mean, there were some really good things explained about growing up and becoming an adult."

"That's a very good observation," responded Jim. "We need to look over those handouts and try to remember what we learned yesterday."

She opened the notebook and showed him the sketches she had made, as well as what she had written down from her recollection of the old woman's teachings.

"I've started this, and I was going to ask you to add whatever else you heard, or already know from your previous visits. However, we can do that another time." She rubbed his chest. "What I really want to tell you about is what happened today in the backyard."

She recounted her experience, and when she mentioned the snowy owl she had his full attention.

"I'm telling you, Jim, it was absolutely amazing, and the really strange part was that we had just heard those powerful words from the old woman. If I hadn't heard those teachings I probably would have simply noticed the beauty of the owl and nothing else.

"Imagine, Jim," she continued with flushed excitement, "can you just see me talking to a white owl? That's when I knew that what you have learned from the old woman over the years far exceeded removing the barrier from around your heart. There's so much more about the Spirit world that you've learned."

Jim leaned over and kissed her. "You do know how much I love you, don't you?"

She nodded and smiled affectionately.

"Well," he continued, "you'd better buckle up, because you are in for a wild ride that you would never have imagined. And, Sarah, I'm so very grateful that we're doing this together, *now*, when the time is right. I could not previously have discussed or even explained anything to you if you had asked me. I just took one thing at a time, and then paid attention. Heck, I still do that. I have no idea where this is going. I'm just 'Following the Snake!'"

"Gracious, I remember you using that phrase with Ruth at the cookout."

"That's right," Jim nodded. "I didn't really understand what it meant until last night. Then I realized how the snake has taken me from one thing to another, or from one person to another, providing the next step to this whole awakening experience."

"Awakening!" gasped Sarah. "That is precisely what I felt after the experience with the owl. I came in and recorded the event, and the only word that popped into my head was 'awakening.'"

She kissed Jim. "What's your take on the snowy owl? And, what do we do next?"

Jim glanced at the clock. "It's been thirty minutes; mind if I stretch that another fifteen?"

"No, please do," she agreed.

"Well, first, I had a hoot owl speak to me when I was at the old woman's. It scared the bejesus out of me at first, and then I realized how excited I was when the owl spoke to me. As I understand it, the snowy owl is blessed with the ability to shape-shift; in others words, it may take other forms, even as a human. It signals a time of great wisdom since they are known in the Native American culture as the Night Eagle. What you heard from the owl was a message for you. Trust it, and see if the owl appears again."

"That's almost exactly what the owl said!" she responded excitedly as she consulted her notebook. "Let's see, the owl's exact words were, '*Listen with your heart, and trust what you hear.*'"

Tenderly, he turned her face toward his and looked directly into her eyes.

"Who knows? Maybe it wasn't just any snowy owl; maybe it was the old woman!"

"Bear with me, Sweetheart, I have two more questions," said Sarah. "First, how does all this fit in with the teachings of our church? And, what was that round marble-like thing you had in your pocket? I had never seen that."

"Those are both great questions. As for the first, I'd say we'll just have to see how it all comes together with religious teachings. It's all the same stuff, but what I've surmised is, it's the Holy Spirit portion of the Holy Trinity. Scripture speaks of the Holy Spirit, but doesn't really explain it, or teach us about its essence. The old woman would say, '*Don't think about it too much.*'

"As for the cat's eye marble," he said as he pulled it from his pocket, "well, it's my understanding that, when someone is ready to commit to awakening, someone who truly *sees* them will offer a gift." He closed his hand around the marble. "The old woman gave it to me. It was a gift from her Teacher; which makes it even more precious.

"But, back to your experience today. Now that I think about it, the hoot owl appeared to me the very next time I visited her after she had given me that marble. Hmmm, very interesting!"

He leaned over and kissed her. "For now, I see a band around your forehead and a belt around your waist, Superwoman. I do believe your powers have intensified and the time is at hand."

"Okay," Sarah teased. "It *is* getting cold in here. Put your cape around me and warm me up, Superman!"

Rick took a hot shower and then packed his lunch for the next day. He placed it on the kitchen counter next to his keys, and glanced at the clock.

"It's 8:15; Mom and Dad will still be up. Better give them a quick call."

Just as he reached for his phone, a text appeared.

"Hey, it's your long-forgotten dad. Would love to hear from you."

No coincidences!

He called his dad's number, and his father answered on the second ring.

"That was quick!"

"Yeah, I know, Dad, and I apologize that it's been so long. I won't give you any excuses."

"No need to, Son; it's good to hear from you. How have you been?"

"Actually, Dad, I've never been better. Is Mom close by?" His stomach fluttered and his mouth felt dry.

Good grief, I've never felt so … nervous!

"Sure, what's up?"

"Put me on speaker so she can hear our conversation."

"Okay, wait a minute."

Within a few moments, his mother was on.

"Hey, Honey, what's up? Should I be nervous?"

"Hey, Mom, quite the contrary; I think you'll be quite happy!"

"Then, I'll bet I know what this call is about," Mom said excitedly.

"I'll get straight to the point," said Rick. "I wanted to tell you this face-to-face, but now's as good a time as any. I'm asking Ruth to be my wife."

"Whoa!" shouted Dad, while his mom squealed and clapped her hands.

"Rick, we're so glad! We just love Ruth. Did she say yes?" Mom inquired.

"Actually, I haven't asked her yet. Her birthday is next week, and I thought I'd pop the question then."

Rick felt as though his heart would burst; everything in his life was falling together. After a few more questions and comments about how happy they were that Ruth would be part of the family, Rick shifted gears.

"It's late and I have a long day tomorrow, so I need to hit the hay."

"Well, thanks for calling and sharing your wonderful news," said Mom. "If you need help with anything, we're here. Your dad and I couldn't be happier for both of you. We love you."

"Thanks, Mom, love you both."

Rick hung up, a very happy man. As he snuggled into bed his thoughts went to Ruth. He grabbed his phone and sent her a text.

"Hey, Beautiful, hope your evening is going well. Sure do miss you. Can't wait to see you Friday; I have lots to share with you. Love you!"

He placed his phone in the charger on the nightstand, and imagined how different his home would feel with Ruth there all the time.

It sure will be nice when we live in the same place; I can hardly wait!

"Okay, everything is exactly how it needs to be. Now to get some sleep!"

Then Rick heard a whisper.

"The Mandala symbolizes the idea that life is never ending and everything is inter-connected."

That's what the old woman said the other day! he thought with excitement.

His heart quickened when he heard the whisper again.

"It is time for The Awakening! Are you ready?"

Reflections

HEAD TALK

What part of the story line so far can you personally relate to?

Was there anything that struck you as "unreal?"

What are you curious about?

What would you like to "think some more about?"

HEART TALK

What stirred your heart the most?

What touched a nerve or a tender part in you?

What memory from your life came to your heart?

What would you like to happen next?

Weaver of Webs / Grandmother Spider

The conversation was lively as Jim, Rick, and Doug made their first trip together to the old woman's cabin. December had been heralded in with frigid temps and large amounts of snow, they were needed to unload and stack the wood on the porch.

Doug and Jim teased Rick about being the "newbie" to married life.

"Once you make a decision, you don't waste any time!" Jim taunted. "It took you five years of dating to finally 'pop the question,' and in less than three weeks you're standin' before a preacher!"

Doug laughed. "Knowing my sister, she probably held you at bay as long as she could, and that unusual engagement ring gave her the nudge she needed!"

"Truth be told," responded Rick with a sheepish grin, "the old woman opened Ruth's heart. I just reaped the benefits. I figured I'd best get her to the preacher before she changed her mind!" They all laughed.

"She did love that ring!" Rick added. "Although, my gramps whittled a snake for her and my grams gave her a hankie and family brooch that she loved as much as that ring!"

"I'll bet she did!" said Doug. "My sis has always had a tender spot for sentimental gifts. I'm just so happy she found a good man who recognized what a gem *she* is!"

"Well, thank you, Doug. I feel like the lucky one; I guess we both are!"

"The jeweler was a very interesting lady," Rick continued. "She appeared to be about the age of the old woman, and when I gave her the sketch, she told me it looked like a Mandala."

Jim raised an eyebrow. "Is that right? Now, that's interesting!"

"From what I've heard a lot lately, there are 'no coincidences,'" replied Rick. "The old woman, the jeweler and my grandparents recanted the same phrase."

"The old woman told me that too," Doug affirmed.

"Then it must be so," responded Jim. "And, speaking of which, I'm pleased that you were able to join us today, Doug, with your new promotion and increased work load. We didn't get to talk much at the wedding."

"I heard you met the old woman. How was that experience for you?"

A long silence ensued before Doug responded.

"Actually, the only word that pops into my head is 'amazing!' That little woman's ability to get straight to the core of what I needed blew me away. Can't say as I've ever felt so visible. I hadn't recognized my own buried feelings until she told a story that opened up the door to my soul." That was it!

"I've not had words to describe that first visit until just now, and that sums up my experience perfectly! I took my wife, Sue, on the second visit, and she felt the same way. It takes time to really grasp such a unusual experience." He paused briefly.

"Sue asked the old woman about our oldest son. He has some unique behaviors that we really weren't certain how to handle. Apparently, she has had first-hand experience with students around our son's age, so she actually helped us to see those unusual behaviors as gifts."

Jim's eyebrow rose. *She finally got to share her "Untold stories!"*

"Sue was speechless when the old woman handed her the tatted chain!" continued Doug. "Thanks for asking, Jim; I understand you've known her for years. You probably know what it is that makes the magic happen. Maybe the energy of the old woman, or the energy of the land opens those doors?"

"I *have* known her a long time," responded Jim, "and, it's probably both; she has deep wisdom, and she weaves that wisdom into her stories. Some sort of connection is made when people hear those stories, which then deepens their connection with family and friends when the stories are shared."

Jim smiled at Rick in the rearview mirror, then glanced at Doug. "Whatever it is, I'm glad to be sharing the web of connection with both of you, *and* with our families."

When they reached the old woman's cabin, Jim backed up the truck to the opening of the path. They slipped on their coats and heavy gloves, and pulled their hats snuggly over their ears. Rick unstrapped a large 4-wheeled cart from the top of the tarp-covered wood, and he and Doug lifted it down onto the ground.

"Hey," Jim noted, "someone has plowed the path. That's handy."

Rick forged the way down the path with the very full cart, as Jim and Doug followed carrying armfuls of smaller pieces.

"We're off to see the 'Weaver of Webs!'" Rick joyfully exclaimed.

After three trips, all the kindling and firewood had been neatly stacked on the porch, and they swept the porch clean.

Jim knocked on the door and the old woman greeted them with a smile. They didn't want to track snow into the cabin, so Doug brought the wood and kindling to the door, where Rick received it and relayed it to Jim, who then filled the kindling basket and stacked the split wood in the iron holder. Jim noticed a new wooden box along the east side of the cabin wall.

"Hey, is that new box for firewood?"

"Yes," she nodded. "My son made it for me. He told me to thank whoever was bringing the wood."

"Well, tell your son he's most welcome; it's the least we can do." Jim glanced at the box. "That will be useful this winter. If today's any indication, we're in for a cold one!"

He turned to Rick. "Tell Doug this may take a bit. We have another box to fill!"

After a dozen or more armfuls had been brought in, Doug joined the others inside. He slipped off his snowy boots, hung up his coat, and placed his gloves in front of the fireplace to warm. Then he took a seat beside Rick.

Jim poured hot coffee for Doug, and Rick handed him a napkin and extended a basket of cinnamon muffins.

"Nice reward for our generosity, huh?" said Rick.

Doug took two muffins and leaned toward the old woman.

"Thank you! I'm certain they're delicious! And the coffee is precisely what I needed!"

The crackling and popping of the fire filled the air with warmth as they all sat in silence and listened to the sacred sounds emitted from the fire. Rick noticed the green glass oil lamp on the far right of mantel, then turned to the old woman.

"It's good to see you." He glanced back at the green lamp. "The items on your mantel are quite intriguing. That green oil lamp has always caught my eye. No doubt there's a story behind it?"

She nodded.

"It looks old and the color is very unique," he said. "Would you mind sharing the story?"

She extended her cup to Jim, who promptly refilled it. She took a sip and glanced up at the antique lamp.

"That green oil lamp reminds me to keep my heart open and share my light with whomever shows up; human *and* nonhuman. My teacher used to say that if I wanted to make a difference in the world, I needed to provide a lamp and a mirror for others. A lamp provides light for those on their path as they move through the maze of life; a mirror offers a person the opportunity to see who they are, and who they want to be.

"In essence, being a lamp and a mirror first requires us to heal our old wounds, and to consciously choose to change what no longer serves us or those around us. That takes both courage and a strong heart, for what we see in another is a mirror of what we need to see within ourselves. We must be diligent and pay attention to *our* thoughts, words and actions, rather than focus on another's behavior. That helps us to 'mind our own business,' rather than someone else's.

"Our essence brightens as we heal our wounds. Others will be drawn to us, like moths to a light. They will want what they see and feel around us. When our light is bright, people will see *their* reflection in us." She glanced at the fire and inhaled.

"This is how we offer mirrors to those around us. This Truth is something of which to be very mindful. We would be wise to consider the energy we emit. Do we view life as a cup half empty or half full? Do we see the best in life or do we wait for the 'other shoe to drop?' Being human is not easy! It is, however, a fascinating journey.

"I chose this lamp because of its translucent green color; you can see a reflection of other colors through the muted glass. Typically, green is associated with the heart chakra, which helps with balance and increases the energy of love in our heart. This deepens our capacity to have compassion for all inhabitants on Mother. When this one came to me, it became a powerful *medicine* piece that has guided my path." She looked at them.

"'Medicine' is a word that references the energy of an object. Always be mindful that whatever you bring into your home will be reflected in your life. Choose carefully those things that bring a sense of lightness and joy, rather than a heaviness that thwarts growth."

She rose, retrieved the lamp from the mantel, dusted it off, and held it close to her heart. Then she took it over to Rick, and extended it to him. He wasn't certain how to respond so he simply held her gaze. With a small grin she leaned over and set it in his lap.

"It's stunning, and carries a magical essence; I can understand it being a 'medicine' piece." he stammered, as his mind whirled. "Ruth has a green vase this very same color that has always felt compelling to me."

Geez, another coincidence?

She stared him in the eyes.

"There are no coincidences. Accept it as a wedding gift," she tenderly responded.

"Oh! I can't take such a special lamp; it's your medicine piece."

"And, now it's yours. Simply accept it from my heart to yours, and let the energy it carries deepen the love you and Ruth share. May it serve as a reminder to treat each other the way you want to be treated."

Rick's heart nearly burst, and his head spun as the sweetness of love embraced him. Doug and Jim smiled as they witnessed the expansion of Rick's heart.

His eyes moist, Rick looked up at the old woman.

"What an amazing gift! And, how did you know we were married? I mean, did you use your gift of seeing?"

Her eyebrows lifted and her wrinkles deepened as she smiled.

"I noticed your ring."

Laughter broke out from the busy minds that had speculated about how and why the old woman knew such things.

She stoked the fire, paid her respects to it, and went back to her chair.

The warmth of the fire kept the four of them comfortably relaxed and connected within their hearts, as snow began to fall outside. Jim got up and added wood to the fire, and the flames again began to dance.

The old woman got up and retrieved a folder from under the walnut table, and handed it to Doug.

"This is for you to take home and share with your wife. When spring arrives, come for a visit and we will sit and speak of these things. Until then, let your mind be still, sit in the silence of winter, and listen to your heart.

"I gave the others these same handouts, and it would be beneficial for you to talk with each other about ways to apply the information into every day life. One of the diagrams will add more understanding to the teachings of the Life cycles; the other will help make everyday life manageable. We make decisions from the time we get up in the morning, and that's what the Problem Solving & Decision Making Mandala offers. If everyone could teach these skills to their children at a very early age, they would have the self-confidence to move through life as responsible, respectful human beings."

Doug nodded. "Thank you!"

"Of course, adults must first demonstrate these skills to their children. Equally important, they must be consistent and follow through with the teachings."

"The wisdoms you share with us are immeasurable," said Rick. "Is there anything we can do for you?" Jim and Doug agreed.

She rose from her chair. "I could use some help in the kitchen; I know you all must be hungry."

Jim glanced out the window. "Actually, we'd better head back before the snow covers the path, which I noticed someone has cleared for you."

She blushed. "My sons are very considerate."

"I know a young man who would love to provide a truckload of wood for you," Rick chimed in. "With the predictions for winter, and your handy new box, we could bring another load to get you through the rest of the winter."

That's a great idea," agreed Jim. "Depending on the weather, how about we bring back another load in a couple of weeks?"

"Before Christmas, of course," Doug added. "How's two weeks from today?"

The old woman smiled.

"Then two weeks from now it is," Jim confirmed. "Would it be okay to bring our wives and celebrate the holiday together, too?"

And," added Rick, "we'll bring all the holiday food."

"Food is never a concern," smiled the old woman tenderly. "In fact, let me box up a few things for you to take home."

Jim followed her to the kitchen. "I'll help you while Rick and Doug gather their things."

Doug moved the chairs back to the dining room while Rick wrapped his "wedding gift" in his vest.

Clad in warm coats, hats and boots, Jim carried the box of goodies, and Rick turned to the old woman.

"Thank you, again, for such a treasured gift. Ruth will be over-the-moon!"

The trip home was relatively quiet as each considered the webs in their life. It was Jim who broke the silence.

"Doug, I believe our oldest sons are about the age to learn about helping elders. How about we consider bringing them out next spring?"

"That's an excellent idea! I was helping elders from our church with chores when I was my son's age. My father was always of service to others, which is probably why I am. That's certainly an admirable trait that will teach our sons about responsibility."

"Count me in," Rick chimed in. "I need practice observing a good father in action!"

"And so, the web extends," Jim offered.

Two weeks flew by quickly and the web of friends settled into their vehicles for the journey.

"Hey, Jim, you lead; we'll follow and keep an eye on the tarp," Rick suggested. Jim nodded and carefully maneuvered his truck heaped with split wood out of his drive.

Rick picked up Ruth's hand and sang, "'*over the river and through the woods, to the old woman's house we go!*' The Gods are smiling on us with this beautiful clear day! Our first visit with the 'Weaver of Webs' as a married couple!"

"What an appropriate name for her, it describes her gifts perfectly!" She leaned over and kissed his cheek, then glanced back at Doug and Sue.

"My heart is happy to be sharing this experience for the first with time with both of you, too!"

The conversation was full and rich as Doug and Sue spoke of the changes in their lives, the dreams they had for the future, and how each day brought a new discovery. Even when issues came up at work or with the kids, they knew that together they could create a solution. They also spoke of how their return to church had blessed their children's lives as well. The youth groups offered a plethora of activities for all ages.

"Interestingly," said Doug, "the same four-step decision-making process the old woman gave us is now being practiced by all members of our church family. And, those steps are introduced to children in grade school. How's that for *coincidence!*"

He chattered away like a magpie as he shared how he and Sue were pleased that classes on Non-violent communication were offered to all age groups, to help participants learn peaceful and clear ways to express feelings, and to actively listen to another person's words. And, that the youth leaders had diverse backgrounds of experience that offered all youth a deeper understanding of life beyond home and school. Everything the church offered was focused on compassion and empathy, to help youth maneuver their way through everyday life, and especially the 'ups and downs' of late childhood and early adolescence.

Rick and Ruth were very attentive; they planned to begin a family soon.

"We found that decision-making handout most helpful," Ruth commented. "As complicated as this world has become, those four steps offer an efficient and simple way to solve concerns and problems with ease. Of course, they need to be practiced and integrated into daily life. Rick and I taped our copy on the refrigerator door."

They arrived at the cabin in about twenty minutes. Jim slowly backed up to the opening of the path, and Rick carefully nestled his car into the remaining space.

"That was a fast trip!" Sue commented. "All our conversation made the time fly!"

The ladies gathered their baskets of goodies and headed toward the cabin, while the men unloaded the wood from the truck.

Sarah wrapped her scarf snuggly around her neck. "Hey, ladies, it's good to share this with both of you. It's definitely a beautiful, clear day, but darned if it isn't cold!"

Ruth glanced up at the sky. "At least the path is relatively short. That wind is fierce; I'm sure grateful there's no snow today!"

They stepped onto the porch and, lo and behold, the men appeared behind them.

"Wow, that was fast!" Sue exclaimed.

"They've done this before," responded Ruth. "This is a larger load, so it'll probably take 'em several trips."

"Better them than us," Sarah chimed in. "They're used to being outside."

The door of the cabin opened before they could knock, and the old woman stood there in a beautiful red corduroy dress, with a charming red and green plaid shawl across her shoulders. Light blush colored her cheeks and red lip-gloss matched her outfit. She was a festive display of the Christmas season.

She held the door as they quickly carried in their baskets and bags, then promptly closed the door behind them. The women finished preparation of the meal, while the men completed their tasks and cleaned up.

Jim carved the turkey onto a beautiful Christmas platter as Ruth filled the red water goblets. The dining room table was draped with a festive green tablecloth, dotted with flecks of gold. Three golden candlesticks with red candles sat on a large, ruby red glass platter in the center of the table. Fresh cedar surrounded the perimeters of the platter, while red cranberries dotted the foliage.

The dinnerware was elegant bone china with red and green poinsettias, and inlaid gold around the edges. Exquisite jeweled napkin rings held bright red napkins that looked too elegant to use. The silverware sparkled, indicating that it had just been freshly polished. It was a table set for royalty!

The three couples circled around the festive Christmas table as the old woman prepared to light the candles. They bowed their heads as she prayed.

"In respect for the birth of Jesus, and to honor the teachings of Love, Faith and Charity, we light these candles to represent the Holy Trinity." She lit the candles, then extended her hands to the person on each side of her. The others followed suit, closed the circle and bowed their heads again.

"May our hearts and hands be of service and may we reveal the gifts of Creator God through our thoughts, words, and actions. We thank you for this bounty, and ask that you bless it to the nourishment of our bodies. Aho, and so it is!"

Doug wasn't certain what "Aho" meant, so he added, "Amen!"

The men had worked up an appetite, and the feast was devoured in a short time. The table was then cleared, dishes washed and put away, and leftovers packed in containers for the trip home. A tray that held a thermos of coffee, cups, napkins, and a tin of decorated Christmas cookies had been set on the ledge of the fireplace.

Jim stoked the fire while the others cozied their chairs together in front of the fire. The mantel was adorned with green garland that snaked around a multitude of Christmas cards. A small Christmas tree sat on the floor to the right of the fireplace. The tree was adorned with a string of popcorn and cranberries draped around colorful twinkling lights, with a sparkling crystal Angel at the top. It was a heartfelt moment for all as a deep abiding presence filled the room with peace and love. It was truly a snapshot of the true meaning behind the holiday season shared by seekers woven together in a magnificent web of beauty and purpose.

Doug picked up the tin of cookies and passed them toward the old woman.

"I remember the story you told me about your family tradition of making Christmas cookies, so our children made these especially for this get-together." He glanced at Ruth. "We cut out and decorated Christmas cookies as kids as long as I can remember."

"Complete with sprinkles!" Ruth affirmed with a smile. Her ring sparkled as she tucked her hair behind her ear and passed the cookie tin to the old woman.

"Thank your children for me; they are beautiful and look delicious," she said.

They all savored the cookies and hot coffee as the flames of the fire danced around and through the burning wood.

"That's a lovely wedding ring, Ruth," commented the old woman.

"Thank you," she smiled, glancing at Rick. "I'm rather partial to it. My *husband* did a great job designing it."

Rick blushed. *It feels strange, and yet completely natural to be called "husband."*

"The jeweler did an excellent job," responded Rick. "She commented that it looked like a Mandala. When my grandparents saw it, they said the same thing."

"What about that brooch, Ruth?" inquired the old woman.

"Why, it's a gift from Rick's grandmother." She touched the brooch. "It *is* beautiful, isn't it? Apparently, it has been in her family for many generations."

The old woman smiled and turned to Rick. "Was the jeweler's name Priscilla, and are your grandparents the Weatherford's?"

Rick smiled and nodded. Somehow, he wasn't at all surprised!

"Guess that's a perfect example of your words, *there are no coincidences.*"

Everyone looked at each other, then at the old woman. She nodded. After a few moments of silence, she scanned the Christmas cards across the mantel and started her story.

"Grandmother Spider spins a web that is planted into the heart of each human being before they arrive on Earth. That web is the silver cord that keeps our souls connected to the Spirit world while we're in a physical body. Once the connection is made, each individual begins to weave his or her web as they walk the Sacred Path of Life.

"You've heard me speak of the wisdom of the natural world, and how nature offers us everything we need to know to move through this Earthly experience. Spiders offer profound teachings about living in balance, being resilient, moving with the flow of life, and *Standing in the Truth*. It all begins with a strong heart."

She stood up and retrieved a picture from the front wall, and brought it back to her chair. It was a simple and beautiful picture of a Spider. She turned to her guests and pointed to the center of the web.

"You see, Spider webs are made up of radical and spiral threads. Radical threads are the strongest, thickest and most durable, because they radiate out from the center of the web. Spiral threads connect the radical threads together to form the familiar circular pattern, and to make the web versatile and adaptive to the various environmental elements.

"When stress is present, the force of the intrusion or damage is redistributed by the spiral threads. The strength of the radical threads that come from the center is what keeps the web intact. It *is* a partnership."

She stood up and placed the picture on the fireplace ledge for all to see.

"Relationships are much the same. When a web is woven with love and the desire to share from the heart, the radical silvery threads will be strengthened and endure. The spiral threads created by the situations or stressors life brings will change or reshape throughout our relationships. If we live in alignment with our hearts, our personal Truths, we can reweave those spiral threads by seeking assistance with learning ways to improve communications and deal with unresolved experiences that hurt our hearts.

"If our actions are not in alignment with our personal Truths, our web will be woven too loosely and we will be caught in our own trap. A web woven too tightly will not allow the gifts of giving, receiving and sharing, and a web woven in fear will attract the lessons needed to overcome that fear."

As if on cue, each of the guests turned to their partners. Rick lifted Ruth's hand and kissed it.

"Newlyweds! How sweet," Jim mocked, then extended his hand to Rick. "Congratulations, my friend! Ruth's a keeper!"

"She's my strongest 'radical thread!'" Rick replied, grinning from ear to ear.

Sarah was the first to applaud, followed by the others. "You're a quick learner; thanks for demonstrating that phrase!" Then she looked at the old woman.

"So, if I understand your words, if Ruth would have said 'no,' that would have been a spiral event that Rick would have had to adjust to. However, his radical heart connection would have remained strong, while his response would have required a spiral reaction such as more conversation or more patience while he waited. Do I have that correct?"

"You do!" nodded the old woman.

Silence ensued for several moments, and Jim stood and tended the fire.

Rick whispered to Ruth, "I'm sure glad you said *yes!*"

Jim sat back down and Sarah retrieved a package wrapped in red sparkling foil paper from the bag under her chair. She extended the gift to the old woman.

"This is a little something from us to you. It feels like a perfect time to give it to you."

The old woman received it with both hands, then moved one hand to her heart, leaned over and touched the floor. She sat up and carefully unwrapped the gift. Within a few moments she continued.

"Grandmother Spider knew what she was doing centuries ago, as do all the inhabitants of the natural world. They offer their wisdoms to anyone who calls to them. Your beautiful gift of a dream-catcher is yet another example of the simple and powerful teachings that will guide us as we Walk the Sacred Path of Life.

"Whereas the spider web begins in the center and moves outward, the dream-catcher begins with a sturdy outer ring. That outer ring represents the heart of the one weaving prayers of love inward to the center circle, which represents the one to whom it's being sent. It's a blessing from one person's heart to another."

She glanced at Jim and Ruth. "Both of you have heard the teaching of Fences and being good Gate Keepers of the sacred energy field around yourself. The dream-catcher begins with that sturdy, yet airy perimeter that holds honor and respect for your Sacred Self. With a solid base within and around your soul, the Light of the Eternal Flame of Love from which you were created is maintained as you Walk the Sacred Path on Earth.

"There is no reason for conflict or confusion to separate us, except by the human reconstruction of Truth. In reality, we are more alike than we are different, and each of us has that silver thread of Truth that keeps us connected to our one true Source, *if* we pay attention."

She looked from the dream-catcher to the fire.

"Rick, your grandparents and the jeweler have shared this journey with me since we were very young. It wasn't until we became adults and entered the fall of our lives that we reconnected, with a common intent to re-member who we truly are, uncloaked by what society taught us. While we do not see each other often these days, they are most certainly an integral part of my heart that has helped me stay awake and move through this human experience."

"We are all connected when we come from our hearts," she continued. "This is a most beautiful gift that I accept with much love. It is my honor and privilege to be a part of your lives."

She rose and retrieved six small, shiny red boxes from under the Christmas tree. She turned to her guests and placed a box in each person's left hand.

Jim was the first to open his gift. He fingered through the gold tissue that revealed a round, black object. Puzzled, he looked at Sarah, who shrugged her shoulders.

"You won't know if you don't open it," Sarah whispered.

Curious, he removed the object, opened it and a light came on, revealing both a regular and a magnifying mirror.

Ruth gasped. "It's a light and a mirror!"

The others opened their boxes to discover the same gift. The men held back their emotions as the woman let their tears flow.

"Sometimes you are simply a small reflection," the old woman tenderly offered, "while other times a closer look is required to see the big picture. The seven of us are honoring a commitment we made before *Grandmother Spider* wove *The Web* that brought us to Earth. Grandmother chose that task to be of service to humanity.

"I wish for each of you to consider making a commitment to serve humanity; to embody what you learn through your thoughts, words and actions, so that other Seekers of Truth that appear on your path will glean Truths they can use while *Walking a Sacred Path*. Let this gift help you be an awakened, *Weaver of Webs*."

With her palms joined in front of her heart, she bowed forward, to show respect and acknowledge the sacredness of her guests.

"These are my words." She picked up the dream-catcher, turned, entered her bedroom, and closed the door behind her.

Life Cycle Teachings

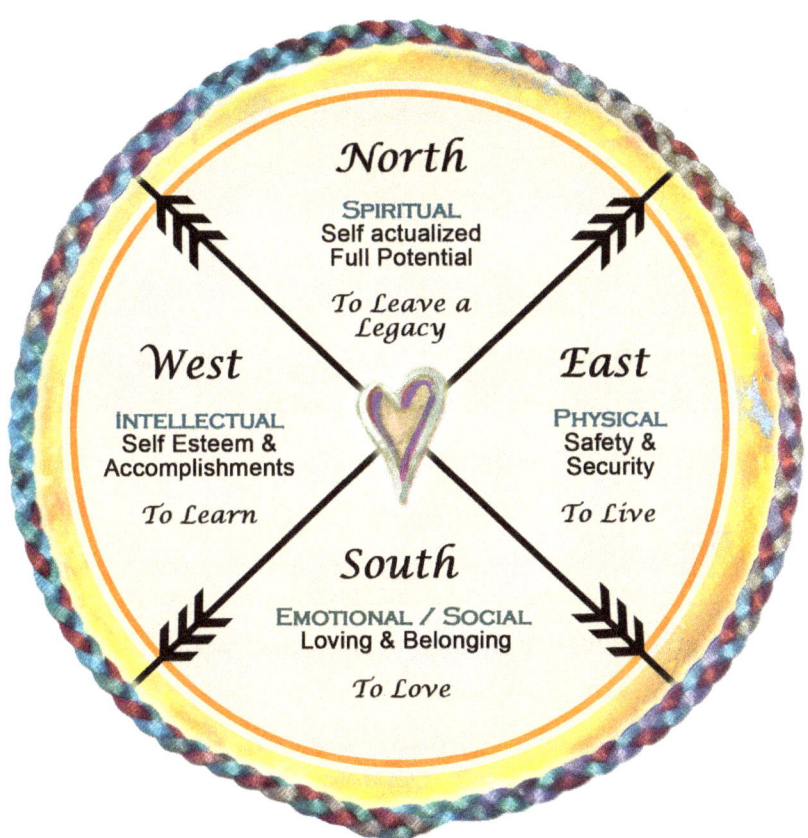

The Four directions each carry an energy that parallels the behavioral qualities needed by humans while *Walking a Sacred Path*. As noted in the Mandala, the four basic needs and how they are met for every human being are: *Physical* (birth/childhood), **Emotional/Social** (school age — young adulthood,) **Intellectual** (adulthood) and **Spiritual** (Old age to death.) According to Maslow's theory in order to become a fully self-actualized human, the developmental need for each stage is listed. Finally, Stephen Covey sums it up as a goal statement for each stage: *To Live, to Love, to Learn, to Leave a Legacy. Coincidence?*

Problem Solving & Decision Making Mandala

Every concern we face in life can be managed with the four easy steps of the Problem Solving & Decision Making Mandala. If everyone would learn these four steps early in life, they would have an invaluable "tool" by which to navigate through the human experience. If every caregiver, teacher, parent, and employer, would consistently encourage the use and follow-through of these four steps, young people would learn from a very early age how to be resourceful and responsible. *Walking a Sacred Path* begins with each of us demonstrating these steps in our lives!

Now it's your turn!

Blank copies of a Mandala are available to download and print from our website: www.HeadToHeartTalks.com. You can create a personal Mandala that will work for your specific needs!

Whether your concerns are personal or professional, or you have a particular dream, vision or situation to resolve, each direction offers gifts to help you move through life. Refer back to the descriptions in this book, or book one, *"Head to Heart Talks: Rediscovering your Authentic Self,"* to fully understand the gifts of each of these directions.

With much gratitude for the courage it takes to step into the next new adventure in your life and to actively co-create the life you truly desire, with your *Heart* and your *Head* as best friends!

From my *Heart* to yours,
Vicky Kelm Williams

Problem Solving & Decision Making

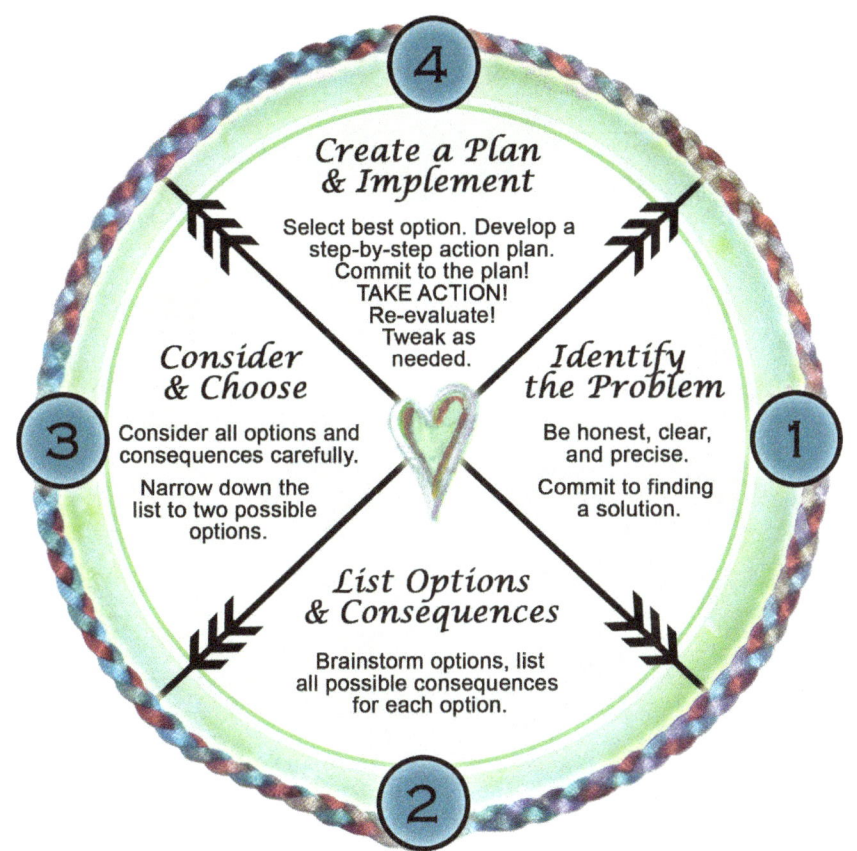

4 Create a Plan & Implement

Select best option. Develop a step-by-step action plan. Commit to the plan! TAKE ACTION! Re-evaluate! Tweak as needed.

1 Identify the Problem

Be honest, clear, and precise.

Commit to finding a solution.

3 Consider & Choose

Consider all options and consequences carefully.

Narrow down the list to two possible options.

2 List Options & Consequences

Brainstorm options, list all possible consequences for each option.